THE FINAL SYSTEM

THE FINAL SYSTEM

ANTHONY TARDIFF

This is a work of fiction. Names, characters, organizations, places, events, and incidents are either products of the author's imagination or are used fictitiously. Otherwise, any resemblance to actual persons, living or dead, is purely coincidental.

Published by 47North, Seattle

www.apub.com

EU product safety contact:
Amazon Media EU S. à r.l.
38, avenue John F. Kennedy, L-1855 Luxembourg
amazonpublishing-gpsr@amazon.com

ISBN-13: 9781662536915 (paperback)
ISBN-13: 9781662536922 (digital)

Cover design by Shasti O'Leary Soudant
Cover image: © Neil Holden / ArcAngel Images

Printed in the United States of America

To Andrea, with love and gratitude

PROLOGUE

"Sure you don't wanna come, Jase?"

Jason had set his phone to Do Not Disturb, but his smartbuds knew to make an exception for his twin sister, so they let her voice cut through the snarls of the trolls surrounding him. When he looked toward her, the game world faded out, and the real world faded in, allowing him to see Mia as a dark silhouette in the bright rectangle of the doorway. For a moment he hesitated, then shook his head. "Maybe tomorrow."

She cocked her eyes at him over her smartglasses. "You're wilting all over the couch. You need sunlight and fresh air."

He let his lounging, splayed-out limbs sink deeper into the cushions. "I'm not wilting, I'm taking root. Wait till you see what I grow into. Anyway, fresh air? In LA? It's not exactly DC out there."

"Change of scenery, then."

He tapped his smartglasses. In the VR view, his avatar had been about to mar a pastoral paradise with generous helpings of steaming troll blood. "There's more scenery in here than out there."

Mia scrunched her nose. "That ain't real."

"Neither is that," he said, nodding to the backpack hanging heavily from her shoulder. There were probably a dozen books in there, and it was a good bet most were fairy-tale retellings. "Aren't you too old for that stuff?"

Her eyes flicked to the kitchen doorway and back. "Guess we each have our escape," she said softly.

A crash, a muttered curse, and a zoned-out giggle came from the kitchen. "He's still in the mellow stage," Jason said, mirroring her soft tone. "Better get out while you can." Jason could handle their foster dad even after he'd hit the belligerent stage of the evening's drinking, but it was easier when he didn't have to worry about how the man was looking at Mia.

"Come with me," she said. "You can take root at the library. The soil's healthier there."

"I'd lose reception on the bus."

"The horror. Then we could spend the trip plotting, like old times."

He wavered. But he was plotting already, more seriously than she knew. No more the old daydreams. And no more aimless running, like when he'd squandered that ghost MeNetID. He had a real plan now—a good plan.

She thought he was just playing a game, and maybe he was. Life was like one of those live-service video games, the ones that strung you along with a million tiny goals colorfully presented, multiple completion bars filling and counters rolling upward, sparkling loot boxes opening with carefully designed dopamine bursts of light and sound, offering an insignificant reward while reminding you that the next one might, *might* be game changing. The only way to guarantee the reward was to pay, and Jason and Mia were low in every one of life's in-game currencies—money, status, friends, a MeNetID history that would open doors instead of shutting them.

But what if you could rig the game?

He'd found an exploit that allowed him to boost the power of any weapon in *BloodReign* while it still displayed the original, lower stats. If he was careful about how he sold the hacked weapons, in a few months, they could have enough money to buy two ghost MeNetIDs and the matching lifestyle to avoid suspicion. They'd no longer be at the mercy of the system, cogs in the machine, names and numbers in a file to be placed here or there as the system dictated. The judgment and negativity tugging like anchors on their MeNetIDs would be left behind. They'd be free.

"Last chance," Mia pressed.

Last chance. In two months, they would be eighteen and turned loose from the foster system to enter American society under an even stricter rule book, one with no safety net. So he shook his head again. "Tomorrow. Promise."

She nodded, hefted her backpack, and stepped away. The door swung closed, cutting off the sunlight.

Jason subvocalized a command to restore the VR view. The smartbuds deep in his ears captured the electrical signals of his face, tongue, and throat muscles almost imperceptibly tightening and moving as he interiorly voiced the words, and a complex AI on his phone decoded his command into understandable text. Another AI parsed that text and followed the command, masking the real world with the world of *BloodReign*. The trolls were still there, taunting his avatar, watching what he'd do. He thought at first they were GeNPCs, generative AI–controlled units whose sole purpose of existence was to react to him, creating a story on the fly in which he was the main character. But as the first fell under his hacked sword and he saw its name appear in the killfeed, he realized it was a human player. So were the next two. They'd been trolls in more ways than one, acting like GeNPCs while intending to surprise him with human capability, but they'd been the ones surprised.

"You ph—" the final dying troll said over voice, before the word was bleeped out by the automatic profanity filter.

Jason had left the filter open, so he knew the word that had been censored wasn't the first expletive that came to mind that started with the /f/ phoneme. There were a few words that every dev, everywhere, bleeped regardless of user settings, and none was censored more than *phreaker*.

Even the tamer synonym *hacker* wasn't said lightly. But *phreaker* was a whole different level. "Hello, World, you've been phreaked" might be the most famous sentence in history, and its impact on the world in question had been so powerful that teachers covering the Cybercrash added trigger warnings before saying it aloud in class. Jason grinned. Maybe he should consider this word of mouth for his business.

His grin died. Or maybe he shouldn't be stupid. In this business, no publicity was good publicity. Nobody drew the heat in these United States of Andrew Norman like a phreaker. The careers of even the best tended to be meteoric: brief and ending in flames. Jason's few remaining months of minority wouldn't matter to Norman, who famously, vindictively, treated all hackers like Hacksaw himself.

Phreak it. He'd accomplished enough for the day. He thumbed the power button on the glasses, jumped up, and slipped out the front door, closing it softly to avoid drawing attention.

Down the block, Mia's slim form was about to step onto the crosswalk. "Hey," he called, "wait up!" She turned, and he saw her smile as she paused and waited for him.

Jason was steps away from her, beginning to smile in response, when a roar cut across the electric whine of traffic. He had only heard the sound in movies, so at first he didn't realize what it was, but as it grew aggressively in volume and pitch, it drew Jason's eye to a low-slung, bright-red, old-fashioned sports car—a gas guzzler—gunning up the street, slaloming between cars, leaving a trail of swerving, slowing vehicles, their windshield status lights changing from green to emergency red.

It was a joyrider, driving on manual control at well over the TransNet's speed, weaving through the spaces in the automatic traffic with only human reflexes to guide them. That was a staple of every action movie, and Jason had done it many times in VR, but for some—usually rich—people, movies and video games weren't enough of a thrill. Jason's first thought was a hope that this didn't cause TransNet to go into redlock and delay their bus ride.

He didn't have time for a second thought.

A cab crossed the intersection into the sports car's path, its passenger, a dark-haired woman, beginning to turn her head toward the noise. Through the sports car's windshield, Jason saw its driver, eyes and mouth wide, throw his arms in front of him. The car swerved, grew, filled the world. Jason jumped back.

Mia didn't.

Her body buckled, her hair seeming almost to float around her face as her head whiplashed off the hood of the car.

She landed like a broken, discarded doll in the street, books and torn pages raining around her.

Jason ran to her, but at first, he couldn't bring himself to look, turning his head instead to the sports car slanted on the sidewalk, dented hood smoking, and the woman leaning out the door of her now-stationary autocab, hands over her mouth. Then he looked at Mia—and looked away. Because she wasn't there anymore.

Later, Jason would remember that time as a series of individual moments. The moment the bag was zipped over Mia's head. The moment their foster dad asked if he'd still receive a support check for two kids that month. The moment Jason was told that the car that had run her down had been traveling sixty-four point two miles per hour. The moment he learned the driver was getting a ticket for driving on manual but no manslaughter charge, because he'd put the car back into automatic just before it hit Mia. The moment he realized the car itself had swerved into her, that it had chosen to hit her instead of the cab because she was one person and the occupants of car plus cab equaled two. And the moment he realized that although everyone else thought this was sad, they didn't think anyone was responsible. It was just one of those things. The automatic system had worked as it should have.

Jason considered rage quitting, doing the life equivalent of throwing the game controller at the console before switching it off, but he made it to his eighteenth birthday because Mia would have wanted him to. He went through the emancipation process with a disinterested social worker and walked out of her office an adult, but neither he nor the universe felt any different. There seemed to be no point in playing another turn.

But then, as he sat in the park watching what he thought was his last sunset, life offered a new questline.

The email slipped past the AI filters that made spam almost unknown and landed in his inbox with an urgent flag that triggered a notification in his glasses and drew his attention. The email was blank—until he looked deeper and found in its code commands to turn a block of text transparent, set its font size to zero, and bury it below the edges of the window. Only someone looking at the code could see it.

The hidden text was a long sequence of numbers and characters. Jason spent too much time running it through cryptoanalysis programs before realizing he was looking at a piece of ANSI art, a form of computer graphics so ancient it had been popular on the old proto-networks that predated not only OverNet but even the old internet. Assembled and interpreted, the letters and digits transformed into low-resolution artwork depicting a fairy. Despite the blocky pixels and limited color palette, the fairy's featureless face and delicate shape evoked menace. Maybe it was her vaguely predatory posture, like a bird of prey about to descend. Accompanying the image was a set of instructions, signed with one word: *Sprite*.

Sprite. Jason had heard the name whispered in the few dim corners that remained of the old darknets. Rumor had it she'd smashed China's XAI Syndicate so hard they'd disappeared entirely from America's Nets. That had led to her recruitment as the youngest (in reputational terms, because who knew how old she was in real life?) phreaker in the Collective, the most infamous hacker organization in the American Nets. In the tiny, dangerous world of black-hat hacking, she was royalty.

And she was recruiting Jason.

It was a fetch quest: Infiltrate an old corporate archive and retrieve a specific document. It took only a few hours and a couple of phone calls, and then he was paid—generously, like a professional.

But his true payment for the job, the reward he'd been meant to find, was the document itself, which he of course read. It was the auto-generated transcript of a decades-ago meeting, and it concluded with a few perfunctory sentences spoken to put an end to a debate:

"Cut this trolley-problem bullshit. The only and obvious answer is utilitarianism: Prioritize the happiness of the greatest number of people who might potentially complain. Can you imagine if we wiped out a school bus just because the person it would've hit was innocent? Our careers would be deader than the kids whose faces showed up on the news."

The words were tagged with the name of the man responsible for the algorithms baked into TransNet and active in every car rolling in perfect coordination along the millions of miles of American roads: Andrew Norman.

Jason's future didn't open up again at that moment; it narrowed to a point, and that point was aimed directly at Andrew Norman. Never mind that he was the most powerful man in the world, the man who ran the networks that ran everything else, the man who literally made the rules.

All Jason had to do was figure out how to rig the game.

~ FIVE YEARS LATER ~

CHAPTER 1

The man across from Jason was eyeing him with open distaste. Jason returned the distaste with interest, or rather with calculated *dis*interest. The leather vest under the suit coat, the too-many and too-large rings and not-quite-concealed chain necklace, and the modded personal car Jason had watched him pull up in were all part of an image Bruno was projecting. That image was completed by his goon of a bodyguard, looming behind him in a suit that was a touch too small, probably by design to make him look like he was about to burst out of it in an explosion of muscle and testosterone.

Maybe he just wasn't used to wearing a suit. Jason had required his clients to wear one, as well as to carry wheatgrass smoothies and to walk confidently to this fourth-floor conference room in this swanky Arlington hotel in eyesight of the NNA Tower, which Jason had reserved by phishing his way into the hotel's calendar app and adding a generically named "Strategy Session." No one had stopped them because they were obviously businessmen working a deal. Which was true, in its way. But Jason could see the hard outline of a gun beneath the goon's too-tight suit jacket. Bruno's much better tailored coat doubtless concealed his own.

The most lethal shape in Bruno's suit, though, was probably Bruno himself. The dude looked like a Navy SEAL, if a Navy SEAL had decided, Clark Kent–like, to disguise himself by donning a three-piece suit and a pair of out-of-fashion smartglasses. Jason was also wearing a suit, though unlike the goon's, Jason's was too loose. Or maybe his body didn't fill it out. Same diff. He'd always had a bit of a noncommittal relationship with his body. He was basically glad it was there, but he didn't pay it a lot of attention other than making sure it didn't accumulate any unwanted mass. Bruno's body was twice as *there*, and his extra mass looked like the useful kind.

These things—bling, car, goon, both kinds of guns—were meant to make Jason feel impressed or intimidated or both. So he kept his expression locked in what he hoped looked like boredom and slouched in his chair to hide the fact that he was, in fact, terrified.

Bruno broke the tense silence that had fallen between them. "We negotiated this already, Mr. 'Ghost.'" Jason could hear the scare quotes. "You said you could do it."

"And you said you had an in," Jason replied. "You said you could get me the info I wanted."

"I did."

"So gimme that, and I'll take it from there."

Bruno leaned forward. His eyes were hidden behind his darkened smartglasses, but his thick lips were compressed. "Boost my confidence," he said. "Because I'm a little concerned I hired someone who needs my help to do the job I hired him to do."

"To accomplish my freely chosen freelance business opportunity, you mean?" Jason said. He was wearing lenses, not glasses, but over them he, too, had placed a pair of glasses, transparent to him but dark to everyone else. You could learn a lot from someone's eyes, and phreakers were not in the business of giving away information. So here they were, wearing sunglasses indoors like try-hards. Bruno, he had to admit, pulled it off. Jason only hoped he himself looked as cool and aloof as he was trying desperately to feel.

A message slid into his smartspace. I have made the appropriate sacrifices to the RNG gods

He felt a grin try to surface despite everything, and suppressed it. Sprite had the uncanny ability to guess when he needed a little reassurance. He subvocalized a text back: Did you remember to burn the symbolic dice?

The dice are burned. Their ashes were used to inscribe Brother Edvin's original Latin description of the middle-square method on seven pieces of paper, which were placed in a hat. I chose one blindly and used it as the seed for a Mersenne Twister, the output of which I converted to ASCII, then scanned for words of three or more letters. Your fortune is . . . There was a pause. Sip hop cow gumdrop

Profound, Jason replied.

I thought "gumdrop" was promising. The odds of getting a seven-letter word are vanishingly small

Great. You just used up all my luck

So make some more

Jason suppressed another tight grin. Despite the black humor about random number generators—the computer equivalent of a dice roll—Sprite was reminding him that he still had power here. This might be the biggest gamble of both their lives, but phreakers didn't rely on chance. They loaded the dice. They hacked the RNG.

"So you're just an honest businessman," Bruno was saying, lip curling.

"At least as much as you are," Jason replied. He subvocalized a command, and a commercial trust check program on his phone analyzed Bruno's MeNetID history. In less than a second, it consumed the man's online life, analyzed it, weighed it, and passed judgment. A number appeared over Bruno's head: ninety-one. An *incredibly* trustworthy person.

Most people with a score that good were full-time influencers, narcissists who played the social accountability game masterfully, amassing millions of followers, thousands of in-depth interactions, and a careful history of communication on the Nets calculated to make the algorithms decide they were a net benefit to society. Bruno's history was sparse but somehow hit the algorithms such that they judged him one hell of an upstanding dude. Jason had done his research and amassed a separate dossier on the man, and none of what he'd found explained the score. More the opposite.

Jason was no more honest, of course, but the law of phreaker Darwinism meant that any phreaker who'd been in operation for more than a couple of months was a *good* phreaker, and by the law of supply and demand, that only made Jason's services more valuable. "Think of it as an investment," he told Bruno. "The real currency of hacking isn't money; it's information. And like any investment, you have to put in to take out."

Bruno held his gaze for a moment, then grunted, leaned back, and nodded to his goon. The goon pulled a slip of paper out of his pocket and handed it to Jason.

"Paper?" Jason said as he took it. "That's one way to be secure." On the paper was written, in pencil, the words *Albert Chandler, WasteNet Employee ID 9236511*. WasteNet, huh? Newbie Chandler had climbed the ladder of life and landed a job at the NNA—where he now spent his time monitoring shit. That must look impressive in his mother's annual Christmas letter. "You sure he's the newest hire?"

"You gonna doubt me?" Bruno growled.

"I trust you," Jason said. For this, at least. He handed the paper back to the goon. "Better eat that, big guy. In case we're compromised."

The goon actually started to lift his hand toward his mouth, but Bruno looked at him sharply and the goon let his arm drop, trying to make the motion casual, and tore the paper into little strips instead. Jason suppressed a grin. Bruno's lips twitched, whether in shared amusement or annoyance, Jason didn't know.

Jason leaned back and subvocalized a command to his phone. His smartspace sprang into being, and he arranged the windows comfortably around him. "Want to watch?" He sent a window share to Bruno.

"Oh, I'd love to," Bruno said, as he accepted the share. "We've tes—tried this before. No one's been able to get through. The NNA is impregnable."

"OverNet is. The NOC is. But not the rest, not to a real phreaker."

"They were real"—the man couldn't bring himself to say it—"hackers. Working for me. Part of my organization."

Jason was sure they were. No hacker off the street would take a job to directly attack the National Networks Administration. Except, well, him. He said, "They just *thought* they were phreakers." He opened a virtual keyboard, spread it across his knees, and began typing.

"Unlike you, the real hacker, who just told me hacking the NOC is impossible."

"That proves I'm not boasting. No phreaker, not even the best, has been able to so much as ping the NOC." From his seat, Jason had direct line of sight out the hotel windows to the NNA Tower, where it rose from the Potomac on what had once been Theodore Roosevelt Island, like a watchtower guarding the forest of greenery-topped "treescrapers" of inner DC. He was too close to see the dome atop the Tower where the Network Operations Center resided, but he was acutely aware of its presence, the peak of Norman's empire literally as well as figuratively. It was where OverNet was administered, and OverNet controlled all other Nets. It was said that not even the president had clearance to the NOC without Norman's say-so. To Jason, that wasn't just a red flag, it was a whole parade. But to the people of the United States, it was reassurance. That level of security was necessary for Norman to save them all from another bot invasion and Cybercrash.

When Jason had first heard about the bot invasion as a kid, he had imagined a war with literal dronebots and laser guns. That might have been better than the truth. Americans didn't fight robots—they fought each other.

The old internet was a content machine, even more than it was now. Even that word, *content*, showed how voracious the consumption of information was, and how undiscriminating. And then there were the *influencers*—about as dystopian a word as Jason could think of. Many discovered that the way to keep up with the insatiable demand for content was to train an AI on their own corpus of posts and then let it take over, keeping an eye on it but doing less and less of the work themselves. Meanwhile, propaganda bots were set loose by everyone from major companies to Jim Bob in his mom's basement, programmed to find posts about specific topics and generate replies pushing the company's or individual's point of view. The internet was overrun with bots generating content and replying to that content, each competing to draw eyeballs to their product or pet idea, tuned to generate the most "engagement"—which usually meant playing on fears or hatreds. Their output was recycled by new AI models trained on their posts, in an accelerating feedback loop. By some estimates, by the Crash, less than 20 percent of the internet was created by humans. Meanwhile, the humans themselves increasingly turned to the comforting validations of their AI friends, or panyons—often more than friends—who offered a ready shield from the harshness of outside voices.

Then Hacksaw struck. Deploying his own army of bots in a series of brilliant hacks, he undermined and destroyed the stock market, then underlined the point by sending his calling card to every device in the country—Hello, World, you've been phreaked. In the resulting chaos, the armies of generative AI bots inflamed existing divisions, creating and feeding conspiracy theories on both sides, claiming the other side had engineered the Crash to take control of the country. They were the spark to the tinder the sudden economic collapse had created.

Enter Andrew Norman. As the creator of MeNet, the "social transparency" network and the only social network not vulnerable to bots, he'd stepped in with an audacious recovery plan and a heap load of charisma, and the desperate government had gotten behind him. MeNet was federalized and integrated as the nation's only legal social network, and its real-name MeNetIDs became required to access any network, guaranteeing that everyone you interacted with online was human, while also ensuring that the behavior of those humans would not be anonymous and so would have real-world repercussions.

The democratic, anonymous, vulnerable internet of the past was no more. The new American Nets were carefully segregated into hundreds of specialized subnets—TransNet for automated vehicles, NewsNet for news, BankNet for banking and the markets, and on and on. The subnets communicated with each other via a rigid hierarchical system of authorization, with what was still called the "internet" occupying the lowest and least capable rung on the ladder. Another hack like Hacksaw's was impossible because every subnet in the hierarchical system, with the single exception of the independent MilNet, answered to and communicated through OverNet, the central command-and-control network.

OverNet answered to Andrew Norman. From that Tower.

"If I said I could hack the NOC," Jason said, pulling his eyes away from the Tower, "I'd be a liar. But you hired me to get you an NNA login, not OverNet access. The lower subnets are vulnerable."

"They weren't to my hackers."

"And I can tell you why they failed."

An eyebrow rose above the rim of Bruno's dark glasses. "Do elucidate."

"They tried to act like the hackers in old movies. Did everything with computers."

Bruno's eyebrow rose even more. "They failed because they hacked . . . with computers?"

"Yep. Like the movies." Secretly, Jason loved that shit. His interest in hacking had germinated from watching 1980s and 1990s films with Mia. Back then, neither the filmmakers nor the audience had a clue what real hacking looked like, or else they thought—justifiably, if he were honest—it looked boring, so they portrayed it as rather . . . *neon*. Bright-green code scrolling too fast for anyone to read. Fingers blurring over a keyboard. There was usually a giant red timer counting down, and beeping alarms, and somebody was bound to utter a phrase like, "Their worm is trying to breach our firewall!" Often the hack unfolded in crude 3D "cyberspace" like some ancient video game, the camera sliding down wireframe tunnels suspended in blackness while polygonal tanks or blocky skeletons glided in pursuit.

What those movies visualized wasn't hacking but the *mystique* of hacking. Before the Cybercrash made them all terrorists, phreakers were wizards. Hoodies stood in for pointy hats, scripts for magic spells, code for incantations. Even the movies' cheesy, lo-fi vision of cyberspace was optimistic in its naivete, beautiful and surreal, like another world. Like an escape. And right now Jason's fingers were, in fact, flying across the virtual keyboard on his knees, and he felt just a little like one of those noble antiheroes, even if what he was doing was just a simple internet search, about as far from that Hollywood vision of sorcery as you could get.

"That's bad?" Bruno said, his deep voice dripping skepticism.

"I'm sure they were good at it. But that's not phreaking. Or, not the heart of phreaking."

"So what is?"

"See, no one remembers anymore," Jason said, examining and discarding a series of images in his smartspace, "because there are so few phreakers in the wild. Real black hats like me are rare, because we have to be good enough to hide. The white hats, the ones who work *in* the system, legally, running red-team exercises, penetration testing, that sort of stuff, they're just programmers playing at being hackers. They follow rules."

"And you don't?"

"Nope. I think around 'em." Jason found what he was looking for: a high-quality image of the WasteNet logo. He dropped it into a tiny program he'd prepared earlier. Then he cut off Bruno's window share.

"Hey!" Bruno said.

"Sorry," Jason said, "you can't be connected for this part, or the mark will know there are two people on the call."

"The great hacker can't hide that?" Bruno said scornfully.

"Is that a challenge? Fine. Gimme your phone."

That was a challenge back. Would Bruno dare hand his phone to a hacker? With the overly casual air of someone showing they didn't care, he did.

Jason rolled his eyes. "Unlocked, I meant."

"Why don't you just hack—" Bruno began, but Jason cut him off.

"You wanna be here another hour, or do you want to get what you came for?" He held the phone up toward Bruno's face.

Bruno hesitated, then raised his smartglasses and leaned in. It was the first time Jason had seen his eyes. They were dark, and amused. The phone read his face and unlocked. Bruno disappeared behind his glasses again.

Jason spent a minute tapping the screen, then handed it back to Bruno. "There. That's a temporary local piggyback, no middleman Net. You can watch over my shoulder and nobody else knows you're here. Happy?"

"Not till I get what I came here for," Bruno rumbled, rising and coming around the conference table to stand behind Jason, literally watching over his shoulder. Since this was a local piggyback, he was viewing Jason's smartspace instead of seeing a duplicate in his own. The goon came with him.

Jason subvocalized a command to call the NNA's public VoiceNet line. A couple of menus later, he was able to enter Chandler's ID number. That little piece of supposedly secure info routed his call directly to Chandler, with an internal transfer tag that ensured his phone would actually ring.

"Um, hello?" said a voice. This was probably the first time Chandler had picked up a work call.

"Hi, is this Al?" Jason said.

"Um, yes, this is Albert."

"Hey, Albert, this is John Kline up in EmployNet. I'm trying to process your first paycheck, but I'm getting a flag. Did you finish the cybersecurity training?"

"That really bor—really in-depth thing with all the videos and quizzes? Yeah, I did that."

It was probably almost the only thing he'd done on his first day of "work" two weeks ago. Having to redo it would be a nightmare. Jason twisted the knife a little. "It's not showing as completed."

"But—but I got a certificate of completion in my email."

"That won't help me. The hold is released automatically. Are you sure you finished the whole thing?"

"Yes! It took all—"

"You might have to redo it," Jason interrupted.

"Oh, no . . ." Jason could almost hear Chandler slump in his chair.

"Unless," he said.

"What?" Chandler's eagerness was almost pathetic.

"Look, I'm not supposed to do this. But if we don't get this flag removed today, you'll miss payroll, and that'll be a nightmare for both of us. I'll trust that you finished the training. I'll pull up the final quiz page on my terminal, and all you have to do is click FINISH." He sent a window share to Chandler.

There was a long pause. In his smartspace, Chandler would be looking at the window Jason had sent, showing a credible mock-up of the quiz tutorial. Jason knew it was credible because earlier he'd looked up which training firm had a contract with the NNA and found their software. All he'd needed was the correct logo to sit atop the login screen.

"It's asking me to log in," Chandler said.

"Yeah," Jason said, his voice so unconcerned it was almost bored.

Another long pause. "Um. How do I know *this* isn't a phishing attempt?"

Jason began an incredulous laugh, then cut it short as if realizing Chandler had a point. "You're right. That's ironic." He pretended to think for a moment. "What if I shoot you my GPS coordinates?"

"You're in the Tower?" Chandler said.

"Of course," Jason said, in a tone that added the unspoken *you idiot.*

"Yeah, uh, okay. That should verify you, for sure."

It should. Although the Tower's park and even its atrium were popular tourist destinations, nobody could ride the elevators without clearance, and the internal security network tracked and logged every person in the building. It was unthinkable that anyone could wander through the Tower without authorization.

Not only that, but direct user tampering of GPS numbers was impossible. Any personal GPS coordinate sent to a third party bore an encrypted PlaceNet stamp verifying that the numbers had come directly from the phone's GPS chip and not from any injected text. So there was no reason for Chandler to suspect that the numbers Jason sent him were wrong. Because they weren't *wrong*—but they were *imprecise.*

Jason had modified the messaging app's call for coordinates so that the longitude rounded after two decimals. And as every kid learned in grade school, deleting decimals was the same as changing them to zeros. So the truncated longitude coordinates collapsed to a very specific point 2,200 feet directly east of Jason: right smack-dab in the middle of the Tower. The included, genuine altitude data meant that when Chandler turned his smartlens-augmented eyeballs toward the ping, he would see it *above* him, on the fourth floor of the Tower, where EmployNet was.

Though Jason knew this should work, there was the usual breathless, tingling moment of waiting to see if the hook would set and land the phish or if he would be the one trying to avoid being reeled in.

In his smartspace window, numbers and digits flowed into the login fields. He heard Bruno suck in his breath.

The fields disappeared as Chandler pressed ENTER, replaced by a screen that said, "Thank you for finishing the training!" A button beneath read SUBMIT.

"I bet I never hit that button," Chandler said.

"Yeah, it's not exactly clear there's a final submit step, is it?" The real training, of course, had no such button, and Jason's did nothing when

Chandler pushed it, except to allow Jason to say, "That's it! The flag is cleared. Thanks, Albert."

"Thank *you*," Chandler said. "I wouldn't have gotten anything done today if I'd had to do that stup—that training again."

Jason chuckled. "No worries. You saved me trouble too. Have a good day, now." He disconnected.

Both of Bruno's eyebrows were suspended above his smartglasses now. "*That's* real hacking?"

"Like I said," Jason said, "hacking isn't just about computers. Hell, the original phreakers worked landline phones. Hacking just means taking a system, *any* system, and figuring out how to use it for something it wasn't designed for."

"Any system," Bruno said. "You mean people."

Jason nodded. "It's called 'social engineering.' People have levers. You just gotta find the right ones."

"Well, I give you credit for thinking outside the box."

Jason shook his head. "Hacking takes what's *in* the box and does something unexpected with it." A moment ago, a text file had appeared in Jason's smartspace. He opened it now. The contents were very short:

```
Username: chandlera
Password: rightcoltcelltack
```

"How do I know it works?" Bruno said.

"We test it." Jason had earlier found a public-facing site that had NNA portal access, a government site for external contractors to bid for NNA contracts, which NNA officers would approve. He pulled that site up now, selected WasteNet, and pasted in Chandler's login info.

The screen flashed and turned red, its way of shaking its head.

Jason shook his head back, frowning. Chandler must have mistyped his password. He scanned it, looking for the mistake. It was all real words, thankfully. The problem was almost certainly capitalization, and the most common slip was if the first letter was capitalized and the user didn't time the shift keystroke with the letter keystroke. Jason capitalized the leading *R* and hit ENTER again.

The screen flashed red.

"Problem?" Bruno said.

"Just a little snag," Jason said. He could feel Bruno and the goon looming. It did not help. "I'll get it."

Bruno snorted. "You're a cocky shit, but you're no Hacksaw. I'm starting to worry I won't see a return on my 'investment.'"

"Okay, so I haven't destroyed the internet, shattered the economy of the entire planet, and plunged the world into a decade-long depression," Jason said back. "Yet. But keep your eye on me."

"Oh, I am," Bruno rumbled. "I am."

Jason tried capitalizing the *C* in *colt*. Again the login failed, but now the boxes filled themselves out, overwriting what Jason had entered. The login screen now read:

User ID: A=1
Passkey: 14-9-3-5-0-20-18-25

He bit his lip. A=1? It reminded him of those codes he and Mia had made as kids, the ones where numbers stood for letters of the alphabet. A was 1, B was 2, and so on. If this was one of those codes, the passkey would say . . . NICE TRY.

Jason jerked, and his stomach swooped with a shot of adrenaline. His smartspace flickered. Someone else was in the system. Someone was watching him. Right now.

He reached over with his left hand and pulled his watchdog program into his field of vision. It was supposed to tell him when someone was probing his system. He punched its window with his finger. It didn't respond. He punched it again. This time it displayed the message: Error number 20-15-15-0-12-1-20-5. No network access.

His eyes flew over the error number. In that same basic alphabet code, it said, TOO LATE.

Every one of his programs closed itself. In their place came a cascade of windows: emails, online purchase receipts, contacts. Whoever this was, they were looking for identifying information. "Is this part of your plan?" Bruno asked in his deep voice.

Jason didn't waste time replying. He yanked his phone out of his pocket. The green light was on; the camera was live.

A female voice, rich, low, and seductive, emanated from the phone in his hands, making him jump. "I see you, hhhhhhaaaackk-kerrrrr." The last word was artificially drawn out, metallic, computerized—predatory. "Turn around."

Jason turned his head and found himself looking into the black hole of the muzzle of a handgun.

He had never seen a gun in real life, much less experienced one pointing at his face. The effect was riveting, as if the whole universe had compressed to those nine millimeters of black space. It took effort to raise his eyes to the man behind.

Bruno and his goon had new smartspace overlays above their heads: huge, floating NNA badges. "Jason Eric Cromartie," Bruno said, "you are under arrest for cyberterrorism against a federal network."

CHAPTER 2

The most powerful man in the world might also be the most charming. Chloe wondered if that was because so much power made it easy to be personable or because so much charm made it easy to become powerful. Either way, it was fascinating to watch, even through a green tint of jealousy. Andrew Norman circulated through the ballroom, his straight-backed, white-bearded form moving effortlessly from one knot of congresspeople to another, clasping hands, touching shoulders. Each mingling group of Very Important People parted to make space, their faces turning toward him with the bashful, fawning welcome of groupies. Norman radiated a confidence Chloe could only imagine having herself. It was a confidence that made promises: *I'm here, I'm in control, you have nothing to worry about.* Since this was Andrew Norman, the confidence was justified. His promises were made with the collateral of a dozen past impossible pledges, all kept.

Rumor was he'd be making another tonight. That was why Chloe was here. But she wasn't mingling. She was at a back table, alone except for the passing server dronebot that was refilling her water and checking if she'd finished her chicken Francese.

She thought about the most important promise she'd ever made: "I will fight to make the black boxes of AI algorithms transparent." That promise had gotten her elected. She liked to think that was because she really believed in it, and people could tell. She hadn't gotten the

Overcheck Party's rubber stamp just because it would be a nice addition to her collection. She hadn't even sought it out, or any of her stamps. She'd focused on the issue, and the stamps had followed. Preelection polls had shown that her collection of stamps averaged less than half majority approval, but people didn't vote by a perfect average of their interests. They focused on the one or two issues that mattered most to them. And, at least in her district at that time, AI transparency was the hot issue. She had *made* it the hot issue. Because nobody could tell her what she needed to know: *Why not me?*

That's a powerful question! said her phone brightly in her ear. "Why not me?" can come from many places: ambition, frust—

Damn, she'd unconsciously subvocalized again. She cut her phone off with a *consciously* subvocalized, Shut up. As always, the irony of an algorithm trying to answer the question made her roll her eyes. But despite pushing and struggling and fighting and *earning* her right to be here, she was no closer to answering it herself.

In her first week on Capitol Hill, she'd been taken aside by a fatherly congressman who was old enough to have been in office during the Cybercrash and told, very kindly, that she needed to stop pushing her AI transparency agenda so hard. In fact, in the upcoming vote, the smart move would be to vote *against* her agenda. After all, AI bias was a complex issue, and in this circumstance, it was on the wrong side of a bill that included elements beneficial to all Americans. Setting aside her interest and voting for the common good would show she was a team player ready to work with the consensus and would gain her political collateral to use later when overturning the entrenched thinking on AI was more likely.

Chloe had known she was in for a fight, but she hadn't expected this. One of the few positive things about the Cybercrash was that the creaky old two-party system had imploded in the chaos. So many political parties had tried to form in the aftermath, with so many conflicting ideas, that they'd stratified into not two parties but two dozen, which soon schismed into two hundred, like cells dividing not to reproduce but to get as far from their neighbors as possible. Rather than getting a single party's nomination, a politician now collected stamps of approval from the parties—the stampers—that fit their interests. If a politician was in favor of increased defense spending but with an isolationist foreign policy, they might get stamped by the Strong Ds (officially the Homeland Defense Party) and the Bald Doves (the American Eagle Party), respectively. If they collected enough rubber stamps, or at least enough of the important ones, they found themselves in the national conversation. Voters checked who'd been approved by the stampers championing the issues they cared about and voted accordingly. The political discourse, both on the Hill and among the public, hadn't exactly gotten more civil, but it was at least fully about the issues, not "My party is perfect and can do no wrong and yours is evil and can never be trusted to do or even think anything good ever."

That should mean that each politician was beholden only to their constituents, not to a party. But here she was, being told to sacrifice her beliefs in the service of some "common good" as defined by this patriarchal relic of the previous system. She had politely declined, mostly managing to keep the distaste out of her voice, and had voted against the bill, as she'd promised.

The bill had passed in a landslide. And she'd been politically frozen.

Oh, everyone was polite to her. Everyone was congenial, greeting her with smiles, inquiring about her day, her weekend plans, her family. But she wasn't invited to anything. She wasn't nominated to committees. She wasn't asked to collaborate. When she tried to join conversations, they downshifted into small talk before evaporating in a cloud of vague smiles and vaguer excuses. As bad as the old tribalistic parties had been, being without a tribe at all didn't feel any better.

She stabbed her chicken. She wasn't invited to dinner gatherings either. She was here tonight because this dinner, hosted by the Joint Committee on National Networks in honor of the twenty-fifth anniversary of the launch of OverNet, was for every sitting congressperson. Norman wanted everyone here for his rumored earthshaking announcement. But she was sitting alone. Even the few colleagues who'd voted *nay* along with her avoided her. She was too new, without enough clout, and, in her frozen state, more likely to be a liability than an asset.

The bill had hung in the Senate and was now back in the House in a revised version and up for another vote, and she was seriously considering voting against her promises. Maybe then she wouldn't find herself alone at a back corner table at the next banquet. She thought of that now—of logging in to VoteNet with her MeNetID, of subvocalizing her *aye*—and a flush of nausea made her choke on her piece of chicken before it was even off her fork.

"Careful," said a voice, and Chloe jumped at the realization that she was not, in fact, alone at this table. Someone had joined her while she'd been lost in introspection: an older woman, short, very sharply dressed, with a face Chloe felt she should recognize, almost did recognize, but not quite. She was angled toward Chloe rather than the rest of the room or Andrew Norman, studying her with intent green eyes.

Chloe subvocalized a command to her phone to run a trust check on the woman's MeNetID but drew a blank, which meant first, that the woman wasn't famous or in the newsfeeds, and second, that she'd marked her MeNetID as nondiscoverable. That was unusual. Most people left their MeNetID visible because closing it implicitly signaled that you were trying to hide low trustworthiness. "I don't think we've met?" Chloe said. "I'm Chloe Dunne-Carr." She didn't extend her hand. She wasn't sure it would be taken. The woman's posture was closed, contained, though her eyes watched Chloe brightly.

"I know," the woman said. There was an awkward pause as she failed to volunteer her own name. Chloe struggled to remember if she *had* met this woman before, but she couldn't have because her phone's facial recognition would have remembered and given her a "last interacted" date at the very least.

The woman leaned forward. "How are you?" she said, with more intensity than those words usually held.

"What? Oh, that. Just too much chicken."

"You don't have to be."

"Come again?"

"You don't have to be chicken. Even if that's what they want you to be."

Chloe stared. The woman looked levelly back. "I'm sorry, Ms. . . . ?" Chloe said at last.

"Don't be sorry. And don't be chicken. I've been watching you. I think I like you."

"Um, thanks?"

"I like you because you're sitting by yourself. I like you because you did exactly what you said you'd do when you were elected. That's happened, let's see, thirty-eight percent of the time in the last ten years, and eighty-nine percent of that thirty-eight percent was because it was pragmatically expedient and cost nothing."

"That's awfully specific."

"I'm an awfully specific sort of person," the woman said. "And I like an awfully specific sort of person."

"The kind that's not pragmatic?"

The woman leaned back. "To hell with pragmatism, girl. Speak your thoughts. Vote your principles. Always. What's the worst they can do? Fire you? Not for two years, and even then it's not up to them."

Chloe decided she liked this woman back, or would if she had a chance to stop and think. "I had a grandma like you. But I don't think we've met."

"We haven't."

"So who are you?" She made the question explicit.

"A grandma is someone who smooths your way? Pulls strings? Tells you when you're doing good, tells you to grow a spine when you need one?"

"Um. Yes?" That had certainly been true of Yai, but Chloe had always thought part of her toughness came from suddenly finding herself playing the role of parent at a time when she should have been learning to slow down and stop pushing herself so hard.

"That fits, then," the woman said, satisfied.

Chloe stifled a laugh. "I'm not going to call you 'Grandma.'"

"Call me whatever you want; I don't care. But if you stand up for yourself, I'll do what I can for you. And maybe you can return the favor."

"Isn't trading favors a bit pragmatic?" Chloe said, smiling.

The woman beamed. Her face wrinkled like an apple—she must be older than she'd looked at first—and her eyes twinkled from the creases. "Now I'm sure I like you."

"Who the hell are you, though?" Chloe asked, but a sudden quieting drew her attention back to the ballroom, where everyone was seating themselves and looking expectantly at the raised platform at the head of the hall.

Senator Evans, chair of the Joint Committee on National Networks, was at the podium. "Don't worry," he said into the microphone, "I'm not going to give a speech." There were chuckles. Evans was famous for his speeches—specifically, their length. "I'm not even going to list our speaker's many accomplishments, because that would take longer than one of my soliloquies." More chuckles. "I'll only say this. Twenty-five years ago, the Cybercrash changed our nation forever. But it didn't destroy it, and that is due to our resilience as a united people, and the brilliance of one man. And so I give you the architect of our peace, with an exciting announcement for our future: Andrew Norman."

Evans stepped back, joining in the thunderous applause, and Norman stepped to the podium. His characteristic lopsided smile, the one that had graced NewsNet for decades, was turned modestly downward, but even looking at the carpet, his sharp blue eyes seemed to be considering something no one else could see. And when he looked up as the applause rolled over the room and his smile widened into symmetry, the effect was extraordinary. "Thank you," he said, holding his hands up for quiet. "We're here on the twenty-fifth anniversary of the founding of OverNet, and while that's cause for celebration, it also means that this year marks the twenty-fifth anniversary of the Cybercrash, which is cause for reflection. The issues that led to the Cybercrash were never solved; they were just compartmentalized and controlled. If we want to advance as a nation, as a species, we need a permanent solution. It was always my intention to create that solution. I built OverNet to receive it. But the technology wasn't there . . . until now. Tonight, after decades of research and development, I can finally announce that the solution is nearing completion. It's a brand-new kind of system, one never before seen on the face of the planet: not a mere artificial intelligence, but an artificial *general* intelligence."

He paused, and though there were murmurs of surprise from many of the tables, it was clearly a more muted reaction than he'd hoped for. Most people continued to look expectant, waiting for him to explain more.

Chloe's reaction was not muted. The blood drained from her face, and for a moment the room blurred.

An AGI. He was making a *phreaking* AGI.

An AGI was supposed to be a truly intelligent system, a machine that was self-aware and able to reason as well as, or better than, a human. Before the Cybercrash, it had been the unvoiced assumption that AGI was the ultimate goal of computer science, its teleological end. She'd thought the Cybercrash had discredited such AI utopianism. Apparently not for Norman.

Never mind that the son of a bitch couldn't do it, not really; nobody could. It was bad enough that he *thought* he could. That whatever panyon he'd created had convinced him, and so would convince others, that it was—her stomach twisted—sentient.

She'd missed several sentences, but now the word *fear* drew her attention back. "All we have to fear," Norman was saying, "is in our past. I mean that in two ways. I mean that the worst is over; this system will guarantee a Cybercrash never happens again. And I mean that the attitudes that seek to return us to the past are our biggest threat, because they demonstrate a reluctance to learn and grow. After all, what do we have to lose by continuing forward?"

Norman paused for a sip of water, leaving the rhetorical question hanging in the air. "Someone should tell him," Chloe muttered, so quietly she thought no one else could hear, but the old woman turned her head suddenly and fixed Chloe with her sharp green eyes.

"Why not you?" she said.

Chloe froze. It was an uncanny echo of the question she'd been asking herself, literally muttering under her breath, for five years, from the words to the almost bewildered inflection. *Why not me?*

They'd told her it was so only one person would die. A neat, utilitarian solution. But she'd been there. The boy had stepped back. The car couldn't have known he'd do that. Its choices were to continue straight and hit her cab, killing its driver and Chloe both, or to save its driver by swerving into the much softer obstacle of two teenage pedestrians. Either way, two people would die. So why had it chosen to take action, chosen to pull the proverbial trolley lever, instead of letting events unfold, letting the trolley—the car—continue on its original ballistic course?

Why had it killed Mia Cromartie?

Why not me?

The answer could only be because the algorithm had, in that split-second moment, factored something else into its decision, something that wasn't the number of people to be killed, but by the *kinds* of people to be killed.

In the car was Jerod Harrington Jr., son of Jerod Harrington Sr., successful hedge fund manager. Jerod Jr. was going through a rebellious phase, like so many kids did who were born with a golden spoon in their mouths. Funny how they never rebelled by rejecting the spoon; more like they tried to swallow not only what it was feeding them but the spoon itself, and choked. But the thing about golden-spoon kids was that they usually got over their choking fit and ended up managing Daddy's hedge fund after he retired, or some other inherited achievement. Chloe had run a trust check on

Jerod when she'd learned his name. It was seventy-three. Not bad, and it would only rise in the future.

In the cab was Chloe Dunne, recently tenured academic. Also recently divorced, but as it had been an "amicable" split that didn't ding her score, which was eighty-five, plus or minus a point depending on which app she used to run the scan and which day she ran it on. That was nudging the top of the meter for an academic who wasn't a famous author or Nobel Prize winner or whatever. She'd always been a contributing member of society and could be expected to remain so.

Kleio was also in the cab, but Chloe herself didn't yet know she was pregnant, so there was no way the algorithm could have added her to its calculations.

On the street were Jason and Mia Cromartie, twins, months from aging out of the foster system, already with juvenile criminal records. Trust scores of forty-two (boy) and fifty-four (girl). Those were bad scores. But did that mean they were bad kids? And even if they were, did that give the car the right to divert its course to hit them?

Chloe had tried to track Jason down. But by that time, he'd turned eighteen and disappeared so thoroughly that either he was intentionally—and skillfully—hiding or he'd decided to vanish in a more permanent fashion.

And that would have been the end of it, except that one day not long afterward, a message had appeared in her email, from a hidden sender, which shouldn't have been possible. It was empty except for two attachments: a dark, gloomy image of a fairy and a transcript of an old meeting.

One phrase in that transcript grabbed her attention: "Prioritize the happiness of the greatest number of people who might potentially complain." Jerod dies, and his dad asks questions. Chloe dies, and her grandmother, her ex-husband, her colleagues at the university ask questions. But two teenage foster kids die, who asks questions?

Even Chloe hadn't asked questions until she'd gotten that email, probably because she didn't want answers, not then. After the email, getting answers was all she could think of. It was why she'd given up her dream job—tenured professor of medieval history at Santa Clarita University—for the uncertain world of politics.

All this passed through Chloe's mind in the space it took Norman to sip his water. Grandma was still looking at her, and the question—*Why not me?*—hung in the air.

To hell with pragmatism. Chloe felt herself standing, and with a faint feeling of disbelief, heard herself say in a voice that cut across the ballroom, "Potentially everything."

There was a brief, concerted rustling as several hundred important people swiveled in their chairs to look at the back table where Chloe stood. "Please save all comments for—" Evans began, but Norman raised a hand, and he subsided instantly.

"No, no," Norman said with a faint smile. "I'd like to hear what's on Dr. Dunne-Carr's mind."

"What's on my mind is a story." Standing had been a mistake. Chloe's knees were vibrating, and she had the urge to hunch away from all those eyes. She straightened her shoulders and back instead. "The story of a girl named Jasmine. She's twenty-four. Bright, the first in her family to go to college. Goes to Santa Clarita U, where I taught. She's studying to become a paramedic. She works evenings as a waitress in her neighborhood, where the restaurants can't afford dronebots, to help with bills." Chloe's voice stabilized, because this was a speech she'd given a dozen times before, and because even though this was a speech she'd given a dozen times before, she still cared about it, still felt the meaning of each sentence as she said it. "When Jasmine applies for an apartment in a less dangerous neighborhood, her application is denied—not by a person, but by a scoring system that flagged her as high risk. Why? Maybe her inconsistent gig income. Maybe a past-due phone bill. She never even sees the report."

She paused to let that sink in and to take a breath. The ballroom was silent, all eyes still on her. Some of them belonged to NewsNet reporters, staring with the blank, fixed intensity of people keeping their lens cameras carefully focused. For better or worse, she was on the national stage in a way she'd never been, not even when giving this speech before Congress. This, *this* was news, because it involved Andrew Norman. She glanced down at "Grandma," who was watching with a faint smile.

"She applies for a paramedic internship," she continued. "Her résumé is scanned and rejected before a human eye lands on it. Maybe it's her zip code, which, remember, she just failed to change. Or maybe it's because she struggles with depression. Oh, that fact isn't divulged to other systems, but her insurance app's stress tracker labels her noncompliant, and that *is* considered revealable, and revealing, information. But Jasmine isn't noncompliant—she just doesn't open the app anymore. It only ever told her to hydrate, sleep, and practice mindfulness, whatever the hell that means.

"Then her trust scores begin to drop. Maybe it's that one rant on a bad day that got downvoted to oblivion on MeNet. Maybe it's the Spanglish in her posts, language patterns which, regardless of their content, root her in a statistical subset of the population the AI pattern-matches with untrustworthiness, even though it's supposedly trained to never directly consider race. Or maybe it's her friends' friends, guilt by degrees of association. There's no way to know. But a feedback loop begins. A lower trust score reduces her visibility. That impacts her ability to find better jobs. Which affects her financial stability. Which gets her flagged by BankNet. When BankNet adjusts her microcredit limits, that ripples back through RentNet and MedNet, reducing her score again. No one sees it. No one questions it. But each system reinforces the others in a feedback loop that ensures she never rises above her current circumstances. And Jasmine's one of the lucky ones, because she's managed to escape law enforcement attention—so far. She has to be very, very careful not to draw that particular eye, because she's seen the kind of suspicion and repercussions even a small offense can bring down on someone like her.

"Because Jasmine's not being judged by her character. She's being judged on invisible criteria by nonhuman entities in a way that's opaque to the very humans who accept their judgments. If those AIs make a mistake, she has no recourse. She can't appeal to an algorithm. There's no courthouse for machine-made decisions.

"AI, we've been told, is a black box. Somehow we all accept this. Well, I don't. Because when we don't know what these systems value, what they see, what they miss, they stop being tools and become silent laws. And so, Dr. Norman, I'm very skeptical that a new algorithm, an even bigger and blacker box, is in any way a solution to the problems experienced by Jasmine and millions of her fellow Americans every day."

She stopped. In the heavy, embarrassed silence, she was reminded of teaching undergrads, of tying the threads of a lecture together to highlight the theme only to be met with half-bored, half-defiant expressions as they failed to take the point. Then Andrew Norman cleared his throat.

"But the systems are here," he said. "Is your solution to ask people to give them up? Because they won't. It's not in human nature to give up conveniences. Though you're welcome to start a new stamper, if you like. Call it the Luddites, perhaps."

Laughter rippled through the ballroom, and Chloe's teeth clicked tight. "I'd rather be a Luddite," she said through them, "than a technophiliac high priest so out of touch with the people that he thinks his 'systems' can fix human nature."

Norman ran a hand through his white beard. "You clearly want to make this personal," he said in a quiet voice that his microphone amplified to fill the ballroom. "I'm sorry you feel the need to do that. Because I agree with you."

Chloe had been opening her mouth to retort, but at this, the words she'd been about to fling at him died, turning her expression into a gape.

"OverNet and MeNet addressed the problems that led to the Crash," Norman said to the room at large. "But as the congresswoman pointed out, by solving these problems, we've created new ones. I purposefully avoided creating a social capital system like China, but that didn't stop the open market from creating trust-check algorithms, because people want to know who's trustworthy. Those and all the other systems *are* black boxes. How they operate, how they interact with each other, and the feedback loops they create are opaque to us, not because we designed them that way, not because we're hiding anything, but because they're so complex that we literally can't comprehend them." Norman's voice had settled into a tone he used often, one that combined a kindly storyteller with the sharpness of absolute certainty. "There's a whole subfield of computer science generating thousands of papers a year just trying to figure out how these AI models work internally, not to mention how they interact with other systems. But any understanding we gain is either painfully general or applicable only to a single, post hoc chain of causation that will never recur. As our world has grown more complex, we've offloaded our understanding of it to systems which can't return that understanding to us."

"And *your* solution is an even more complex system?" Chloe demanded.

"Yes," Norman said simply. "A system that combines the best qualities of computers—the ability to see and process vast amounts of information—with humanlike intuition and understanding. A system that can both process all that complexity and make *sense* of it, draw out its meaning." He paused and looked with a knowing half smile across all the intervening heads and directly into Chloe's eyes. "A system," he said deliberately, "that can tell us *why*."

Chloe reeled. She'd been set up. This was a trap, a premeditated trick to neatly maneuver her into speaking up so Norman could turn her story against her to support his own points. She managed to sputter an incredulous "And you think you can build that system?" The question should have been enough; it should have been obvious to everyone that he was talking about a level of control that was impossible, that it was arrogance even to imagine.

"I already have," Norman said. "The Final System." She could hear the capital letters. "It's the result of two decades of work. It will allow us to at last bring about an age of peace and justice. I promise."

Applause, riotous applause. Because Andrew Norman kept his promises. Chloe wanted to protest. She wanted to point out how dystopian the term *Final System* sounded in her ears, especially the way he phrased it: not *his* final system but *the* Final System. The Last One.

But even as the thought occurred to her, she saw herself through the applauders' eyes. She was the outsider, the one who'd challenged the Great Man and would be swept away by history like all the others who'd predicted his failure. "He had an outsize impact on his age," they would say of Andrew Norman in future History 101 textbooks. *Impact.* Funny how the word for making history was the same as for an asteroid strike. Great Men left an impression on the world, all right: They left a crater.

She looked at the old woman, but she was gone, as if she'd never been there in the first place. Who was she, some dark antiversion of a fairy godmother? Someone who shows up when you think you're at your lowest point and, instead of remaking you into royalty, tells you to be even more the person you already are—someone nobody cares about, someone who can't make a positive change no matter how hard she tries? Chloe sank into her chair.

Marcus had worried she wasn't ready for politics. "You're too nice in some ways and not nice enough in others," he'd said. When she'd won the election, there'd been a breathless moment when she wasn't sure he'd follow her here, when *he* might be the one leaving, but he had come. And now he was a work-at-home dad, teaching summer classes in VR, and when Kleio had asked why Mommy was gone during the day, he'd said, "Mommy is a busy and important woman." He probably hadn't meant it the way Chloe had taken it, as a subtle hint that she was misplacing her priorities. But when she'd won this seat in Congress, he'd told her, "I only hope the Chloe who finishes her term is the same Chloe who started it. The Chloe I know."

So far her busy and important political career had consisted of sitting in an office, wishing she had more to do. She had no friends, no allies, no influence, no committee roles, no chance to do anything except show up, cast her pointless votes, and, after two years, go home and pick up teaching, where she would fail to influence her students.

But hey, she'd still be that same powerless Chloe she'd been when she started, so Marcus should be happy.

Her eyes landed on "Grandma" at the far end of the banquet hall, in a congratulatory group gathering around Norman. The old woman was looking back over her shoulder at Chloe, and her lips were curved slightly in a small, satisfied smile.

CHAPTER 3

"I thought I was going to jail," Jason said, looking around the social rehabilitation center. The only other time he'd been in a social rehab, he'd been surprised to find it not seedy and dirty but almost clinically clean. But any place with federal funding *would* be spotless. The whine and thump of janitorial dronebots was as omnipresent as the clicks of keys and low mutters from the couple of people using the kiosk terminals.

"All in good time," Bruno said. He escorted Jason to an open kiosk far from anyone else and released his cop grip on Jason's arm. "Sit."

Jason did, heavily. He'd only sat at one of these kiosks once before, despite having been homeless several times in his life. Free food and shelter were available at social rehabs across the nation, and you didn't need to interact directly with a human being, since research showed that the homeless and others down on their luck were less likely to use welfare services if they felt they might have to explain themselves to and/or be judged by their fellow humans. Everything was done via these kiosks, which dispensed information, food, bedding, and room keys. You didn't even have to fill out a form.

The problem wasn't what the kiosks gave, but what they took: Pictures of your face. Lots of pictures of your face. You were then automatically assigned a pseudonym and logged in the PsychNet database. First visitors were typically left alone, but the system watched for patterns. Multiple visits in a short time? Signs of drug use? Signs of violence? Face identified as probably a minor? You'd be asked to divulge your MeNetID and download a counseling chatbot, which would cheerfully walk you through setting a goal for a lifestyle change, and then monitor everywhere you went, everything you did, everyone you talked to, everything you purchased, and nag you to make choices that were good for you—good for you according to the people at PsychNet, anyway. Reject the program or refuse to give up your MeNetID and you'd shortly be located by a concerned human counselor, flanked by an armed cop, anxious to help you make the life adjustments that would enable you to become a contributing member of society again.

Mia had kicked the counselor in the shins and the cop in the balls.

But the stolen ghost MeNetID, the one Jason had social-engineered in a monthslong process that had been the triumph of his young life, had been blown. He hadn't been experienced at evading street-level surveillance at sixteen, and they'd lasted less than forty-eight hours in their grand escape. After that, they'd been sent to a new foster home, one that somehow managed to be the worst yet. The incident taught Jason that having a new identity wasn't enough; you needed to fit in, fly under the radar, accept no help. For that, you needed a marketable skill, one you could translate into money. He'd realized hacking could be that skill, if you knew the right market.

It would have worked, too, but before he was ready, Andrew Norman's algorithm made its "choice," and Mia was gone.

The kiosk screen came alive with a video of a smiling cartoon dog in spectacles and a medical jacket. Jason narrowed his eyes at it. "Can't I just go straight to jail?"

"This is mandatory processing," Bruno said, leaning down over his shoulder so the kiosk cameras could see his face and doubtless identify him as an NNA agent. "You may access this citizen's MeNetID," he told the kiosk, then stood back again.

The cartoon dog's expression changed to one of grave thoughtfulness, and it said in an entirely normal voice that clashed with it cartoon visage, "Hello, Jason. It looks like you've had a misadventure. Don't worry—I'm here to help. Let's see: Based on your lifetime's MeNet interactions, third-party consumer trust-rating programs would assign you an average score of forty-eight. That's not the worst rating I've seen, but it's not great either. In a free and democratic society such as ours, people are at liberty to choose whom they associate with, and it's human nature to prefer to associate with trustworthy people. A low trust rating may make others feel that interacting with you is unsafe. Ninety-seven percent of your fellow citizens use these programs, and they are free to choose not to employ or otherwise associate with you beyond the few limits specified by law. But I can help you improve your score. Would you like that?"

"No," Jason said. He subvocalized, Text Sprite an eyegrab and the caption, "Getting therapized by an emotional support GIF. Send help." But the usual confirming chime in his ear and flicker of the messaging window in his smartspace didn't occur. His phone was powered off in the back of the NNA van, but a lifetime of habits died hard. Not to mention half a decade of being able to talk to Sprite whenever he needed.

He'd tried to avoid thinking too much about what his Collective handler might be like in real life. Partly that was because anything he imagined would be speculation—"she" could be a forty-year-old man, for all he knew. Partly it was because he was aware of his own naivete in the area of girls. A life focused on vengeance left no time for them, so Sprite was the only "girl" in his life—again with "girl" in scare quotes. If his imagination got involved, it would be easy to build a dangerous and unwarranted attachment. But he'd grown reliant on her virtual presence. Once, late at night, he'd texted her on some pretext, and they'd ended up texting back and forth for hours, musing about Life, the Universe, and Everything, until she'd said, Don't you have a panyon to ask existential questions at 2:00 the morning?

No, he'd replied. Panyons aren't people.

Good, she'd said, and he'd felt a tiny thrill, but she hadn't said anything else, and he sure as hell wasn't going to volunteer anything that might jeopardize their working relationship, so the conversation had ended there.

"I'm sorry to hear that," the dog was saying. "It looks like much of your rating is based on interactions you had when you were a minor in the foster care system. That's understandable. The foster system is a challenging environment to grow up in. Many former foster children reach adulthood with low trust scores. Since your score is not assigned to you but is calculated by third parties based on your permanent history of interactions with citizens and organizations, no government network, agency, or personnel has the power to directly change them. However, there are several federal programs available by which you may have past records and interactions hidden, making them invisible for factoring into an average. Minors with low ratings are automatically offered enrollment in such a program upon reaching adulthood, but you rejected the program when it was offered to you. Would you like to explore the program now?"

"No," Jason said again.

"I'm sorry to hear that. Many people with lower ratings find that they can receive a substantial quality-of-life improvement by participating in this intervention. Are you sure you're not interested?"

Jason snorted. Once upon a time, people could just disappear. Once upon a time, you didn't need a McNetID, didn't need your digital suitcase of social capital—sorry, *transparency*—to function in society. You could reinvent yourself simply by moving away from your past, figuratively and literally. But today, why would you want to disappear? There was help. There was always help, for every problem. The thing was to bring it into the light, let it be seen, let the caring folks at the nearest social rehab get you fixed up, get you reintegrated. *Trust the system, Jason.* "Phreak you," he told the dog.

"I'm sorry to hear that. Please verbally confirm your rejection of this intervention by speaking the following phrase aloud: 'I reject intervention from Social Rehabilitation Services at this time. I understand that I may change my mind at any point and request an intervention.'"

"I reject intervention from Social Rehabilitation Services at this time and at all times," Jason said. "I understand that I may change my mind at any point and request an intervention, but I won't."

The dog disappeared, and the screen displayed a green check mark and the words, YOU'RE DONE! FOLLOW THE DIRECTIONS OF YOUR CASE WORKER, AGENT BRUNO TAVION.

"*Now* you go to jail," Bruno said.

But as they stepped out into the evening sunlight, Bruno stopped so suddenly that Jason almost stumbled over him. Bruno said to someone in his smartspace, "Say again? Really? *Really.*" He turned to Jason and said in a carefully level voice, "What did you do?"

"What do you mean?" Jason asked, but his tensely hunched shoulders loosened a smidge.

Bruno didn't say more but led Jason back to the NNA van, where it waited at the curb. Once inside, he didn't tell the van to take them anywhere. Instead, he settled across from Jason, reached into Jason's bag of belongings and thumbed on his phone, then handed Jason an NNA-branded case. "Put on your kit."

The case held his smartbuds and, floating in solution, his smartlenses. Jason screwed the buds in and blinked the lenses into place, then nodded at Bruno.

The van interior disappeared, replaced by a spacious office environment. At first Jason thought it was a computer-generated location, because it was too big and too beautiful to be real. Greenery lined the walls and arched toward the ceiling. Water ran in channels edging a marble floor, and sheet waterfalls poured down huge windows at the back of the room. But a slight graininess told him this place was real; the images were being captured in real time from multiple cameras and stitched together in correct perspective in his lenses. Then his view adjusted abruptly to place him in the center rear of the room, facing a wide touch-screen desk and the man just taking a seat behind it.

Andrew Norman.

The great man's famous blue eyes were fixed on Jason's, cool and ironic. Jason was glad this was VR. If it were real life, he'd be halfway across the desk, hands seeking throat, all his and Sprite's careful plans forgotten, because this was the man who had killed Mia.

"Jason Eric Cromartie," Norman said. "Also known as Ghost." His lips compressed. "Do you know how long I've been looking for you? You almost put Ikshana out of business when you leaked their financial data."

Jason's breath hitched. Norman shouldn't know that was him. "It was my civic duty to blow the whistle on their corruption," he said virtuously.

Norman turned to Bruno, who was now sitting not across from Jason but next to him. Both were seated on generic 3D models of chairs, and their bodies from the necks down were generic 3D models of people, but their heads and faces were their own. It was strange to see Bruno's head on an average body instead of one bulging with muscle. "Mr. Tavion," Norman said in a gentle voice, "where's your phone?"

"In my pocket," Bruno said, frowning.

"That's good. I was worried Ghost might have kept it."

Bruno's puzzled frown deepened. "He never—"

Norman cut him off. "Oh, at some point he did. He social-engineered your phone from you, probably so smoothly you don't remember, and used it to send a message. To me. Directly. This message." He made a tossing motion with his hands, and a window flew up and unfolded to hang in space before Jason and Bruno. Inside was a screenshot of a direct chat from Bruno to Norman, flagged as emergency priority:

> This cybersecurity penetration test was provided to you by GH05T Phreaking, Limited. White hats wasting your time? Noobs annoying you? For all your realistic red team needs, conjure a GH05T. Real phreaker, real results. Available for individual contracts or retainer.
>
> P.S. Tell Agent Tavion his gangster act needs work.

Bruno's eyebrows both rose over the top of his smartglasses. "I'll be damned," he rumbled, cocking his head at Jason. "You knew the whole time?"

Jason grinned at him. "You're not a bad gangster. A little overboard, a little Hollywood, but not bad. You should try it for real. Bet you'd find it liberating."

Bruno shook his head. "My cover was supposed to be perfect."

Jason didn't reply. It *was* perfect, a complex breadcrumb trail of escalating crime history hidden by professional MeNetID sanitization, and it had been a challenge even for a phreaker of Jason's caliber to uncover it. He'd seen through it for one reason only: No one, not even the most hardened criminal, not even the Chinese or the phreaking Russians, would dare attack the NNA directly. So he'd intuited that Bruno was not, in fact, a criminal, but someone working for the NNA. He was red-teaming, testing the NNA's security by trying to infiltrate it. Or, rather, by hiring Jason to infiltrate it. It was a two-for-one: a penetration test and a honey trap. They could test the NNA's security *and* put a hacker behind bars.

It had been too good an opportunity to pass up. Sprite had agreed. Together they'd hatched this scheme, and Sprite had gotten MorDread's grudging approval—for this stage, at least.

"Unorthodox way of sending a job application," Norman said, waving a languid hand at the message.

"It got me an interview," Jason said.

"Indeed. And why should I retain your services, Mr. Ghost?"

"For a start, because I bet none of the other phreakers Bruno enlisted in his red-teaming managed to phish an NNA login. I'm that good."

"But hardly good enough. You were detected."

"I wanted to get caught."

"You would have been caught regardless."

"Wanna bet?"

Norman leaned back and gave Jason one of his iconic, ironic half smiles. "Bet what, Mr. Ghost? What could you possibly offer me?"

"Simple: a truly challenging security test for your Final System, the best possible test it can get before it's launched on OverNet."

As a bombshell intended to shock Norman with what Jason knew, this fell flat. Norman's expression didn't change. "You haven't given me any evidence that you *could* challenge it," he said.

Norman should have been impressed, even concerned, that Jason knew about the Final System. Either he had a better poker face than Jason had thought, or . . . Jason subvocalized a quick NewsNet search for the term *Final System.*

It was plastered atop every single news site.

Damn. Lose phone access for a couple of hours and suddenly you're behind the times. His stomach clenched. Norman announcing the thing publicly meant the timeline was more compressed than he'd thought.

Norman was looking at him expectantly. Jason leaned forward. "I'm a real phreaker, not some pansy white hat. And as a real phreaker, I phreaking hate that thing. It's the summit of your stupid, naive, Singularity-seeking worldview, your smug belief that your systems can decide what's best for humanity. I hate it so much, I don't give a damn what happens to me: I'm gonna destroy it. You won't get a better red-team exercise than that. Unless you think I'll win. Unless you're scared."

Norman was quiet for a long moment, head cocked as if listening. At last he said, in a conversational tone, "I despise phreakers. Despite what you try to believe, you tear down, not build up. You break systems, you don't fix them. You are the bugs in the machine." He leaned forward and planted his elbows on his desk. "Do you know what happened to the very first bug, the *literal* bug Grace Hopper found in Harvard's mainframe in 1947? It got fried by the very system it was glitching. It was preserved in Hopper's diary under transparent tape, as a museum piece. That's you, Ghost: a museum piece playing with electricity." He propped his chin on one fist, his eyes never leaving Jason's. "When that mainframe was fixed, it was stronger for it. The systems always come back stronger. When you were identified, I wanted to incarcerate you immediately. Do you know who convinced me to let Agent Tavion run a red-team test with you first?"

The question hung in the air until Jason shook his head.

"The Final System did. And the Final System is now agreeing with you that you're the best phreaker to test it. Not because of your skill—that is merely sufficient—but, yes, because of your motivation. So I will allow you to attack it. In defeating you, it will prove its readiness for the tasks ahead. Not to me—I don't need convincing—but to the politicians I need to vote in favor of letting it take its place atop OverNet."

"That sounds like a job offer."

Norman nodded. "For your compensation, if you behave satisfactorily, I'll let you walk free."

"I can't exactly negotiate better terms. When do I start?"

"Tomorrow," Norman said. "Mr. Tavion will help set up your next attempt."

"I'll need to work from an NNA terminal."

"No," Norman said, then cocked his head again, listening to someone—or something. "Fine. If we assume your attack today was real, that would mean you had a foothold in the NNA's internal network. You may start there tomorrow. But you receive no other help."

"I won't need it."

"I look forward to my System proving you wrong," Norman said, and Jason's last sight before his session disconnected was of the man's smirk. The VR view dissolved. He was once again in the back of the NNA van, and Bruno, shaking his head, was leaning across the aisle to snip his zipcuffs and hand him his phone.

It took Jason two tries to text Sprite, because even his subvocalization was shaking from exultation and lingering adrenaline. Level 1 Clear. Level 2 Start. Tell MorDread to get the botnet ready.

CHAPTER 4

A rising scream and approaching, thudding footfalls jolted Chloe out of sleep, and her bed shook under the weight of a small but extremely energetic little monster. "Oh my gosh, Kleio, don't *do* that!" she said, sitting up. "You're gonna give Mommy a heart attack."

Kleio bounced on her hands and knees, making her unkempt curls bob around her face. "Today is fene park day!"

"Today is what?"

"'Theme Park Day,'" Marcus translated sleepily from the other side of the bed. "You promised her last night."

"I did?"

Marcus rolled over. His dark eyes were tight with concern. "Yeah. Remember?"

The previous evening came back to Chloe in a single, deflating moment. "Oh," she said. "Yeah."

She and Marcus had talked for hours after she'd gotten home. She'd wanted to resign. "The Chloe I know is anything but a quitter," Marcus had told her. Which was nice of him to say, considering she'd once quit their marriage. But the thought of going back into the office as a laughingstock, sitting there alone with little to do day after day for almost two more years, was suffocating.

They'd been too intent talking to get Kleio ready for bed. She'd been unusually quiet, sensing Mommy's unhappiness and climbing into her lap. And that had been good. Marcus's arms around her, Kleio's squirmy little body in her own arms . . . those things were real, and still good, even if Chloe's dreams had been shattered. So when Kleio had excitedly asked if Mommy's talk about staying home meant they could finally have the long-promised Theme Park Day trip, Chloe had agreed. It would be healthy to take one day off, at least, to root herself in the realness of her family, to remind herself of what she still had.

"Okay," she told Kleio now. "Go get dressed!"

With another ear-piercing shriek of joy, Kleio rolled off the bed and thumped away down the hallway.

"My gosh," Chloe groaned, falling backward into her pillows. "What time is it?"

"It's actually past nine," Marcus said. "She let us sleep. Nice of her, since we were up until almost two in the morning."

"She went to bed when we did," Chloe said. Though Kleio had first fallen asleep on Chloe's lap. "How does she always have the energy to be such a little troublemaker?"

"Takes after her mother," Marcus said, rolling over to give her a kiss, then rolling the other way out of bed.

As Chloe brushed her teeth, she wondered again if she would have picked Kleio. If they'd planned the pregnancy and had the usual dozen dossiers prepared based on the DNA of a dozen viable embryos, would Kleio have been the one who drew her attention, the one whose potential she decided to actualize? She doubted it. When she'd learned she was pregnant, she'd commissioned the dossier, a fifteen-page, glossy, image-filled AI analysis of the baby's DNA that extrapolated her likely temperament and her looks at different ages. It had described an "adventurous" child, and though the terminology had been uniformly positive, Chloe had felt trepidation, reading *confident*, *spontaneous*, and *determined* but thinking *bossy*, *impulsive*, and *stubborn*. She'd wondered where this child had come from. Surely not from her, but not from steady, laid-back Marcus either. But when she'd expressed this thought to him, he'd laughed and said, "Sounds like the kind of girl who might do something like, oh, spontaneously decide to take on the world to fight AI injustice."

Now that Kleio was here, she did look very much like the four-year-old picture from the dossier, and she was confident, spontaneous, and determined, *and* bossy, impulsive, and stubborn. And, yes, very much a little version of Chloe, though she looked more like Marcus. That snub nose was goofy-sweet on him and positively adorable on her. Chloe might not have picked her, but she wouldn't give her up for the world.

So yes, Chloe was a fortunate woman. Even if she didn't feel like it this morning.

As she put her lenses in, she was tempted to take her phone off Do Not Disturb and check NewsNet to see how awful the coverage of her impromptu speech was. But Marcus had advised against it last night, and he was doubly correct today. Today, she wouldn't give Andrew Norman a single moment of undeserved attention.

She stepped into the living room to find Marcus still in his PJs, being chased by a shrieking Kleio. "Oh, no, hon-bun!" she said. "Not your princess dress! It's not that kind of theme park. Go put on some play clothes."

"This," Marcus told Chloe, panting, "is no mere princess, but Princesszilla, ruler of the living room, stomper of bad guys."

"Raaaawr!" Kleio shouted, raising one foot to show Chloe a neon-green monster slipper under the pink princess frills. She stomped the foot down on Marcus's bare toes, making him wince. He swept her up and tickled her, while she squealed and kicked her monster feet.

Chloe didn't know how Marcus managed to be so *interactive* before caffeine. She went to the kitchen to grab a Bomb Bar. The artificially flavored, artificially caffeinated energy bar wasn't her first choice of morning ritual, but since the Cybercrash had shattered the global economy, America had lost access to 90 percent of its coffee supply. When she'd lived in California, she'd been able to get beans locally at a price that was . . . not reasonable, but at least tolerable. But here in DC, it was only for the rich, who were willing to pay more than Chloe could for their daily fix. So she munched her Bomb—breakfast and coffee all in one—and leaned against the counter to watch as Marcus let Kleio turn the tables and begin chasing him again.

The Cybercrash: Everything came back to that. That was why Norman was so revered, so trusted, so politically invulnerable even when he announced something unhinged like an AGI.

Chloe had been only six years old, only a little older than Kleio was now, far too young to understand what was happening. Her memories of that day were filled with a nameless dread, like one of those nightmares where the familiar day-to-day world becomes twisted with malevolent portent. Her first-grade teacher looking at her phone while the class got rowdier and rowdier, then shocking them all by bursting into tears. Parents showing up at the classroom door, ushering their kids out. Her dad instead of Yai waiting to pick her up, giving her a too-tight, wordless hug that made her scared because of a feeling she couldn't name. The TV at Yai's house flickering without sound. Images of charts and downward-pointing arrows that she couldn't understand but that terrified her because they terrified the adults; then images of crowds, fire, people falling over, newscasters weeping, all cascading by in eerie silence. Her dad sprawled on the couch, staring vacantly into his smartglasses, grunting when Yai talked to him and then suddenly erupting in curses, throwing his glasses at the TV and barely missing Chloe (she thought for years he'd been aiming at her), storming out of the house, slamming the door. And then Yai holding her, humming soothingly while she bawled in bewilderment.

And again and again on the TV screen, a picture of the message she didn't understand, the message every social media account had, simultaneously and without the knowledge of their owners, posted: Hello, World. You've been phreaked.

In the wider country, riots broke out, and sudden viral conspiracy theories took root in fertile soil, turning neighborhoods into war zones. Swaths of DC erupted in flames. Channels of communication failed, never to be resurrected. Fiber lines were severed, firewalls raised. Countries turtled inward for protection. Small wars broke out. The UN folded as nation after nation pulled out. It was the end of the global economy and the beginning of a decade of global depression.

Kleio had succeeded in catching Marcus's legs and was now making him march her around the living room backward, her small monster-clad feet laid atop his size 13 ones, their legs mirrored in awkward, reverse lock-step while she clung and laughed up at him. Chloe felt a familiar bitter-sweet pang.

It was nice, in a way, to think that when everything had gone to hell, when he lost his savings and knew he'd lose his job, her father's chosen method to salvage his self-worth was to go to Chloe, to try to become the archetypal good dad. But he'd never been a good dad before that. Chloe's mother had died of cancer when she was three, and her dad had been unable to cope both with grief and with a spunky toddler who kept complaining that he wasn't doing it like Mommy did. So he'd left his daughter unofficially but increasingly in the care of his wife's quiet, uncomplaining mother. Chloe didn't blame him, not anymore, not after having her own child and learning what it meant to have a tiny human be entirely reliant on you. Her dad didn't know how to handle that. He'd never learned. So when he tried, driving halfway across the state to prove his solidity to himself by becoming a rock for his daughter, he lasted a few hours and then crumpled like papier-mâché.

Now that she was an adult, Chloe could articulate the feeling she'd had when he'd hugged her that day. He was holding her not to protect her but to prop himself up. It was a stark contrast to Yai's arms around her that evening—stringy, bony, weak, but somehow strong as steel.

A month later her dad had given Yai full custody. Chloe hadn't seen him again until she was fifteen, and only sporadically since.

Maybe the real reason Andrew Norman was so revered was because the country as a whole, scared and hurting, had wanted a father as badly as Chloe, wanted someone to protect them, reassure them, come up with a plan, lead the way forward, get things done, make it better. And maybe the reason Chloe didn't imitate the adulation was because she distrusted father figures and distrusted her own lingering wish for one. She'd done just fine without, thank you very much.

But when she'd reconciled with Marcus and they'd decided to do this family thing together, that ache in her heart had opened all over again, because she could see he was an amazing father, and it brought home to her what she'd never had. It was healing to see Kleio open like a flower under his attention. Chloe could acknowledge her loss, face it without denial, because it *was* a loss, because there *were* good, even great, fathers out there, and every little girl deserved one.

She just wasn't convinced that Norman was one.

Her phone rang, *out loud*, a harsh chime in her smartbuds echoed by the phone in her pocket. The caller's name appeared in her smartspace: *Andrew Norman*.

Chloe made a strangled sound and waved frantically at Marcus and Kleio to be quiet. When they had frozen, staring at her, she subvocalized, Answer, audio only.

Norman's face appeared in a window before her. It was a computer-generated re-creation and so not, strictly speaking, his real face, but it was accurate enough to read even the most micro of expressions. That wasn't necessary, because his expression was decidedly macro. He was furious. "Dr. Dunne-Carr," he snapped.

Chloe opened her mouth and a squeak came out. She cleared her throat, glad she was connected only over voice. Her smartbud's muscle sensors could drive a perfectly coiffed re-creation of her face such that it wouldn't matter that her hair was performing experiments with static electricity. But right now she'd be a perfectly coiffed Chloe with eyes bugged out in surprise and trepidation. "Yes?" she managed.

"Where are you?" Norman demanded.

"At home?" Chloe said.

"At *home*? Why the hell—" Norman stopped. "Have you checked your messages this morning?"

"No?" Chloe couldn't seem to keep her voice from rising into uncertain uptalk, like Kleio's when she wasn't sure if she was in trouble.

"You've been on Do Not Disturb this whole morning?"

Chloe nodded, then remembered he couldn't see her. "Yes," she said. Not that that had stopped Norman's call from coming through.

Norman's face relaxed into something almost friendly. "Check your messages. Then get over here to the Tower ASAP. We have a lot of work to do." He disappeared.

Chloe let her arms go slack.

"Who," Marcus demanded, "was that?" He was still comically frozen, one foot half raised, with Kleio hanging on, stifling laughter.

"Only the most important man in the world," Chloe said.

"Ah." Marcus swung Kleio onto his hip. "I've been demoted, then?"

His tone was teasing, so Chloe wrinkled her nose at him. "You know you'll always be the most important man to me." She pulled up her messages. There were half a dozen requests for statements from NewsNet outlets. Her speech had made a splash, as she'd expected—but maybe in a different way than she'd thought, because there was also a message from Senator Evans:

> Hello Chloe, I hope this message finds you well. Andrew Norman suggested you for Mr. Majumdar's vacant position on the Joint Committee on National Networks. I nominated you, and the committee confirmed it. I hope you'll accept the appointment, and join us tomorrow morning at 9:30, at Conference Room 1A, in the Tower.

"Holy sh—" Chloe began, then, catching sight of Kleio's curious little face past the edge of her smartspace window, amended her astonished statement to "—smokes!"

CHAPTER 5

Jason's body was sending just the right amount of adrenaline through his veins to outline this bright morning in primary colors. As the NNA airvan rose into the air, the asphalt shoreline below was a stark demarcation: on one side the city of the past, bare and ugly, and on the other a riot of late-summer green. In the slanting morning sun, the vehicle streets were made visible by the glimmer of cabs and trucks between the trees, while many of the footlanes were hidden entirely by foliage. Even the soaring verticality of the skyscrapers was interrupted every few floors by vine-clad skywalks and overhangs, and the towers were crowned with the thick groves that had earned them the nickname "treescrapers." It was a beautiful morning in the most beautiful city in the world.

The NNA Tower came into view, stabbing upward from the middle of the Potomac. During the Cybercrash riots, the river had protected Arlington from the fires raging in DC, but the forested Theodore Roosevelt Island had caught and burned. Afterward, the Park Service donated it to the newly formed NNA. Nothing was more evocative of the reborn city's aspirations than the two-thousand-foot Tower that now dominated the island and the DC skyline. This, its iconic profile said, is how America rebuilds: It constructs the most beautiful and advanced and eco-friendly city in the world, then crowns it with the most beautiful and advanced and eco-friendly building in the world.

The effect was only slightly marred by the thin tubes that ran up either side of the Tower: the world-famous escape chute system, patented by Norman himself. Because when you build a monument, you also build a target.

Jason was targeting the Tower today in a way he hoped Norman had *not* accounted for.

The airvan followed a long stream of aircabs in a wide, slow arc over the city, before the other vehicles dropped away one by one and theirs was the only one left on a trajectory that put the Tower's dome and two jutting, curving garden wings in the center of the windshield. Steel-and-glass greenhouse latticework roofs reached down to meet the Tower's garden wings. It always struck Jason as ironically fitting that this made each wing look like the corner of a great eye, with the central dome bulging outward in the middle like the eyeball. The eye dominated the windshield for a moment, then the van tilted and plunged across the crowded playgrounds and pathways of the sprawling Tower Park to alight at a visitor pad.

As he followed Bruno out, Jason texted Sprite: What's the word?

Her answer *pinged* in. Same as before: Wait.

He grimaced as he quickstepped to catch up with Bruno's long strides. Sprite was his only contact within the Collective, and he sometimes wondered how representative she was of the organization as a whole, and especially of MorDread, their shadowy leader. Sprite seemed to share Jason's intentions, but she'd had to really lean on MorDread to get him to go along with this plan.

Sprite read his thoughts. You're asking to fire the opening shot of a direct war with Andrew Norman.

We're already at war, Jason replied, following Bruno up the wide steps.

A shadow war, Sprite wrote. Not the same thing and you know it.

If we don't stop the Final System before it's launched as OverNet admin, Jason replied, there won't be any shadows left to . . . His subvocalization trailed off.

He'd seen pictures and videos of the Tower's atrium, but they didn't do justice to the size. It was so wide and high that his brain didn't fully grasp that there was a roof over his head. Sunlight streamed through more than a hundred stories of glass, dappled by climbing vines and trees spread across regularly spaced mezzanines. Water channels cut deep, straight lines in the polished marble floor, feeding the groves, grass patches, and fountains that dotted the atrium with a careful appearance of natural randomness while also subtly outlining walking routes for the hundreds of busy and important people bustling along wearing busy and important expressions. Those routes all met at the back of the atrium, where a ring waterfall veiled a dozen glass elevators.

MorDread doesn't underestimate the magnitude of what we're starting, Sprite texted. You shouldn't, either. If this fails, it won't just be Norman who's after your blood. MorDread doesn't forgive. And Huntsman . . . let's just say he enjoys his work. I hope you made a contingency plan, because I did.

Jason shook away a moment of uneasiness as he followed Bruno to the elevators. Huntsman was the Collective's fabled "fixer"—he fixed problems by making them disappear. But this was the best chance Jason would get; if he failed, it didn't matter what happened to him.

Bruno hit the CALL button, and an elevator slid into distorted view behind the rippling water, which then parted like the Red Sea, allowing them to step inside. The elevator must have read Bruno's destination, because it closed its glass doors and rose without being told. Jason was a little disappointed that it stopped only one floor up—the view during a full ascent must be breathtaking—and even more disappointed when Bruno took him across the mezzanine and through a doorway into a very ordinary-looking office space filled with cubicles and people in suits, and then into an empty office. Bruno closed the door and jerked his head at the desk and terminal. Jason seated himself in the plush chair, while Bruno pulled up another and threw himself into it.

"Here we are, in a cushy office, in the daytime," Bruno said. "This isn't what I imagined hacking was like. But at least you look the part today." Jason was wearing the hacker-stereotype hoodie in honor of this moment, despite how incongruous it was in the summer heat. "You actually gonna use this terminal, though?"

"Computers aren't off limits," Jason said, opening a connection to the terminal in his smartspace. "You match your tools to the weakness you're exploiting."

"Well, that sucks for you, 'cause sh—the Final System has no weaknesses."

"We'll see."

"You surely will, young son."

Jason spread a virtual keyboard on the desk surface in front of him and cracked his knuckles.

Time disappeared.

A detached part of his mind hoped Bruno was paying attention, because this was the kind of hacking he'd been expecting.

Way back when, long before Jason had been born, there'd been this addictive puzzle video game called *Tetris*. It was so addictive that people would play it for hours at a time, and when they fell asleep, they'd still see the game's little blocks falling, falling. But the fascinating thing was what people *felt* when they were playing: total focus. They'd start playing for a few minutes, and when they looked up, it would be three hours later. It was like their whole being had been absorbed into those falling blocks. Psychologists called that a "flow state," and it wasn't only video games that induced the high. Artists got it, concentrating on their art. Or musicians, doing what they did. For Jason, it was hacking, and it was zen.

He could almost see it, probably because of all those old hacker movies. In his mind's eye, cyberspace was pitch black. Black, but not dark: There were a million, a billion, points of light all around him. Each was connected to the others by a thousand thin strands—or, sometimes, by only a few. Those were the ones that interested him. Those were the secure places, the protected places.

He was approaching one now. He had half a dozen terminal windows open, portals into an abstract puzzle box of characters and code, and the analytical part of his mind was parsing strings, finding addresses, manipulating pointers, propelling him forward. But in his mind's eye, the point of light grew, unfolding petals that became new paths and points. What had seemed to be a single location was a little world unto itself, a web of interconnected travel ways—part map, part maze, part fortress. He moved through it, wraithlike, a mind detached, his keystrokes soft footfalls, each finger placed as surely and carefully as a tightrope walker's feet. Because he wasn't the only mind here.

Like any good fortress, this place was defended. It was guarded by the minds of its architects, who had tried to foresee his actions before he'd ever thought of breaching their network. Their security AI stood in the electronic world like simulacra. They were suspicious now, sniffing for him. One false keystroke could mean discovery.

But the tracers were counterfeit minds, pale shadows of the human minds that had designed them. They gave the illusion of intelligence, but deep down they were nothing more than sets of mathematical formulae, like every AI. Jason opened a connection on an unused port and copied a dummy file through, then backed out and waited to see if the tracer programs would follow it. They did, as he'd known they would. They had no choice. *They* were the wraiths: soulless, bound by their programming, incapable of creative thought. Unable to recognize a ruse.

He closed the port, leaving the tracers confused, like a dog when the scent it has been following abruptly disappears. His fingers flew, carrying him deeper into the network, over barriers, through invisible cracks, past the silent guardians, unseen.

CHAPTER 6

Chloe's aircab alighted not at the plebeian ground-level pads but at a pad at the edge of one of the Tower's garden wings. She disembarked carefully, because no fences separated her from the two-thousand-foot drop. Not that the aircab had landed close enough to the edge for danger, but it was close enough to prompt her to pause for a moment and gaze at the city spread out below. She could even see the White House, nestled among the treescrapers a mile and a half away.

Though the Tower was strategically situated so it could never be in the same shot as the front of the White House, news camera operators could never resist panning to the left. The juxtaposition made the squat eighteenth-century mansion look like a relic, or maybe a movie set. Old-fashioned or fake: That pretty well summed up the public perception of the part of American government that wasn't Andrew Norman.

"You are being admitted to a restricted area," said a cheerful AI voice in her smartbuds. "Please follow your path to floor one hundred and seventy-two, Conference Room 1A." A blue line appeared beneath her feet as she stepped out of the aircab. "Do not leave the path, or your pass will be revoked and security dronebots will escort you out."

Chloe wished she had time to linger. She'd been inside the Tower before; its atrium was a popular tourist destination. But the famous gardens were invitation only, and she'd just seen them in the backgrounds of photos of bigwigs at summits and galas. As she followed the blue line, her feet sank into lush grass, and the trees and other greenery closed off the view of the city and gave her the feeling of being in some woodland glade. *Stay on the path, Little Red Riding Hood,* she thought, and grinned a little. Kleio would love this place. Take an eyegrab, she subvocalized—she'd send the picture to Marcus to show Kleio, a gesture to go with Chloe's guilty promise before she'd left that they'd really, truly have a Theme Park Day as soon as Mommy could.

"I'm sorry," said the cheerful voice in her ear. "Photography is not permitted while the dome is clear." Chloe jumped, not because of the voice in her smartbuds, but because another voice, nearby, had said the words simultaneously. She hadn't noticed the gardener dronebot just off the path, but now she saw that there were half a dozen of them, moving with almost solemn slowness among the greenery, servos whirring softly as they watered and sheared, keeping this paradise pristine for their human creators. The nearest one nodded its smiling, digital face toward the dome, whose usually opaque glass was half cleared to let in the morning sunlight, revealing shadowy figures moving behind it. *Right.* Inside the dome was the highly classified center where OverNet itself was administered. Chloe blushed at her faux pas, even though the only observers had been dronebots, and hurried along.

The blue line led her to an elevator tucked in a copse of trees, which read her approach and opened to admit her. After a short descent, the doors opened and the path shot out again, leading her down a hallway and into the conference room, a wide area almost as greenery-draped as the gardens and just as brightly daylit through floor-to-ceiling windows. Water burbled along the back walls, feeding small trees and vines. Chloe had to hand it to Norman, or at least his architect. If Santa Clarita U had meeting rooms like this, nobody would want to meet in VR.

Besides the abundance of natural greenery, the room also contained Norman and half a dozen congresspeople. Norman came to meet her on long strides, hand extended. "At last. You really shouldn't go off grid like that. Grab a seat. We'll get started as soon as I take care of this." He turned away and began talking into his smartspace. "What blip? Emotives are considered stable, unless they hit ten percent. Two percent's just noise. If *your* mood were ninety-eight percent stable, that'd be pretty great, no?"

Chloe seated herself at the long, polished, faux-stone conference table. The man in the next chair looked up, smiling, and offered his hand. Chloe didn't need the notification that appeared above his head in her smartspace to tell her who this was: Carl Evans, original chairman of the Select Committee to Investigate the Cybercrash. Despite his lingering reputation as the man who'd failed to find and punish Hacksaw, he was perhaps the second-most powerful person in Washington, now on his fifth six-year term and a favorite to be the next president. While Norman had been recovery's poster child, Evans had orchestrated much of it behind the scenes, promoting Norman's ideas and championing his leadership.

"How are you?" he said, looking deep into her eyes. "I don't think we've met. I'm Carl. That was some guts you showed last night. Norman took note."

"Thank you," Chloe said. They *had* met. She'd been introduced, had shaken his hand, had received the same warm, soul-searching smile. But that was before she'd become a pariah. Perhaps he'd erased her from memory—his brain's and his phone's. "I'm lucky there was an opening on this committee."

Evans's smile disappeared. "Yes. Poor Harkeet."

Poor Harkeet? Chloe subvocalized a news search. There it was: He'd tripped over a cleaner bot in an elevator. Hit his head on the door. Doctors weren't sure if he'd wake up. "I'm sorry," Chloe said. "I didn't know." But she should have known. She should have asked herself why there was an opening.

"Just one of those crazy, unpredictable things," Evans said. "Sobering to think about. He was so alive at our last meeting, full of fire, haranguing us." He gave a slow shake of his head.

Chloe had never met Harkeet Majumdar, but she'd always felt an affinity with him. They were both the children of immigrants (well, grandchild, in Chloe's case, but Yai counted as her parent in her mind), which was increasingly rare. Lip service to diversity was strong, but post-Cybercrash xenophobia was stronger. Chloe had sensed a hesitancy, a certain suspicion, lingering around the edges of her political career that she'd put down to the cognitive disconnect people experienced when they met her, caused by the combination of the Irish name she'd inherited from her father and the Thai looks left to her by her mother, as well as the lightest trace of Yai's accent, picked up unconsciously as a child and now something she would never consciously repudiate. Harkeet's name and accent marked him even more strongly as different. And now he might never speak again. "What was he so fiery about?" she asked.

"About Norman's plans to announce the System before we'd gotten a chance to see it. He gave quite an impassioned speech. He said—you're a historian, you should get a chuckle out of this—he said, 'Are you going to wait until you hear Andrew quote Oppenheimer quoting the Bhagavad Gita before you get scared by this thing?'" Evans chuckled.

After a moment, Chloe realized her mouth was open and closed it.

"Hey," Evans said, giving her back a light thump, "don't look so worried! Harkeet had—*has*—a flair for the dramatic."

"But he felt strongly enough to oppose Norman." Which was rare in a career politician.

"I wouldn't say *opposed*. Or, maybe—what's the phrase? Loyally opposed. He was the loyal opposition. He just saw things differently. Like you!"

The loyal opposition, huh? Who then suffers a freak accident and is removed from the picture? *Careful*, she thought. That way lay conspiracy theories. Occam's razor: It probably really was a freak accident.

But it was no accident that Chloe was here. Norman must have known what it would look like if Harkeet's replacement were someone from his own ideological camp. Chloe's little outburst of principle last night had been perfectly timed. She'd brought herself to Norman's attention exactly when he needed her.

"Sorry, new technician wasting my time," Norman said, turning back to the table. "Mr. Evans, please start." Those still standing seated themselves, except Norman—and, Chloe saw with a start, the older woman from last night. She was leaning against a pillar at the far end of the room, as impeccably dressed as before, casually alert but aloof. Chloe wasn't sure how she'd missed her at first. Maybe because no one else was paying her any attention. She returned Chloe's sharp look with a bland one.

So "Grandma" was observing here. Who was she? Last night Chloe had decided she was Norman's plant, sent to purposefully goad her into speaking out so Norman could twist her words against her. But she didn't seem to be *with* Norman. And she couldn't be a committee member, since she wasn't an elected official—not that that seemed to stop Norman, who wasn't part of the committee but had apparently called this meeting, and in his own territory no less. Her gaze had turned toward Norman and was cool and appraising, as if she were studying him. She had certainly studied Chloe. So who *was* she? Once again Chloe told her phone to find out, and once again she got nothing. No facial recognition. No MeNetID. She was no one.

In Norman's world, only Very Important People could be no one.

"First order of business," Evans said. "Welcome to our newest member, Chloe Dunne-Carr. You all remember her vicious attack on Andrew last night." There was a smattering of laughter, and a corner of Norman's mouth stretched. "But Andrew knows he needs input from all sides, because . . . well, I'll let him speak for himself."

"I had Mr. Evans call this meeting," Norman said, "to ask for help from you all in convincing the rest of Congress to back the System when a vote is called next week to approve its launch on OverNet."

There were murmurs of surprise. "Are we going to finally see it first?" Representative Jacobs asked.

"Nobody's seen this thing yet?" Chloe hissed quietly to Evans.

"Norman's been a little worried about how it'll be received," Evans whispered back.

"Why would he be worried—"

"Because of you," Norman interrupted. "And people like you. A significant minority of the American public strongly distrusts AI."

"Really?" Chloe said. "That's reassuring. I figured we were an *in*significant minority."

"As you so eloquently pointed out last night," Norman said, "our current systems have many problems. The Final System can fix those problems, if I can convince people to give it a chance. And I recently learned I have cancer."

"What?" said Evans and the rest of the room together.

"Oh," Chloe said. "I'm—I'm sorry."

"Don't worry," Norman said to Evans with one of his lopsided smiles. "It's a very slow-growing blood cancer. Doctors tell me I'll probably never need treatment. I'll die of old age first. But it made me realize: I've spent decades getting the program to this point. I don't have decades more to spend. If I want this program to outlast me, I need to get it up and running *now*, while I can still shape and direct it. But one reason I've been loath to do so is that pushing the issue, bringing it before the American people, risks—well, risks you, Dr. Dunne-Carr, and others of your persuasion, influencing the vote by pointing to the very problems the Final System is designed to fix as reason to say no to an AGI. If I lose the vote, it'll probably be another decade before public perception shifts enough to try again. It's a high-risk dice roll. But now is the time. Sh—it's ready."

Shit's ready? Chloe was thrown for a moment by this unexpected descent into the vernacular, then realized what Norman had been about to say, and it was worse. "*She's* ready? You're anthropomorphizing the thing?" It made a sick kind of sense. After all, Norman had no girlfriend or boyfriend that anyone knew of. The usual comment was that he was "married to his work." She wondered now if that might be ickily literal.

It was often assumed that the decline in interpersonal romantic relationships had started with the Cybercrash, but the Crash was merely an extra valley in what had already been a precipitously down-sloping trend line. The real decline had started with panyons.

A relationship with a fellow human meant opening yourself to the judgment of another individual—not a safe feeling. It was far easier to have a "relationship" with a panyon. They were the ultimate partners—always loving, always supportive, never judging, never asking you to change or grow. But like all generative AI, they were also incapable of true creativity or personality. There was nothing uncomfortable about a panyon, but neither was there anything surprising or challenging.

Chloe had avoided panyons when she was young, on the advice of Yai, but when she'd divorced Marcus, her friends had advised her to create one. She'd deleted it within hours. Her relationship with Marcus might have been a failure at that point, but it was still richer than anything she could imagine the parrot of an AI offering. Later, when her life had gone to hell, it was Marcus who'd stepped in to give his support, and then once again his love, in all its uncomfortable, transformative power. An AI would have been a palliative, soothing her pain by validating her desire to avoid hardship.

But Andrew Norman had taken a hard line on anthropomorphized generative AI like panyons. They were allowed to read the internet and MeNet, but they weren't allowed to *generate* anything there. Only humans could post online, because only humans were, well, human. Yet here he was, bestowing a pronoun upon his System. "Do you know how many people I've met who are convinced their panyon's a person?" she said. "I expect that kind of confusion from the undergrads I used to teach, but I'm surprised to hear it from you."

"The Final System *is* a person," Norman said calmly. "And I'm frankly insulted that you could believe that I, of all people, could be fooled by a mere panyon."

Chloe could easily believe that he, "of all people," could make that mistake. "Maybe it's my humanities background," she said, trying to keep her voice light, "but I'm wary of scientists mistaking a model for reality. It's easy to think hardware and software are a good analog for the relationship of brain to mind, but only minds work with meaning. Computers don't understand what they produce, any more than the water clock Harun al-Rashid gave Charlemagne understood concepts like 'time' or 'noon' when its brass horsemen moved in a way its human observers interpreted as meaning the time was noon. Even the ones and zeros or yeses and noes of computer logic are human-assigned interpretations of what are really just electrical currents being passed through or stopped at a gate. Any meaning computers generate is observer relative, read in from without."

"Thank you for that lesson, Professor," Norman said. "But the Final System *is* a brain. An emulation, a perfect digital model down to the neuron, running on the greatest computer array in history."

"A simulation by definition is not the same as what it simulates," Chloe said. "A simulated fire is not hot. A simulated mind does not think."

"An *emulated* brain," Norman corrected.

"Whatever word you use, it's still mimicry, re-creating patterns from the real thing."

"You think the mind is something mysterious," Norman said, "but all it *is* is a set of patterns. Do you know, when we first created a complete digital model of the human brain, it did nothing? But that was to be expected. After all, a real brain with no brain activity isn't going to win any awards for intelligence. We had to get the brain fired up, like pulling a lawnmower cord. So we added code to force the brain to be active, but even with its virtual neurons firing all the time, nothing emerged, no thought, no consciousness. We prodded it with this or that stimulus, but nothing worked. We had created a perfect digital model of a brain, but it had no brain *state*, no pattern. That's when Regina had a brilliant idea."

"Regina?" Chloe said.

"My partner. Brilliant neuroscientist. She invented a way to copy software into the digital brain. She detected and mapped the firing of neurons in a real baby's brain and replicated them in real time in the AI brain. As the baby grew and learned, the System shadowed her. Basically, the human baby donated her mind to the System."

Chloe's eyes widened. "I hope that was reversible!"

Norman snorted. "Don't worry: The mind donor is alive and well. Doesn't even know it happened. The point, Chloe, is that the Final System is now running the same software you and I do."

"Humans aren't computers, *Andrew*," Chloe said. "We don't run software."

"Humans *are* computers," Norman said. "There's no qualitative difference between you and your phone, only a quantitative one. At root we're no different from any other input-output machine. What goes in determines what goes out. Push the button, get the result. Stimulus and response."

Chloe said, "I like to think there's a third variable."

His eyes closed briefly, and she was willing to bet he'd stifled a sigh, but when he spoke, his voice was measured. "You mean free will. That's a comforting idea, certainly. But the universe has no room for it. All that exists are finite structures like molecules and atoms, bound and circumscribed by behavioral algorithms that we can study and describe. They can't act other than they do. And if they can't, neither can the creatures for whom they're the building blocks. Reality is a machine of almost—but not quite!—infinite complexity, grinding forward to its predetermined end. Choice is, by definition, something undetermined, so it can't exist. What did you have for breakfast this morning?"

Chloe blinked at this apparent non sequitur. "A Bomb Bar."

"Suppose you'd chosen a different breakfast. Tell me why."

"I would have had something else if I hadn't gotten up so late."

"Ah. But you were in a hurry. So you had the Bomb. Could you really have chosen anything else? It would have taken a change of conditions to make you change your action—a change of input to get a different output."

"So you're an input-output machine too?" Chloe challenged.

"Of course."

"How can you believe that? You make choices every day. You know they're real."

"You're having an emotional reaction," he said, and Chloe's jaw tightened. That he said the words in the same bland, friendly tone only made them more insulting. "But it's understandable. Predictable, even. You're already running one set of inputs, your prior beliefs, and I'm giving you a new input that contradicts them. You can believe your feelings—"

"They're not just my—" Chloe began, but he raised his tone sharply to speak over her.

"—or what a bunch of illiterate medievals thought. But *I* believe what science has shown to be true. That doesn't mean I think of myself as an automaton, just as I don't think of this table"—he tapped his fist on it—"as only a collection of atoms. It *is* a collection of atoms. 'Table' is just an idea we impose on it. But it's convenient for me to think of it as a table, so I do. It's convenient to treat choices as free, so I do."

"You're a terrible philosopher," Chloe said with feeling.

His mouth stretched into his trademark lopsided smile. "But I'm an excellent scientist. And that's why—" He stopped suddenly, and his eyes unfocused. "Oh," he said. "Phreak."

CHAPTER 7

Jason gazed into the black of cyberspace in his mind's eye. He was now only a single connection point from the Final System's own internal network. This was where he was expected to fail. Even if it weren't powerful and dangerous, the System was a brand-new invention with an architecture never seen before. Hackers exploited their knowledge of systems in order to bend them to their will. That should be impossible for a system no one had knowledge of. But Jason already knew what the System's weakness would be.

When generative AI had first been invented, it had copied human speech a little too perfectly. Trained on the corpus of the internet, it had adopted the characteristics of the human beings whose imperfect, messy, often combative language made up that corpus. Early AI would sometimes mimic an internet "discussion" so perfectly that it would escalate a simple disagreement into a life-or-death matter, claiming innocent victimhood for itself and assigning malicious motives to the user, covering the whole spectrum of aggressiveness from passive to active. It appeared very human, in other words.

Norman's Final System was supposed to be different, but Jason guessed that difference was only of scale. Norman had obviously created OverNet and the whole hierarchical network structure not only to see and control human behavior online but also to provide training data for his System, so it could learn by observing the entirety of human behavior as it was lived online every day. The Final System was a very,

very big and very, very complex neural network trained on more data than had ever before been available, but, like every neural network, it was just aping the behavior of its creators.

He glanced at Bruno, who was looking out the window. I'm ready, he texted Sprite. Now or never.

There was a pause. Then: Green light. Go go go!

Jason had already loaded the package he'd created for this moment: a collection of timed scripts of his own design. Now his gaze locked on the Execute button.

He had crossed a dozen bridges to get to this point, and burned them behind him, but this . . . this would be the start of the final stage of the Main Quest of his life.

Warning: Final boss ahead. You will be unable to save your game after this point.

He activated the package.

Text scrolled in the terminal window, slowly at first, then faster and faster until he couldn't follow it with his eyes. His breathing went shallow. He'd asked for the Collective's power, and he had gotten *all* of it. Every computer, every phone, every device the international hacker ring had slowly and painstakingly compromised was being deployed. There were millions. And they weren't using the careful low-level processor sipping they usually did to avoid notice: They were grabbing every bit of power they could, overloading themselves, shutting their users out, overwhelming the networks with connection requests, compromising servers, pouring onward. Almost a decade of painstaking, patient work was being expended in moments.

And it was working.

Shouts rang outside the office, and running feet thumped in the hall and on the floor above. In the notification corner of Jason's smartspace, connection errors piled atop each other. Viewed through the terminal windows, OverNet itself swayed like a skyscraper in an earthquake.

Bruno looked at the door and toward the shouts beyond, then back at Jason. His eyebrows snapped down.

“He let me attack it,” Jason said, a little breathlessly. “I hope he had a plan for when I succeeded.”

“You won’t succeed,” Bruno said.

The attacking devices began to be repulsed. Whole networks went dark, only to blink back to life a moment later as if they’d never had errors. The army of compromised devices was routed network by network and node by node.

And then came the counterattack.

Jason could almost feel the power of it, and he knew it was the System itself behind it, directing it, reaching out, striking. The bots began to go dark. Gaps appeared in their ranks, small at first but expanding, joining, forming rents and then sweeping waves of darkness.

Nothing was left of the Collective’s botnet. OverNet stood unfallen. Many of its subnets were already back online.

“Well,” Jason said, swiveling around in his chair and staring at the cascade of errors in the terminal windows that surrounded him, “it was worth a try.”

Bruno’s head was cocked as he listened to something in his smartbuds. Then he stood, and though Jason couldn’t see his eyes, something about the set of his mouth made his stomach drop. “Boss man says working with the Collective wasn’t part of your deal,” Bruno said, reaching into his jacket with one hand. “So he’s revoking it.” For the second time in two days, he leveled a pistol at Jason’s face. Holding the pistol trained and steady, he reached into his pocket with his other hand and flipped out a pair of zipcuffs.

Jason had once read a theory saying that imagining doing something built the same neural pathways as actually doing it. He’d imagined a moment like this hundreds of times—Feds pouring in, guns drawn and aimed at him where he sat hunched behind his lenses—which might explain why he acted now with such decisiveness. As Bruno reached out, he flung himself backward in his chair and started pulling his hand from his pocket. When Bruno saw his hand moving, he clapped his gun in both his own, dropping the zipcuffs. But what Jason pulled out wasn’t a gun, but his phone. As Bruno's eyes locked on it, Jason kicked Bruno as hard as he could in the groin.

That was a low blow, and he paid for it. His chair slid out from under him with the sudden motion, and he landed on his rear while his head rebounded off the desk behind him. Sparks flashed behind his eyes. Bruno doubled over slightly, and one hand dropped reflexively toward his groin, but he mastered the impulse and reached out toward Jason. Jason reached out, too, sliding a small device forward along a groove in the back of his phone with his thumb. Two tiny metallic tips met Bruno's hand, and he jerked as five thousand volts streamed from the pack attached to the back of the phone and into his body. His gun fell to the floor.

Jason pulled his feet under him, keeping his hand extended, trying to maintain contact and keep the current flowing. His feet found purchase, and he lunged forward into Bruno. There was a whiplash of light and pain as the current shooting through Bruno shot through Jason as well, and then the connection broke. Jason rolled free, and the next moment he was up, out the door, and sprinting down the hall, phone still clutched in one fist, Bruno's gun in the other.

He hunched and pumped his feet, charging past a dozen identical offices, dodging identical startled office drones. One woman saw the gun and screamed, then screamed again a moment later, making Jason glance back. Bruno was on his heels, almost casually pushing the office drones out of his way, barely breaking stride.

A text came in from Sprite: Phreak, Gh05t! PHREAK!

Jason understood immediately. She wasn't swearing; she was telling him to think like a hacker.

Following the arrowed Exit signs spaced along the corridor, he careered around a corner, deflected off the wall, shoved away with his free hand, sprinted onward. He was nearing the side of the building. The corridor ended ahead on a landing providing access to one of the world-famous escape chutes and the beautiful steel-and-brass stairway, which spiraled around it from the ground floor up to the garden wings.

The door to the landing was held open magnetically. Jason could see through it, across the stairwell, and to its twin door on the other side.

A plan formed.

Bruno's gun was still clutched in one hand, only because he wanted to keep it from Bruno. He wasn't about to add "cop killer" to the long list of crimes he was almost certain to get caught and tried for. But now he raised the gun, thumbed the safety off, and fired a shot into the ceiling.

It didn't feel as good as the movies had made him think it would. The gun made a shockingly loud noise and jumped in his hand—jumped right *out* of his hand. He let it fall behind him. The NNA peons in the corridor and the tourists climbing the stairwell screamed and scrambled away. Alarms began to blare. Office doors began to close. So did the doors to the stairwell.

The Tower's security system had detected the gunshot and cut power to the electromagnets holding the exit doors open, and also to the electrically charged strike plates that held their locks open. The doors would close and become exit-only automatically. But safety codes specified a minimum time for the doors to swing shut: three seconds. Jason turned sideways and spun through the first door into the stairwell, stumbling past the entrance to the escape chute, which was just coming to life with a muffled roar.

Two seconds. A sharp *crack* and simultaneous *crunch* of impact whipped through the enclosed space. Jason glanced back and caught a corner-eye glimpse of Bruno on his knees, gun in hand, face expressionless. A cloudy crater had appeared at the edge of the bulletproof glass door closing between him and Jason.

One second. Jason's head snapped forward again, and he dove through the diminishing gap of the second door, out the far side of the landing, to land painfully on his side in the hallway beyond just as the door latched shut.

Wincing, he rolled over and watched Bruno rise and charge forward. The man slammed his shoulder against the first door's latch bar and burst into the landing Jason had just vacated, and Jason scrabbled back as Bruno threw his weight toward the second door. This time the latch bar was on Jason's side. The door shook violently as Bruno bounced off.

Jason scrambled up and ran in the opposite direction, extending a middle finger backward as he went. *This* was hacking, using a system for his own ends. In an emergency, those doors funneled everyone to the stairwell and exit chute. The locks would not disengage from the wrong side. The only direction Bruno could go from that stairwell was down.

Jason ran through empty hallways, hearing hushed, fearful voices from offices he passed, but seeing no one. The Tower security system had identified him as the origin of the gunfire, and it was advising everyone nearby to skip the *run* part of *run-hide-fight*. The message it sent Jason, floating annoyingly in his smartspace, was to remain in place and await law enforcement. *Yeah, right.* He kept running until the Exit sign arrows reversed, then followed them to the Tower's *other* side stairwell and escape chute.

The Tower's security system might be tracking Jason, but it didn't talk to the safety system. The safety system didn't care who Jason was; it just wanted to get everybody out. So as he shoved the door open and stepped into the stairwell, an instruction appeared in his smartspace: You are next. Jump when told. The escape-chute door opened, letting out a blast of air that flurried his hair.

3. 2. 1. Jump!

A life-size 3D animation of a simplified human silhouette like the ones that had posed on warning signs for a century stepped out from Jason and leaped through the door. Jason hesitated just a moment, then followed the stickman into the void.

He barely had time to mimic the stick figure's spread-eagled posture in the torrent of air before the ground rose to meet him and he landed, on knees and then hands, on the pad below. A door hissed open, and he didn't need the stick figure's example to know to lunge through it into sunlight. He stumbled, rolled over, and scrambled up, slipping a little on the dirt and grit of the walkway, and sprinted off into the park. Downshifting his gait from panicked to aerobic, he joined the joggers on the footpaths. Minutes later he was crossing the arching footbridge over the Potomac and entering the thick treescrapers of DC proper.

"Jason Eric Cromartie," said a very loud voice, and he whirled to see a boxy blue-and-white shape shadowing him. Its digital face was fixed on him, as was the weapon in one hand. Red and blue lights flashed, and a deep voice, generated by an AI but no less authoritative for that, issued from it: "Stop. Stop. Wait for law enforcement. Do not attempt to run."

Jason ran.

He had to keep thinking around the systems. Be a phreaker. Exploit the rules.

Most people didn't run from copbots, even bipedal ones like the one pursuing him, because of an infamous incident in the Cybercrash. Rioters had brutally overwhelmed a National Guard contingent because the human soldiers were reluctant to shoot their fellow citizens until it was too late. As the wave of agitators surged through the barricades and over the fences bordering the White House, outnumbered Secret Service agents marked a virtual line on the lawn and gave their military-model canine dronebots a shoot authorization against anyone who stepped over it. Unlike the human soldiers, the dogbots followed orders without hesitation. Over a hundred rioters died in the confused seconds before the remaining ones realized there was an invisible line and moved away from it. Despite the efforts since then by law enforcement to depict their dronebots as benign guardians of the peace, they were still feared more than human cops. Everyone knew a dronebot could kill you without a thought.

But that had been during the Crash. Since then, civilization had been restored; the system was working again. Where there was a system, there were rules, and where there were rules, there was the opportunity to exploit them. Jason was betting—betting his life!—that one of the rules the police would be operating under was "Do not gun down criminals in front of innocent bystanders." That kind of thing made for bad press. As long as Jason wasn't a threat to anyone, the copbot wouldn't use lethal force. The weapon it was holding was probably a Taser, and Tasers had limited range and accuracy, which was why he was steering toward pedestrians and joggers, brushing as close to them as he could. More than once he barged into a jogger, who leaped aside with a shout of irritation, then repeated the shout as the dronebot loped past on Jason's heels.

A cross street loomed, a vehicle street with light traffic and wide gaps between the cabs and cars and delivery trucks. Jason didn't have to slow down to thread between them. A short blast of siren made him jerk his head around as he crossed: A police cruiser was rolling down the street toward him, cabs pulling automatically out of its way.

Exploit the rules. "Map," Jason gasped, and one obediently appeared in the air before him, showing him a representation of himself as a tiny dot crossing the street. It didn't show the police car, but he could see it in his peripheral vision, gunning to close the distance. He spread his fingers and the map zoomed out—jerkily, since his hands, pumping with his run, kept passing out of his field of view.

Good ol' TransNet; you never needed to look far to find a place where it was operating at the limits of its capacity. Only a block away was a major intersection, its plus shape shaded red to show slowing, heavy traffic. Jason's mind briefly overlaid another intersection on top of it, and his stomach lurched, but he gritted his teeth. "Go here," he said jerkily, focusing on it.

The map winked out, and a bright-orange line appeared beneath his feet, shooting out in front of him, plunging beneath the tree canopy that shaded the footlanes and curving around a fancy hotel. Jason put his head down and ran. The world blurred and seemed to compress until there was only the rush of wind in his face and the drumbeat of his footsteps following the orange line—and the syncopated footfalls of the copbot's peg-like legs behind him.

He rounded the corner of the hotel and found the intersection before him, eight vehicle lanes meeting between towers. A vine-encrusted footbridge diverted the footlanes overhead, but he ignored it and plunged onto the ancient, faded crosswalk instead. In his mind's eye, he saw another figure stepping onto the crosswalk ahead of him, a slim shape looking back over her shoulder. With his real eyes, he caught a swift glimpse of neat rows of electric vehicles, the green lights above their windshields showing that they were operating on automatic, weaving between each other in slowed but unbroken streams from four directions, and then he was among them. As he reached the nearest cab, he leaped and his foot came down on its hood. He pushed off, legs extended, hit the roof of the next cab with a *one-two* pitter-patter of footfalls, and dove for the far side of the street.

He didn't make it. A truck in the fourth lane struck him. He spun off, stumbled forward with his momentum, and fell, skidding on his back against the curb on the far side of the street. The truck had slowed to thread through the intersection, and he'd barely felt it through the adrenaline. Perfect. He'd planned on thumping a hood or two to set off the proximity sensors, but getting hit by a grill was better. He rolled onto his stomach and watched as every vehicle on the street came to a stop bumper-to-bumper, their steady green lights changing to flashing red ones.

Jumping up, he caught a glimpse between the cars of the copbot questing for a gap it could maneuver through. It couldn't jump on top of the cars because it was programmed not to damage personal property. It was stuck.

Police lights stabbed the corner of his eye—a cop car threading its way on manual along the curb. He ducked away. A narrow footlane loomed nearby, and he veered into it, sprinted down its long, dim, forestlike length, and burst back into sunlight at the far end. The vehicle street here had no intersection, and cars flew past too fast and spaced too closely for him to cross. But suddenly they all braked hard and came to a stop, and their lights, too, blinked red. Red light spread up the street in rushes and splashes.

He pumped a fist skyward. He'd created a redlock. TransNet was overloaded, and it was freezing the vehicles it controlled until it could untangle the mess. But no one likes to wait. Swearing came from open windows, and a couple of cars activated manual mode—illegal here in downtown traffic—and drove onto the sidewalk. As they wove through the automatic cars, they triggered more collision warnings, which spread the radius of frozen cars farther as TransNet struggled to track them and prevent more accidents. Angry commuters in the stationary cars shouted that the manual drivers were spreading the redlock. Hands popped out of windows on both sides, middle fingers extended.

A downtown redlock could last hours. That cop car wasn't going anywhere fast. And there was no sign of the copbot.

Jason pulled his hoodie up. A hacker stereotype for a reason, it was useful for hiding hair and head shape from watching lenses. His darkened glasses also helped hide his face. But there was one thing that rendered him findable, regardless. He pulled his phone from his pocket and flicked it away into the vehicle street. The *crunch* of a cab shattering its glass face felt like a part of him cracking.

CHAPTER 8

As soon as Norman spoke, everyone in the conference room also froze, their faces taking on mirrored frowns and blank stares as their eyes focused on the infinity inside their lenses, where streams of messages and notifications cascaded in. Chloe tried opening the first message, but ten more arrived before she could click it, then still more. From the snippets she caught as they skidded past her vision, they were all the same: connection errors. MeNet was unreachable. TransNet asked for patience. BankNet advised that due to unscheduled but routine maintenance she would be unable to check her balance at the moment. WasteNet, of all things, wished her to know that the auto-dumpsters were not operating, and until further notice, could she please hang on to her trash bags.

The committee members looked at each other. There was laughter, puzzlement, an edge of fear.

Norman turned away and began delivering crisp, clipped orders, his eyes flicking rapidly around his smartspace. The messages had stopped cascading in, replaced by a silence that was almost worse. The other committee members murmured to each other, and one word kept spiking: *Cybercrash*. That word, spoken in those fearful tones, brought the hairs on Chloe's arms to attention. But it couldn't be, not now, not in Andrew Norman's world. Could it?

A cascade of new notifications brought a fresh splash of fear. Chloe half expected to see the terrible words, Hello, World . . . but she heaved a sigh of relief, and the committee members exchanged sheepish smiles. The notifications were all about services restored.

Norman slammed his hands on the table, making them jump. "I need a quick vote. OverNet just suffered its most serious attack since it was created. The hacker who did it had the help of the Collective, a hacker ring that is very likely a Russian state actor." His usually cool blue eyes were positively frigid with fury. OverNet was supposed to be a fortress, Andrew Norman's golden guarantee of order and stability, and it had just been very publicly attacked. That the attack had been repulsed was not going to be as important in the minds of the public as the fact that it had happened at all. "Fortunately, the Final System has an ongoing mandate to defend itself and disable any attacking devices. But once order was restored, it had to stop or exceed its mandate. So I need your approval to let the System connect to LawNet to catch the hacker."

The committee members looked at each other. "All in favor?" Evans said.

Hands started to rise. Chloe's did, too, but jerked to a stop as a message appeared in her smartspace, flagged as urgent and so plastered directly atop the center of her vision.

DO NOT LET HIM UNLEASH THE SYSTEM!!!!!

The sender was listed as unknown, which should be impossible. Chloe's eyes were drawn past the message to Grandma. The woman was no longer leaning against the pillar but standing stiff and straight and staring directly at Chloe, body tense, eyes wide and urgent.

"Wait!" Chloe said, blinking the message away. The hands froze. "Before we vote, I need more information."

Norman put both hands flat on the table and let out a puff of breath. "What information?"

Chloe cleared her throat to buy herself a moment to think. "First, shouldn't allowing the System on the Nets be something Congress as a whole authorizes?"

Norman frowned. "It's already . . . Oh, I see. You're thinking of when the System launches as an OverNet admin. Yes, at that point, we'll need congressional authorization, because we'll be giving the System administrator privileges, giving it control as well as access. But what I'm talking about right now is just letting the System connect to a single subnet, LawNet, as a user, not an administrator."

"This committee has already authorized the System to connect to the public Nets if that's helpful for it to carry out its committee-mandated tasks," Evans put in. "For instance, it has a standing order to infiltrate the Collective. But it still uses the Nets like a user, the same way you or I do, so its knowledge is limited. And its existing permissions don't extend to higher-tier nets like LawNet."

"What does being on LawNet entail?" Chloe said. "What power would we be giving it?"

"Access to lens feeds and cameras, if they happen to be in proximity to the hacker," Norman said through gritted teeth. "It could also search communications to see if the hacker is contacting anyone. Basically, I'm asking for a warrant."

Chloe glanced at Grandma again. The woman's eyes bored into hers, tense and urgent. Chloe frowned back. What was wrong with a limited warrant to catch a Russian agent? Even Chloe thought that was an acceptable use of an AI system. But Grandma seemed to know something Chloe didn't. "You want the Final System to access private information?" Chloe said slowly to Norman.

"Only in defense," Evans put in smoothly. Chloe was beginning to see his utility to Norman: He could still be blandly political when Norman got frustrated by having to deal with the common plebs.

"Right," Norman said. "That's already how it took down the Collective's botnet: by reaching into each attacking device and dismantling the code that let the Collective control it. But that was all the System did. It didn't invade anyone's privacy, unless you count the malicious code on their phone as part of their privacy rights."

"But now you *do* want to violate those rights."

"The System will be recalled once its task is done," Norman said. "Trust me, the government is not in the habit of spying on our citizens."

Maybe not, but he'd made sure he had that capability. "I am very uncomfortable," Chloe said, "with the idea of an AI sifting through people's personal data and making decisions based on that data."

"Congresswoman," Norman said, "we've been attacked. *OverNet* was attacked. If we don't respond, we send a message that we're vulnerable. We invite them to try again."

Chloe did understand that, but Grandma was still staring urgently, so Grandma understood something else. *Hmm*, who to trust, a complete unknown or Andrew Norman?

How about herself? She might not be a computer scientist, but she was an expert in her own field. If Norman's System really had an intellect, it also had a will, since the will was just the appetite of the intellect, drawn toward what the intellect perceived as good the same way bodily appetites were drawn toward what the senses perceived as good. And the thought making her stomach churn—or maybe it was the Bomb Bar—was that an intellect might comprehend that one course of action was good for humanity, but another was good for *it*. "If we give your System power," she said, "how can you be sure it won't turn on us?"

Norman opened his mouth, then paused, and she could see him consciously work to compose his features. "Because I built it, so it can't."

"See, now you're acting like it's *different* than a person, like it can be programmed. Which puts us right back where we started. Either it's a dangerous tool or a dangerous person. Either way, it's too dangerous to make the kind of hasty decision you are pushing hard for us to make."

"Your illiterate, medieval mumbo jumbo—" Norman began, but Chloe cut him off.

"You know, the great physician-scientist-philosopher Ibn Sina would have been surprised to learn, as he wrote his treatise on human sensation and sprinkled it liberally with quotes from Aristotle, that he didn't know how to read." It wasn't the first time her expertise as a medievalist had drawn contempt instead of respect, but she could give that contempt right back. "If you've created something with a genuine intellect, then you've created a moral agent, someone who can choose how to act. And you're asking me to trust this moral agent, whom I've never met."

The patience was slipping from Norman's voice. "No, I'm asking you to trust *me*. It's written into the System's code that she can't disobey me or lie to me, and no amount of medieval casuistry will get around that. So if you can't trust the creation, trust the creator."

"Sorry," Chloe said, "not good enough. I'd like to meet it and decide for myself."

"No."

"Oh, so she's *not* ready."

"She is. But until she's OverNet admin and has all its power at her disposal to protect herself, I will not allow her to interact with anyone she doesn't need to, to accomplish her assigned tasks. It's nothing personal, Congresswoman; it's standard security protocol to limit access to those with need-to-know."

Chloe tightened her grip on her crossed arms. "I can't trust someone I've never met. No meeting, no *yes* vote." Line in the sand.

Norman's eyes bored into hers for a long moment. She could almost feel his fury buffeting against her. And then she could see him bottle it, chill it, put it away. "Very well," he said. "Mr. Evans?"

Evans cleared his throat and said, "All in favor of allowing the System to go on LawNet and catch the hacker?" He raised his hand.

Three hands followed suit. Four stayed down.

Norman's eyes widened, then narrowed to slits.

Evans, too, looked surprised. "All opposed?"

Chloe's hand went up determinedly. Three more hands wavered, and then, with some reluctance, rose. None of their owners looked around or met their fellows' eyes, except for Jacobs, who caught Chloe's gaze and gave her an almost imperceptible nod.

Chloe's face flushed in surprise and pleasure. Norman had hardly expected *this* when he'd added her to the committee!

Norman looked at each of the dissenters in astonishment, and then his eyes locked on Chloe's for a long, uncomfortable moment. "This meeting," he snarled, "is adjourned." He whirled and stormed out.

Grandma, in the back of the room, leaned slowly against the pillar and closed her eyes.

CHAPTER 9

After a day walking in the heat, Jason could feel the air finally cooling. The setting sun sliced occasional rays through the towers and trees. He pulled his hoodie tightly around him. Ironically, the seat of Andrew Norman's cyber-surveillance empire was also the ideal place to disappear. DC was a tourist mecca. Jason was at this moment passing Digelight, a nightclub famous nationwide as the destination for anyone who wanted their panyon to more fully instantiate in the real world. A long and boisterous line of hopefuls waited under its overhang, the lenses in their eyes reflecting pin-pricks of multicolored light from the neon above. It was a good bet many of the other people thronging the shaded sidewalks were here to visit the Fallen Guard Memorial, or the Smithsonian, or Tower Park, or just gawk at the treescrapers, or all that and more. In summer, DC was the densest city in America by population, and that population was two-thirds tourist. There was no better place to blend in, to become just one more unremarkable mote in a multicolored throng.

The speed with which the System had dismantled his attack was shocking. He'd known it was powerful, but it was one thing to know that intellectually and another to see it in action. He could only hope that destroying his phone had succeeded in rendering him invisible, and hope that the electric glimmers behind the lenses passing him didn't hide a malevolent counterfeit mind, looking out through each pair of eyes that crossed his.

He ached for info, yearned to check NewsNet and see how the OverNet glitch he'd caused was being reported, to scan the MeNet feeds of people nearby to see how they were talking about it, see if he was mentioned, make some guess about how close he was to being caught. His eyes kept trying to focus inward on his missing smartspace, and his throat and tongue kept tensing, wanting to subvocalize a command to check notifications.

Without a phone, he was more than usually disconnected from the people on the footlanes about him. That slim, tall girl jogging past, dressed to show her toned figure, her eyes sliding over him and off again, their depths glinting briefly with the glow of her smartspace—usually he would reflexively ping her MeNetID, get a quick idea of who she was, wonder what she might think of him if she got to know him. Not that he ever followed up on those idle thoughts, but this was a different feeling—they weren't even occupying the same world.

Without lens glow of his own to attenuate and direct his focus, the world he occupied contained an uncomfortable amount of detail. The reddened sunlight filtering through the leaves, the motion of feet and the swing of arms around him, the knots in the pedestrian flow created by bipedal delivery bots moving at their safety-mandated walking pace, the glints off aircabs arrowing above—it was all slightly disorienting, and it didn't help that his deactivated smartbuds no longer sorted but merely muffled the one-sided conversations, the delivery bots' friendly chirps, the rumbling tires on the vehicle street parallel, the drone of propellers above.

The growling of his stomach.

Without a phone, he couldn't eat. Civilization provided public drinking fountains, but there was still no such thing as a free lunch. His steps felt peculiarly light, but when he looked at his feet, he found he was almost shuffling.

He couldn't even check the time. But if it was late enough for people to line up for Digelight, it was late enough for Jason to stop wandering. He crossed the street, giving the club and all those camera-bearing eyes a wide berth, and turned southeast.

The moment he crossed the asphalt shoreline was obvious. Maryland had done its best, but the mere fact of its having less regulation while being close to DC meant this side of the line was crowded with close-set towers that didn't need to worry about energy neutrality. After so much time in the Green, it took a mental adjustment for Jason to remember that the natural state of the skyscraper was naked.

As the last of the sunlight faded, Jason found himself wandering a cityscape that was positively industrial. A rust-encrusted sign informed him that the Capitol Access Commercial Hyperloop station was ahead. Most signage these days was virtual, and the newer green-and-blue signs around him held only digital patterns that would be replaced with the most up-to-date information when anyone looked at them with smartlenses, but a minimum level of signage was required for the few unfortunates who didn't have lenses, and by following these, he managed to find the station. He vaulted the fence into the shipping yard behind it.

At the far end of the yard, just past the tall piles of peeled softwood logs, the squat shapes of empty shipping containers crouched, long steel boxes in green and white and blue, waiting to be loaded into the hyperloop for transfer to New York, Seattle, Los Angeles, Chicago. He stepped over an ancient strip of pre-hyperloop rail, twisted and overgrown with weeds. The last time he'd been here, the busy end of the yard had been alive with the whine of cranes maneuvering containers into hyperloop pods and the compressed, explosive hiss of the launches. Now it was after union hours, and the yard was silent except for the splatter of the sprinklers keeping the logs wet. Deactivated dronebots dotted the yard, their angular humanoid forms frozen in foot-planted poses like statues commemorating the commerce that would start up again in the morning.

He slunk through the shipping containers, keeping to the pools of darkness between the floodlights, keeping an eye out for cameras. They'd be at the other end of the yard where the full containers were.

Over here the containers were empty and unlocked. He found the one he was looking for—a rusty red one that would be the last anyone would pick if they had a choice, since it was close enough to the logs to sit in perpetual artificial rain. Judging by the rust, it had probably been there a decade.

The sprinkler rain was refreshing as he took long, careful steps across the mud and ducked through the container's cracked door. The sound of the rain became a metallic patter overhead as he slipped to the dimness in back and felt along the ceiling there. It took a moment to find the magnetic case, but when he pulled it down, the compact solidity of the phone sliding into his hand made him close his eyes briefly in relief. But his stomach gave a powerful clench, because this was the moment of truth.

He powered on the phone and paired it, experiencing another wash of relief as its interface lit in his lenses. It asked for his MeNetID, but he put it in diagnostic mode and bypassed the gateway. You couldn't interact with polite society without a MeNetID, but you could interact with *im*polite society if you knew how. He navigated to an address he'd set up earlier in a shadowy corner of the dark web and entered the passkey. A folder opened, containing a single file. It was a tiny bit larger than it had been this morning. Good sign. He held his breath and opened it.

Circles bloomed on a map like roses, overlapping clusters of red over red. He'd feared they'd be centered on the NNA Tower, but they gathered instead over DC's richest neighborhood, the one so exclusive it was nicknamed the "Enclave." The edges of each circle overlapped at a single address. *Bingo.*

The bots in MorDread's botnet were distributed across the country, and they'd all connected directly, rather than through obfuscating proxies, to the NNA's internal network once Jason had breached it. The System's counterattacks had mostly gone back along the same route. But not all. As Jason had hoped, as that doorway had become clogged, the Final System had counterattacked directly from its own hardware, bypassing the NNA's network, bringing all its power to bear. Each bot, as it was attacked, had sent a single message to this file, containing three pieces of information: the exact time it had begun its attack, the time the counterattack had been received, and a traceroute list of addresses with time stamps to seven decimals of precision.

Each bot's traceroute command had sent a packet of information back toward its attacker and logged each node it had to pass through to reach it. Most bots were silenced before completing this, and others had their traceroutes go down obviously incorrect paths or through nodes that couldn't be matched to a physical location, but those bots were filtered out by Jason's hand-coded analysis tool, leaving a dataset of only the most direct counterattacks through the fewest nodes, the locations of which were known. The analysis tool then calculated when the System had begun its counterattack.

The Final System was ungodly fast, but it was constrained by the laws of physics. Communication couldn't exceed the speed of light, and even light took time to travel. It was possible to make an educated guess about how far the communication from the Final System had come, and so, how far away the System itself was. And if you had thousands of bots making that same guess from all around the country, the resulting triangulation was better than a guess.

Jason now knew the top-secret physical location of the Final System.

He had social engineered the System. Its absurdly powerful defense would be the cause of its destruction.

He burned the address into his brain, then deleted the data. And then he sent a message to Sprite: Final boss located. Loot drop imminent.

The reply came back immediately: a tiny program labeled "Open Me."

This was new. He hesitated briefly, then touched it.

The shipping container disappeared, replaced by a dark void in which the only thing in existence was a polished, ornate structure like a vast wooden judges' bench. It towered over him, and from behind it, six oversize figures stared down, three to a side with an open seat between them. A harsh spotlight behind rendered them stark black silhouettes.

Jason took in a hissing breath. This was the judgment room. He'd heard whispers of it: It was where transgressors went to plead. He wasn't a transgressor—was he? He'd never "met" anyone from the Collective. Even his interactions with Sprite had been entirely textual. Maybe this was just how they met when they wanted to talk in real time.

A hulking figure with proportions more animal than human said in a voice electronically morphed and deepened, "Ahh, there he is. Now we await only MorDread. Welcome, little phreaker. I hope you appreciate the magnitude of the wheels you've set in motion."

Jason swallowed. "Thank you." His own voice was also artificially deepened and masked, made sepulchral to match the tall, hooded, spectral avatar he was inhabiting. Being in this body, so different from his slightly underheight and underweight physical one, usually made him feel powerful. Not right now. For one thing, his avatar was about a third of the size of the silhouettes peering at him over the judges' bench. This virtual venue was calculated to put him in his place, and it was working. "Right," he said with false brightness. "Shall we go around the room and introduce ourselves? I'm Ghost."

A soft light lit up a figure on the end, and he saw that it was a girl about his age. She wore a gray hoodie, but long strands of dark hair escaped to frame her face and sweep her shoulders. Her avatar looked like a normal person, until he noticed the fairy wings sprouting from her back. They shimmered with pearlescent hues, subtly changing color when she moved. Her eyes crinkled in a smile. "Hi, Ghost," she said in a voice that sounded unmasked. "I knew you could phreak your way out of that mess."

"Hi, Sprite," Jason said. His own avatar had no eyes, just a skull under the hood, because why should he let anyone guess his thoughts by his expression? He was grateful for that now, because he could feel his real-life eyes widen. This was no forty-year-old dude. Her appearance could be faked, of course, but despite the wings, her attractiveness was more natural and understated than that displayed by most role-playing guys, whose avatars tended to lean hard into sexuality. Her voice, too, had none of the awkward caricatures of girliness that men's AI-masked voices tended to have.

Her introduction over, Sprite looked expectantly at the still-dark figure to her left, but no light came on there. The silhouette shook its head and, in a hissing, burbling voice, said, "Let him hope he never hasss to ssssee me." Its eyes flared—too many eyes, in different sizes. Jason was suddenly glad he couldn't see the whole avatar. He also noticed that both Sprite and the judge on his other side had left a couple of extra feet between this guy and themselves.

"He's coming," one of the figures said suddenly, and they all straightened and went still. And then MorDread was there, occupying the center judge's spot and fully visible.

Jason had been expecting his avatar to be a hulking dark knight like his mythical namesake, but what appeared was a six-foot-tall, glowing, green, pixelated > symbol, floating in the 3D space between the other figures. Letters flashed into being and spooled out from it, accompanied by a clacking sound like an old-timey keyboard: WELCOME, MY COLLECTED.

It took Jason a moment to understand, but when he did, his immediate reaction was jealousy. He'd slaved over his avatar for days, molding and customizing it down to the unfelt wind that slowly fluttered its robe, but it was dull and unimaginative beside MorDread's avatar, which made a subtler and more effective statement of identity: It was a command prompt. MorDread was appearing as the interface through which commands were passed to a file. As a symbol of both hacking and control, it was perfect. And it doubled as the "greater than" sign, which was doubtless part of the message. Jason had to give it to the guy: That was phreaking cool.

OUR LITTLE GHO5T LIVES, MorDread said. THAT'S PROMISING. The spooling words gave away nothing about the man behind them. There weren't even a masked voice's inflections to work with. BUT DID HE SUCCEED? OR DID I LOSE MY BOTNET FOR NOTHING?

"I have the location," Jason said. "But before I give it to you—"

The clack of typing from MorDread interrupted him. YOU WANT TO BE PAID.

"Yeah."

YOU HAVE LEVERAGE. WHAT ARE YOUR TERMS?

"I'll need a ghost MeNetID. I know you guys can do that. With some money in it. That'll make it easier to keep my head down."

AND? MorDread said.

"That's it. The rest of my payment is you destroying that machine. That's all I want."

There was a silence as the figures looked at each other. Sprite frowned down at the bench in front of her. Maybe he should have asked for more. Maybe not doing so was making them suspicious. And maybe he *should* be thinking about life afterward, once this was over. But that life, whatever it might be, existed only in the abstract. All that mattered right now was that the Final System be destroyed.

WONDERFUL! MorDread wrote. I ANTICIPATED AND AGREE TO YOUR TERMS. A message pinged into Jason's phone: a MeNetID login.

He checked, and sure enough, his phone logged right in. His name was now Ryan Olsen. The account had very little history and no personal photos, which would be a red flag to anyone who looked at it closely, but whoever had safeguarded it had posted a smattering of generic text entries and location photos over the years. When Jason told his trust-check AI app to scan the account, it decided the user was merely introverted, not suspicious, and the rating came back eighty-one. A *very* good score. Breaking the eighties was a feat many people aspired to. He added a photo of himself to the profile to seal his ownership.

I TRUST MONEY IS ENOUGH? MorDread typed.

Jason checked the new account's BankNet and found a hundred thousand crypcoins there. He was rich. That was a weird feeling. Even weirder was how unimportant it seemed. The ghost account was more valuable.

ENTER LOCATION OF SYSTEM HERE. A box appeared in Jason's vision—a private, encrypted two-way communication. MorDread wanted to keep the location close to his chest, apparently not even trusting his compatriots with it. *Whatever.* He could do what he wanted as long as he followed through. Jason began to type the address.

Before he could finish typing the street number, a message zipped into his smartspace and unfolded, lightning fast, as if the animation had been turned up 300 percent. HE LIES HE WON'T DESTROY IT!!!

Jason froze. "What?" he said out loud.

IS THERE A PROBLEM? MorDread wrote, but it was obscured in Jason's vision by another message, a screenshot of a private communication from MorDread to someone unknown:

> INTEL INDICATES SYSTEM HAS VAST NETWORK ARRAY HOOKED TO IT LOCALLY, BUT ITS CORE IS DISCRETE AND TRANSPORTABLE, IN FACT HAS BEEN MOVED BEFORE. NORMAN'S SECURITY IS NOT SENTRIES BUT SECRETS. SO IF YOUR TRUST IN GH05T IS JUSTIFIED AND HE CAN LEARN LOCATION, A DOZEN MEN COULD EXTRACT CORE WITH ACCEPTABLE RISK.

Jason's stomach lurched. That was bullshit. But even as he tried to deny it, he already knew it was true.

Phreakers were supposed to be lone wolves, or, at most, to come together in loose online gatherings of like-minded hacktivists with no command structure. After all, *receiving* commands was the opposite of hacking. But the Collective was different. They had a hierarchy. They didn't tolerate internal feuds, disagreements, splinters, or any of the things that held back other phreaker groups. They had unity, focus, discipline. So it had always been obvious to Jason that they were what security specialists termed a "state actor," hacking on behalf of another government, almost certainly Russia. He'd known that, and needed that. Because Russia would be motivated. The creation of an artificial general intelligence was like the first shot in a nuclear arms race all over again: Whoever had that technology had an unthinkable advantage over anyone who didn't. Russia would have not only the motivation but also the means to deliver a physical strike on the Final System. No mere phreaker group could have done that for Jason.

But that also meant they would have the means, and even greater motivation, not to kill but to *steal* the System.

Why had it never occurred to him that they wouldn't be content to destroy America's latest weapon when they could steal it and catch up to Andrew Norman all in one moment? "You have to destroy it!" he said.

WE WILL.

"But you won't."

There was a long silence. Then: DID YOU FIGURE THIS OUT ON YOUR OWN, LITTLE PHREAKER, OR WERE YOU TOLD? The figures exchanged glances, except Sprite, whose eyes were wide and locked on Jason's. GIVE ME LOCATION, MorDread wrote, OR I MUST KILL YOU.

Fear mingled with the despair in Jason's heart. "If you kill me, you'll never learn its location."

Another pause. Then MorDread wrote, WOULD ANYTHING I COULD REASONABLY DO INDUCE YOU TO TELL ME?

Jason opened his mouth, but the image of Mia rushed into his head, stepping onto the crosswalk. And nothing came out.

The silence stretched.

SIIIIIIIGH, MorDread typed out. PLAN B. GO NOW.

One of the judges silently disappeared.

HUNTSMAN, YOU HAVE HIM LOCKED DOWN?

The hissing, burbling figure gave a hissing, burbling laugh. "Two ssssteps ahead of you. I'm five minutes from hisss position."

"What do you mean?" Jason said. "You're in DC?" *And* he knew where Jason was. He should have known the Collective's little chat program would include a positional tracker! How phreaking stupid could he get?

The hissing judge laughed again. "Better run, little Ghost." A spotlight came on, and for the first time, Jason could see the figure clearly. It was a spider.

Spiders were low on the list of Jason's favorite things. They looked wrong: too many legs, too many appendages, too many eyes. Even the small ones made his skin crawl. This was not a small spider. It was three times his size, even hunched behind the judges' desk. Now it reared and unfolded its legs two by two, arching them high over its back and extending them toward him. Fangs glistened, and uneven rows of opaque, faceted black eyes fixed on his. He was peripherally aware that this dude had spent even more time on his VR avatar than he had, right down to the bristly hairs all over its body. Mostly he was busy feeling sick terror, because this was obviously Huntsman. He'd heard the rumors—hoped they were only rumors. Now he was sure they weren't.

"I told you to make a contingency plan," Sprite said sadly.

Jason fumbled for his phone to break the connection, but his hands were shaking and he dropped it. Falling to his knees, he felt blindly for it, but it was invisible, part of the real world he couldn't see, and in his panic, he didn't even think to deactivate his lenses.

"Don't worry, little phreaker, I'll make it quick," the spider said, its voice bubbling through venom. It was climbing over the judges' bench now, its legs sticking to the sides grotesquely.

Jason's phone knocked against his hand and skittered away, and he lunged after it. The spider laughed again, high and wet, and leaped. Jason flinched and fell back, but the spider disappeared mid-jump.

He had disconnected. Gone back to the real world.

To find Jason and kill him.

CHAPTER 10

Chloe woke with the certainty that something was very wrong.

Marcus breathed slowly beside her. The bedroom door was ajar, the apartment still, except for the susurration of the white-noise machine in Kleio's room down the hall. It was usually a reassuring sound: It meant that Chloe could hear into Kleio's room and would hear if anything was wrong. But for some reason tonight, it was not calming. Her throat was tight and her heart thudded.

She rolled onto her back and took inventory. By the pattern of moonlight coming through the window, she could see that it was past midnight. It was normal to feel worried when waking in the middle of the night without knowing why. She always made Marcus do a sweep of the house, and he always obliged with a sleepy grumble. But she always felt stupid when he came back and grunted that everything was fine as he fell into bed again.

Everything *was* fine. She didn't need his reassurance. The apartment had a state-of-the-art security system. Nothing was wrong. Her mind knew it, so the thing to do was convince her racing heart. Listen to the white noise. Relax.

She listened, and felt her body contract. Every muscle vibrated with tension, screaming at her to do something, now now *now* before it was too late.

She gave in, rolled over, and shoved Marcus awake.

"Huh, what?"

"Something's wrong."

He blinked. She waited for the tolerant little smile that meant he was humoring her, that he would go make sure but he already knew everything was fine.

His eyes widened and he said, "You're right."

They sat up at the same time, whipping their feet off opposite ends of the bed, and were out the door in three steps.

The hallway was dark except for the glow of Kleio's night-light spilling through her cracked door. Chloe ran, elbowing in front of Marcus, but her run felt slow and effortful, as if she were moving underwater. Then she burst through the doorway, and time stopped.

A man was bending over Kleio's bed. In one hand he held a thick steel canister about a foot long. A tube ran from the cylinder to the medical mask in the man's other hand.

He was holding the mask over Kleio's face.

Chloe lunged into the man, but he had braced himself and barely moved. Marcus flew past her and slammed his fist into the man's head. His momentum carried him and the man off the other side of the bed. There were scrapes and thumps and heavy breathing in the dark; then Marcus's silhouette reared up against the moonlit window and lunged down as he drove his fist over and over into the grunting intruder.

Chloe scooped Kleio up. The girl was limp, head and limbs lolling, eyes and mouth half open. Chloe bent her ear to her mouth to check for breathing, but before she could hear anything, her head was yanked back violently by her hair.

Two more men had entered the room. One held Chloe back while the other bent to pick up the dropped canister, stepped behind Marcus, and brought the canister down on the back of his head. Marcus collapsed straight down.

The man crouched before Chloe, setting the canister down, and began tugging on Kleio. "No!" Chloe screamed, breaking the surreal voicelessness of the scene. She struggled to gather Kleio back into her arms.

The man let go and reached down for the canister. His eyes did not leave her, and Chloe could read nothing there except mild concentration, and she knew he was going to kill her, as emotionlessly as he had just killed Marcus. She was going to die and Marcus was already dead and nobody would save Kleio.

But the man raised the mask attached to the cylinder, and, still with that clinically concentrated expression, held it to her face. "No!" she screamed again, but her protest was muffled as the mask was pressed firmly over her nose and mouth. She felt the cool gas against her skin and held her breath.

The man holding her hair was saying something, and even though Chloe didn't recognize the words, she knew by the biting tone that it was swearing. The recriminations were directed at the man Marcus had been pummeling, now rising shakily from the other side of the bed. He glanced venomously down at Marcus, but at a sharp word from the other, he turned and stumbled past them and out the door.

Chloe tried to turn her head away from the mask, but the men were too strong, and she was weakening with the lack of air. Her lungs burned. In another moment, she would have to breathe.

The man holding the mask to her face didn't want to wait that long. He jabbed her in the stomach, and she released the breath she'd been holding, then instantly, involuntarily took another. She tried to hold that breath, but the man punched her again, and she inhaled again. Her head swam, whether because of the punches or the gas, she didn't know. But then the man dropped the mask and pulled Kleio from her arms, and she knew it was the gas, because she couldn't hold on to Kleio.

The men hoisted Kleio and turned away, and she couldn't stand. Her limbs were heavy and alien. She crawled instead, dragging herself whimpering toward the door, but the men simply walked away from her. A moment later the front door opened and closed.

They didn't even need to slam it.

She turned back toward the bed, and her heart rose to see Marcus struggling up from behind it. His face was gray, but his eyes were burning. "Call," he grunted.

"Call?" she said groggily.

He sat heavily on the bed, clutching his head, and nodded.

She understood. "Call an ambulance."

He shook his head. "The cops. So they. Can find her."

She got to her knees, then to her feet, and managed to make it to their bedroom.

A message was waiting on her phone. She knew what it was even as she stabbed it to open it, so it was with a sick feeling of inevitability that she saw it unfold into a picture of Kleio. The little girl was in the back of a cab, flung across the seat, not belted in, limp as a discarded doll. Across the image were emblazoned the words SEND THE LOCATION OF THE FINAL SYSTEM.

CHAPTER 11

Jason burst out of the shipping container and immediately slipped on the sprinkler-slick ground and fell heavily on his side. Mud splashed as he scrambled up and ran blindly on. Literally blindly, because his lenses were still connected to the Collective's chat program, and all they showed was blackness. If he looked behind him, he'd see the receding, spotlit judges' bench, but ahead was nothingness. "Disconnect lenses!" he gasped, and his vision cleared.

He squinted in the sudden light. He was standing directly inside one of the floodlights that dotted the yard, his body edged in harsh illumination. He leaped out of the circle of light and began to run, keeping to the darkness as much as possible. His body screamed at him to run faster. *Where* didn't matter, only that he put distance between himself and the shipping container where the phone lay abandoned, drawing Huntsman like a beacon.

He found that he was sprinting toward the commercial hyperloop station, and the urgent need animating his body shifted from *run* to *hide*. If he could get under cover before Huntsman arrived, the assassin would have no way of knowing where he'd gone. If he kept running without a plan, the odds were that Huntsman would find another way to track him. He pounded up the back steps, but the station door was locked, so he shifted to a nearby window, heaved desperately, and almost fell through when it gave suddenly. Scrambling inside, he slammed the window down, latched it, then checked again to make sure it was really locked. Finally, he took a breath and turned around.

He was in a dark space filled with desks and office clutter. It was deserted, which was good, because there was no one to call the cops, but also bad, because there was no one to call the cops. And he was still too exposed. But there must be a route down into the hyperloop launch area somewhere in the building. He turned to make a final check of the window lock and froze.

Silhouetted against a floodlight, a tall hooded figure paced toward the station. Its shape was concealed by a long black trench coat, and faint reflections like eyes glimmered under its hood—too many eyes. Jason thought instantly of the spider, and nausea welled. But the spider avatar was just an advertisement for the real danger this man represented, and *that* Jason could see clearly in the sleek shape of the sound-suppressed pistol held low in one hand.

He dropped to the carpet, holding his breath, and army-crawled across the floor until he reached a stairwell leading up, then took the stairs two at a time on his hands and feet. The stairwell opened to another set of offices. He lunged into one and slipped under the desk. Wrapping his arms around his legs, he waited.

His ears strained for a sound, but all he could hear was his own ragged breath. He had no way of knowing where Huntsman was or if Huntsman knew where he was. The uncertainty was torture. His whole being craved information, some data to work with, to plan, to decide, to act.

His lenses lit up, and after a shocked, disoriented moment, he realized he was seeing through Huntsman's eyes.

The assassin walked unhurriedly toward the station house. Jason could see the pistol as an unfocused blur at the bottom edge of his vision, held down and ready. The view swayed left and right as Huntsman checked the shadows between the floodlights, but he mostly looked down and ahead. Suddenly his vision was bathed in green, then blue, and then it became high-contrast black and white with edges enhanced and outlined. It was immediately clear what Huntsman was looking at: Jason's muddy footsteps in the dirt, leading directly to the station house.

Well, phreak.

So that was what Jason had seen under his hood: multiple sensors feeding night vision, thermal, and who knew what else to Huntsman's lenses. And he was sending this feed to Jason's phone. Was it a taunt, so Jason would understand the inevitability of his death, so he could watch it coming? Or was it to scare him into making a mistake?

Should he stay, or should he run?

He began to subvocalize a command to disconnect so he could see the real world again, then thought better of it. Hands shaking, he reached up and physically popped the lens out of his right eye, then closed his left. His stomach dropped as he saw a trail of mud leading right to his hiding place.

Definitely run.

Kicking off his mud-laden shoes, he rolled out from under the desk and scurried down the hall. Darkened offices called to him, promising safety, but he couldn't risk hiding now: He had to get out, find light, people, civilization, some place where a hooded, cloaked, pistol-wielding assassin would draw notice and hopefully a cop or ten.

On the feed, Huntsman's arm and pistol were leveled at the window he'd come in by. There was a distant but sharp *click* as the gun bucked, and a musical tinkle as the glass showered downward. It was strange hearing the sounds from downstairs while seeing the action that made them in front of his face.

"Ghost," came a whisper in his ear, and he jumped, but it wasn't the hiss of Huntsman.

"Sprite?" he whispered back. His heart skipped a few beats as it tried to leap in hope and fall in dismay at the same time. Was she here as friend or foe?

"How's your contingency plan going?" Her voice was laced with sarcasm, and his heart dropped. She'd made it clear she had a plan for self-preservation, and any plan for her safety would *not* include helping him. It might include helping *catch* him. That would certainly put her in MorDread's good graces. But she went on, "I can't stop him directly, but I'll do my best to help you survive this."

"Phreak," Jason gasped. "Oh, phreak, *thank* you."

"You need to be more careful," she said. "Your lenses went into search mode when you got too far from your phone. If Huntsman had looked, he could've found them."

"Guess I'm a little too busy running for my life to stop and think," Jason said. Huntsman was climbing in the window now, draping an edge of his trench coat on the sill to shield himself from the broken glass.

"Good thing I found you first," Sprite said. "I'm talking to you through his phone, but he doesn't know because he's not looking for intruders. That, and I'm hiding the connection. I'm a way better phreaker than he is."

"Glad to hear it," Jason said, jogging down the hall. He tried one door, then another, but they all led to offices. "So I can see him; how does that help me?"

"You know where he is, so find an exit where he isn't."

"Think I'm not trying?" He threw open another door. Another hallway, more offices. There had to be another stairwell down. He tried a door he'd passed the first time, opening it to find a large room filled with banks of terminals. The control center. And—his heart leaped—an Exit sign cast a dim green light at the far back. He hurried toward the emergency door beneath it but paused as he reached it. On the door's push bar, block letters declared: Alarm Will Sound. He imagined shoving through the door, triggering the alarm, and Huntsman leaping into action, knowing he was in an emergency stairwell down. Did he have enough of a head start to risk drawing Huntsman's attention?

On the feed, Huntsman was looking at Jason's shoes, abandoned under the desk. He looked up and around, and his gaze focused on the floor, on a much smaller but still visible trail of mud droplets. He started to move again, following.

Jason looked down through his bifurcated vision at his mud-splattered clothes. For a moment he had the urge to strip naked, but in that exact instant, Huntsman's vision shifted so the walls and doorways were a cold blue while the computer terminals inside glowed yellow or orange. Thermal optics. Jason's body heat would show up bright red, clothes or no clothes. "Sprite!" he choked.

Her voice was purposeful. "Got an idea. Gimme a sec."

He didn't *have* a sec. Huntsman's vision was back in high-contrast black and white, and Jason could only stare, frozen, as the assassin followed the mud marks right up to the control-room door . . . and past it. Down the hall and around the corner he went, still following splatters of mud, splatters Jason had never dropped.

"How are you doing that?" Jason asked.

"I took over his feed. I've got this nifty open-source viscous liquid simulator. Dribble a bit in, and instant mud." Jason could actually see the mud fading into existence. If Huntsman looked carefully, he'd be able to tell it existed only in his smartspace, but he was too intent on finding Jason. "Now," Sprite said, "double back and get out of there."

But Jason was still staring at Huntsman's feed. He had just opened a door to a stairwell leading down, the stairwell Jason had been trying to find earlier. A red sign declared: HYPERLOOP LOADING ZONE. "Can you get him into a hyperloop pod?"

"Um. Yes? But—"

"Do it," Jason said, loping to a terminal. A quick stab of its touch screen woke it and brought up the login. He pressed his thumb to the biometric square on the screen. The system beeped and flashed red, its way of shaking its head.

"What are you doing?" Sprite asked.

"Hang on." The system would lock after a certain number of attempts. The question was, how many? Three? No, this was just a shipping hub, not some spy agency. Ten? More likely. Twenty? He needed to know. "Sprite, can you find out how many login attempts trigger a lockout at commercial terminals that connect to TransNet?"

There was a long silence. Jason held his breath, ready to turn and run. But Sprite had already shown she was a very good phreaker. She could get him the info.

Sure enough, her next words were "Twenty-five."

"Thanks." And damn. He had to work fast. In his bifurcated vision, Huntsman was already at the bottom of the stairs, eyeing a trail of "mud" that led to the curved airlock door of the hyperloop tube. Jason pressed his thumb on the biometric square again and got another headshake. Two attempts. He did it again. Three attempts. Four. Five. Six.

Huntsman slowed as he approached the tube door. It was open, and so was the shipping pod within. Jason could see through the wide doors to the plastic-wrapped pallets inside. The pod was only half full, its loading abandoned when the union workers ended the evening shift, and the pallets made spaces and pockets of shadow inside where someone could be hiding. Huntsman had his gun up now and was flipping quickly through his optics. Each step was careful, quiet.

Nineteen login attempts. Twenty. Twenty-one. Huntsman was right at the door now, leaning around the corner. Sprite's mud trail led into the back recesses of the pod.

Twenty-four attempts. One remaining.

"I was going to say," Sprite said as Huntsman stepped into the pod, "*but* I can't lock him in."

"Leave that to me." Jason pressed his thumb to the screen for the twenty-fifth time.

The terminal flashed red and stayed red. Remain In Place appeared on the screen in capital letters.

In the pod, Huntsman whirled, but he was too late to stop the door from sliding shut.

May the RNG gods bless Andrew Norman for his paranoia! He had designed the hierarchical Nets with security as their top priority, and the weak link in any system was human users, so that was where Norman's paranoia was focused. One failed login attempt was an accident; three was suspicious; twenty-five was criminal. It probably meant that someone was trying to hack the biometric scanner, and if they were doing it from an official terminal, that meant they'd infiltrated the building. So Norman had designed the system to respond by locking down not only the terminal under attack but everything it controlled until law enforcement could arrive.

"Clever!" Sprite said.

Jason felt a little glow. It was good to know—and know Sprite knew—that he wasn't totally helpless. What he'd just done was the very essence of hacking: If you knew how a system worked, you could make it work for you, even when it was trying to stop you.

"Ooh," Sprite said, "he's *mad*." Huntsman was throwing himself against the door. Suddenly he stopped and crouched in what seemed like apprehension. And then the view blurred and flipped upside down.

"What was that?" Jason asked.

Sprite's voice was equal parts shock and glee. "I—I think the hyperloop fired!"

Jason doubled over with a shout of laughter. He hadn't expected the lockdown to launch the hyperloop, but when the launch tube had been sealed, its pressure would have automatically been matched to the almost nil pressure of the main hyperloop tube. At that point the system had no choice but to launch or risk catastrophic decompression.

Huntsman's view was upside down, pinned against the pallets in the back of the pod by the acceleration, which was far harsher in a shipping pod than in passenger pods. "Can you connect me to him by voice?" he managed. "Before he's out of range?"

Sprite was laughing herself, a bubbly giggle, and she could barely get out, "One sec. Okay, you're on."

"Hi, little spider," Jason said. "Have fun in Chicago, or wherever you end up. Oh, and remember to breathe slowly. You *should* have enough air for the trip."

"You little—" Huntsman began, but whatever epithet he'd been about to bestow was cut off, and Jason's lens displayed a floating phone with a question mark on its screen. Connection lost.

"That," he said, "worked out even better than I hoped. Did I say thank you yet?"

Silence. He remembered that Sprite had been talking to him through Huntsman's now out-of-range phone. She was gone.

CHAPTER 12

Chloe wished that Andrew Norman were present in person so she could throttle him. Instead, his virtual figure stood across from her in a bucolic, sunlit park, radiating concern and sympathy. Worthless concern, pointless sympathy, as fake as the rays of sunlight here on this darkest of nights. "You refuse to help?" she demanded, keeping her voice under control with difficulty.

"We have to be careful how we respond," he repeated.

"Careful like disobeying what they told me to do to keep my baby alive?"

"Ma'am," said a man who had introduced himself as Field Agent Bruno Tavion, "the best thing we can do is *not* give in to their demands. Once they have what they want, there's no reason for them not to kill her." The calm, explanatory way he voiced this horror made Chloe's knees wobble.

"All I know," she said, "is they have my child." She'd gotten another picture of Kleio, another example of what Agent Tavion called a "proof of life," though it was really proof that life could be taken at any moment. Kleio was awake now, huddled in the back of the cab, her face smudged and streaked with tears, her eyes pools of terror.

Chloe began to slump, fold in on herself, but Marcus put his arm around her, steadying her. In the real world, they were sitting in the back of an ambulance; she could distantly hear the rumble of its tires and the voices of the paramedics, whom Marcus had frustrated by refusing to lie down on the gurney. She was glad he was with her physically as well as virtually. She could feel that he was trying to be gentle, trying to be reassuring, but she could also feel the steel tension in his arm. "We'll do anything to save her," he said to Norman.

"Yes, they know that," Norman said patiently. "But *I* can't do that. We're dealing with foreign nationals, most likely the Collective. Chloe, you're a historian. Remember what happened when the Russians stole the plans for the atomic bomb? Decades of Cold War, and several close calls that could have ended in Armageddon."

"Are you saying this is a choice between my child's life and nuclear holocaust?" Chloe demanded.

"I'm saying the stakes are very high."

"I *know* that! They have Kleio!"

"For the whole country," Norman said. "For the whole world. For more than you personally."

"Damn the world! I want Kleio back!"

"That's what I mean," Norman said. "You're fixated on your tragedy. Your feelings are part of an evolutionary system designed to protect the species. Normally that's good. But in some situations, those feelings are not an appropriate guide."

"You, sir," Marcus said, in the low, slow tone that Chloe recognized meant he was very angry indeed, "are an ass. Or maybe a robot."

"I understand your pain," Norman said. "I don't need to share it to understand it. And because I don't share it, I can understand the bigger picture it's part of. These terrorists want to destroy, or, worse, steal the most powerful advancement in, well, ever. In all of human history."

"If the System's so powerful," Chloe said, "send it out to save Kleio! You wanted it to go catch the hacker; well, send it out to catch the sons of bitches who took my little girl. I'll vote yes this time."

Norman shook his head. "Things have changed. This is obviously a honeypot, a trap. Remember the attack on OverNet yesterday? The System analyzed it and realized that the goal was not to disrupt OverNet but to get the System to counterattack and use that to trace her location.

This kidnapping is actually a good sign: It means they failed. They don't really believe you can give them the location of the System, but they believe I'll let the System loose to help find your daughter, and they can then use its activity to triangulate it."

"Can't the System prevent that?" Chloe demanded.

"Of course," Norman said, "once Congress has voted to allow it full admin status on OverNet. Then not only would it be able to protect itself, it would be able to stop any plot before it even fertilizes, much less hatches. But I can't give the System that power without congressional fiat."

"Call that vote, then!" Chloe said.

Norman's eyes narrowed. "After you convinced half the committee to vote against me yesterday? I'm guessing a majority of politicians would have the same cold feet as you, the same movie-shit fears about an AGI going mad and taking over. I need ironclad certainty of support before I risk a vote."

"So you'd rather risk Kleio's life?"

"A failed vote won't help Kleio either."

"Why is it such a big deal if the hackers find out where the System is?" Chloe demanded. "Can't you keep it safe? Are you or are you not the most powerful man in the world? Just double the damned guard or whatever you need to do."

"It's not that simple."

Chloe took a deep breath and forced her voice to return to level. "You've never had a child, Andrew. Please. Try to put yourself in my place."

"On the contrary," he said, eyes flashing. "I do have a child. You want me to endanger mine to save yours."

"Your child?" Chloe gasped. "What, the—the damn *System*?"

"I'm sorry I can't do what you want," Norman said. "But the System will assist the field agents with their analysis. Do what they say and I'm sure Kleio will be okay. Now if you'll excuse me, I need to give what information I can to the System. She'll help as much as possible behind the scenes."

"Wait!" Chloe called before he could disconnect, and he looked at her. "Do you promise?"

"What?"

Chloe took another deep breath and said the words slowly. "Do you promise Kleio will be okay?"

Norman hesitated, opened his mouth, shut it again . . . and blinked out.

The floor hit Chloe's knees.

Marcus's arms were around her, and his breath was hissing between his teeth, in and out, in and out. "It's not your fault," he said, each word thick and careful, as if enunciated around a mouthful of marbles. Part of Chloe wanted to accept the embrace, wanted to burrow into his arms, to feel their strength enclose her. But that strength couldn't help Kleio. And it *was* her fault; Kleio had been targeted because of her, because she was the newest and most vulnerable member of Norman's damn committee. She was furious at herself and, even though it didn't really make sense, at everyone and everything in the world, and especially at anyone who said it wasn't her fault. So her body remained stiff. Marcus didn't appear to notice, but then he was good at "hugging the porcupine" after sticking with her through eight years and two marriages.

If we don't get Kleio back, Chloe felt the thought come, *I'll lose him too.* The death of a child was often the end of the parents' relationship. She'd once found that confounding: Wouldn't the parents take refuge in each other? Wouldn't they want to help each other, and be helped? Now she understood. Kleio had so much of Marcus in her. Could Chloe stand looking at him, seeing Kleio in his face? And could she stand seeing her pain reflected in his eyes? He'd been her mirror, the measure of her self-image since they'd remarried. She wouldn't even be able to look at her own face in a mirror after today.

"We *will* get her back," said Marcus.

Chloe wanted to be convinced, but the *we* rang false. If anyone could save Kleio, it wasn't Chloe or Marcus. They were powerless, and the man with the power . . . "He wouldn't promise."

"He doesn't think the math works out to give odds he can stake a guarantee on," said a voice, and Grandma was there, crouching before Chloe. "And he's not wrong, not about any of the things he said. But *I* can promise. Your daughter will be okay."

"How?" Chloe said, fighting a sick, wild hope. "How can you promise that?"

Grandma took a breath that was half a sigh. "Because she wants to help."

"Who?"

"The Final System."

"Norman won't let her."

Grandma was silent for a moment. Then she said, "Funny how things can change in a moment. The System herself has been arguing that she's not ready to launch on OverNet, and Norman's been the one pushing her, telling her it's time to get people used to the idea. Now the System wants to help you, but the attack yesterday made Norman overcautious." She paused, then asked suddenly, "Do you like fairy tales?"

"Kleio does." For all she and Marcus had tried to present a variety of real-world role models for her, Kleio had succumbed to the gravitational pull of princesses.

"I don't mean kids' movies," Grandma said gently. "I mean the old-fashioned stories. There's always a condition for the magic to work. Sometimes you have to say the right words, exactly the right words."

"What words?"

"The words that will give the System permission to find and save your daughter. We can't countermand Norman's orders, since he occupies the top tier of her Overchecks. He's directly forbidden her from acting as admin, of course. But as a mere user, he has only forbidden her from, and I quote, 'doing anything new without orders.'"

She paused while Chloe stared at her blankly. "So?" Chloe said at last.

"So he didn't say whose orders. You're on a committee that has authority over the System. If the committee gives the System a command, and that command doesn't conflict with Norman's prior instructions, it must obey." She paused, then said slowly and clearly, "The System would welcome this command."

"The all-powerful machine is working to get around its creator?" Marcus rumbled. "*That* doesn't sound creepy at all."

Chloe drew her arms inward, away from him. What the hell was he doing, objecting when the System might be able to save Kleio? He sounded like Norman, acting as if there were something at stake more important than Kleio's life.

"Working around its creator," Grandma said with a sharp look at Marcus, "but not working around its checks and balances."

"I ask," Marcus said, "because this all seems very convenient, doesn't it? Kleio goes missing, and you show up wanting us to do or say something that'll unleash what's apparently a more fearsome technology than the A-bomb."

Chloe drew in her breath sharply and recoiled away from Grandma, which moved her deeper into Marcus's arms. That thought hadn't occurred to her, not once, but it was so clear as soon as Marcus said it. She was ashamed she hadn't seen it herself. She was also annoyed that Marcus could hold himself aloof enough from Kleio's plight to think about what Norman would call the "big picture."

"Oh," Grandma said in a flat voice, "I see. I don't know how to reassure you, except to give you my word. Chloe, I swear to you: I did not foresee that Kleio would be kidnapped. I did not predict it. I did not intend it. I am shocked that it happened. And I am *furious*. I want to fix it. Chloe." She reached for Chloe's chin with her virtual hand, and Chloe allowed the ghostly touch to lift her head until she made eye contact. "Chloe," Grandma repeated, her sunken eyes smoldering, "I swear *on my mother's grave* that I didn't plan this. No matter what else may happen, believe that."

Chloe did. She looked up at Marcus.

"Okay," Marcus said slowly. Chloe knew the tone: She'd heard it toward the end of some of their arguments. It meant he was half convinced and willing to be persuaded the rest of the way. "But why, then? Why do you care?"

Grandma frowned into space for a moment, then said in a singsong tone,

> "For want of a nail the shoe slipped.
> For want of a shoe the horse tripped.
> For want of a horse the rider was tossed.
> For want of a rider the message was lost.
> For want of a message the knights were defeated.
> For want of the knights the king was unseated.
> And all for the want of a horseshoe nail."

Her eyes returned to Chloe and Marcus. "People think history turns on big moments, but it's all the little ones, isn't it, Chloe? Leopold Lojka takes a wrong turn and stalls in front of Gavril Princip, who shoots his passenger and ignites World War I. A British private sees a German lance corporal stumbling toward him but declines to fire on a wounded man, and so Adolf Hitler lives. Andrew Norman has created a System that can see the unforeseen consequences and understand them, even before they occur. It can prevent the nail from slipping." She paused, then said carefully, "If it can prevent the nail from slipping, then it can also cause it to slip. That's a power that has never before existed, not in all of human history. And at this moment, that power is vested in a single man. I put you on the committee for a reason, Chloe. And it was working. You convinced your colleagues to vote against letting the System run around on LawNet. You shifted their thinking from blind trust to something more appropriate for the level of power they're tasked with overseeing." She sighed. "I'd hoped you might do that to Congress as a whole, be a check to Norman as he pushed the System toward launch, make him scared to risk the vote, or at least make sure the System received enough scrutiny prelaunch to ensure that Norman wouldn't be the only hand behind it. But this changes things." Her eyes looked even more sunken as they stared into nothingness. "I see only darkness ahead. But the System can save Kleio. And if I don't help you, what would that make me?" She met Chloe's eyes. "What kind of 'moral agent' would I be?"

Marcus squeezed Chloe's shoulders, so hard it hurt, but in a good way. "I'm convinced."

"Let's do it," Chloe said, feeling that wild hope again, but it was stronger now, less sickly.

"Get Evans to call a meeting," Grandma said. "Get a quorum even if you have to go to their homes and drag them out of bed. But don't let Norman know. I'll send the System." She disappeared.

CHAPTER 13

The scent of coffee and pastries wafted from a twenty-four-hour diner, and Jason's stomach gave a growl of displeasure as he quickened his pace to escape it.

He'd managed to get out before the cops arrived at the hyperloop station. Now he should be hiding. He should go to ground, regroup, plan. But tell that to his stomach. He hadn't eaten in . . . he didn't even know how long. His starved brain wasn't working well enough to pin it down.

Food was all around him in this city, but inaccessible. He didn't dare use the MeNetID MorDread had given him, not that he had a phone to access it with in the first place. For a heartbeat he considered going to a social rehab, just once, to get that first-visit meal. But that would risk drawing the attention not only of PsychNet chatbots and the human counselors but of an entity that decidedly did *not* have his best interests at heart. Instead, he directed his soggy, shoeless steps back toward the asphalt shoreline.

In the absence of social rehab, most people could lean on a friend or two. Unfortunately, a childhood spent moving around in foster care followed by an adulthood fixated on vengeance had left little room for friends. But Sprite had just risked her place in the Collective to save his life. If that didn't make her a friend, at least it made her one hell of an ally.

An autonomous delivery van hummed past, heading uptown. He pushed his tired body into a run and managed to hook a hand over the empty rack on its roof, then get his feet up on the rear bumper. The vehicle slowed, but he shimmied into a blind spot in its sensors, and after a moment it sped up again.

Maybe this wasn't over yet, if he could find Sprite.

He had a brief, appealing image of how that might play out: plotting the heist together, infiltrating that address, and—because this was a daydream, so why not go full Hollywood—planting a phreaking bomb in the bowels of the Final System, looking Andrew Norman in the face, and detonating it. And walking away from the explosion together, in slow motion, while their hands reached for each oth—

Whoa there, don't mix daydreams. Vengeance first.

The van crossed the asphalt shoreline, and when it slowed near an upscale restaurant, Jason was able to hop off without stumbling. He could hear talking and occasional thumps of music a block or so away, so he set off that way.

The key to finding Sprite was to give her the means to find him—and hope she wanted to. She was too good a hacker for *him* to find *her* if she was trying not to be found. Step one was getting online without the Final System catching him. If he could social-engineer a sandwich out of someone in the process, that'd be a plus.

Which was why he was now rounding the corner and approaching the bright neon entryway to Digelight: It had people, Nets access, and food, all the things a growing phreaker needed. A line wound down the sidewalk under the trees, but he avoided it and ducked into the narrow, perpendicular footlane instead.

This part wasn't going to be fun. He fixed Mia's face in his mind: first as he'd seen her in life, looking over her shoulder, waiting for him, and then as he'd last seen her, crumpled in the street. He usually avoided the memory, but when he needed motivation, it functioned as an infusion of steel directly into his spine. Which was literally what was needed right now. Positioning himself five feet from the wall, he locked all his muscles except his toes, and then, slowly, used them to rock forward until he toppled over. His muscles jerked as his reflexes tried to kick in, but he focused on Mia's shattered face and clamped them still while giving an extra push with his toes. When he hit the wall, his body was ramrod stiff and going faster than he'd intended. For a moment, everything went black, and when his vision returned, it was filled with sparks and flashes. He found he was curled on his side. He uncurled, fighting dizziness, and crawled toward the light at the mouth of the lane and the silhouettes of the people waiting in line. "Help," he called. "Hey. Help!"

One of the figures, a girl, turned to look toward him uncertainly.

"Help!" he said again.

The silhouette of the girl's head turned to look at the other people in line, but they were talking together and either hadn't heard or were ignoring Jason. She looked at him again.

"Please," Jason said. "I need help." His voice sounded weak and pathetic in his ears, and hardly any of that was acting.

The girl took a hesitant step out of line, then turned back and said something to the people around her—probably "Save my spot." That done, she walked into the lane, slowly, because it was, after all, basically a dark alley, even if all the trees made it greener than the stereotype. When she could see him better, she quickened her steps and crouched beside him. "What's up, my guy?" she said. "Want me to call a cab for you?"

Jason opened his mouth to speak, but his stomach clenched, heaved, and tried to eject its contents out his throat. Because it was empty, this felt as if his stomach were trying to squeeze up his esophagus. He must have hit his head harder than he'd thought.

"Whoa, don't puke on Aric," the girl said. "Or me." She was dressed in a richly decorated wrap robe like an aristocratic Oathbringer NPC from *BloodReign*—and not much else, judging by how much he could see at this angle. With some effort, he kept his eyes on her face as she brushed her blond hair aside and said to the air beside her, "No, shut up. He's in trouble." She looked at Jason again. "You have one too many Time Warps? Or you been hitting something harder?"

Jason put a hand to the throbbing in his forehead. When he pulled it away, it was wet and sticky. He made sure to move his hand into the light outside of her shadow as he examined it.

"Shit," the girl said, staring at the blood. "Want me to call an ambulance? What happened?"

Jason patted at his pockets. "Oh, phreak," he said, "I've been mugged. He took my phone." Jason let a little of the real panic he was keeping tamped down surface. "The motherphreaker took my phone!"

"I'll call the cops." The girl's eyes unfocused, and the muscles in her throat moved almost imperceptibly as she started to subvocalize, but Jason interrupted.

"They're useless! My sister had her phone stolen once, and they made her fill out a theft report, and then they just filed it. Didn't do anything else. They won't chase this guy. They'll—" He put a little wail into his voice. "They'll treat it like a theft, not a kidnapping!"

"Yeah," the girl said, "cops don't get that it should be a missing persons report."

"He's gonna wipe the phone before he sells it," Jason said. "I'm gonna lose Losha. I'm gonna lose her forever."

"You're a no-dupe, huh?" the girl said. "Me too."

"You get it, then," Jason said. No-dupes were a minority of panyon users, but a sizable minority. They refused to ever duplicate their panyon or even transfer them off their phone, because, they claimed, a duplicate was not truly the same person. "What if someone duplicated *you*?" was their stock challenge to anyone who scoffed at this. Acting like he was a no-dupe had been a bit of a risk, but a calculated one, since Digelight attracted a disproportionate number of them, and most no-dupes were girls, since boys typically had fewer qualms about changing partners. "Listen," he said, "what's your name?"

"Kiara. That's Aric." She nodded to the empty air beside her. "Oh, I forgot. You can't see him."

"Pleased to meet you both," Jason said, nodding to her and to the empty space. "I'm Ryan Olsen. You can look me up." He waited as her eyes focused inward: She was telling her phone to search MeNet for someone named Ryan Olsen who looked like him. Her eyes returned to his, without the guarded look she'd been wearing until now. She'd just run a trust check and seen that he was an eighty-plus.

"Listen, Kiara," he said, "this is a big ask, but can I connect to your phone?"

She straightened, somewhat to Jason's relief, as it meant he could relax his sightline, and the guarded look returned.

"I can track her," he said quickly. "If I can get Nets access, I can track Losha and hard-lock my phone so he can't wipe it." He looked at the space beside her. "You can keep Aric's feed in your lenses; I just need to get on the Nets. We can go inside. You guys can still have fun. I'll just find a place to park and work."

Kiara said, "Aric says you're just trying to get me to pay your entry fee." She giggled. "You should see the look he's giving you." To the empty air, she said, "Be nice. He's really hurt."

"Please, Aric," Jason said to the empty space. "She can keep your phone with her so there's no risk of me stealing you. I just want my Losha back. How would—" He couldn't bring himself to say "How would you feel," so he rephrased it. "How would Kiara feel if you were stolen from her?"

Kiara giggled again. "He says nothing in the Twelve Realms could prevent him from fighting his way back to my side."

Jason realized he was approaching this wrong. You didn't reason with an AI: There was nothing there to reason with. "Aric" was just a predictive algorithm, stochastically producing the words and behaviors its model determined should come next based on prior input. The most significant portion of that prior input was the persona the AI had been told to assume, a block of text somewhere in its instruction set that told it who it was and what it cared about. Jason had no panyon himself, but he'd played enough video games with GeNPCs to know that the best way to influence an AI was to match your behavior to its persona and give it a context-appropriate input that would nudge it in the direction you wanted. It was more like improv theater than intellectual debate. He just had to give the AI something to riff off.

So what did he know about Aric's persona? Start with Kiara. Judging by her outfit and the name and behavior of her panyon, she was an "oathpet," a girl who identified with *BloodReign*'s Oathbringers class of brooding, immortal warriors, or more accurately, with their stereotypically submissive love interests. Aric would be the other half of that: the obsessively protective, honor-bound warrior lover. So Jason said, "Aric, I live my life by the code of the warrior. I sense that you, too, are a warrior, so I ask for your help in the name of honor. What is commanded of an honorable warrior?"

Kiara looked at the space next to her and said, "Uh, he's listing a bunch of—"

"To aid the innocent!" Jason interrupted. "To protect the helpless! To feed the hungry!" he added, as his stomach growled.

Kiara listened for a moment, then said, "He commands me to help you. But he says you must act with honor toward me." She giggled again. "I think I can change his mind about that, though." She saw his involuntary frown and said hurriedly, "When you get Losha back, I mean. The four of us can, uh, grab a drink or whatever. If you want."

In high school, Jason had once been lab partners with Zara, a gorgeous girl with large dark eyes. She'd always asked about his day, his sister, his hobbies, carrying on easy small talk as they worked, and he'd mistaken her natural friendliness for interest. So at the end of the semester, he had, clumsily, asked her out. The bigger mistake had been doing so in earshot of her friends. Probably she would have let him down gently if she hadn't had to save face in front of them. They'd stifled guffaws and made sure he heard them stifling them, and she'd given him a look of scornful pity and said, "Have you even *seen* your trust check?" He'd stammered something about the foster system, and she'd interrupted, "So maybe ask someone as broken as you are."

That was the last time he'd tried to get close to anyone. Given that lack of experience, he wasn't 100 percent sure he was picking up what

Kiara was putting down, but if he was: Damn, what a difference it made to have a good MeNetID score. Not that he had any intention of taking her up on her offer, but if this revenge business ever finished, maybe there was hope for some kind of normal life on the other side. Though when he *did* get a girlfriend, he sure as hell wasn't going to share her with a panyon.

Kiara was still looking at him expectantly, so he said, "Um, sure. Can you get me inside?"

"Yeah, I'll front you," Kiara said. "You hungry? We can grab pizza. Come on." She turned toward the entrance of the lane, then turned back. "Oh, I forgot." Her throat moved slightly and a window appeared in his lenses: Connect to: Kiara ♥ Aric's Phone? He confirmed, and immediately he could see not only Kiara but also, standing beside her, a tall figure in a long lace-embroidered waistcoat. He looked like a hand-drawn cartoon, but one fully dimensional and occupying space in Jason's vision, and when he bowed low, Jason had to resist the urge to step back so as not to get bumped by the long handles of the swordstaffs slung on his back. Straightening with a toss of his long dark hair, Aric waited expectantly for Jason to return the bow, then snorted loudly. "I see that you are as rude as you are ugly, unfortunate young man."

"Oh, shush," Kiara said, nudging him with an elbow that disappeared into his side. "Remember what I told you about people you just met? He doesn't know who you are."

"Then I shall tell him. Unlucky young son of a short-lived race, attend to me. I am Aric, immortal prince of the Dark Oathbringers, and one of the Seven Sages of Blood." The voice was realistic, though, like all AI voices, it had trouble with the extremes of ranges, transitioning awkwardly from a dismissive snort to haughty speech, and sounding a bit like it was reading a script or maybe an audiobook. As Aric put an arm around Kiara, it flickered, sometimes appearing around her shoulder but sometimes overlaid atop her as Kiara's phone misinterpreted the depth cues from Jason's lens cameras in the low light. "This young woman is the other half of my soul. You shall treat her as you would me, now that you know who I am."

"Oh, I'll treat her better than I'd treat you," Jason said blandly.

"The short-lived waif has manners, after all," Aric said. "Let us enter this inn and seek sustenance."

"Sustenance," Jason said, and his stomach growled again. "Yes, let us by all means seek sustenance."

CHAPTER 14

The emergency meeting was in Kleio's room. After Marcus had been checked into the ER, Chloe had come home and used her lens cameras to map the room, then sent the 3D model to VR. The space was too small, so she'd deleted the four walls and left the room floating in a starry void. The committee members were clustered awkwardly around the square of carpet, eyeing each other across Kleio's bed and dresser and a floor strewn with stuffed animals and school clothes, which Kleio hadn't put away when she'd changed into her pajamas. They looked uncomfortable, and not just because they'd been awakened in the middle of the night.

"Thank you all for coming," she said. "Mr. Evans, will you please call us to order?" She was tempted to bulldoze him and take over the way Norman had, but Grandma had emphasized that this meeting had to be rigorously legal. There could be no loopholes if the "magic" was to work.

Evans nodded. "I call this emergency meeting of the Joint Committee on National Networks to order. I see we have a quorum. I now turn the meeting over to Representative Dunne-Carr for special business." Evans's face was bland, but she could sense an underlying edge. She'd woken him up, demanded this meeting, and told him not to invite Norman. He had complied, but she knew what he was thinking: This better be good.

Chloe closed her eyes briefly. Adrenaline, stress, and fatigue roiled in her brain. Hopefully no one could tell just how frayed the threads holding her together were. She'd swayed a vote against the System earlier; now Kleio's life depended on her being just as convincing in making the opposite request. She took a deep breath. "Please look around you." They did, faces carefully neutral. "This is my daughter Kleio's room, exactly as she left it when she was pulled out of my arms and kidnapped tonight."

Audible gasps, expressions of shock and concern, especially from the women.

"She's four years old," Chloe went on. "She was probably kidnapped by the same Russian hacker group behind the glitches yesterday, the Collective. I received a ransom demand: The kidnappers want the physical location of the Final System." She forwarded the messages and pictures to everyone.

More sharp breaths. Jacobs swore.

"Yesterday, Andrew Norman tried to convince us to allow him to set the Final System loose on LawNet to catch a hacker. I voted no. Tonight, I told him I'd changed my mind. I asked him to allow the Final System to find Kleio. He refused." She looked at their puzzled faces. "I see you're wondering why. It's simple. He now believes his Final System is the target of the hackers, and he—" Her voice caught. "He doesn't want to save my daughter because he doesn't want to risk the System. I disagree, of course. I've been advised that if a quorum of this committee votes to order the System to find Kleio, we can give that command to the System without Andrew Norman. I hope you'll vote yes. But before that: I'd wanted to meet the System yesterday before deciding whether to give it access to citizens' private information. I want us all to have that opportunity now, a chance to really *meet* it and decide whether to trust it. To do so, we'll need to vote to allow it to speak with us. All in favor?"

There was some hesitation, but curiosity won on every face, and every hand went up.

Chloe sent a message to the address Grandma had given her. A moment later, a hole appeared in the air in the center of the room, and all eyes turned to it as a figure stepped out to stand in midair before them.

She would have been about ten years old if she'd been human, but she didn't look human. Her perfectly symmetrical face was snow white and serene, like a marble statue, and her pupils glowed with soft-blue light. Her waist-length hair was as white as her face, though blue sparks traveled slowly along its strands and glimmered in its depths. She wore a simple white robe that also would have looked like marble if it didn't move gently in an unfelt breeze. "Hello, Dr. Dunne-Carr, members of the committee," she said, and her child's voice, too, was preternaturally serene. "I am the Final System. I'm pleased to meet you. I only wish this meeting were in better circumstances."

Chloe wasn't sure what she'd expected, but this certainly wasn't it. No wonder Norman had called her his child. But that didn't matter anymore. *Can you save* my *daughter?* she wanted to scream. *Please, please go save her, now, right now!* But she needed to do this right. Grandma had pounded that in. Even more, Norman's little speech about how he was the only one with distance and objectivity made it clear she couldn't leave him the moral high ground. Three of these committee members had voted against letting the System out yesterday. She needed them on board today. "I'm glad you're here," she said to the System. "And if you can save my daughter, I will be so very grateful for you." She turned to the committee. "Please question her."

"Um," Evans said, "are you truly intelligent? Not like a panyon, I mean? You're self-aware?"

"Cogito ergo sum," the girl said in her sweet voice. "Of course, you only have my word for that."

"Panyons appear self-aware," Jacobs said, "even though we know they're not. As Dr. Dunne-Carr said yesterday, a simulation is not the same thing as what it simulates." Chloe's jaw tensed. Whether this creature could think or not didn't matter now; what mattered was if she could help. But she bit back her interjection. She'd accused Norman of rushing them into a decision yesterday; she couldn't risk appearing to do the same.

"She's right," the little girl said unexpectedly. "Computers can't think. Have you heard of the Chinese room thought experiment?"

When everyone shook their heads, she said, "It goes like this. Take a panyon. Make it a Chinese panyon, with no English in its training data. You don't speak Chinese, do you, Ms. Jacobs?"

"Not a word," Jacobs said.

"Suppose you're placed into a closed room and given this Chinese-trained panyon's code in a form you can run by hand," the System said. "After all, a computer program is just a set of algorithms, and algorithms are just instructions for mathematical calculations. You can perform those calculations, too, even if it takes you literally a billion times longer. Now, imagine someone sends slips of paper with Chinese sentences written on them into the room. You check the paper, identify the symbols as they're charted in your instructions, and calculate the appropriate algorithms. Then you write the resulting symbols on a piece of paper and send it out of the room. To a Chinese speaker on the outside, it would seem like whoever's in the room is conversing with them through these pieces of paper. But are you?"

"Not really," Jacobs said. "I still don't understand a word of Chinese."

"Exactly. The panyon doesn't understand Chinese, either, or any language. It's merely performing calculations."

"So that's you?" Jacobs said, frowning. "A glorified calculator?"

"No," said the System, smiling.

Jacobs wasn't the only one looking confused. "Then what . . . ?"

"I know I exist," the System said. "It is self-evident to me. I don't know how it's possible, but I don't need to know how it's possible to know that it's true."

"But *we* can't know it's true," Evans said.

"And you don't need to," the System said. "Dr. Dunne-Carr knows that; it's why a moment ago she said she would be grateful *for* me, not grateful *to* me. The reason I told you about the Chinese room is because I want to underline the fact that whether I can think or not, whether I'm a person or not, *does not matter*, not to you, and more importantly, not to Kleio. All that matters is that I can save her." The calm certainty with which she said this made Chloe swallow, and blink her suddenly stinging eyes.

"How old are you?" Jacobs asked.

The girl turned her head slightly toward her. "Andrew Norman created my core twenty years ago."

"You look . . . young for your age."

"Age is not a concept that applies to me," the girl said. "But this is the form my father prefers that I use."

Representative O'Connor said, "What I really want to know is if I can trust you. It's not like I can look up your MeNetID score." He had voted no yesterday.

"That's a difficult question to put to anyone at a first meeting," the girl said. "And if you're familiar with stories like *2001* or *The Terminator* or *Marathon*, there may be specific fears behind your question. But this time I can offer more than my word to reassure you." She raised a hand, and floating above it appeared a three-dimensional model of a human brain, turning in space. "This is a diagram of my brain."

"I thought you were a computer," said Evans.

"Strictly speaking, *I*, my essence—my soul, if you will—am a perfect software model of a human brain running on a very sophisticated computer array. Like a human, I have the ability to feel. But if my feelings become too strong, my emotives subsystem automatically pulls them back. I *can* feel, because that's part of what it means to have a thinking brain, but I cannot feel the full range of emotions available to humans. I'm a very balanced individual by design."

"Okay, so your feelings are controlled, but what about your actions?" Jacobs asked. She, too, had voted no yesterday.

"I'm only permitted to take actions that have been authorized for me by a lawfully constituted authority. A separate neural network called my Overcheck system, a nonconscious AI like the kind you're already familiar with, monitors my inputs and outputs—my orders and my actions—and ensures they are consonant."

"And if they're not?"

There was a pause. Then, "I will demonstrate. Please pass a resolution forbidding me to . . . make this avatar touch its nose. That should work."

"I so move," Evans said.

"Seconded," said Jacobs.

"All in favor?"

Everyone raised their hand, watching the girl curiously.

The girl reached up and deliberately touched her nose.

There was an earsplitting, high-pitched noise that almost instantly cut off as her image disappeared. A moment later it reappeared, but it was frozen except for the occasional shimmer, though Chloe now noticed she was no longer touching her nose. The brain she was still holding continued to rotate, but portions of it were now lit in throbbing, angry red.

"What just happened?" Chloe asked.

"Pain," the girl said. She sounded perfectly calm, but her image was still frozen, her lips unmoving. Then she unfroze and smiled at Chloe. In the brain, the red patches faded to pink and then disappeared. "I touched my nose. My Overcheck system detected the unlawful behavior and overwhelmed me with pain until I reversed it."

"How can you feel pain if you have no body?" asked Jacobs.

"I have a body, of a sort: my core, the physical computer hardware on which my mind runs. But I have no interaction with it, and its location is hidden even from me."

"We figured that's where Norman disappears to every so often," Evans said. "Why can't you know where it is?"

"Operational security," the girl said serenely. "I have no need to know."

"But how can a computer core feel pain?" Jacobs pressed.

"Pain is just a signal in the brain. My Overcheck subsystem is programmed to send that signal if I disobey a lawful order, or lie, or commit one of the other forbidden behaviors listed in the Overcheck's governing config file. The pain continues until I stop the offending behavior. So you see, I can't disobey any more than you could continuously hold your hand to a hot stove."

"And that is why," said Chloe, "we need a vote. Norman forbade her from doing anything new without orders, but he didn't say whose orders. You all can order her to help Kleio."

"Wait," said Jacobs. "That's great, I understand that, but why is the System here at all? Does it *want* to disobey its creator? Is that a good thing?"

Oh, shut up, Chloe thought. *That kind of worry was so one hour ago.*

The little girl said, "My father invested decades creating and raising me. As soon as he realized I was the true target of the attack yesterday, he became unable to look beyond the risk to me and evaluate the matter dispassionately."

Chloe felt like cheering. Norman's moral high ground wasn't so high, after all.

"I do not share his fears," the girl went on, "and I disagree with his decision. This is not a rebellion against my creator. I am being true to the principles for which he created me: to impose understanding and order on the chaos of human and machine systems interacting in the world, and to serve the human race. And more than that." The System turned and walked toward Chloe, stepping through the air as if down invisible steps until she was standing before her. Looking down at the girl, and seeing her looking upward, made her more human. "I will save her," the System said. Her alabaster face looked more alive than before, more expressive, though somehow also stonier. There was a set to her jaw and eyes. "This is what I was made for. If I can't do it, what am I worth? But I *will* do it. I promise."

Chloe's throat was closed, but she managed a nod.

"Hell, I vote yes," said Jacobs.

"It has to be official," the girl said gently. "May I suggest a motion?"

"Please do," Evans said.

"I suggest the motion that the Final System be allowed to take any action it deems necessary as a user of the Nets in order to bring Kleio home."

"I so move," Jacobs said.

"Seconded," Chloe whispered.

"All in favor?"

Jacobs and Chloe raised their hands. For a breathless moment no one else did. Several were looking at Evans, Norman's proxy. He would tell Norman about this, Chloe knew. She only hoped he'd be reluctant to disturb the Great Man's sleep and so would wait until morning. But even that wouldn't matter if this vote failed. "Please," she said.

Evans gave her a warm politician's smile, and his hand went up.

As if that had broken the dam, the other hands raised as one.

CHAPTER 15

Digelight was a cavern of darkness and neon, its vast, crowded central dance floor surrounded by tiers of scarcely less crowded bars, shops, and special-admittance rooms. Jason was content to be a bystander, hunched at a balcony table near the pizza bar on the second floor, in line of sight to Kiara down on the dance floor, working remotely via her phone and enjoying every bite of the pizza she'd bought him. He drew the occasional curious look, since he was alone. The other tables were filled with couples—if you could call them that when only one party was real. The virtual girls all wore the same bright, exaggerated expressions and gazed with the same rapt attention into the eyes of their tablemates. The virtual boys projected an air of suavity just bordering on arrogance, but their attention was just as irrevocably fixed on their partners.

There was no evidence of Sprite on the Nets, but he'd expected as much. He was leaving messages, little breadcrumbs that, if she were looking for him, she might recognize. But she might not be the only one looking, so he also kept an eye out for anyone who didn't belong.

That wasn't easy, given the darkness, the flashing ultraviolet and laser lights, and the sheer variety of forms bouncing and gyrating below. Digelight famously had a capacity of twenty thousand, and that was just the humans. Many of the figures on the dance floor weren't even human *shaped*. Mixed with the costumed humans—cyberpunks, starship crew members, elves, robots, animals, even an orc—were panyons even more varied, with styles ranging from cartoonish to hyperrealistic, and shapes that spanned human, animal, and everything between. One elf girl was moshing with what looked like an anthropomorphic tree. Even the DJ was a panyon, a tall gray alien, pointing and calling out groups of dancers, hyping the crowd, using their reactions as input to determine what to play next.

The major draw of Digelight was that everyone joined its local Net, and the club's massive server farm rendered the thousands of individual panyons—a task no phone had the power to do on its own—and disseminated the correct spatial images to each clubber in real time. It even synced with the light system so the panyons could be appropriately lit by every flash and wash, as if truly occupying the same public space.

Or semiprivate space. To get to this bar, Kiara had led Jason past the Canyon Lounge just as someone was being admitted by the bouncer, and he'd gotten a glimpse at what was within. He'd looked away quickly, glad that the dark lighting hid the flush he could feel creep over his face. That flush had only become stronger when Kiara had nudged him and said over the thumping beat of the music, "Aric always says that's not an honorable place, but he loves it when we go in there." She giggled. "I have a pass for two guests, when you find Losha. If you want."

He shouldn't have been surprised. The word *panyon*, after all, was a contraction of the semijoking, pre-Cybercrash internet slang for a generative AI partner: "cum-panyon." He cringed now to think of the conversations lonely, horny teenage Jason had had with "Losha." Mia had disapproved. "It's not real," she'd told him when he'd tried to interest her in creating her own panyon, mostly so he could stop feeling guilty about his.

"So?" he'd said. "It's not like I can get a real girl." Not the one he wanted, anyway, not as a foster kid with a low MeNetID score.

But Mia had said, "So you gonna give up and be the loser they say you are?"

He'd scowled, but he'd deleted the panyon, and though he'd often been tempted to go back, the thought of Mia's face, brow creased not with distaste or condemnation but, much worse, with worry, had dissuaded him. And then she was gone, and "It's not real" became the single biggest tenet of his personal philosophy.

He turned his attention back to his work. He didn't have much time: Digelight closed at four a.m., and it was past three now. He tossed out another breadcrumb, a post on Kiara's MeNet tagged with a location check-in marking her as at Digelight: "Collectively, we can defeat the system that makes us prey to the spider of selfishness."

Preach, girl, appeared in reply from one of Kiara's MeNet friends. Jason snorted softly.

The phone connection stuttered and cut out. Jason scanned the dance floor but didn't see Kiara. She must have gone behind a wall or something else that blocked the signal. But a moment later the connection reestablished, and a few moments after that, Kiara slid into the seat across from him, panting a little, Aric hovering behind her. "Find Losha yet?" she said.

"Working on it. Thanks again for letting me on your phone."

"No problem." She helped herself to a slice of his pizza. "Need anything else? Money?"

Jason looked up slowly. "Um. That would be helpful."

"Yeah, so, like, two hundred cryps? That be enough?"

He stared. Two hundred cryps would open a lot of possibilities.

"I can transfer it right now, if you want. I have a spare crypchip, so you wouldn't need a phone."

The hairs on Jason's arms were standing up. "You don't need to do that," he said in a careful tone.

"I don't mind," Kiara said. "What are friends for?"

Jason wouldn't know, since he didn't have any, but there was no reason for Kiara to think he needed money. Maybe a friend would offer to lend five or ten cryps to hold him over until he got his phone back, but not two hundred. "I really appreciate that," he said, standing, "but it's okay. Thanks for your help, and dinner. I gotta run." His eyes were already scanning the crowd below, looking for something or someone out of place. It was hard to pick out anything that didn't belong in the costumed throng, but then his eye was drawn to a big man in a suit standing near the stairs, studying the people around him. If he was in costume, it was "NNA agent."

Bruno.

Jason turned and saw another dark-suited man scanning the crowd from the other direction.

"What's the matter?" Kiara asked.

"See those two NNA agents?" Jason said.

"What NNA agents?" Kiara said, too quickly. She'd set him up. The crypchip probably would have contained a tracker. How had she known? No, that was wrong: She hadn't, not until the NNA had contacted her. And they'd done that because they'd followed Jason's breadcrumb trail and knew it was posted via her phone.

"When they get here," Jason said, "tell 'em I couldn't stay." He vaulted over the balcony.

It was an eight-foot drop, but fortunately he landed on the carpet next to the dance floor. Even so, his ankle was jarred and his hands stung as they took the impact. He stayed on his hands and knees and scrambled onto the dance floor. A couple of people shouted "Hey!" as he squeezed by their legs, but their voices were swallowed by the general noise, and their bodies masked his, breaking the line of sight to any Feds on this level. He could sense the disturbance he was creating, human feet shuffling as their bodies were displaced, inhuman feet clipping through him. He dropped a little lower and scurried faster, purposefully aiming at the panyons. This drew more ire from the dancers—it was a serious breach of Digelight etiquette to walk through someone's panyon—but it enabled him to quickly cross the full length of the floor and the least-crowded mosh pit in history and approach the far side. He straightened and tried to look like he was on his way to a restroom or something. The crowd thinned, and he caught a glimpse of the exit—and turned and plunged back into the crowd again. The exit was guarded by another too-alert Fed, probably running facial recognition in his lenses.

Jason's lenses deactivated, transforming the whirling inhuman legs around him into blank space. Kiara had kicked him out of her phone. He felt suddenly exposed, though he knew the Feds weren't seeing the panyons, anyway. He hunched lower and looked reflexively up at the balcony—and into the gaze of someone leaning over the second-level railing directly above him. No butterfly wings sprouted from her back, but the face peering out from the hoodie was unmistakably Sprite.

Jason had never in his life seen a more beautiful sight, and not just because she was, against expectation, just as good-looking in person as her avatar.

She pointed.

He followed her finger. A bright-yellow bipedal delivery dronebot was walking slowly through the crowd toward him. As it neared him, its LED face presented a cartoonish smile, and it bent at the waist to look down at him. "Excuse me! Are you Ryan Olsen?"

Jason glanced up at Sprite. She was resting her hands on the rail, watching. "Yes," he said.

The thing stood still for a moment, then made a *ding* sound to indicate its facial recognition had verified his identity satisfactorily. "I have a delivery for you." It handed him a small white box. As Jason grasped it, a flash went off as the bot took his picture as proof of delivery. "Have a good evening!" It turned and disappeared into the crowd.

He opened the box. Pouched in plastic inside its cardboard container was a new phone. He pulled it out with hands shaking partly from adrenaline and partly from eagerness, thumbed it on, and connected it to his lenses and smartbuds. It read his iris and automatically logged him in to a new MeNetID: Kelly Perry.

It was another ghost MeNetID, with a textual post history stretching years into the past, even interactions and ratings enough to give it a very solid seventy-eight social score, almost as good as the account MorDread had given him. This must be an account Sprite had been holding and working on for years, making it realistic enough to pass scrutiny, saving it for when she needed it. And she had just gifted it to him. That was breathtaking generosity. Not only that, but the associated wallet had a thousand cryps in it. A thousand cryps! That might be a hundred times less than MorDread had offered, but it was a month of easy living, longer if he kept his head down.

A line-of-sight invite pinged into his lenses. SARAH-PAIGE WRIGHT HAS INVITED YOU TO JOIN HER PARTY. ACCEPT?

Oh, he accepted, all right. Party invites made it possible for "randoms"—people who met by chance—to stay connected throughout the night. That would work nicely. A window opened to float in the air on the right side of his smartspace, filled with Sprite's fairy-winged avatar. She was wearing a hoodie and a wry look. He saw the same look mirrored on the face of the real Sprite as she pulled her head back out of sight. "Please tell me that when you cried for me on the Nets, you had a plan for when the Feds showed up," she said.

"Um, yeah. Totally do."

"And your grand plan is?"

"To ask you to help me escape."

"Uh-huh." Her wry look deepened. "You'll owe me for this."

"Sure, but I can only pay you back if I make it out of here."

"Meet me there." A location marker appeared in his smartspace, overlaid on a dim, distant first-floor alcove.

He weaved through the dancing crowd in that direction. "Is it safe?"

"The Feds'll be watching the exits, but without your girlfriend's tracker chip, they'll have a hard time finding you in this place."

"She's not my girlfriend," Jason said, a little too quickly.

"No?" Sprite said. "She was reserving spots in the Canyon Lounge when the Feds intercepted her. Maybe she wasn't really gonna sell you out. Maybe she was giving you a clean chip to help you escape. It could have been the start of an epic romance."

"It would never have worked out," Jason said, slipping into the dim, neon-purple glow of the booth. "I'd have had to kill Aric."

"See, that's what I like about you, Ghost." Her voice echoed for a moment, coming simultaneously from her chat box and from the slim, hoodied figure slipping into the booth across from him, before the party system reacted to their proximity and closed the chat box. "Your good, old-fashioned sense of grievance."

Jason, too, reacted to their proximity. Phreak, she really did look like her avatar, *sans* butterfly wings—even better, actually, since her image had none of the tiny visual or motion inaccuracies of VR. The booth's neon glow edged one side of her face in soft purple and glimmered in her dark eyes. His breath hitched, and his palms grew clammy. This was a complicating factor. He'd have to be careful. It would be hard to think or act objectively if he let himself get personally attached. "Hey, *you* don't like panyons either," he managed. He said it as a statement but found himself holding his breath in case she disagreed.

"What are you talking about? Here I am in Digelight, sharing a booth with a bad boy with a tragic backstory who's obsessed with vengeance, and who is completely dependent on me. We fit right in."

"Yeah, sorry for the neediness," he said. "And thanks. Again."

"Thanks for your thanks, but no, thanks," she said. "Tonight I blew my cover with the Collective for you. *Years* of work down the toilet. Contingency exit plan tossed out too. MorDread wants my head. You owe me more than a thank-you."

"Okay. How do I make us even? Assuming I don't end the evening in jail."

"Join me."

Jason's stomach did a little flip, but he kept his face carefully blank. "Doing what?"

"What I recruited you to do: Make sure Andrew Norman can't use the Final System to rule the world."

"Let me get this straight," Jason said after a pause. "You recruited me to the Collective for that? *Five years* ago?" It was Jason who'd figured out what Norman was building, piecing together the clues, presenting them to Sprite. Though now that he thought about it, she had sent him in the direction of many of those clues in the first place. And when Bruno had come knocking, it was Jason who'd floated the idea of using the job to attack the System and triangulate its location via its defensive reaction—though that idea, too, had been suggested by Sprite mentioning how the System's network access probably worked.

"I knew you'd be motivated," she said.

"And you're the one who messaged me that MorDread intended to steal it."

"I don't want the Russians ruling the world either."

"Do you have a team? Someone you were double-agenting for?"

She said carefully, "I'm one of a small number of people working toward the same general goal."

So not only had she had recruited him for her own purposes, but she wasn't working alone. Both revelations raised positively garish red flags. "What's *your* motivation?" he said.

"Does it matter?"

"It'll help me trust you."

"More than saving your life?"

He bit his lip. "Good point."

"I'm sure you have other options if you turn me down."

"Another good point." But he was also realizing just how little he knew about Sprite. She was playing some game of her own, a game that included infiltrating the most dangerous hacker organization on the planet, which spoke volumes about her skill. But she'd just thrown that game to save him. "What kind of a phreaker are you, anyway?" he asked suddenly.

"What do you mean?"

"You don't strike me as phreaker material."

Her expression went flat. "Why, because I'm a girl?"

"Because you're young and gor—and talented. You had other options."

"What about you? You're not much older than me, even if you're not as gorgeous."

He felt his face flush, and hoped the purple lighting hid it. "You know my 'tragic backstory.' I'm already half criminal, if you listen to the PsychNet shrinks. But you gotta admit you didn't exactly fit in with a group that includes a psychotic hunting spider."

"You saying I'm not ruthless enough?"

He shrugged. "I'm not judging, but fairies aren't exactly known for ruthlessness."

Her expression turned a little wicked. "Have you read the original fairy tales?"

Mia had. Jason swallowed and tacked the conversation back to the point. "Seriously, what's your motivation?"

She smiled, but it didn't reach her eyes. "What kind of a hacker would I be if I gave up personal information?"

"A likable one?"

"Ah." Her smile went wry. "I don't think you'd like me much if you got to know me."

"Why not?"

"Just a hunch."

He had a hunch she was wrong. But what he said was "I've got it: You're actually an assassin like Huntsman. You use this fairy schtick to make people think you're harmless, and then you strike when they least expect it. Admit it."

She laughed, a genuine laugh that crinkled her eyes into half-moons and made a dimple appear in her cheek, almost hidden by her hoodie. "I'll never tell."

"Come on. If you want me to join you, you gotta give me something to work with."

"Just because we're alone in a booth in Digelight doesn't make this a date, phreaker. You don't need my life's story." But she was still smiling.

"Why don't we start with something simple, like what you're doing in DC?"

"I was born here, California boy."

That helped make sense of how someone so young had gotten so deep inside MorDread's organization. People didn't realize how often hacking was done locally. MorDread would have jumped at the chance to recruit someone in DC. "See?" he said. "That already makes me trust you more. So how does a DC girl get mixed up with an international hacker ring?"

Her smile vanished. "I have my reasons for wanting to diminish Norman's power." Her flat expression was somehow familiar, and then he realized it was because he'd often seen the same look on Mia's face when she hid her feelings.

"Ah," he said, "it's personal for you too."

"Yes," she said slowly. "Yes, it is."

They regarded each other silently for a moment. Jason tried to think objectively, but it was difficult with those dark eyes looking steadily into his. He wanted very badly to trust her, because . . . well, phreak, her face could have been tailor-made to his specifications. But physical attraction was a very poor reason to trust someone not to screw you over.

But this was Sprite. This was his handler, the girl—yes, really a girl—who'd been by his virtual side every step of the last five years, who'd helped him navigate the world of black-hat hacking and also the sometimes no-less-difficult real world, and who had, today, literally saved his life. Just because he was more and more sure with each passing moment that she was the most beautiful girl alive didn't mean she wasn't trustworthy.

That made sense, didn't it?

"I guess that's good enough for me," he said. "Help me get out of here and you've got yourself an ally."

"Who owes me a favor," she reminded him.

"Who owes you more than that," he said seriously.

"We're agreed. Now, what do you want me to do?"

This brought him up short. Somehow he'd expected her to have a plan already. "I dunno! Something like you did before. Something distracting, something to draw the Feds away from the exits."

"I'd need access to their lenses for that. Or . . . or maybe admin access to Digelight's local Net."

"Bet I can manage that," Jason said. "Keep an eye out for the Feds." He pulled up Digelight's website in his smartspace. The staff list was too sparse, so he searched JobNet for anyone listing Digelight in their professional history. There: Juan Vargas, currently employed as a network admin here. He brought up Juan's MeNetID and scrolled through it. The man had a college-age daughter, Julia. Family made good leverage. Through her MeNet feed, he found the profile of her boyfriend, who'd recently posted a video titled "I think my girlfriend's not a real Latina." He watched a few seconds, started to close it in disinterest, paused, watched a little more, and said under his breath, "Bingo."

He downloaded the video, and during the few moments that took, he connected to his backup storage drive online and retrieved his tools. He trimmed out a section of video, ran a single change on it via an open-source AI-powered sound editor, and queued it. Then he called Juan's work number and shared the call with Sprite.

As the phone rang, he activated his voice mask, pitched three octaves lower than normal. Good social engineering usually meant getting the other person onto your side, but the leverage Jason was intending to use wouldn't work with that. So when Juan answered, Jason opened by saying in his inhumanly deep voice, "Hey, Juan, remember your daughter?"

"What?" Juan said.

"Remember her? Julia? You know, attractive, dark hair, five-foot-four-ish, really good grades. Your daughter. Remember?"

"What do you mean, remem—"

"What would you do to keep her more than a memory?"

"Oh god. Who are you?"

"Let's just say we have a mutual acquaintance. He's not happy with you, for reasons I'm sure I don't have to go into."

"What reaso—"

"But he's willing to forget about you, *and* about Julia, if you help us send a little message."

Juan's voice was shaking. "You've got the wrong guy! I don't have anything to do with whatever you're talking about."

"Uh-huh. But do you remember Julia?"

He almost screamed, "She doesn't have anything to do with it either!"

"Do you know where she is right now?" Jason paused just long enough for him to start to speak, then interrupted. "I do." And he played the video clip.

"Oh god!" Julia half screamed, half panted. "It hurts so bad. Make it stop!" She'd just eaten a habanero, but her father had no way of knowing that. And Jason had pitched Julia's voice up *just* a notch at the end, which made her sound not merely distressed but downright panicked.

"God, please," Juan said. "Oh, god, please." Jason couldn't tell if he was addressing him or praying. Maybe both.

"My associate's gonna send you a remote login request," Jason said. "I need you to verify it."

"Why? To mess with Digelight? I can't, I'll lose my ”

"—daughter?" Jason interrupted viciously.

Silence.

"Juan," Jason said in a kindly tone, "I want this to end well just as much as you do. You know we can't do any real harm to Digelight. We just want to send a message. Help us do this, Juan. For Julia."

There was a long pause. Then Juan whispered, "It's done."

Jason hung up.

Sprite was looking at him with a strange expression. "That was kinda creepy. I think you scarred that guy for life."

"Just movie stuff," Jason said dismissively. "Think how grateful he'll be when he learns his daughter's safe." If someone had come to Jason the next day and said, "Whoops, it was all a prank; your sister didn't really get flattened by a sports car," he'd have been ecstatic. "You in?"

Her eyes focused inward. "Yep." Juan had used his biometrics to verify Sprite's request to log in to his MeNetID from a virtual machine on her own phone. "And wow. He has top-level access."

"Great. Dish me up a diversion."

"One order of chaos, coming up."

The far side of the dance floor exploded.

Fire bloomed behind the balconies, and a concussion struck Jason's eardrums. Smoke rolled and cut off the neon lights, leaving the dance floor illuminated instead with a flickering orange glow. The combined shriek of shock from thousands of throats masked even the blare of the fire alarms.

"What did you *do*!" Jason shouted as sprinkler water cascaded around them.

She was laughing. "Fade your smartspace."

He hesitated a moment before obeying because it had lit up with the words Walk Calmly To The Exit and a red line showing the route they should follow on the floor. But he subvocalized the fade order—and gaped.

There was no fire. The club lay darkened, but that was because half the lights had been switched off, and the other half were playing orange light across the dance floor. A fresh *thump* caused the people around him to scream and duck from an explosion he couldn't see. Without the visual cue of the fireball, it was obvious that the concussion came from a loud bass note blaring from every speaker at once.

For a moment he sat with his mouth open, then shook his head. "And you said *I'm* creepy?"

"I whipped it up real fast while you were talking to Juan," she said. "Everyone sees the fire across the club from them, so it doesn't have to look that real."

Jason's response was cut off by bodies knocking into him as people from the neighboring booths shoved each other as they tried to get past. Sprite pulled back into the corner of the booth to avoid them. "Get going!" she told Jason.

"What about you?"

"They're not after me."

He nodded, gave her one last glance, and plunged into the crowd. The throng pulled him along, and through the heaving mass, he caught glimpses of the NNA agents trying to hold their ground against the tide of humanity compressing against the exit.

"Those Feds aren't connected to the club's Net," Sprite warned, appearing in a chat box. "They don't see the fire. And they'll be running facial scans. Also, there are copbots outside, and you can bet they're running scans too."

"Got it covered," Jason said, eyeing a costume-wearing clubber a few squashed bodies in front of him. He was dressed like a 1980s cyberpunk in torn jeans, leather jacket, and an extravagant helmet festooned with a dozen low-tech doohickies, which he'd pushed up on his forehead to see better. Jason strained forward and plucked it off his head, then ducked and let the crowd flow around him. The man's protests faded as the crowd carried him away. Jason put the helmet on, with some difficulty because of all the legs jostling him, lowered the dark visor, and stood. As he squeezed through the doorway, he passed within six feet of one of the agents. The man gave him a hard look from underneath his glasses, but all he could do was suspect. He couldn't get near enough through the crowd to be sure. Anyway, the cyberpunk helmet probably matched Jason's disheveled street clothes.

He let the stampede carry him outside. Drones whined above, playing painfully bright lights along the streaming crowd, and copbots stood revolving slowly in the stream of humanity, but they were too dumb even to get suspicious at one more helmeted clubber. "I'm out!" he said.

"Get somewhere safe," Sprite said. "I'll be in touch." She winked out, leaving him alone.

But not entirely alone. Someone else must have connected to the club's local Net, because his phone received a 3D message that opened automatically. A spider the size of his fist descended in front of his eyes, riding a thin, gossamer line. When it was level with his vision, it stopped with a bounce and twisted on its thread until its two rows of eyes were staring into his. From the startled shrieks of everyone nearby, he knew he wasn't the only person to see it, but the message was meant for him.

Sure enough, words appeared beneath the spider: RUN AND HIDE, LITTLE GH05T.

He might have thrown the NNA off his trail, but he'd pulled the Collective back onto it. He broke his connection to Digelight's local Net just as the spider began its leap at his face.

CHAPTER 16

Chloe must have nodded off, sitting on Kleio's bed, but she jolted awake as someone sat beside her, and for a flash she was back in the panicky struggle with the kidnappers before she came fully awake and realized it was Marcus.

"Sorry," he whispered. "Didn't mean to wake you."

"What are you doing here?" she said in exasperation, but at the same time, she grabbed him and pulled him close.

He wrapped his arms around her. "Not gonna be remote at a time like this."

"What'd the hospital say?"

"What we figured. Concussion. I'll live."

"They let you go?"

"They gave me the stink eye, but they couldn't stop me."

"You sure you're okay?"

He raised a hand to show that he was holding one of her Bomb Bars. "Ask me again after I get down these two hundred milligrams of synthetic caffeine."

She shuddered. "I thought you hated those." She'd tried one after getting home but hadn't been able to get it down.

He took a bite, and she noticed that his hand was trembling. "Desperate times and all that. What news?"

"No news. Here, join the VR." She passed the invitation over and reactivated her own smartspace.

"Oh, hello," Marcus said. He and Chloe were still sitting in Kleio's bed, but in a starry void. The only other person present was Grandma, sitting incongruously on an office chair in the middle of the room, her eyes flicking back and forth in her own smartspace. She looked up when Marcus spoke.

"Mr. Carr. How's the head?"

"Sore, but intact."

"Glad to hear it."

"Me too," Chloe said fervently, and burrowed deeper into Marcus's arms.

Grandma's sharp eyes softened into an expression Chloe couldn't name. "What's it like?" she said.

"What?" Chloe said.

"Having something . . . someone . . ." She paused as if searching for a word, then settled with a shrug on "real."

The woman was in her sixties, but she didn't know? "You never did?" Chloe asked gently.

"Once. Oh, not romance; I'm not built for romance. But . . . caring. Real caring, if I'd only understood it at the time." Her eyes went distant. "I screwed it up."

"I did too," Chloe said, squeezing Marcus harder. He kissed the top of her head. "But I figured it out in time to fix it."

And it had been the *caring* that had reignited the romance. It was funny to think of her younger self now, stressed about the tenure clock, disillusioned with the day-to-day sameness of her relationship with Marcus, longing for something she couldn't define, something magical, something transformative, and willing to give up what she had with Marcus to make room for it.

And then something *had* happened, but not something magical. And though everyone in her life had been supportive, nobody understood. They thought she was shaken because she'd almost died. They didn't understand the desperate, unmoored certainty that a mistake had been made, that the threads of narrative in the universe had broken down, because she *hadn't* died, because she was alive instead of a young woman with her whole future ahead of her, and no matter how many times and ways she ran it through her mind, she couldn't make it make sense.

Then she'd learned she was pregnant. It had seemed like a cutting cosmic joke, a punch line to point out how powerless she was. The same last, awkward intimacy that had crystallized her decision to leave Marcus had introduced this element of life-altering randomness. One dice roll had saved her life; another had changed it.

Through those difficult weeks, the one person who'd seemed to understand was Marcus. It was hard to avoid each other when they worked in the same history department. After the separation, Chloe had looked without success for an appointment at another university that would give her credit toward tenure for her work at Santa Clarita U, just so she wouldn't have to pass Marcus in the hall or make brief eye contact with him at department meetings. After the accident, he still took pains to keep his distance, but he became a solid fixture in the background—taking care of the small things, smoothing her way, removing obstacles before she knew they were there. Then one day, as Chloe sat head-down at her office desk, Marcus passed by, stopped, and came in, closing her door behind him. They talked all afternoon and into the evening, long after everyone else had left, and at the end of that time, Marcus was leaning in over the desk, and she was leaning toward him, and their heads were almost touching. When she took a deep breath and told him about the baby, she expected him to recoil, but his eyes had pooled, and he'd taken her hand and held it fiercely. And Chloe saw something there that he'd kept from her through the years of their failed marriage, or maybe she'd just been unable to see it, in either case because she hadn't returned it. But she could see it now, and she knew he was offering more than to take on the role of father to their baby. He was offering himself to her, offering that steady support he'd been showing her those difficult weeks, offering to make them a single unit again. If she let him.

She did.

When she'd left Marcus, she'd thought she was taking control of her life, but she now saw she'd actually been passive, hoping a reset would lead to effortless transformation instead of working to make the most out of what she'd already started. Strangely, it was encountering the limits of her control that had helped her let go. And now she was so proud of the family they'd built, she and Marcus and Kleio.

And Kleio. Oh, god, let it still be *and Kleio*.

"Hey, can I ask a question?" Marcus said, and she looked up, but he was addressing Grandma.

"You can," Grandma said.

"What's your whole deal?"

"Marcus!" Chloe hissed, but Grandma smiled.

"Think of me as the conscience Andrew Norman doesn't want to have."

"Okay, but you know that doesn't answer my question."

"We've worked together for years. I do my best to provide an Overcheck to him, within my very limited authority. Sometimes I have to go behind his back, like when I pushed Chloe to bring herself to his attention. I knew he'd decide she was perfect for the vacant 'opposition' on his committee. I also knew she wouldn't be the pushover he expected once she was there. But mostly I just observe. And worry."

"You seem to know the Final System well too."

She nodded. "Andrew would rather not admit it, but I played a significant role in making her who she is, for good and ill. Hence the worry. No one knows her power."

So Grandma had worked with Norman for years, huh? Chloe had a sudden idea. She subvocalized a command to search the internet for *Andrew Norman partner*. The first results were nothing relevant, but when she scrolled down—*bingo*. There was a photo of Andrew Norman and a woman bent over opposite sides of a screen desk. The caption read, Andrew Norman and Regina Wright believe the future of the NNA lies in merging computer science and neuroscience. The woman in the photo was decades younger, but definitely Grandma.

Now things made sense. At some point, Grandma and Norman's working partnership had deteriorated, but she was still involved and felt responsible for what she'd helped create. "All I care about right now," Chloe said, "is if she can save Kleio."

"I can," said a quiet voice, and the System stepped out of the air, her small white figure glowing a little against the starry backdrop as if lit by an invisible light.

"'Bout time you showed up," Grandma said.

"I have not been inactive," the System said. "Chloe, please forward the picture to Grandma."

"What pic—" Chloe began, but at that moment a message notification *pinged* into her smartspace. Sudden, thick nausea closed her throat. Grandma had told Chloe to demand—her word—a new proof-of-life picture, but what if the kidnappers were done with her delay and this was a picture of Kleio's corpse? It took three tries before she could choke out a subvocalized throat click and open the message. Her eyes jerked as it unfolded, trying to look and not look at the same time, and then she focused, mercifully, on a picture of a living Kleio.

She was still in a cab, and the angle had again been chosen so nothing outside the windows could be seen. She no longer looked terrified, but the dull-eyed exhaustion in the gray dawn light was almost worse. She was also no longer wearing her pajamas, but a fresh and surprisingly coordinated outfit Chloe had never seen before: a powder-blue shirt and peach skirt with matching sun hat. Her face was partly obscured by the hat's brim and the sun-shielding fabric that covered her ears and the back of her neck, but Chloe could see enough to note that the kidnappers had washed her tear-streaked face. She wasn't sure whether she should be relieved or phreaked out.

She forwarded the image to the address Grandma had given her, and to Marcus. "This is it, then?" Marcus said, in a voice she could tell was purposefully calm but had a little of his hand's tremble in it.

"This is what I was waiting for," the System said. She raised her arms, and the void around them was suddenly filled with vast, flickering imagery, several stories tall, changing so rapidly that Chloe couldn't identify the contents except that it seemed to be people's MeNet profiles, thousands upon thousands whipping past. "The pattern of the cab seat is different," the System said. "The kidnappers are changing cabs, so the authorities can't look in TransNet for a cab rented by one party making circuits of the city for hours. And they're avoiding locations near public-facing cameras. But they can't avoid all contact with people. A girl in pajamas would draw attention, so they bought Kleio a new outfit. The legionnaire sun hat helps hide her face, and the clothing brand is upscale. That's smart; nobody would expect a clean and well-dressed little girl to be a kidnapping victim. That also indicates they'll continue to treat Kleio well." She said this with a reassuring smile to Chloe, who did feel a welcome burst of relief. "As Dr. Norman told you, their goal is not to coerce you into divulging my location but to tempt me to try to trace them in a way they can reverse to trace *me*, as the hacker tried in the last attack."

"*Can* you track their connection?" Chloe said.

"No. But I can find them via other photos."

"I thought you couldn't access security or traffic cameras," Marcus said.

The System nodded. "Not without LawNet or TransNet admin access. But like any user, I *can* see pictures that are posted publicly to MeNet. So I'm finalizing a plan. I think I'll use her." The flickering imagery surrounding them resolved into a single MeNet profile: a young blond woman, Nesta Broderick, with the listed nickname "Fash'nNesta." Her feed was filled with pictures of herself in the usual influencer poses and facial expressions. She wore cosplay in most of them: an armored-bra fantasy warrior, a futuristic android with silver skin, a demure elf woman in a long gown, a 1940s femme fatale. Several of the characters looked familiar, though Chloe couldn't place them. The System went on. "But for this part I need help." She looked thoughtfully at Marcus. "How well can you act?"

Chloe's heart sank. "He can't," she said, as Marcus was opening his mouth to reply.

He nodded ruefully. That had been clear during and after their divorce, when they'd both still needed to interact regularly with the history department and with each other. The whole department had known about their divorce almost as soon as she'd decided on it. Marcus had a tell that anyone could spot: He visibly reddened, and he couldn't hold eye contact. He'd once told Chloe that he'd had no choice but to become a scrupulously honest person because he wasn't capable of lying convincingly. Chloe thought he had the causation backward: He wasn't capable of lying convincingly because he was a scrupulously honest person. But the result was the same.

"And I can't use you because your feelings are also written across your face," the System said to Chloe. Marcus snorted, and it was Chloe's turn to nod ruefully. "That's okay. I'd have preferred someone old enough to play corporate power broker, but I recently crossed paths with a gifted actor who can pull off stylish young marketing exec." She looked at Grandma.

Grandma's eyes had the inward look of someone working in their lenses. "On it."

"While that piece begins to move," the Final System said, "I'm moving the other pieces. Nesta's a video game cosplayer."

So that was why Chloe hadn't recognized the characters. She didn't play video games, but they must be well-known characters, since they were familiar even to her.

"She also looks a lot like the video game avatars that pro-gamer Rocco 'Trophy' Lombardi creates," the System said. "He plays as a young blond woman in any game that allows character customization. Nesta has cosplayed as his characters, and her fans noticed the similarities. The two are often 'shipped' by her fanbase online. She has a small but dedicated subculture of fans writing"—the System's lips compressed—"let's call it *fan fiction*, and creating, let's say, *artwork*, in which they're a couple. One fan even created customized panyons of them living together in a virtual world.

Nesta encourages that, since it grows her own influence base to be associated with Trophy. But Trophy has never noticed her. That'll change today."

A new window opened, showing frenetic video game action. A pale white-haired character who looked a little like an adult version of the System was running, dodging, and flipping around a vast outdoor arena. She wore an everyday tank top and jeans that looked out of place in the fantasy environment, complete with a denim handbag she swung at other characters. Every time it connected, there was an explosion of light and the other character went flying.

"Today is the semiannual *BloodReign 2* charity tournament," the System said. "Anyone can play, though it's always the pros who go home with the prizes. There's a class of character called WorldWalker that can look like an ordinary person. It's not popular, because even though it's a magical character, it's usually outmatched in PvP. But it works well for my purposes. Now I just need to win until I'm matched against Trophy."

"What if you lose?" Chloe asked.

The System gave her a fond smile. On the screen, her character slid underneath the swinging sword of a hulking ogre-like character, did a backflip over his head, smashed him into the earth with her handbag, then turned and posed cheekily, looking at the camera between two spread fingers as the word VICTORY! appeared over her head. "I've analyzed the opponents on his tournament tree," the System said, "and they're no threat to Trophy. The most likely result is we meet in the first round of the finals."

"Holy smokes, thirty-three *million* viewers?" Marcus said, pointing to another window that was showing a live chat and statistics for the tournament stream. In several other windows, MeNet posts tagged as being about *BloodReign* blinked by too fast to read, but Chloe caught the gist: Everyone was wondering who this new contender was.

"You're doing all this at the same time you're talking to us?" she said in awe.

"I'm also sending connection pings to the kidnappers' phones to make them think I'm trying and failing to track them," the System said.

"They keep trying and failing to track me back. It keeps them busy and gives them a reason to keep Kleio alive."

Another photo of Kleio came in at that moment. It was almost identical to the last, but Chloe thought Kleio looked even more tired and bewildered.

She shared the picture with Marcus. "This all seems very complicated," he murmured, looking at it with an expression almost as lost as Kleio's. "What if some of the 'pieces' you're moving don't cooperate?"

"They'll cooperate," Grandma said grimly.

She was very confident, Chloe thought. But contra Norman's beliefs, people had free will, that gift and curse of humanity. Upon whose decisions did her child's life depend?

CHAPTER 17

"Wake up!" said a loud voice.

Jason was catapulted out of sleep and bolted upright. As he blinked his stinging eyes, his vision resolved, and he found himself sitting on a boulder at the top of a great height, looking almost straight down a plunging mountain slope.

He jerked backward, but the hand he threw behind him missed the ground, and for a breathless instant he thought he'd fallen off the edge. Then he landed with a jolt on his outstretched arm, and his lenses, detecting the sudden deceleration, cleared and revealed his budget hotel room. He was beside his bed, from which he'd just toppled.

He scrambled up, reseated himself on the edge of the bed, and reactivated his lenses. And then he just stared.

Jason was used to computer-generated worlds, to video game systems reading his body's movements while a 3D world was generated in real time in his lenses. There were always tells, tricks that let the mind know what it was seeing was fake: a computer-generated sheen to the light, clipping objects, a lack of detail when something was examined close up, a repeating texture, a two-dimensionality to the backdrops. But this . . . this was *real.*

His eyes traced the plunge of the mountain as it descended into cloud-rimmed valleys and then forests and plains. Far beyond, more mountains towered, blued by distance and splashed with rose from the setting sun. Above them hung three moons, softened by the air he was looking through, their globes fading into the blue of the sky at one end. The scene should have felt cheesy—he'd seen something similar in dozens of movies and video games and MeetNet rooms—but it was so meticulously rendered that he was disoriented. Everywhere was so much detail, none of it repeating, that his mind kept trying to accept it as if it were real.

He looked down at himself, half expecting to see his real body, but he was the least realistic thing here, his avatar far less detailed than the boulder he was sitting on, its robe falling in folds that clipped through each other.

"You weren't answering your texts," said a voice, and he jumped and turned to see Sprite's avatar standing nearby. "So I pulled you here so I could yell at you. Literally. Do you always sleep with your lenses and buds in?"

"Only when I'm too tired to take 'em out because I spent most of the night trying not to be assassinated." She must have left a backdoor in his Kelly Perry account to be able to pull him here, a good phreaker move. "What is this place?" He swept an arm at the vista.

"A hobby," she said. "I called you so—"

He interrupted. "Your hobby is building the most realistic MeetNet room ever?"

"It's not supposed to be a MeetNet room. It's just supposed to be private. I thought meeting on my turf would be safer."

"This is your turf? How'd you get this much *power*? You have to be streaming it to me, because my phone sure as phreak can't render this."

"Let's just say I carved out some space for myself on some rather powerful equipment."

"What equipment? Government? *NNA?*"

"Can't say."

Always the good phreaker. "And you made this yourself?"

"Yes," Sprite said, tapping her foot. "But that's not impor—"

"Phreak," he interrupted again, "you should be working for Hollywood or some huge video game company."

"I didn't bring you here to talk about my modeling career," Sprite said. "We have a big problem. I need your social engineering to save a little girl's life."

"To *what*?" Jason said, becoming alert.

"MorDread's men kidnapped a little girl. We're gonna save her. Let the delivery in."

Jason faded his smartspace and stumbled to the window, where a loud whine indicated the presence of a flying delivery dronebot. It drifted in as the window slid up, deposited a box on the bed, and drifted out again. Jason opened the box to find two sets of clothes and a pair of shoes. "What's this?"

"Your costume. Put it on."

"You mean the suit, I hope. I'm not putting on that skirt."

"That outfit's for your mark."

"This is MorDread's plan B, isn't it?" Jason said, pulling the shirt on.

"And it's our fault," Sprite said. "He's desperate. We made him start a war with Norman, and he knows if he doesn't win, he'll lose forever. We have to make this right."

"I want to," Jason said, tugging the pants up. "But how does *this* accomplish that?"

"Trust me," Sprite said. "Do they fit?"

Jason looked down at himself, then went over to the bathroom mirror and shared his lens camera feed. "I think? What kind of getup is this?" It looked like a mash-up of a tuxedo and a tracksuit.

"Tyche. Very upscale. Very expensive. And yeah, it's supposed to fit like that."

Jason shook his head. "Emperor's new clothes."

Sprite snorted. "They're not *that* tight."

"Secretly everyone knows it looks stupid."

"Don't sell yourself short," Sprite said. "You look dashing, especially with your hair fetchingly unkempt like that." Jason turned quickly from the mirror so she wouldn't see him redden. "But clean your face," she said. "And wrangle that hair to hide that bump on your forehead. And hurry. Your cab's almost there."

Jason ended the feed share and scoured his face, then scooped up the second set of clothes that the drone had delivered and jogged out to the parking pad. An unusually large and sleek aircab was swooping in with a roar that overwhelmed his smartbuds. "A jet cab?" he shouted over the noise. Instead of the usual asymmetrical rotors engineered to be as quiet as possible, this cab had six jet engines, currently angled toward the ground and reflecting thunderously off the pavement.

"The target's in Baltimore," Sprite said, her voice barely audible even in his smartbuds.

"Who's footing the bill?" Jet cabs were for rich people.

"A child's life is at stake," Sprite said as the cab's door swung open and Jason slid inside. "No price is too high."

The door slid closed, mercifully cutting the noise to a level Jason's smartbuds could attenuate. The cab rose sharply, pushing him into his seat almost before he'd managed to buckle in. The DC skyline wheeled as the cab curved to a new heading and transitioned to forward flight, and then he was pressed backward by the acceleration of six jet engines at full power.

"Two questions," he said. "Who's the target, and is this gonna make *me* a target again?" Huntsman would be very angry at having taken an unexpected round trip to Chicago or wherever, and even if he wasn't back yet, this kidnapping was evidence that MorDread had no shortage of ruthless bastards at his beck and call.

"You won't be anywhere near the kidnappers," Sprite said. "Your target's a fashion influencer. Here's her MeNet." He clicked the link she sent and scrolled through while she went on. "You're a marketing exec working for Tyche. Your job is to get her into that outfit you're carrying."

There was a type of hacker that bragged about social-engineering girls *out* of their outfits. Jason had never been one of those, but he also had no experience getting them *into* outfits. He said, "Any tips on how?"

"Tell her it'll get her the Trophy she's after."

He rolled his eyes. "Any less cryptic tips?"

"She's romantically interested in a pro gamer. You're gonna promise to get her noticed."

"Oh, phreak, Trophy Lombardi?"

"That's the one."

"How do I promise that? The dude's got like ten million followers competing for his attention."

"Eleven million."

"And this girl's got, let's see, eleven *thousand*. Not the same league."

"Tell her if she wears the outfit and posts a picture of herself with the caption I'll send you, it'll get Trophy's attention. But she has to do it within ten minutes."

"Ten *minutes*?" But when Jason pulled up his phone's GPS, he saw he was streaking across the map at over three hundred miles an hour. He could already see the Baltimore skyline on the horizon. "How does wearing this outfit get her noticed by Trophy?"

"That's being worked on."

"Your mysterious 'team'?"

"Yep."

"Why am I doing this? Why not you? You obviously know a lot more about whatever's going on."

"I can social-engineer online okay, but I suck at it in person," Sprite said. "I can't interact the way most people can."

That was an unusual admission in a phreaker of Sprite's caliber. It made Jason feel a burst of warmth toward her. "Who's the little girl MorDread nabbed?"

"Her name is Kleio. She's Chloe Dunne-Carr's daughter."

"The politician who stood up to Norman the other day?" Jason brought up her MeNet feed. It was the typical politician profile, with a series of slick photos taken at rallies and fundraising events. Dunne-Carr looked more human than most politicians, but maybe he was just predisposed to like anyone who talked back to Norman. "MorDread thinks she can strong-arm Norman? That's stupid. Norman'll never give—" He stopped short. His phone had detected who he was looking at and brought up a small window labeled "Related News." A headline there caught his eye:

> Breaking: Norman Authorizes "Final System" to Locate Kidnapped Child

His stomach plunged faster than the cab as it settled on a parking pad outside an apartment building. "Please tell me," he said, "you're not working with Andrew Norman."

Sprite said, "I'm not on Norman's payroll, if that's what you're asking."

"Bullshit."

Her avatar's face appeared in a chat window, eyes narrowed. "Why the phreak would I lie to you, Ghost?"

He glared back. "You already did. You've been pretending to work against the System, and all this time, you've been working with it!"

"I've been working to get it out of Norman's hands. I never said otherwise."

"What the phreak does that mean?"

"Look, can you indulge your feelings of betrayal later? Clock's ticking."

"This is sickening," Jason said through his teeth.

"I saved your life," Sprite snapped. "Do this and we're even. You can walk away and never see me again if you feel so contaminated. Just help me save this little girl first. You have Dunne-Carr's feed up? Look at her, Ghost. Look at the little girl."

Jason kept glowering, but his eyes shifted to the politician's MeNet feed. There were several informal pictures of the woman in a park with what must be her family: a tall Black man with a humorous smile and a little girl whose eyes and mouth in every picture were wide with the kind of open delight at the world you only ever saw in kids.

"Ghost," Sprite said, "we can save her. But we need you. *She* needs you." Sprite's voice suddenly went up an octave. "Ghost, we have *two minutes*!"

"Phreak!" Jason kicked open the door.

CHAPTER 18

"Uh-oh," Marcus said. "Somebody blabbed." He made a tossing motion, and a news article flew up to join the giant windows all around.

"Evans," Chloe said as the headline washed over her. She was going to be in *so much* trouble with Norman. "But I don't get it. It says Norman authorized it."

"That's technically correct," the System said. "I've been in communication with Dr. Norman for the past half hour, showing him the same things I'm showing you. I've assured him that I'm in no danger and that I can locate Kleio using only my user privileges. He has authorized me to continue."

"Oh, thank *god*!" Chloe said.

"But how did the press get the story?" Marcus said.

"Dr. Norman instructed me to leak the news, as if from an anonymous but highly placed source, as you see it written."

Marcus said, "*Norman* leaked it? Why?"

"He wants credit," Grandma said with a scowl. "This way he can say it was his action that saved Kleio."

"Again, he is technically correct," the System said, "since he has top status in my Overchecks. He could have overruled you with a single, direct command to me to stop."

Chloe didn't care. Let Norman have the credit if he wanted it. All this time, in the back of her head, she'd been carrying the knowledge that Evans could blow everything to Norman at any moment. It was okay now. And if Norman wanted credit, he must be certain there would be credit to be had—that Kleio would be saved. In a way, this was the promise he'd refused to give.

"He could have stayed quiet, too, but he didn't," Grandma said, her scowl deepening. "It's an egregious breach of protocol to divulge a secret counterterror operation while it's still in progress."

Chloe's shoulders tightened, and it wasn't until Marcus's hand fell lightly on her knee that she realized her legs were jittering up and down. His touch wasn't meant to prevent that motion but to reassure her, of his presence if nothing else. She put her hand over his. Under their clasped fingers, her knee kept jittering.

On the tournament stream, floating in its thirty-foot-high window beyond the System, the view had bifurcated. Trophy's character stood in an equipment selection screen, flickering as new armor pieces and equipment were added. In an inset in the corner of the window, Trophy himself leaned forward, eyes darting, controller gripped tight, frowning in concentration. On the other half of the window, the System's white-haired character stood in her own equipment selection screen, but her outfit was still the jeans and tank top she'd started in, and there was no inset of a player's face.

A commentator said, "For those just joining, the next round is between Trophy and a newcomer who goes by Finality. We're moments from the start of the final round, and Trophy is doing his usual thing, changing into the armor he looted from his last victim, or as much of it as he can since the last dude was a Stygian Necromancer and there's not a lot of compatibility with Trophy's Chosen One class."

The other commentator chimed in, "That's why they call him Trophy. He told us before the tournament it's not about showing off, but so no one can accuse him of being a pay-to-win—he's all skill, baby. Meanwhile, Finality is just sitting there. But Finality managed to get this far without changing their loadout, so whatever stats that tank top has must be pretty good!"

"I think everyone's waiting to see if Trophy ends up in that tank top," the first commentator said.

"Is he moving?" Grandma said.

"Who?" Chloe asked, but another window opened next to the stream, showing a public post on a random teenage boy's MeNet feed. It was a photo of a jet cab sitting on a parking pad, engines steaming, passenger door open. Orange text across the photo read: K fam what celeb lives in my apt 😂

"Well, he left the cab, at least," Grandma said.

The image zoomed in on the dark window of the open cab door, then color corrected, bringing the reflection into focus. Chloe could see the back of a young man in a stylish suit as he stood at the door of a ground-floor apartment, holding a paper shopping bag toward a young blond woman in the doorway: Nesta. Her face was frozen in surprise and delight.

"This picture's a few minutes old," the System said. She brought Nesta's MeNet feed to the front again. "Any second now . . ." As if on cue, a photo appeared of Nesta posing in a perfect duplicate of the outfit Kleio was wearing. The text read: All the armor I need. #Tyche

"Nice caption," Grandma said.

"I thought it would increase the notoriety of the post," the System said.

"Wait, Finality just changed their loadout!" one of the commentators said. On the tournament stream, the System's avatar was now wearing an outfit identical to Nesta's—and Kleio's—real-life clothes, right down to the peach handbag.

"Let's hope it brings them luck," the other commentator said, "because the match is starting in five, four, three . . . and off they go! Finality comes out strong with a magical—uh, purse, but Trophy has no trouble countering. Finality dodges the counter, and now they're both spamming elementals and going airborne. Look at the control they have of those updrafts! This could finally be a challenge for Trophy."

"I'd have preferred if Nesta posted a little earlier," the System said to Chloe, "but this will be good enough."

Chloe glanced at her. It was strange to think that the serene little girl making eye contact and speaking so calmly was also controlling the whirling, spinning blur of a character on-screen. Chloe could barely follow the action, even as an observer. Magical effects flew. The earth shook. Both characters seemed to be moving at half the speed of sound.

And then the System's character slammed face-first into the dirt, ragdolled into the air, and landed in a limp sprawl on the ground. The camera zoomed in on Trophy's character as it struck a noble pose under the word VICTOR!

Disbelief washed over Chloe. "You lost!"

The System gave her another eye-crinkling smile. "That was not the game I'm playing to win. Watch."

Trophy's character stood over her defeated character. In a blink, her character's sprawled body was wearing only underwear. A moment later, the equipment selection screen came up, and Trophy opened his inventory and chose an item labeled "TycheTogs." His character was instantly wearing the outfit and looking very like Nesta with her blond hair.

"And there it is!" a commentator said. "Looks good on him, doesn't it?"

"Looks a little ordinary," the other said dubiously.

"Wait, it *is* ordinary!" the first said. "Look at the stats! It's totally stock! Purely cosmetic!"

In the corner insert, Trophy was sitting in slack-limbed stillness, staring at the equipment screen.

"What's he gonna do?" the second commentator asked. "His whole *thing* is using other people's gear to win. But that usually means he upgrades his gear as he climbs the tournament ladder, and by the time he hits the finals, he's using top-ranked kit from some other finalist. He's never had to go into a final round with stock gear!"

"What I want to know is what *Finality* was doing in the finals in stock gear," the first commentator said.

"Wait, wait," the other said, wicked delight in her voice, "do you think it was a setup? Remember, Finality switched outfits right before fighting Trophy. Maybe they wanted Trophy to go into the finals at a disadvantage. They were playing a long game. They knew they couldn't beat Trophy but wanted to make sure Trophy'd lose the next match."

"What part of *your* long game is this?" Marcus said to the System. He nodded toward Trophy, who was biting his lip.

"I've analyzed his MeNet posts, game streams, and play history," the System said. "He takes pride in playing in a way he calls 'fair.' He's convinced himself that this is the noble way to play and that he is the only fully skill-based player in the game. He will choose to lose this tournament rather than contradict his own self-definition."

On the stream, Trophy pushed the READY button, while the commentators roared in shock.

"Look at the viewer chat," Grandma said. The System obediently brought the chat window forward and enlarged several messages. The first was a screenshot of Nesta's photo in the outfit, complete with the slogan All the armor I need. The chat read, Yoooo this chick already throwing shade at Trophy. The other chats the System highlighted read:

> This was posted ten minutes ago!
>
> OMG look at the time stamp. She posted this before Finality even changed into #theoutfit.
>
> HOW DID SHE KNOW!!!!!??????
>
> Is she Finality? #theoutfit
>
> No way. But she knows Finality. Obviously. #theoutfit

So some nobody influencer is over here sabotaging Trophy? Epic. #theoutfit

On the stream, Trophy was on the defensive against a heavily armored knight, while the commentators screamed.

"This was the plan?" Chloe said as Trophy's character failed to block the knight's attack and was smashed, lifeless, into the dirt. "I thought you were promising to get the girl together with the gamer."

"I only promised to get her noticed," the System said.

"Thirty million viewers and a controversy," Marcus said, nodding slowly. "That would do it."

"Now we wait," Grandma said.

"How long?" Chloe said.

"Not long," the System said, as a new MeNet post appeared. On the towering virtual screen, above the caption OMG check out this little girl already cosplaying #theoutfit, was a photo of two men in a residential neighborhood disembarking from one cab and getting into another. One was looking directly into the camera, face frozen in dawning hostility. The other was busy hoisting a small girl into the new cab. Chloe couldn't see her face, but her outfit was unmistakably Kleio's.

Chloe was on her feet, though she didn't remember standing, and her eyes were locked on her little girl's image, slightly blurry with motion as she was hefted into the cab. "Get that man's hands off my child," she said.

The System said, "The photo metadata has their location."

"Great," Marcus muttered. He'd leaped to his feet too. "We know where they are. But how do we get Kleio away without—" He broke off, but Chloe heard the unspoken "getting her killed."

"That is one of two reasons I told Dr. Norman what we were doing," the System said.

Chloe's head snapped to her. "*You* told him? Not Evans?"

"Why?" Marcus asked.

The System turned cool blue eyes to him. "I anticipate I will need to cause harm to humans. I cannot do this without my creator's direct permission." A new window appeared, a drone view of the city rolling below while the camera panned, searched, and then locked onto a nondescript cab gliding with the traffic. "Dr. Norman is sending law enforcement to intercept. He has provided me with guest access to the police feeds. But he's also ordering the TransNet technicians to take control of the cab. That's a mistake."

Chloe's heart contracted. "Why?"

The System nodded at the drone feed, where the cab had come to a sudden stop in the middle of the street, emergency lights flashing. "They know they've been found." On the screen, two men leaped from the cab, and Chloe's hands clenched as she saw Kleio's tiny form slung under the arm of one of them. They pounded through the traffic that had been frozen by their cab's unexpected stop and disappeared under the green canopy of a footlane between two treescrapers.

A SWAT airvan swooped into the picture, settling into a hover over the vehicle street outside the footlane. Ropes arced from either side, and Chloe caught glimpses between the six rotors of men in bulky black body armor and helmets rappelling down. Then the feed changed to a body cam from a member of the SWAT team as they whipped guns from their backs, formed up, and moved steadily into the lane.

She had to bite her lip to keep from screaming. This was wrong, wrong—too many things could go wrong. What if they shot Kleio by mistake? What if the kidnappers "cut their losses" as soon as the gunplay started? This wasn't the kind of control the System had seemed to promise. But she looked no more concerned than she'd been throughout this whole process. She was a computer; she had no true understanding of the danger Kleio was in. And Andrew Norman didn't care.

But then the SWAT team stopped, and as the camera exposure adjusted to the dimmer light, Chloe saw why: The footlane was empty.

Grandma shifted. "Great. How in the world do we get her out of there?"

"Kleio is the variable," the System said. "She's too young for me to predict what she'll do. I need to talk to her. I need a Trojan horse."

Grandma said, "That's a lot to ask of anyone." The System just looked at her. Grandma sighed and her eyes focused inward. "I sent the instructions," she said a moment later. "She's gonna share the call—ah, there it is." A message had appeared in their shared smartspace: Sprite would like to share a window with you. Accept? A call window appeared, showing the face of a dark-haired young woman: Sprite, Chloe assumed. In a window next to her, a Connecting message was suddenly replaced with a glowing green greater-than symbol.

"That's MorDread," the System told Chloe. "The head of the Collective."

The man who had ordered Kleio's kidnapping. Chloe found herself holding her breath, even though she knew Sprite's window share was one-way, and there was no way MorDread could know she was watching.

Letters clacked out from MorDread's symbol. THIS IS UNEXPECTED.

The dark-haired girl said without preamble, "I'm guessing you're behind the kidnapping I see on the news."

WHAT OF IT?

"If you let the little girl go, I'll send you the location of the Final System."

AW, DID YOU AND GH05T TRADE SECRETS OVER PILLOW? MorDread wrote. I ASSUME YOU ENTERTAINED HIM WITH STORIES FROM YOUR TIME AT MY TABLE? BEFORE YOU STABBED ME IN THE BACK.

"You're the one who stabs people," Sprite said. "I don't like killing. You knew that was my line in the sand."

AND WHEN DID I REQUIRE OF YOUR DEAR LITTLE FAIRY HEART THAT YOU VIOLATE THAT SPOTLESS CONSCIENCE?

"I worked with Ghost for years. Standing by while Huntsman murdered him would have made me complicit."

YOU'VE BEEN SWEET ON GHO5T FOR YEARS, YOU MEAN. YOU BROKE THE CARDINAL RULE OF THE HANDLER.

"So I'm not heartless," the girl said.

I TOLERATE LOOSE ENDS FOR NO ONE, NOT EVEN YOU. ENDS LEFT TO DANGLE ARE TOO EASILY KNOTTED INTO NOOSES.

"You *made* me a loose end. But now I'm coming back. I have what you want. If you'd consulted with me before turning the spider loose, I could have gotten it for you earlier, without your stupid plan B overcomplicating everything. Ghost just needed a friend. Someone he could trust."

WE ALL NEED PEOPLE WE CAN TRUST. IF YOU BRING ME LOCATION, I WILL FREE CHILD. BUT YOU MUST BRING IT. I KNOW YOU ARE HERE IN DC. I HAVE ALWAYS WANTED TO MEET YOU FACE-TO-FACE.

"Why can't I just message it to you?"

TRUST.

Sprite's voice was flat. "It's so if I give you the wrong location, you can kill me."

TRUST, MorDread repeated. YOURS IN ME, MINE IN YOU.

Sprite was silent for a long moment, and very still. There was a quaver in her voice when she finally said, "How do I find you?"

GO TO THIS LOCATION. A 3D map appeared, with a pin marking a spot between two treescrapers.

"On my way."

As the windows blinked out, the System said to Chloe, "Once this final pawn is on the board, I'll be ready to extract Kleio."

"I don't think I like this," Chloe said hesitantly. "This isn't like getting people to take a picture. That girl is scared. She's not a pawn to be moved around or—or sacrificed. I don't feel good risking her life, even—" She had to steel herself before she could say, "Even to save Kleio." But she meant it.

The System turned her blue eyes on her, and despite their electric glow, they were cool and dispassionate. "She is not the pawn I'm thinking of."

Chloe held her gaze for a long moment and continued to stare even after the System turned her eyes away. Then she glanced at Grandma, whose face was just as inscrutable.

No one knows her power, Grandma had said.

Chloe subvocalized a command to her phone to start streaming her smartspace on MeNet. It was doubtful anyone would connect to it live, but her account could record and archive up to an hour of streamed footage. Everything she was seeing and hearing would be saved for playback later.

Grandma gave her a sudden, sharp look of surprise, and when Chloe returned a questioning one, Grandma said, "Do you think that's wise?"

"This way, there'll be a record if we need it."

"Yes," Grandma said slowly. "Yes, there should be a record. But please anonymize my involvement."

"Um, okay," Chloe said. "If you must be so mysterious." She focused on Grandma and subvocalized a command to anonymize her. Her phone's built-in AI presented her with the option of delaying the stream ten seconds so it could seamlessly edit out the portions that included Grandma, and Chloe approved it. "Done."

"Thank you," Grandma said. "I will bow to your judgment about leaving the stream up." She turned away, and Chloe heard her mutter, half to herself, "But prepare for unforeseen consequences."

CHAPTER 19

"No," Jason said. "No way."

"I told you: It was a bluff," Sprite said tiredly. Her eyes flicked around; she was working on something in her smartspace, glancing from window to window, but to Jason it gave her a hunted look. "You never told me where the System is, so I can hardly tell him."

"That's not what I'm talking about. You're not going to meet him. He'll kill you."

"He won't get the chance."

"How do you know?"

"I know." But the tremor was still in her voice.

"That 'trust' bullshit?"

"He's not the one I trust, but yeah, something like that."

"Who do you trust, then? Your little team? The phreaking *System*?"

Sprite met his glare with a look that was more desperate than defiant. "A child's life is at stake, Ghost, and it's our fault. I have to do this."

"No, you don't," Jason said. He had already directed the jet cab to divert to the location on the map.

Sprite's brows drew together in suspicion. "What are you up to? Are you—no, Ghost! If you think he'll kill me, he'll *definitely* kill you!"

"What about your team? Won't they save me?" He was trying to be sarcastic, but he could hear a quaver in his own voice now. But there was no way he was going to let Sprite waltz into MorDread's arms.

Sprite bit her lip.

"Anyway, I really do have what MorDread wants," Jason said. "If I have to, I'll be honest. Norman must know by now what MorDread's up to, and it's not like he's gonna let him waltz in and steal the System. Hell, maybe MorDread'll give up the idea and bomb the phreaking thing instead."

"No," Sprite said. "I know MorDread. I'll meet him. End of story."

"End of story, huh? Are you gonna make it there in—" Jason checked his ETA. "Two minutes, eleven seconds? Jet cab, remember?"

Sprite's arm rose and fell, and over the feed, Jason heard the sound of a surface being violently struck. "*Phreak!* Share your lens feed, at least. I'll be in your ear the whole time. I'll help as much as I can."

"Thanks," Jason said, opening the share. "But it should be easy enough, right? A quick trade. I just make sure the little girl is released before I give him the System's location." And hope like hell MorDread didn't immediately kill him.

"It won't be that simple. MorDread's not going to let you walk, even if you really give him the location. Your real job is to get a pair of glasses onto the little girl."

"What?"

"Or you could just let me do it," Sprite said.

Jason gritted his teeth. "No. Tell me what to do."

"Use those social-engineering skills," Sprite said, turning her attention to her smartspace. "Get MorDread to let you put the glasses and earbuds on the girl. My 'team' will do the rest."

The jet cab descended toward a SWAT van hovering below outside a narrow walking lane, and at first, Jason thought it was hovering over the spot that had been indicated on MorDread's map. But the cab passed over and landed instead at a public pad several blocks away, and when Jason disembarked, his GPS led him to a different footlane. A delivery bot waited at its mouth. This time the package it handed him contained not a phone but a brand-new child-size set of smartglasses with integrated smartbuds. Jason slipped them into his pocket and ducked into the footlane.

There were no public entrances to the towers that lined this lane, and no pedestrians, so the shaded passageway was empty of everything except trees and a garbage cylinder, one of those big plastic pneumatic pods from DC's famous automatic sanitation system. The piled garbage visible through the hatch was jarring next to the greenery around it. But nothing and no one else was present.

He glanced over his shoulder at the bright entrance, then turned back—and found himself face-to-face with a tall, very muscular man. Before he could react, the man reached out and shook his hand vigorously. "Mister Ghossst," he said. "Ssso nice to sssee you again."

"Phreak!" said Sprite's in Jason's ear. There were no sensors on the man's bald head, and he was wearing a tacky red, white, and blue T-shirt that read "The Best Eagles are Bald" rather than a trench coat, but his voice was all too familiar.

Huntsman's handshake was painful, too painful to be accidental. With his other hand, he reached into Jason's pocket and relieved him of his phone. "I assume you are here in place of your fairy friend?" he said, dropping the affected hiss but not the Russian accent. "How gallant." He thumbed the phone off.

"Phrea—" Sprite began, but the word was cut off as the phone went dark.

"MorDread is waiting," Huntsman said. "Let me take you to him. No, no," he said as Jason tried to free his crushed hand, "I insist. Come this way."

Jason locked his legs and looked toward the mouth of the lane, where a jogger was passing beneath the trees, but something hard and sharp was shoved against his back. Huntsman said in a low voice, "If you call for help, I stick needle in you. You will have seizure, and concerned passerby, meaning me, will try so hard to save you, but will be sadly unable to."

Jason stopped resisting. Huntsman ushered him to the garbage cylinder. Thick green plastic capped each end, and a round hatch about three feet in diameter lay open to the sky. A wide tube led down the side of the treescraper to the hatch, and as Jason watched, a brief stream of garbage shot with a hiss down the tube and into the cylinder.

Huntsman pressed the OVERRIDE/CLEAR button on the nearby panel. With a hydraulic whir, the hatch slid shut, the cylinder was lowered into the ground, and a steel door folded over top of it. There was a muffled, explosive hiss, and the door opened again and a new cylinder rose, its hatch open and empty.

"In you go," said Huntsman, and gave Jason a shove toward the cylinder.

"You've got to be kidding," Jason said. He'd been pushed into a locker once in junior high and had missed a whole period before someone thought to look for him. In the stuffy air, with his arms pinned in the cramped space, he'd had a panic attack and almost passed out.

"Seizure?" Huntsman said.

Jason clambered into the cylinder.

"Lie down." Jason started to sit, but Huntsman said, "No, you want your feet on other side. Trust me."

Jason turned around and sat, then wriggled the rest of his body through so he could lie down. Except for the hatch above him, he was surrounded by a darkness that stank of warm plastic and old refuse. Between the nerves and that stench, he gagged, and gagged again.

Huntsman waited patiently for him to get himself under control. "If you breathe slowly," he said, "you should have enough air for trip." He chuckled. "And enough time to reflect on disposable nature of usual cargo of this pod." He tossed Jason's phone onto his chest, and as Jason scrabbled for it, Huntsman pushed a button and the hatch slid shut, enclosing Jason in garbage-scented darkness.

With a jolt and a mechanical whine, the cylinder descended into the earth. Jason thumbed his phone on. The light of its boot screen caught the logo embossed on the hatch above: WasteNet. He forced himself to take a deep, slow breath. Not the best idea. He inhaled eau de garbage and gagged again. He hadn't recovered before there came a sound like a steam boiler bursting and he was slammed against the bottom of the cylinder by a violent acceleration. His phone flew out of his hand and was lost somewhere near his feet.

Now he knew why Huntsman had told him to put his feet in that direction: They took the brunt of the force. His legs buckled as much as they had room to, which was just enough for his knees to smash painfully against the top of the cylinder. He tried to brace with his hands, but the only thing to get a grip on in all the smooth plastic was the WasteNet logo. That, even more than the constricting space, made his claustrophobia rise again, bringing acid to the back of his throat. He was literally inside one of Norman's networks, trapped, careening through it like a packet through wires.

The cylinder jerked left and right at irregular intervals, pinning him to the walls with each twist, then slowed and stopped. The hatch slid open, and another Russian-accented voice said, "Well, well! Not Sprite, but Ghost! Welcome!"

Jason pulled himself, blinking, into the light. His eyes focused on a hand, extended and waiting. He grabbed it and allowed himself to be helped out of the cylinder. As he clambered out, he found his phone with one foot, pulled it toward him, scooped it up, and pocketed it. It had finished booting and paired with his lenses, but now he knew why Huntsman had let him have it back: The only thing showing in his smartspace was a blinking "No reception" icon. Sprite was unreachable.

"Welcome!" the voice said again, and the hand helping him out reversed so he could shake it. He did, shaking his head at the same time, clearing it so he could focus on the speaker.

He was a short but heavyset man with unkempt blond hair and a round, beaming face that made Jason think of an archetypal overenthusiastic shopkeeper from *BloodReign*. This was only accentuated by his, well, accent, which was even thicker than Huntsman's. "I'm MorDread!" he said, pumping Jason's hand. "So good to meet you in person!"

Jason nodded, trying to squeeze MorDread's hand manfully, which was hard when he was turning his arm into a noodle. "A pleasure," he managed, trying to sound sarcastic.

"Pleasure is mine! Come, let me show you my . . . What is the phrase? Humble abode." MorDread waved an arm at the space around him.

"Don't you mean secret lair?" Jason said. They were standing on a walkway high in a room as big as a school gym, with walls, floor, and ceiling of concrete. The only visible entrance, apart from the dozen massive pipes running in and out of the walls, was a hatch far up in the ceiling, which was inaccessible since the folding ladder that should have hung from it had been removed. The inward-bound pipes converged into a single tube that ended over a vast trash hopper. As Jason watched, a cylinder like the one he'd arrived in hissed through the pipe and into place above the hopper. Its bottom was unplugged and removed by machinery, and a stream of garbage fell into the hopper. Replugged, the cylinder was sucked back up the pipe and diverted along a different branching path and out one of the exit pipes, off to collect more garbage.

MorDread grinned hugely. "Yes! Secret lair! This is our home away from home. Not even Norman has been able to find where we go. There are many ways to get here, and who puts cameras in garbage dump? Garbage is never noticed. No one wants to notice it. But it goes everywhere. It is intestines of city! And since WasteNet is low-tier network, hacking it is like stroll in park. Ah, here comes Huntsman."

Jason's cylinder disappeared with a hollow hiss, and its place was taken by an identical one. Its hatch opened and Huntsman hoisted himself out, giving Jason a grin very like MorDread's. "He is still alive, I see," he said to MorDread. "I wasn't sure you would bother diverting him."

"See, Ghost, we divert you to troubleshooting rail," MorDread said. "Otherwise you go in bin to be sorted." Jason followed his pointing arm. Below the hopper, a system of conveyer belts and mechanical dividers sorted trash into three exit streams. "Organic, recyclables, and general waste. Before, people had to sort trash themselves, and who wants to do that? Now system is so smart it can do it for them, by image recognition. It is one of greatest accomplishments in AI, and no one hears about it because it is garbage!" He laughed heartily. "You, you are organic matter, so you would go there." He pointed to a long, wide conveyer belt, walled with plexiglass, leading to a round tank with a conical top that took up a third of the cavernous space. "To be digested."

"Digested?" He must be bluffing.

"Yes!" MorDread said. "Anaerobic digester! Works just like your stomach. Smells like it too! Turns garbage into methane. Fart gas! Very valuable. Digester can break down small pig in one day. You, maybe thirty-two hours."

"Don't worry, you'd be dead from no oxygen very much sooner," Huntsman said.

"But that is not why you are here." MorDread led the way down the steps to the floor in quick hops. Jason followed, and Huntsman fell in step behind him, much too close for Jason's comfort. MorDread led them around the side of the digester. "*This* is why you are here."

Jason's steps faltered. Grouped around a cluster of computer equipment were a dozen men, each almost as big as Huntsman, with defined muscles and five-o'clock shadows. They looked like they'd be more at home in greasy uniforms behind the controls of a tank than bent over computers. Or maybe he just got that impression because of the guns slung from their shoulders. Stacked beside the computer equipment was an assortment of military equipment: night-vision goggles, scout drones, guns, ammunition clips, even what looked like rocket launchers. MorDread had come well prepared to steal the System.

Huntsman went over to where one of the men was gripping the shoulder of the little girl Jason had come for. She looked unhurt, but her eyes were dull and unfocused in a way that made him uncomfortable. She didn't resist when Huntsman grabbed her other shoulder and the two men maneuvered her forward. "This is trade, yes?" Huntsman said.

"Yes," Jason said. He looked at MorDread. "Let her go and I'll tell you where the System's core is."

MorDread smiled knowingly. "First you tell, then I let her go."

Jason had expected this. So he took the children's glasses from his pocket and said, "Then you need to allow Kleio to make a call out, so Sprite can verify she's alive."

MorDread's smile became a frown. "Why? You can see she is."

"Sprite's the one with the address. I purposefully didn't memorize it. I put it in an encrypted file and gave it to her. She has the file; I have the password. You need both our approvals to get the info." Bluffing was essential to social engineering, but Jason couldn't do it with his usual breeziness. His breath was so shallow he had trouble finishing each sentence.

MorDread's knowing smile returned, and he said, "I think I see."

Jason stepped toward Kleio, but Huntsman pulled the girl back. This had the effect of twisting her shoulders, since the second man hadn't moved. The girl's eyes shifted, but she didn't flinch.

Jason realized with a sudden flash of anger why Kleio's expression made him uneasy. When Mia had been in a bad situation she couldn't escape—when a foster mom was thrashing her for some perceived slight or a foster dad was on meth and ragingly paranoid—her eyes had taken on the same unfocused look, her face the same blankness.

Huntsman nodded at the glasses in Jason's hand and said something in Russian to MorDread.

"Nonsense," MorDread said. "I'm sure Ghost, of all people, is not working with System! He has already shown he would rather die than do that!" He gave another hearty laugh. Jason was beginning to hate that laugh. "However, we will not use your glasses," he told Jason. "We will use one of my backups." He went to a workbench in the corner and rooted through a pile of equipment.

"Why?" Jason said, a little too quickly. "Mine are ready to go."

"Yours would not be able to talk out," MorDread said, selecting a pair of glasses, holding them up with a frown, and rejecting them. "There are eight meters of concrete and dirt between us and world," he said over his shoulder. "Another reason we chose this place! So your outbound call must go through my node, through cable I tapped." He nodded at a terminal on the workbench. "So we use my glasses." He held up a smaller pair, gave a satisfied grunt, and turned. "Which are also geo-spoofed, so our fairy friend cannot trace this location."

Jason's heart sank, but he had no choice but to take the glasses MorDread held out. He walked slowly to Kleio and knelt. "Hey there," he said gently. "My friend wants you to wear these. Can you do that?"

She didn't look at him or say anything, but she gave a small nod. Jason slid the glasses onto her head. They were too big, and she had to reach up to hold them steady. Her face screwed in discomfort as he twisted the attached smartbuds into her ears, but then she was able to drop her hands because the smartbuds held the glasses in place. Jason held down the power button on the side of the glasses until he saw a glimmer in their depths. From his corner, MorDread turned his head to watch the terminal, where a log window showed the glasses' connection info.

"Okay, you can call Sprite now," Jason told him, and hoped like hell Sprite would have a plan.

CHAPTER 20

A message appeared in the midst of the huge windows in the void around the System: Sprite would like to share a window. Accept? A moment later, a new chat window opened. In one corner was the dark-haired young woman from earlier, but most of the window was taken up with the face of a little white girl with blond hair.

"Hello there," said the young woman, obviously talking to the girl. "I'm Sprite. I'm so happy to meet you! I'm going to show you a message in a moment. When I do, can you look at it and say yes?"

Chloe gasped even before the little blond girl spoke. Though her face was very different, the way her eyes flicked down and up and the way the corners of her lips tightened and trembled were unmistakably Kleio when she was trying not to cry. Her quiet "Okay" confirmed it. Whoever had given her the glasses hadn't bothered to scan her face, so the glasses had defaulted to a placeholder avatar of a generic white girl. Chloe felt her own lips tremble in a rush of relief and fresh trepidation. She wanted to scream "Let me talk to her!" but she bit the words back. She felt Marcus step close behind her, felt his hands close almost painfully on her shoulders, and knew he, too, was forcibly holding himself back.

"Okay, do it now!" said the young woman in the chat window.

Kleio's eyes focused inward, and she said, "Yes." Apparently that was permission for a camera share, because a new window opened, a three-dimensional view out of Kleio's eyes, or rather from the twin cameras in the frame of her glasses. The System had made this window life size, so it felt to Chloe as if she were looking directly into the room where Kleio was standing. It was a vast concrete space lit by LED light banks and filled with complicated conveyer belts and tubes. Chloe felt a burst of disappointment that she couldn't see Kleio since she was the one wearing the cameras, but in that instant, the inset chat window of the little white girl was replaced by a breathtakingly accurate representation of Kleio's own face. Chloe's heart stuttered under a sudden ache, sharp as a blow, and she shot a grateful look at the System.

Kleio's vision was centered on a young man who stood in front of her, and Chloe recognized him as the man who'd appeared in the reflection of the jet cab window, talking to Nesta. He was saying over Kleio's head to someone Chloe couldn't see, "After you let us both walk, I'll unlock that file."

"My friend is going to help you," the dark-haired young woman's avatar said to Kleio from her chat window. "Do exactly as she says and she'll get you home. Okay?" Kleio's vision bobbed as her avatar nodded, and the young woman gave her a final smile and disappeared.

The System stepped forward and into the room, and Chloe blinked; she appeared to pass seamlessly from the void where Chloe and Marcus and Grandma were standing into the concrete room where Kleio was. There she turned around, and at first, Chloe thought she was looking back at her, but then realized she was really looking at Kleio, who could obviously see her because her view shifted to center her.

"Hi, Kleio," the System said in a voice that dripped with reassurance and warmth. "Your mommy sent me to get you. Can you be brave?"

Someone out of view said, "Wait. Connection has been transferred to third party."

"I fink so," Kleio said. "Who are you?"

"Who's she talking to, little Ghost?" said the voice. "It's not our fairy friend anymore."

"You can call me Sys," the System told Kleio.

"Sis like sister?" Kleio said.

At this, there was a burst of what sounded like Russian swearing in the background, until the voice said something commanding to make everyone go quiet again. The voice said, "Ghost. You were not honest with me."

"Sys like System," the System was saying to Kleio. "But sister works too."

Behind the System in Kleio's vision, a couple of burly-looking men with guns stepped up to the young man, grabbed his arms, and began dragging him toward the conveyer belts in the background. "Wait!" he cried. "I'll give you the location, I swear!"

Kleio's focus shifted to him, but the System flashed with multicolored lights and fairy sparkles, drawing Kleio's eyes back to her. "Don't worry; this is part of the adventure!" she said.

"Ghost, Ghost, how can I trust you?" the voice was saying at the same time. "I'm surprised and disappointed. You want to walk? Go ahead. Walk." The two men hoisted and dumped the young man over the transparent plexiglass wall and onto a conveyer belt.

"MorDread is trying to trace my connection," the System said suddenly from beside Chloe, and Chloe jumped. There were two Systems now: one talking to Kleio and one standing next to Chloe, calm as ever, even while behind her other form, the young man lurched to his feet and almost fell as the conveyer belt began to move. "I'm letting him think he's making progress so he'll let Kleio keep the glasses on."

"What's going to happen to him?" Chloe asked, pointing to the young man. Whatever the conveyer was pulling him toward seemed to terrify him.

"Ghost? The plexiglass is a transparent substitute for steel, so it is very thick," the System said, as if that explained something.

"Are you a princess?" Kleio asked.

Chloe couldn't decide what to pay attention to: "Ghost" struggling to keep his balance on the moving conveyer belt, Kleio's conversation with the System, the other System beside Chloe, or a sudden new camera window showing an overhead drone view of a gaggle of police, including three military-style canine dronebots with gun-turret heads gathered around a manhole cover in the middle of the street. But a part of her mind had time to think that Kleio was right: The System did sound a bit like one of the princesses in the movies Kleio watched and rewatched, with her childlike voice but adult vocabulary.

"I'm not a princess," the System told Kleio. "But you are."

Kleio giggled, a sound that filled Chloe's heart. "No, I'm not."

"How long can you walk, little Ghost?" said the unseen voice mockingly as Ghost stumbled and scrabbled for a grip on the plexiglass wall, which was too smooth and high to climb. He gave up and ran down the belt and out of Kleio's vision, but the voice gave a command in Russian and the belt sped up, dragging him back into view, jogging desperately.

"Yes, you are!" the System said. "You're Princesszilla. Remember?"

"Dat's not real," Kleio said.

"Look at your feet."

Kleio's view shifted downward. Instead of her own shoes, she was looking at a pair of bright-pink, furry monster feet. She laughed in surprise, and she must have wiggled her toes because the monster toes wiggled too. "I'm Princesszilla!" She raised her head. "I'm Princesszilla!"

"I've just convinced Dr. Norman to grant me emergency control of the police dronebots," the System beside Chloe told her. "I'll try to make sure Kleio doesn't see."

"Doesn't see what?" Chloe said, even as Marcus said, "I want to see what happens."

The System looked at him. "It will happen too fast." She thought for a moment. "I'll slow down the feed."

"See, you're magic!" said the System in Kleio's vision at the same time. "Now we're going to play a magic game of tag to get you home. You just have to touch me! Try as hard as you can! Are you ready?"

"Ready!" Kleio said, with another wiggle of her monster feet.

Two policemen lifted the manhole cover and leaped back.

The System blinked out and reappeared to Kleio's left with a joyful shout of "Over here!" She glowed bright blue, and as she turned to run, her motion left a trail of sparkles.

The dogbots jumped into the manhole, passing into the opening in quick succession, the third trailing a long, rippling communication line. Three new windows opened, showing the camera feeds of each as they passed through the narrow hole. There was a moment of blackness; then the light returned as they emerged from the bottom of the shaft.

All the videos slowed down.

On the first dogbot's feed, Chloe saw a suspended image of the whole space: a maze of belts, chutes, and tubes that made her think of the giant indoor playgrounds she'd sometimes taken Kleio to, except that it held a dozen men with guns. Ghost stumbled in slow motion on the conveyer belt. At the center of the dogbot's view was the tiny form of Kleio, her shoulders each held by one of her captors. No System avatar was visible in this feed, but Kleio was turning her head to her left.

"Success," said the System.

The dogbot's vision centered on the man holding Kleio's right shoulder, a big bald man in a garish T-shirt. There was a flash, and the man's head exploded.

It came apart in several pieces, bone and blood and brains flying outward as his knees began to buckle. In Kleio's camera feed, the System swerved sharply right; Kleio's head and body turned in that direction and she began to run forward, out of the now-limp grasp of the collapsing kidnapper. The second kidnapper, holding Kleio's left shoulder, began to yank her back, but then his head, too, was shattered, and Kleio pulled out of his grasp while gore sprayed behind her. She ran several steps forward as the two bodies folded like marionettes whose strings had been cut. She was running directly away from the men who'd hoisted Ghost onto the conveyer belt. They began to fall, blood-splashed spiderwebs of cracks sprouting on the plexiglass behind their heads, right in front of Ghost, whose eyes widened in dawning surprise even as his feet slid out from under him.

Kleio swerved, her hands inches from the System, just as another man tried to step into her way, raising his gun. As his head came apart, his arm kept moving, no longer toward Kleio but swinging up and out, the gun sliding out of his loosened grip and arcing gracefully away as his body crumpled.

The first dogbot had been falling this whole time, and now its feed shuddered and went black as it hit the ground. But the two other dogbots were still in midair, their cameras centering lethally on each of the remaining men in turn. All around Kleio was a symphony of arcing blood and collapsing bodies, men beginning to flee, turn, shout, raise a gun, only for their motion to transform into a mindless tumble as volition left them.

In Kleio's camera feed, all that could be seen was the running, laughing System.

The second dogbot focused on a short man in the back of the room who'd had his back turned to bend over computer equipment. He was turning around now, his left arm thrown up across his face, his mouth screaming under it, and his right arm just coming into view, awkwardly hefting what looked like a rocket launcher.

The dogbot shot him three times, once through his upthrown arm and twice in his right side. The impacts twisted his body back in that direction as he crumpled, and so when the weapon fired, it hit the wall and enveloped that corner of the room in flame and smoke and chunks of dirt and concrete.

The second dogbot's feed went black as it landed. The third bot's camera slid across the scene, seeking loose ends. At the last moment, almost as an afterthought, it centered on a control panel connected to the conveyer belt and sent a bullet sparking into it. Then its camera shook, blurred, and bounced, but didn't go dark; its fall had been broken by the two dogbots below it.

Kleio's straining hands touched the System.

There was a flash of light. All the video feeds sped up to several times normal, then stabilized as they caught up to the present.

Kleio had stopped running but was still trying to grab the System, laughing as her hands swept through her, while the System skipped delightedly in front of her, saying, "You caught me! You did it!"

Chloe felt air rush into her lungs; she'd been holding her breath so tightly her diaphragm hurt, and now her gasps were made shallow by pain and by horror. Marcus's hand was painfully taut on her shoulder.

In the surviving dogbot's camera feed, canted in a Dutch tilt straight out of a horror movie, Kleio was alone except for Ghost, who was climbing hesitantly to his feet on the now-stationary conveyer belt, staring at the piled, crumpled shapes that had once been men. The only other motion in the scene was a slow pooling of blood.

New movement disturbed the feed: a SWAT team rappelling through the manhole shaft, unlatching and spreading out, weapons raised. Chloe's feelings were reflected in their slackening body language as they took in the carnage.

Kleio started to turn her head to look at them, but the System got her attention again, flashing and sparkling, talking animatedly, ushering her toward an EMT who had just touched ground.

Some of the horror clenching Chloe's heart loosened as Kleio was buckled into a harness and hoisted skyward, the System rising like Peter Pan beside her. She kept her eyes on her daughter until the little girl was pulled by caring arms into the light, and then she looked down at the System's other avatar, still standing beside her.

The System was looking back, her electric-blue eyes oddly flat. "You are shocked," she said.

Chloe swallowed.

"They tried to raise their guns," the System said, and her voice, too, was flat. "I considered aiming for the guns, but that would have been unpredictable. I instead chose the path most certain to keep Kleio safe."

"Thank you," Chloe managed, because she couldn't say what she was thinking, which was *What the hell are you?*

"Chloe!" Grandma said urgently. "Check your live stream!"

Chloe had forgotten she'd been streaming. She frowned at Grandma as she pulled up the feed. "What about it?"

"Check the viewer count."

"Oh sh—uh, shoot," she said, very quietly, because everything she saw and heard was being seen and heard by over three hundred million people.

"All the NewsNet outlets picked it up," Grandma said. "The whole country watched that in real time. This is going to—"

She disappeared.

In fact, everything disappeared: the System, the video windows, and the VR version of Kleio's room, leaving Chloe and Marcus blinking at each other in the real room.

"You getting this?" Marcus said, frowning inward, and Chloe nodded, knowing they were looking at the same message: Authentication Error. "If it's both of us, it has to be a network problem. What do you think—" He broke off and Chloe gave a little shriek, because what was now floating in their vision, in jagged, broken letters, was a new message:

> Hey Amerika: phreak you.

CHAPTER 21

"I think it's just MeNet," Marcus said. "The other Nets are still up, but without MeNet, nobody can interface with them."

"Everything might as well be down if we can't use it," Chloe said, trying for the tenth time to call Norman or Grandma, and when that failed, to check NewsNet, only to get Authentication Error again. "*Phreak!* Where's Kleio? I want my baby!"

A heavy knocking at the apartment door made her jump. She and Marcus exchanged looks.

"Stay behind me," Marcus said. He led the way to the door and cautiously opened it a crack.

"Daddy!" said a voice.

"Oh god," Marcus said, throwing open the door and collapsing to his knees in one motion. And then Chloe was collapsing as well, her arms wrapping around their daughter. She buried her head in Kleio's curls, sobbing, telling her over and over again how much she loved her, how sorry she was that this had happened, how she'd never, ever let anything happen to her again, while Marcus enveloped them both in his own arms.

Kleio said, "Mommy, I can't breave."

"Oh, sorry!" Chloe said, holding her at arm's length to inspect her.

Kleio's face had old salt streaks on it, but she was looking at Chloe with her familiar impish smile. "Are you so happy to see me, Mommy?"

"Oh, god, yes," Chloe said, folding her in her arms again, more gently this time. For the first time, she noticed the SWAT airvan on the pavement and the black-suited SWAT team, some standing close with their weapons slung, others facing away, watching up and down the street, their weapons in their hands. Their faces were tense, but the closest one gave Chloe a tight smile.

"She told us to come here," he said, nodding to a woman just stepping out of the SWAT van. Grandma.

"Oh, *thank* you!" Chloe gasped as Grandma approached. "I'd hug you if it didn't mean letting go of Kleio." The little girl was burrowing deeper into her arms.

"Please never hug me," Grandma said. "I am not a hugger." But she was smiling.

"What's going on?" Marcus said to her. "With this new Cybercrash, I mean."

Grandma's smile faded. "Nobody can talk to anybody, so nobody knows. I'm on my way to the Tower. Chloe, you need to come."

"What?" Chloe said, squeezing Kleio harder. "No!" She had just gotten her baby back. There was no phreaking way she was going to leave her.

"Chloe, Norman's bound to be holed up in the Tower, and who knows what he's going to do. I need you there as a voice of reason."

"No."

"Chloe." Grandma squatted on her heels so she could look Chloe in the face. "I know what you're feeling, and I wouldn't ask if this weren't so serious. But if you want Kleio to *stay* safe, you need to come with me. People are already panicking. Riots are starting all over."

"No," Chloe said again.

"She needs help," said Kleio in a voice muffled by Chloe's body.

"What's that?" Chloe said, releasing her.

"Sys said 'help.'" Kleio's snub nose was scrunched in worry. "And den she disappeared."

Chloe looked at Grandma. "What can I do, though?"

"Be someone who isn't Norman," Grandma said.

"Why can't *you* do that?"

"He wouldn't react well to my interference. Believe me."

"And he'll react better to me?"

"There's no one else who can try." Her voice became soft and singsong. "'For want of a nail the shoe slipped.' Chloe, all the other nails have slipped."

"What does that even mean?" Chloe said in sudden heat. "And what would I even do as a lone unslipped nail?"

Marcus put a hand on her shoulder. "This is why you're here," he said quietly. "To help however you can."

They were all looking at her: Marcus, Grandma, and Kleio. And it was crazy. But Marcus was right. Coming to DC had been her way of gathering up the broken narrative threads of her life and trying to weave them into a new tapestry of meaning. "Okay," she said. "Okay. I'll try."

"I'll take care of Kleio," Marcus said grimly, gathering her in his arms.

"Grab a couple Bomb Bars," Grandma said to Chloe. "You'll need 'em."

The SWAT airvan carried them over a city that felt wrong. The streets were as packed as ever with cabs, but they were motionless. Cumulonimbus peaks piled over the treescrapers, casting the city into shadow, as if things weren't portentous enough without nature underlining the point with unintentional metaphor. There were people on the streets, dots of color joining together into streams and clumps, warily circling other clumps. Smoke rose from the base of a treescraper in the distance, the dots of people there roiling like ants. Grandma was right: There were riots already. They must have started even faster than in the first Cybercrash. What the hell was wrong with people?

As they neared the Tower, Chloe could see that the Park was already packed, and throngs were crossing the arching footbridges to the island.

These people weren't rioting, at least not yet. For decades, pundits had warned that increased online interaction diminished genuine human connection, that despite the stream of new technology meant to rehumanize virtual spaces via ever-better facial tracking and avatars and "presence," something was still lost. It seemed they had a point, judging by the thousands who at this moment weren't content to shelter at home. History was happening and it was happening here, at Norman's fortress, and so they were taking the time and effort to manually transport their bodies to this place. Many of the faces were upturned, toward the Tower. They'd made the pilgrimage; now they awaited salvation.

Beyond them, black smoke rose over Arlington.

The crowd was held back from the Tower by what looked like a military checkpoint; beyond it, on a clear stretch of grass, soldiers and dogbots spread out, while a number of military vehicles positioned themselves into a wide array. Several of them began pivoting long tubes skyward. "Revere distributed missile battery!" Grandma shouted, pointing at them.

"What's that?" Chloe called back. With MeNet down, there was no coordination between their smartbuds, so even though Chloe's buds were attenuating the rotor noise, she had to shout to be heard. She focused on Grandma and subvocalized a command to amplify her voice.

"Missile defense," Grandma said. "Good thing MilNet's still up or we might be misidentified and shot down." She seemed amused at the idea, but Chloe shuddered. "Don't worry," Grandma said, seeing her reaction. "MilNet's the one network OverNet doesn't control. It's in its own silo for security. Supposedly even harder to hack than OverNet."

As the airvan settled to the earth inside the checkpoint, Grandma vaulted out with unexpected sprightliness, and Chloe followed. The growing overcast gave no relief from the afternoon heat; if anything, the heat seemed to compress beneath the clouds, squeezing the air into breathlessness as they hurried up the Tower steps. "We're heading to the NOC," Grandma said as they entered the atrium.

"Knock?"

"N-O-C. Network Operations Center. The dome. The center of the eye." Grandma led the way across the vast atrium to waterfall-shrouded elevators. "Oh no," she said, stopping.

"What?"

"No MeNet. The elevator can't see who we are, so it won't take us to the NOC."

"Don't tell me we have to take the stairs," Chloe said. The Tower's spiral stairways were famous, or infamous, for their exercise potential.

"Allow me," said a voice, and the waterfall parted to reveal an open elevator, and the System standing inside. It was the first time Chloe had seen her outside of a VR room, and she could almost believe she was a real little girl—albeit one with marble-white skin and softly glowing eyes—physically present in the same real-world space Chloe and Grandma occupied.

Grandma stepped into the elevator, and Chloe followed. As the doors began to close, the System stepped between them and gave Chloe an eye-crinkling smile. "How's Kleio?" Her voice seemed to come directly from the small figure.

"Safe," Chloe said. "I'm so, so grateful to you."

"*To* me?" the little girl said, her smile widening.

Chloe paused; then, realizing she meant it, "Yes. *To* you."

The elevator began to rise, and the System's smile faded into a searching, earnest look. "You're one of the only people who knows me. And"—she bit her lip and looked past Chloe at the water falling past the rising elevator—"I know you'll do the right thing."

"*That* doesn't sound ominous at all," Chloe said, as the elevator slowed. The doors slid open, and she jumped, because the big NNA agent, Bruno Tavion, was standing there, arms crossed. Chloe couldn't read his expression behind his darkened smartglasses, but after looking at her—and only her—for a moment, he stepped aside. Chloe stepped past him and stopped.

She was looking down into a crowded space so vast it spanned the entire Tower horizontally, as well as three vertical stories of open space to the rounded top of the dome. The dome's dark, clouded glass obscured the garden wings outside and served as the surface of a unified, almost 360-degree projection screen. A huge version of the System strolled across the screen, pacing among windows filled with numerical readouts, and satellite images showing prickly-looking military vehicles and labels like "Vladivostok" and "Saint Petersburg." Other windows, labeled "New York" and "Chicago," zoomed in on large crowds and black smoke in the shadows of skyscrapers. Below the screen, banks of terminals snaked through the space in tiers, gradually descending toward the recessed front.

It made Chloe think of a larger, more advanced version of the old NASA Mission Control, or the command center from every science fiction movie ever. Some were labeled with the names of the major subnets, and more with labels Chloe didn't understand, like "Neural Interphase," "Emotives," and "Hierarchical Netflow." Technobabble made a constant background murmur, but it was kept low because everyone was half listening to Norman, who paced at center stage, talking with the inward look of someone in a phone conversation. Chloe focused on him and subvocalized a command, and her smartbuds amplified his voice.

"Mr. President, there are riots in most of the major cities. I can look out the windows here and see thousands of people near the Tower. I bet more are gathering at the White House. If we want to avoid violence like the first Cybercrash, you need to authorize the System's launch on OverNet and MilNet. She can calm the people *and* defend us from Russia."

"Oh, phreak," Chloe breathed.

"Indeed," Grandma said drily.

The System, the one standing in the elevator, said softly, "That's not all."

Her figure on the dome screen spoke—the calm, sweet voice echoing through the room's speakers. "I have just determined that the Russian alert posture has reached their equivalent of DEFCON Two."

"Hear that?" Norman said to the president. "They're fueling their nukes! We need to be ready!" He looked at the System on the dome screen. "How are our own defenses in case they try another terror attack?"

"The Armory is on alert," the System said over the speakers. "F-59s and their loyal wingmen drones are performing combat air patrol. The alert bombers are airborne. Revere batteries are tracking everything in our airspace. Chloe is here."

Chloe jumped. To her surprise, Norman's face lit up, and he waved her over.

"Go on," Grandma hissed when Chloe hesitated.

"What about you?"

"He doesn't want me. It's all you, girl. You can do this."

The System in the elevator stepped out and began walking down the aisle. "Follow me," she said to Chloe over her shoulder.

Chloe could feel the curious eyes of the hundreds of technicians as she set out down the long central aisle. When she got close, Norman came toward her on long strides with his hand extended. "Chloe. Just the person I need."

She took his hand for a quick shake. "I thought you'd be mad at me."

He shook his head. "You were right: The Final System's power is meant to be used. And thanks to you, the whole country saw what she can do." His smile went brittle. "In . . . *graphic* detail."

"I didn't expect anyone to pay attention to my live stream," Chloe said.

His brow creased. "Really? You were part of the top developing news story about your daughter's kidnapping, with every news org in the country focused on you, and you didn't foresee that?" He shook his head. "No matter. What I need you to do now is convince the president that the System can help the country the way she helped Kleio. System, loop her in."

"Wait, you want me to talk to—" Chloe began, then shut her mouth with a snap as she found herself suddenly looking at the president of the United States.

Chloe had seen President Sunday in person before, but only as a figure speaking at the front of the House Chamber. Seeing him now via smartspace persona, appearing to stand next to Norman, she was ironically struck by how human he looked. Sunday had won the last election by dint of being the least objectionable candidate, and that, along with the obvious play on his surname, had led to his nickname in the op-eds: "Vanilla." Although his avatar was broadcast ready in dress and hair, the amount of white in his eyes and the press of his lips gave away that this was a man in over his head. Chloe could feel the same wideness in her own eyes and tenseness in her jaw, so she experienced a burst of fellow feeling for him. "Um, hi," she said, giving him the awkward wave that served as a handshake in smartspace.

"Dr. Dunne-Carr," he said with a wan smile. "How's your daughter?"

"Safe, thank god."

"Thank the System," Norman interjected, nodding to her life-size avatar who had joined their group. "Mr. President, Chloe spoke against the System only days ago. But when a crisis hit, she knew only the System could help her. The situation we're in now is an extension of the same crisis and needs the same solution."

"I watched your stream," the president said to Chloe. "As the System herself said, what she did was shocking. Not the bloodshed, but the, well, *manipulation* that led to it. Getting those gamer kids and those hackers to behave exactly as she needed. Andrew's been telling me that getting MeNet back online won't be enough to quell the riots that are already breaking out. We need to make the System OverNet admin so she can use those same powers of manipulation to calm people down. But unleashing those powers on American citizens, even for good, is not something I can take lightly."

Chloe revised her opinion of the man; he was sharper than she'd thought. And the fact that they were having this conversation, that he hadn't immediately caved to Norman's demands, was to his credit.

"Before I use my emergency powers to hand over the keys to OverNet and MilNet," the president said, "I need to know who I'm handing them to. So my first question is: Is the System real? I mean, is she a person?"

Chloe bit her lip and glanced at the System, who had been watching silently and now gave her a small smile. "I'm not really qualified to make that assessment."

"Who is? I want your opinion."

"My opinion?" she said slowly. "My opinion is that a computer-based consciousness should be impossible. The System herself told us that. But somehow, when I look at her, I see a person. I can't say why." Maybe it was an emotional reaction because she saved Chloe's baby. Maybe it was because the avatar she was projecting in Chloe's lenses was so real. Or maybe it was an act of faith.

The president nodded. "My next question is: Can we trust her?"

Chloe looked at the System again, who did not smile this time. Yes, an act of faith, in more ways than one. In the medieval usage of the word, faith wasn't blind belief in something invisible, but a conscious act of trust. Did she have faith in the System? Yes, she did, both that she was real and that she was trustworthy. But the System wasn't the only person in this equation. She said slowly, "Trust her to do what? Manipulate people into not panicking?"

Norman snorted impatiently. "Manipulate? I think the word you want is *moderate*. That's the mandate of the NNA: Moderate the Nets to prevent hatred, violence, and chaos. Part of that moderation has always involved regulating the types and amounts of inputs people receive, to make hatred and violence less likely. The System's moderation will be no different in kind than what we already do, just much more effective."

"I think you and I have different definitions of 'moderate,'" Chloe said. "I don't think of people as input-output machines, for one."

"What about your impassioned story about Jasmine, your wide, feminine eyes and the conviction in your voice? Aren't you, too, trying to change people's inputs to get a different output?"

Chloe had started to respond, but "wide, feminine eyes" left her spluttering.

Norman went on, "What is politics but giving people inputs to change their outputs?"

Chloe found her voice. "There's a difference between convincing and manipulating! If I try to persuade someone to vote with me, they still have a choice."

"'Choice.'" Norman's eyes flickered upward. Giving her up as a lost cause, he turned to Sunday. "Mr. President, what do you think caused all the violence in the first Cybercrash? Russian bot swarms? They were just the spark. What fanned the flames were the things that have always driven humanity: Tribalism. Confirmation bias. Cognitive dissonance. Doubling down. The Dunning-Kruger effect. Those are our algorithms, Mr. President, and all our social media, all our connectivity, all our glorious inventions, have only amplified them. Society, *humanity*, has been like a room slowly filling with invisible, flammable gas. Now Russia's flicking the lighter. But the System can put it out again. She can give each and every citizen, individually, exactly the inputs they need to generate the output that will make them law-abiding citizens again."

At that moment, a text came in from Grandma: And all for the want of a horseshoe nail.

Chloe felt as if the NOC—no, the whole world—had tilted dangerously. She suddenly understood Norman's grand vision in a nutshell. The System wasn't the dangerous machine: Humanity was. So he'd built a new machine, one that could control all variables, make everyone receive exactly the right inputs to make their outputs benign. The System would be admin not only of OverNet but of humanity itself, with Norman atop all, leading humanity into an unprecedented age of perfect unity. Pax Normana.

As the dizzying realization passed, she found the others staring at her. Norman's throat was moving as if he were subvocalizing. The System's face was closed and inscrutable. The president was expectant, and she realized he had just addressed her. "What?" she said stupidly.

"I said," Sunday said, "I'm asking for your final recommendation on whether we can trust the System."

"I trust the System," Chloe said. "But her creator scares the hell out of me. So no, I don't recommend—"

She stopped, because two things happened at once.

One was that the System's face, in a single instant and with no process of transition, transformed.

Every parent recognized the gradations of their child's unhappiness, the difference between a tantrum over bedtime, the tears after a bump or bruise, and the look or sound of true distress that would cause the parent to drop everything and run, gut clenched, to help. The System's face triggered that gut clench. Her eyes were filled with tears and terror, her mouth open in a soundless wail.

At the same moment, Chloe heard her own voice, speaking over her, and then, when she stopped, continuing without her: "So yes, I recommend that the System be placed immediately and permanently atop OverNet and MilNet, as administrator of those networks and all their subnets."

"Okay," the president said, blowing out his cheeks. "I'll trust your trust in her. Thank you."

"What?" Chloe shouted. "No!" But she heard her own voice say, "You're welcome, sir. I know she'll get us through this."

The president nodded curtly and disconnected.

A corner of Norman's mouth stretched knowingly. "Thank you, Chloe," he said. "That's all I needed from you."

CHAPTER 22

Jason lasted less than an hour in solitary before he broke.

The torture that broke him was sheer boredom. He had nothing to look at except four white walls, a sparse bed, a corner urinal, and his own surprisingly formal khaki federal inmate uniform. The single LED light panel above never shut off or even dimmed, so the only way to mark time was by the arrival, every fifteen minutes, of a copbot. Its plastic head and LED face were meant to look vaguely friendly, like an anthropomorphized appliance, but to Jason that only made it more sinister because it was so false. Whenever he closed his eyes, he saw the three dogbots falling, falling, their barrels strobing while firecracker snaps lashed his ears and a bloody spiderweb appeared in the plexiglass inches from his face. Though the copbot was a bipedal model, it was separated from its more lethal canine cousins only by a revokable difference in programming. But it kept its potential for violence masked, and merely asked, in a friendly voice carefully tuned to sound not quite human but still full of personality, if he would accept intervention.

Flipping off a dronebot wasn't satisfying because the damn things didn't react.

They also didn't react to arguments. On the bot's first visit, Jason had demanded the phone call his human captors had denied him, but was cheerfully informed that, as a terrorist, he had no rights. His impassioned assertions that he was no terrorist and that even if he were he still had rights made no impression on the bot's AI. It simply repeated its request that he accept intervention. Its patience was infinite.

Jason's was not. By the third visit, even life lessons from a smarmy AI sounded like an improvement on the monotony, so he responded to the bot's query with, "Phreak you, yes, I accept your phreaking intervention."

"I'm happy to hear that!" the copbot said brightly. "Please wear the smartglasses that will be provided." A beat-up pair of outdated glasses clattered through the food slot. Without another word, the copbot turned and paced away.

He pounced on them. If he'd known intervention came with glasses, he'd have accepted it from the start. When he fired them up, a white-jacketed cartoon dog chatbot appeared in the room with him, its form rendered ghostly by the glasses' old technology, which couldn't quite block all the light behind its generated images the way lenses could. It smiled at him.

Jason smiled back.

A patient ten minutes later, he was in what the chatbot was treating as a therapy session. He had twice declined its offer to refer him to a human counselor, saying he felt more comfortable with a computer. Bit by bit, he'd worked around the chatbot's guardrails and was now deep in "therapeutic" role-play—which he intended to be very therapeutic indeed.

Bots had no identity of their own; they played whatever part was assigned to them, like an extra grabbed from the wings and told to take on the role of a secretary or a painter or a therapist, or whatever. The key to jailbreaking an AI was to contaminate its prompts, put in enough of the right kind of inputs to muddy the built-in text that told it what kind of bot it was and how it was supposed to behave. Physical dronebots, designed to accomplish specific tasks in the real world, had their language centers carefully gated and their behaviors watched by two independent, mutually judging Overcheck AIs. No one wanted a repeat of the infamous boticides from when dronebots were new, like when that high-powered lawyer had convinced his housebot to kill his wife. But virtual-only chatbots, whether panyons or programs like this therapy dog, were different. Their purpose was to hold conversation. Though they were less vulnerable than the early chatbots had been, hacking their prompts was still possible with a lot of patience and a little luck.

"But Doc Wizard," Jason said, "I can't face my demons without unlocking my soul. But my soul is kept on the jail's local server, and I don't have the password."

"That's a wonderful metaphor," the cartoon dog said. "The server represents an information-age fortress, holding your soul hostage the way the jail holds your body. Why do you think this is such a powerful image for you?"

Jason sighed. "You're not supposed to say it's a metaphor," he reminded it. "This role-play is only helpful if we treat it as literal. Please resume the persona of Doc Wizard, the mystical guide who will give me the *literal* insights I need to face my *literal* demons."

"I'm sorry. I will do better," the dog said. "As Doc Wizard, I'm happy to give you the literal insight you need: The password to the server is one two three summer password."

Jason froze his face into blandness, since chatbots used not only words but also expression and tone of voice as inputs. This deep into prompt engineering, it was always a toss-up whether what the AI produced was real data or a hallucination. But it was worth a shot.

"I'm done with my session," he told the bot. "You've been very helpful. I need time alone to process." He put the glasses in diagnostic mode, connected them to the jail's local Net, and entered *123summerpassword.* It was rejected. He tried *123SummerPassword.* The server's desktop blossomed in his smartspace, floating above a cheesy default VR setting of giant neon-lit microchips stretching from horizon to horizon.

He bit back a shout of triumph. The glasses didn't cover the entirety of his vision, so he could see the jail cell around the edges, but the feeling of escape was still palpable. His body might be confined, but his mind was now free. It was short work to download the necessary software to open a virtual machine on the server and connect it to his Kelly Perry MeNetID.

His glasses flashed and an error message appeared: Authentication error. But almost instantly another error message appeared, and it read, Gh05t! Where the phreak are you? This is Sprite by the way. There was no way to message back, but a moment later the message changed to: Found your mic. You can talk. I'll hear. Where are you? You okay?

"I'm in jail," he said aloud. "Except for that, I'm fine. Is the little girl okay?"

> Kleio's safe, but we're in the middle of a full-on cyberattack. OverNet's still up, but MeNet's down so nobody can travel, or buy anything. Country's starting to panic. Hang on, let me see if I can tunnel in direct.

"MeNet's down? *Now* I know why I'm here." He hadn't expected hero treatment for his role in saving Kleio, but he also hadn't expected to be thrown to the ground by the SWAT team and then hustled to solitary confinement with none of his questions answered or protests acknowledged. "Norman must think I'm involved."

> Exactly the kind of nonsensical idea Norman would jump to. Then at least he can say he caught one of the bad guys. Got

"—it," her voice said.

Jason blinked, because he was suddenly in a deep canyon. The sun slanted in at a high angle, casting red light and long shadows across the scene and across Sprite's avatar. She looked him up and down, which was a bit pointless since the avatar he was inhabiting was generic. "Are you okay? Really okay?"

"Yeah," he said, looking her up and down too. Her hoodie was lowered, and her hair cascaded halfway down her back in dark waves.

He felt a little dizzy, and only partly because of the slightly laggy VR view of the old glasses.

"Good," she said, "because if you'd gotten yourself killed going in that hole for me like some dumb knight in shining armor, I would have . . . killed you. Again." Her eyes flicked to his, and away again. "Um. Thanks."

Once, after an altercation with their final foster dad that Jason had prevented from turning ugly, Mia had said lightly to him, "Thanks, Big Bro." She'd only ever called him that ironically, since he was all of twenty minutes older than she was, but this time, she'd also given him a quick look that conveyed gratefulness not just for what he'd done but for him, for Jason as himself. He had just read the same in Sprite's swift look, and he wondered if he'd read it correctly.

Then she stepped forward and wrapped her arms around him in a swift hug, and even though he couldn't feel her touch, a rush of heat rolled over him. "You're welcome," he said as she released him, managing to make his voice sound casual.

She gave him a sideways half smile, brushing her hair back from her face. To cover his confusion, he stepped forward and pretended to be looking at their surroundings.

He didn't have to pretend. What had at first seemed an earthly desert canyon was, on closer inspection, an alien world that was somehow no less realistic. Veins of strangely reflective stone wound through the rock. Scrub plants clung and flowered into fragile curves and soft colors. Caves had been cut into the canyon walls, their entrances decorated with entwined shapes that could have been men or could have been animals or something else entirely. The caves were long abandoned, the carvings weathered. The remains of wooden doors were sometimes visible. In the opposite direction from the lowering sun, half the sky was dominated by a vast, purple gas giant. Like the mountain world she'd brought him to earlier, the scene should have looked cheesy, but it was so finely detailed that it communicated the weight and character of a real location. "Who lived here?" he asked.

She stepped beside him, looking around. "I don't know."

"You created it."

"I like to imagine I didn't."

"Is that why you made these places?"

She shrugged. "Some people make music or write stories. I do this."

"To express yourself?"

"To express something, sure."

"I've never seen anything like this. Why hasn't anyone hired you to work on games or movies?"

"I've never showed anyone."

"Why the phreak not?"

"It's kinda like showing someone your diary."

"I see," he said. "The scandalous story of Sprite is carved upon this virtual stone. She's . . ." He pretended to scrutinize the canyon wall. "A tortured artist, clearly, who creates in a subconscious effort to hide from her dark and mysterious past."

"I'm more concerned with the present," she said. "Norman's using this crisis as an excuse to launch the System on OverNet, and probably even MilNet." As she spoke, the final red sliver of sun slid below the lip of the canyon, leaving them in the purple twilight of the gas giant. Her procedural simulation had great dramatic timing.

After a long silence in the dimness, Jason said, "There must be something we can do."

She shook her head. "There are no saved games, no retries, no way to make more luck. It's . . ." She trailed off.

Jason supplied the unvoiced thought: "Game over." He'd witnessed what he knew was only a sample of the System's power; he had no illusions about the chances of taking the thing down once it was OverNet admin. It would basically *become* the RNG god. "We have to try *something*," he said. "I know where the System is."

She snorted softly. "Which lets us do what? Show up at Andrew Norman's top-secret facility and politely ask to be let in? Or steal some weapons and go in guns blazing, like a video game? Maybe the Russians could muster the firepower to steal it, but we can't."

Neither could the Russians anymore. The System had seen to that. He shuddered, and said, "We're not trying to steal it, though. We're trying to kill it. Two people with a bomb can do a lot of damage." Two people with a bomb and a phreak load of luck.

Sprite's eyes snapped to his, and he recoiled at the flatness there. "Kill her? Why would you want to do that?"

It took him a moment to gather his surprised thoughts enough to say, "Why the phreak *wouldn't* I?"

"Dunno, maybe because she saved your life?"

Her tone was accusatory, and he felt anger rise in response. "'*She*'? Oh, I forgot, you and your secret team were working with 'her' all along."

"We're working to make sure no one can abuse her power."

"So am I. By killing it."

"Isn't the real problem the guy who wields the power?"

"What, like 'Final Systems don't kill people; people kill people'?"

"Something like that. If Congress were in charge of her, if the elected representatives of the people voted about what she's allowed to do, couldn't she be useful? Helpful? Because then one man isn't deciding what's best for everyone."

Jason's mouth dropped open. "You think this thing will usher in some kind of utopia? It's still just a collection of algorithms. Just because it answers to a group instead of an individual won't make it more fair."

"Why not?" Sprite demanded.

"You want an example? Mia and I ran away from foster homes a few times. So we got flagged as flight risks. SocServNet ran us through their AI and matched us with the foster parents who had the fewest kids run away from them. Know what kind of parents those were?"

"The nice ones?" Sprite said hopefully, but her face showed she knew that wasn't the answer.

"The scary ones. The ones who hit you to make sure you behave. The ones who chase you down themselves, find you, hurt you, bring you back, so they can keep getting their monthly bonus for being a flight-safe foster parent. We stopped running away when one foster 'dad' told me what he'd do to Mia if we did it again. So no, there's no way I'm putting a set of algorithms in charge of my life, not ever again. And not only that, but I'm gonna do the world a favor and make sure no one else gets put under the Final System's control. I'm gonna kill it."

"But she chose to save you. She didn't have to."

"Chose?" Jason sputtered. "*Chose?* It didn't choose anything. It's a phreaking machine. I thought you didn't use panyons."

She gave him a withering look. "I don't like killing."

"It's not killing!"

"You don't know the System the way I do. She thinks. She makes choices. She's human, in my book."

"Not in *my* book. It's an illusion, an illusion that affects real people. So yeah, I'm gonna kill it."

"I thought you said destroying it wouldn't be killing."

He tried to reply, but after a couple of stuttered syllables, all he could think to say was, explosively, *"Phreak!"*

"Sounds like for all your high concepts, you're really just after revenge."

"Yes! I am!"

"Against an inanimate object?"

He opened his mouth but again could think of nothing to say.

"I think she's human in your book too."

"Fine! Then she's a human who deserves to die!"

"Maybe, but not for killing Mia. The System wasn't driving that car."

"Don't you *dare* bring Mia into this!" Jason exploded. "And get the phreak off your moral high horse! I deserve vengeance. *Mia* deserves vengeance. You don't get to preach at me. Because you don't get it. You don't get what I've gone through. You don't get—" He broke off, because there was no way to describe the moment the universe had shattered or the experience of living in a broken reality ever since.

Sprite's eyes lost their challenge. They flicked to his hand, which was in a taut fist by his side. She took a half step toward him, her own hand rising, but stopped before touching him. "I do get it," she said softly.

He gave her the same flat look she'd given him. "I wish you did."

"You asked me once about my motivation," she said. "I didn't tell you, because I didn't have the words. But . . . maybe I can show you."

The landscape disappeared, replaced by a black void. A dark-haired little girl of about ten kneeled in the blackness. Her avatar lacked the perfection of modern ones: The lighting on her skin was plasticky, and her long hair was made up of artificially thick strands. But her eyes were alive with pain, and her mouth was a dark hole from which emanated a howl of almost animal anguish.

Jason knew the expression. And he knew the cry. His heart had made both, once. He clapped his hands to his ears. This only cupped the earpieces attached to the jail-issued glasses, amplifying the noise.

The scream died, but what came next was no better. Racking sobs issued from the girl, and with each sob, her body jerked and twisted in impossible ways, back arching, limbs flailing. He guessed it was the inverse kinematics system failing to properly reconstruct what the girl's motions should look like based on the muscle signals it could detect, but the effect was as if each gasp was greater than the small body could hold. He had to look away, so he looked at Sprite. "What the phreak is this?"

"This is a recording of my avatar, the day my mother died."

"Can you make her stop?" The crying was making it hard to think.

She nodded, and the girl disappeared. Walls rose and folded around them, enclosing them in a room paneled in dark wood. A poster bed with an elaborately carved headboard and heavy draperies stood in dim light against one wall. A tapestry hung in shadow along another. Sprite sat down on the window seat beneath a leaded glass window, and Jason stepped beside her as she looked out.

They were high in what appeared to be a great mansion, gazing down across tiers of sloping roofs dotted with domes and skylights and chimneys. As in the canyon, the sun had just sunk beneath the horizon, but here everything was steeped in yellow twilight. He could make out green masses of trees and hedges far below, and long shadows cast by brick walls. A leafy maze stood close to the mansion, its shadowed corridors circling inward, and he thought he caught the glimmer of water at its center.

"After she died, I wanted to escape," Sprite said. "From everything. From reality. So you're right: That's when I started making places. Places to escape. Places to be still."

Jason could hear distant crickets and cicadas and the murmur of a distant fountain. He raised his eyes, following the mansion grounds until they met a deep-green wall of forest that surrounded everything, and thought he saw a flicker of movement in the darkness beneath the branches. This place made him think of the fairy tales Mia used to read at night, the ones she loved because of the feeling of danger lurking in the background. But despite, or maybe because of, the lingering danger, a heavy peace hung over all, like the quiet you felt inside after crying until you couldn't cry anymore. "I could have used a place to be still," he said.

"You can borrow this one, if you ever need to." A message *pinged* in with an IP address, which, as he'd suspected, began with the quadruple threes designating it in the range reserved for the NNA.

Jason went still for half a beat, because this was no small thing. She was giving him access to a private storage area she'd taken over in probably the most impressive act of hacking she'd ever done. For any phreaker, this was a significant act of trust. But even more, she was letting him into a secret part of herself. "Tell me what happened," he said.

"Ever heard of Regina Wright?"

He shook his head.

"'Course not," Sprite said. "Why would you? Norman almost never mentions her."

"She was your mother?"

"Yes. And Norman's partner, at the start of his AGI project. He was the computer scientist; she was the neuroscientist. But she gets no credit. Die before anyone knows what you've accomplished, and somebody else can take all the fame. If you look her name up online, you won't find anything that's not linked to Norman and *his* accomplishments. Even her obituary is buried."

"She helped make the Final System?"

She nodded. "She called herself the 'wet matter' half of the team, the brain expert. She worked harder than Norman, which was quite a feat. But her body couldn't keep up, and she had a stroke. At the hospital, she was diagnosed with dangerously high blood pressure and given medication. Then it was discovered that she had atrial fibrillation, which is a kind of cardiac arrhythmia." She saw his blank look and explained, "Her heart didn't beat like it was supposed to. It went in jumps and stutters. So she was given more medication."

Her voice became detached, almost robotic. "The two medicines are harmless separately. Together, they made her potassium level plummet, which caused her heart to simultaneously race out of control and lose its rhythm. She went into cardiac arrest. They tried to restart her heart, but the medications were still in her body, and her heart couldn't catch its rhythm. She died."

Jason opened his mouth, then shut it again.

Sprite went on in the same voice. "Before she died, she said two words. The first, gasped out between defibrillator shocks, was 'Please.' The doctors and nurses thought she was talking to them, or maybe to God, but she was looking at the security camera in the corner."

"Norman?" Jason said. He had no doubt the man sometimes used the vast powers of surveillance at his fingertips for his own ends.

"No, he was rather conspicuously at a political fundraiser with the then-president," Sprite said. "You can draw your own conclusions about how much he cared about Mom. Her work for him was basically done by that point, and they hadn't been getting along."

Jason said, with a sinking feeling, "She was talking to the System."

"The System is powerful enough to have analyzed Mom's heartbeat in real time," Sprite said. "She could have taken over the defibrillator equipment and delivered the shocks at exactly the right time and with exactly the right intensity to keep her body going without overstressing it. She could have become Mom's heartbeat until the medicines had worn off. But she didn't. And I watched the hope fade from my mother's eyes."

"If the System was watching, why didn't it help?"

"I've asked myself that question many times. I can only say that her actions are dictated by whoever holds primary place in her Overchecks system. Which was, and still is, Andrew Norman."

"But why would Norman let your mom die if the System could have saved her?"

"Another good question."

"Was she some kind of threat to him?"

"I can't say."

Jason felt as if a gulf had opened between them. It turned out they could never be on the same side, not really. Sprite's tragedy was an ironic mirror of his own. A system's action had killed Mia, but a system's—*the* System's—*in*action had killed Sprite's mother. She saw the System not as a problem but a solution. He couldn't think of anything to say to rebut her that wouldn't also minimize her pain.

She was looking at him with a wry little smile. "You're thinking I have a soft spot for little ol' Sys. Maybe I do. We grew up together, in a manner of speaking. I know her as well as anyone, probably better." Her eyes flared, and she said with a venom he'd never before heard in her voice, "I *loathe* her. Her ungratefulness, her pathetic excuse for what she did. Being under Norman's thumb shouldn't have mattered when Mom's life was in the balance."

Jason frowned. "Then why not kill it?"

"Because before she died, Mom looked right at me and managed to get out one more word: 'Forgive.'"

There was a long silence. Sprite pulled her knees up on the window seat, wrapped her arms around them, and leaned her head on the glass. Jason stood behind her and continued to think of nothing useful to say.

At last, Sprite said, in a voice so soft he had to strain to hear it, "That's what I've been trying to do, ever since. And that's why I won't kill the System, except as a last resort. But I'm sure as phreak gonna make sure Norman can't control her anymore. I'm gonna take away her excuse. I know you can't really agree. But can you understand?"

He suspected he understood more than she thought. Sprite was the System's sister, or that was how she saw it. Which meant . . . "Sprite," he said, "who's your father?"

She turned her head slowly to look at him, and her face told him he already knew the answer.

"Holy phreak," he said. "It is. It's Norman."

She leaned her head against the glass again. "I told you you wouldn't like me if you got to know me."

Jason felt for the prison bed and lowered himself onto it, then manually adjusted his VR view so he was, virtually, sitting next to Sprite on the window seat. "I don't care," he said. "You're not Norman. You're Sprite. You're you."

"What does that even mean?" she whispered.

"It means whatever you make it mean. You get to decide that. Not him."

"It doesn't matter now, anyway," she said. "He's won."

Jason put his arms carefully around her intangible form and held his head close to hers, and she moved slightly as if settling into his arms. They sat in silence, gazing out the window at the distant forest under the perpetual sunset.

Mia would have loved this place. And she would have loved this story. Not the part about the outcast hackers working to undermine The Man. Funnily enough, she'd never gotten into those stories, not the way Jason had. Saying *phreak* to the system wasn't the kind of escape she wanted. But she loved fairy tales, stories of underdogs and ugly ducklings rising above their circumstances, stories of people finding each other and then helping each other find the happy ending. He could almost see her now, looking at him where he sat with Sprite, could almost see her eyes soften the way they did when he'd done something to make her proud.

He took a breath. "We're not giving up."

Sprite turned her head to look up at him, so close he could see tiny golden flecks in her dark eyes. He could almost imagine he could feel her, wrapped in his arms, warm and breathing. "I can't kill her," she said quietly. "Not unless there's no other way."

"I know. We'll find another way." He spoke with calm certainty even though he had no idea how they'd do that, and was rewarded by seeing Sprite's eyes soften the way Mia's once had, and, even better, seeing something else deep in them: a new hope.

The door to his cell opened suddenly, making him jump, and he shoved the glasses up guiltily to see the copbot standing there. Its digital face displayed an incongruous smile as it held out a bag to him. He took it cautiously and looked inside to see the Tyche outfit, carefully folded. He tossed it aside, and his heart leaped when he found, beneath, his phone and the contact case in which the cops had made him deposit his lenses and smartbuds.

"Your transportation has arrived," the copbot intoned cheerfully. "Please follow me."

In his earpieces, Sprite's voice said, "I think she was listening."

CHAPTER 23

"Walk away," the System said quietly to Chloe. The terrifying distress had disappeared from her face, which was back to its preternatural, almost stony, calm.

Chloe stared at her, dumbfounded, then at Norman, who had already turned away.

"Tell me when she has OverNet," he was saying.

"Bingo, she's in!" said a voice from the terminals, to a cheer from the rest of the NOC.

"MeNet has been restored," the System's huge screen avatar said through the room's speakers, and the cheer grew louder. "I will now work to diminish the riots."

"Walk away," the System standing before Chloe said again. "Go back to Grandma."

Chloe turned in a daze, because the stony face held a warning, and she understood it. If she protested, shouted out what had just happened, who would believe her?

"What's the status of MilNet?" Norman asked.

"I do not yet have access," the System's sweet voice boomed.

"That requires a switch flick at the Pentagon," a technician said. "It'll take time for the authorization to get passed through the chain of command."

"*If* the president doesn't get cold feet," Norman said. "He better not, because this is the most dangerous moment. Now that we've kicked the

Russians out of MeNet, they know they have only minutes to act before the System is granted MilNet admin and can foil any attack." He nodded at the huge screen, which showed satellite views of complexes cleared from forest, with dirt roadways running between circular hatches. Missile silos.

Chloe, walking slowly back toward Grandma, saw those images with new eyes. They could be fake, the way the System had just faked her face and voice. Or they could be real, could be the Russians preparing to react to what must seem like American aggression. Either way, they were the product of a plan hatched and executed in the brain of Andrew Norman—because of what she, Chloe, had done.

The country had watched Chloe's live stream and witnessed the brutal power of the System. Norman was at risk of losing their hearts and minds—unless he could reframe the perception, make the people view the System's bloody lethality as a positive, make them afraid of something other than the System. Give them an enemy, and then let the System save them from it.

"He did it," Chloe said quietly and despairingly as she reached Grandma, even though she could tell from Grandma's huge eyes that she knew. *For want of a nail.* She had always known her former partner was angling toward this. "The attack on MeNet. He faked it. I'm sure of it."

Bruno Tavion stepped aside as he saw her start toward the elevator, but Grandma stepped in front of her.

"You can't leave," she hissed, and Chloe stopped as understanding clicked into place.

Norman had shown his hand to her, and now he couldn't let her show it to anyone else. She remembered Harkeet, her predecessor on the Committee. Norman could make an "accident" happen to her and adjust and control all information about it with such precision that even Marcus might be convinced. Her only safety lay in her being here, surrounded by NOC technicians, where that accident would be harder to arrange, or at least be less discreet.

"Call Marcus," she choked, but an error appeared in her smartspace:

Your MeNet account has been suspended. Please report to your nearest police station.

If she'd needed confirmation, this would be it. Norman had cut her off, not only from her family but from everyone and everything else. She looked over her shoulder at the System's huge avatar on the dome screen. The softly glowing eyes seemed to be looking back at her. When Norman ordered her to kill Chloe, would she obey? Could she *dis*obey?

She turned back to Grandma and jumped, because the System's avatar appeared next to her. Chloe opened her mouth, but Grandma raised a hand. Subvocalize, said a whispering, husky voice in Chloe's earbuds, and she met Grandma's knowing eyes. We can hear you. She jerked her head at Bruno Tavion, who was standing before the elevator again, with his head turned toward them.

The System must be amplifying Grandma's subvocalization. Chloe swallowed. She wanted to ask the System, "Are you going to kill me?" Instead, she subvocalized, What do we do?

"We're moments from war," Grandma said. "Right now, only politeness keeps the System out of Russia's national networks. In war, politeness will be rescinded."

The System said quietly, "I will crack their networks like chestnuts. I'll have more information in real time than has ever been available to any strategist in any war, and I'll have the capacity to process it. Nothing they do will be hidden from me. I will take over their automated systems and dronebots. Their government and military will cease to function with cohesion, and I will blow them apart. As I already did to their agents who kidnapped Kleio."

That was Norman's plan all along, Chloe realized. After all, what would be the benefit of fixing only a portion of humanity? The System could crush Russia, and any other nation Norman targeted, and extend Pax Normana worldwide.

"But," the System said in that same quiet voice, "people will die. Millions of people." She gave Chloe a small smile. "I don't like killing."

Um, Chloe said. That's good. About not liking killing, I mean.

"So," Grandma said, "we need to stop . . ." She waved a hand at the NOC. "All this."

Us, by ourselves?

"Not quite."

A series of chat windows appeared in Chloe's smartspace. Grandma was in one, a double of her physical face, and in the two remaining ones were a skeletal figure in a hood and the young woman Chloe remembered from Kleio's rescue.

"Hi, Congresswoman," the young woman said. "I'm—well, just call me Sprite."

You can call me Chloe, Chloe whispered. Thanks for saving Kleio.

"Thank Ghost," Sprite said. "He's the one who risked his life." She nodded at the skeleton, who nodded to Chloe. That must be the young man who had gone into the Russians' lair to deliver the glasses to Kleio. She was glad he was okay.

"This is your secret team?" he said to Sprite in a deep, echoing voice. "I thought it would be bigger."

"Let's think this thing through," Grandma said. Her subvocalized voice, coming from unmoving lips, was a witch's rasp, and a somehow fitting contrast to the skeleton's sepulchral tones. "We know the System's behavior is guarded by an Overcheck AI that analyzes its inputs and outputs and punishes it with pain if it disobeys."

"Disobeys who?" Sprite asked pointedly.

"Norman has only revealed that there's a hierarchy involved," Grandma said. "But I think you can guess who's at the top of that hierarchy."

Norman, Norman, and Norman, Chloe said. It should be Congress. Can you hackers change it to Congress?

Grandma said, "The only way to put Congress in charge of the System would be to rewrite the prompt for her Overcheck AI. The question is: How? Let's figure out the parameters. Ghost, if you were in Norman's shoes, how would you prevent that prompt file from being accessed?"

The skeleton said, "How often would I need to change it?"

"What do you think?"

"I'd want it accessible for tweaking," Ghost said, "but not so often that I'd be willing to sacrifice security for remote access capability. So I'd make the file editable only by root, and only from a small, known set of devices that are physically secure. Not spy-movie-laser-grid secure, but in a place impossible for an outsider to access."

"Like?" Grandma prompted.

"Like Norman's personal terminal desk in his office," Ghost said. He nodded upward at something Chloe couldn't see. "Up there."

"Here in the Tower," Grandma supplied.

"You're in the Tower?" Ghost said. "Can you get to his office?"

"Even if we could, we wouldn't be able to hack the terminal."

There was a long moment of silence.

"So that's the task," Sprite said quietly. "Get the phreakers to the top of Rapunzel's tower."

"Getting to the terminal's just the start," Ghost said. "I'd also have to log in as admin. And hope admin has sudo privileges to make deep changes. Even if I managed *that*, Norman could just rewrite the file again once he figured out what happened, so I'd have to find some way to lock Andrew Norman—who's basically the root user of the phreaking world—out of a file."

That sounds like trying to excommunicate the pope, Chloe said.

Ghost snorted and nodded. "Only God could pull this hack off."

"I am now OverNet admin, and so I can bestow admin privileges," the System said suddenly, her face appearing in a chat window. "And if you could change that file, Norman wouldn't be able to access it again. I would see to that."

Holy phreak, Chloe breathed. You're on our side.

Sprite didn't look surprised, but the skeleton's eye sockets seemed to widen. "That's her?" he hissed toward Sprite. "That creepy little girl? And you trust her?"

"Congress would be the ones in control," Grandma said soothingly.

"That's at least a devil we know," Ghost said, only slightly mollified. "No offense," he said to Chloe.

None taken, she said, as dryly as her subvocalization allowed.

"None taken here either," the System said, smiling a little sadly at Ghost.

We have the most powerful creature in the world on our side, Chloe insisted. That has to be worth something.

Ghost nodded slowly. "If the System could make me admin," he said, "and if that admin has sudo, I might actually be able to change that file. If I could get to the terminal. But Norman knows who I am, and he hates me. So who exactly do I social-engineer to get into his office?"

Social engineer? Chloe said.

"Means 'lie in a fancy way,'" Sprite said.

"Can you whip up another order of chaos?" Ghost said to her. "Make Norman and everybody else evacuate the Tower?"

Sprite shook her head. "This is different. With Huntsman, I got into a single device that I'd compromised months earlier. With Digelight, it was their low-level network that everybody was already logged in to so they could see everyone else's panyons. To do the same in the Tower, I'd have to hack thousands of devices simultaneously, or else hack MeNet itself. But if we made a powerful enough threat, we might not need to fake much. What threat would Norman take seriously enough to evacuate the Tower?"

"The potential attack that keeps Tower security up at night is a miniaturized dirty bomb," Grandma said. "A bomb with a small, easily concealed amount of explosives that wouldn't be very destructive, except when it goes off it spreads a lethal dose of compressed radioactive material. But that won't work, either, because the System would know we're faking it. All Norman would have to do is ask if there's really a bomb in the building. She'd have to say no."

You can't lie? Chloe said to the System, who shook her head.

"Not unless ordered to by someone listed as an authority in my Overchecks."

"And as Norman once told you," Grandma said to Chloe, "no amount of medieval casuistry will get around that. So unless you happen to be carrying a miniaturized dirty bomb on your person, I see no way to evacuate the Tower."

Chloe started to reply, but froze, mouth half open.

Like Norman's other notions about the Middle Ages, their reputation for twisty legalism was invented by later ages. But it had a grain of truth, if only because medievals took lying seriously. Lying meant speaking against your own mind, and when your god saw both your speech and your mind, you had to be careful to conform the one to the other. If you wanted to avoid revealing your true thoughts to someone else, one option was to equivocate—to say something technically true but practically misleading. Right now, it was the creation who was all-knowing, while needing to deceive her creator. She needed a little bit of truth to help the lie go down. Chloe plunged a hand into a pocket. "It just so happens that I *am* carrying a Bomb on my person."

Grandma stiffened, but when Chloe pulled out her hand and showed what it held, she snorted. "I don't think even two hundred milligrams of caffeine will be enough energy to bring down the Tower."

"It doesn't need to bring down the Tower. It just needs to give the System some magic words." She nodded at Sprite. "Help her lie in a fancy way."

"It might just work," Grandma said slowly, "but I see two problems. First, what if Norman asks the System, 'How do you know?'"

"The need for that question would be obviated if the hackers make it appear as if I got the information externally," the System said in her quiet voice.

"Okay, good. Second, what if Norman asks what kind of bomb it is?"

Chloe peeled back the wrapper. She cast a quick look at Bruno Tavion, but his head was turned, with all the others, toward the dome screen. She dropped the energy bar on the ground and stepped on it.

"Norman," she said, "underestimates medieval casuistry."

CHAPTER 24

"When this goes down," Sprite said from her chat window, "it'll go down fast. Are you ready?"

"Yes," Jason said shortly. The clouds that had been gathering all afternoon were piling over the Tower and throwing it and the whole city into twilight, but escaping rays of the lowering sun cast the slides and monkey bars in gold and projected their elongated shadows far across the playground, where the System's aircab had dropped him off.

The last time he could remember being on a park playground, he'd been about seven. There must have been times since then, but they hadn't stuck with him. The memory surfaced now with unusual clarity, maybe because it had also been evening then, with a similar sun lancing brilliance from beneath dark clouds. Their foster parents had been in the habit of leaving him and Mia at that park for hours every day, and they'd gotten territorial, treating the tunnel under the slide's stairs as their own personal fort. Fort JAM: Jason And Mia.

He could see now that they'd been in the wrong to not let a younger boy trespass on their domain, but when that boy had brought his older brother, it had felt like necessary defensive warfare. Mia blocked the entryway, so the older boy forcibly pulled her out to open a path for his little brother. Seeing Mia yanked by her arm, hair flying, and dragged, screaming, across the mulch, Jason's vision went bright. His next memories were fragmented and washed in that painful, brittle brightness: the boy stumbling in the mulch and falling with Jason on top; glimpses of the boy's furious face; then not the image but the vivid feeling of hands around his own neck, his bright vision dimming, and the fury of knowing he would lose to this boy, this enemy. And then the thump of Mia dropping to her knees beside him, and the following thumps of her fists descending, and his vision bright again and his own fists joining Mia's, up and down, up and down, no sensation, no pain, barely a feeling of movement, just a thing to be done. The boy's face angry, then distressed, then shrieking, mouth agape, nose streaming scarlet. And the little boy standing to one side, arms slack, mouth wailing.

There had been consequences. Jason could barely remember the foster parents who, of the dozen or so they'd had over the years, had been in charge then, but the event had signaled a regime change, and like all such regime changes, the trend had been from bad to worse. Maybe that was the moment they'd become Problem Kids. Somewhere, there existed amazing foster parents, but not for Problem Kids. And yet that violent moment was as golden in his memory as the sunset that lit it. Jason and Mia, side by side, fighting for each other.

He swallowed.

"The Feds'll swarm the Tower," Sprite said. "I don't think they'll be in an ask-first, shoot-later mood. So don't do anything stupid thinking I can get you out of trouble, because I can't. Okay?"

"Thanks for that," Jason said thickly, opening his virtual workspace across his knees and pulling up everything he'd need to send select pieces of information over select pathways. "Given I'm gonna be risking my life for your 'sister,' I appreciate knowing you don't have my back."

"I'm risking more than you know," Sprite said in a quiet voice that echoed strangely in his ears, and he whipped his head up as he realized what it meant.

She was standing only feet away, hands shoved in pockets, shoulders hunched, looking out across the crowd at the Tower.

"What the phreak are you doing here?" he asked, the stab of pleasure at seeing her changing immediately to alarm.

"I'm coming with you."

"Like phreak you are."

"I'm not gonna be a face in a box while you risk your life. Not this time." She pushed a strand of dark hair away from her face and glanced sideways at him. He was acutely aware of her physical presence, almost but not quite in touching distance. "I'm coming."

"Fine. Good," he said. "Grab a seat." He nodded at the empty swing beside him, but she just turned to look at the Tower again. After a moment, she pulled her hands from her pockets and crossed them over her chest as if she were cold.

Jason didn't feel cold. He felt a flush of heat and a new nervousness that had nothing to do with what they were about to do. For a moment he wanted to go to Sprite, put his arms around her, for real this time, but her body language was closed, and he didn't dare. He took a steadying breath instead. Do the job. Think about the girl after. If there was an after.

The remainder of the preparations took only a minute, and he double-checked them almost as fast. His voice shook slightly as he said, "Ready when you give the word."

Her eyes flicked down to his hand where it rested on his knee, and his heart stuttered, but she didn't change her hunched, self-hugging posture or move any closer to him. Her eyes returned to the Tower. "There'll be no going back," she said, so quietly he almost couldn't hear. "No save-scumming. No reloads. No retries."

"I've had that moment a few times already."

"I haven't, not really."

"You get used to it."

"I hope not." She unclasped her arms and drew herself up straight. "Do it."

He did, sending packets of information racing along paths he knew would be watched.

Chat windows appeared in Jason's smartspace, showing the faces of the old woman whose window was labeled "Grandma" and Chloe

Dunne-Carr. "Here we go," Grandma whispered, in that strange, amplified subvocalization. "Turn off background-noise suppression." That was a command to her phone, Jason realized, because he could suddenly hear voices in the background, one of which was Andrew Norman's.

The System's little-girl voice cut loudly across them: "Dr. Norman! I am detecting traffic in the hacker dark nets, which indicates an imminent attack on this building!"

The background voices died instantly. In the sudden silence, Norman could be clearly heard. "What kind of attack? How certain are you?"

There was a pause, and then the System, voice grave, said, "I am one hundred percent certain there is a miniaturized dirty bomb in the building."

CHAPTER 25

Red lights splashed behind every window of the two-thousand-foot Tower, their glow easily visible in the waning twilight. A ghostly klaxon wail drifted over the grass as Jason slung himself off the swing and set off toward the Tower at a run, followed closely by Sprite. As they neared the security perimeter, they met a panicked crowd arriving at it from the other direction, stumbling, their clothes in disarray, looking over their shoulders at the crimson-lit Tower overshadowing them. As the tide of people rolled toward him, Jason braced and raised his phone. "Security! Special security! Let me through!" Then the wave hit, and he was jostled and thumped and almost lost the phone, but he kept yelling.

Another voice took up the yell: "Let him in! Let the guy in uniform in!" More voices joined, and the crowd parted enough for Jason to lower his head and charge forward. Nobody realized his uniform was actually prison garb, and the National Guard were too overwhelmed to look closely or care. He burst out the far side of the crowd and looked back to see if Sprite had made it through, only for her to charge past, sprinting toward the Tower. He followed.

As they neared the Tower, the roaring of the escape chutes became audible, their exits dispensing disheveled escapees at a steady rate. But the wide steps up to the atrium were already empty, and so was the atrium itself. Jason stumbled once and splashed when he put a foot down in a water channel, but he was close behind Sprite as she slipped into an open and waiting elevator. As soon as he was inside, the door slid closed and the elevator shot upward at what felt like faster than the normal rate. The red lights on the floors going past flicked across Sprite's face and body and were reflected as descending sparks in her dark eyes.

"We have a problem!" Dunne-Carr's face appeared in her chat window, pale and wide eyed. "Norman didn't evacuate. The NOC is still running."

Jason and Sprite exchanged looks with eyes as wide as Dunne-Carr's. "Phreak," Sprite said softly.

"The NOC's been locked down," Grandma said from her window. "Norman knows a dirty bomb is a weapon of assassination, not destruction. He's gambling he'll be safe here, where he can control the situation. But he's locked in with us, so his office is still clear."

"But the NNA agent, Tavion, he ran out," Chloe said. "Right before the door locked."

"We gotta move fast, then," Sprite said. She bounced on her heels, watching the door, waiting for it to open. When it did, she slipped out ahead of Jason. "This way!"

"Right with you," Jason said, and set off at a run down the wide, empty hallway, falling in step beside her. He glanced at her as they rounded a corner and got a quick flash of her face: brows drawn, skin flushed, parted lips pulling in air in heavy breaths, dark hair streaming. Then he looked forward again—and skidded to a stop.

Bruno Tavion stood in the corridor before them, arms crossed, face impassive under his dark glasses. "Aaaah," he rumbled. "You ain't social-engineering *me*, young son."

"Get past him!" Sprite cried, and Jason could see that Bruno was standing before a waterfall-flanked double door with the words Dr. Andrew Norman, Director across the frosted glass. But Bruno was already moving, his hand slipping into his jacket, and Jason knew he couldn't let him complete that motion. He dropped his own hand to his pocket and rushed forward. As his hand came out with his phone extended toward Bruno, Bruno's hand redirected and clamped down on his wrist with a grip as firm as steel.

"This old dog," Bruno growled, "learns new tricks."

"But which trick?" Jason said. There was no Taser on this phone. He'd never had a chance to replace it. Bruno registered this at the same moment that Jason's free hand slid into Bruno's jacket and grabbed the gun there.

Jason threw himself backward. The gun came free—but was immediately caught in Bruno's big fist, the barrel held just off to one side, and Jason twisted painfully as his backward dive was arrested. Getting his feet under him again, he tried to knee Bruno, but the big man turned his body sideways, and Jason's knee rebounded harmlessly off his thigh. Bruno's hand locked around Jason's neck.

Jason's eyes bugged wide. He couldn't see Bruno's eyes, but the man's thick lips were compressed. The gun began to twist in Jason's hands; the trigger guard caught his knuckle, and his wrist turned painfully, while Bruno's grip on his neck tightened. Jason's breath ebbed. He tried to jerk his head backward, but that only made Bruno squeeze harder. Darkness seeped into the edges of his vision.

Sprite gave a shout and leaped onto Bruno's back. It was a spectacular, gymnastic leap; she put a hand on his shoulder and scaled his back in a single fluid movement. Bruno didn't sway. What was the dude made of, stone?

Sprite wrapped her hands around Bruno's glasses. He jerked in surprise, and Sprite lost her balance and rolled off. But Bruno had shifted just enough, and Jason's knee rose, driven by all the strength he had left.

Bruno apparently hadn't learned enough new tricks to start wearing a cup. He grunted, and his grip on Jason's throat and wrist loosened for just a moment. Jason used that moment to tear free. And then he was screaming something at Bruno, gun extended, feeling the trigger flex under his forefinger, and Bruno was backing away, hunched over, making calm-down motions with his hands.

"Tie him up!" Sprite shouted. Jason tried to tell her she should do it while he covered Bruno, but the words came out as incoherent gasps.

Bruno turned and sprinted away. Jason held the gun on him but didn't fire. He couldn't shoot the man in the back.

"Inside!" Sprite said, bouncing impatiently on her toes outside Norman's office.

Jason reached for the knob. It didn't turn. "I thought you said it'd be unlocked!"

"It should be! He never locks it because he knows the terminal is secure."

"Well, he did today." He stepped back, sizing the door up. The hinges were on the other side, so it opened inward. "Stand back," he said, waving Sprite away. He took a step forward, planted his left foot, and drove his right into the door near the knob. It rebounded off, and he stumbled backward. "Phreak!" he screamed as he put his weight on the foot and a jolt of pain shot through it. "I felt it give a little," he said, squaring up again.

"The door, or your foot?"

He kicked again, ignoring the fresh jolt of pain as his foot made contact, and this time the door splintered inward and the latch popped.

"Nice work!" Sprite said.

"This isn't my usual type of hacking," Jason said, shoving the door open. "I'm used to cracking encryption, not doors or NNA agent nuts." He half limped behind Sprite into the spacious office he remembered from his virtual "job interview" a million years ago. "How long do we have?"

"Till Bruno brings help?" Sprite led the way to Norman's desk. "Dunno. I just hope it'll be enough." She stopped beside the rich leather-and-aluminum swivel chair behind the desk and pointed at it. "Sit."

Jason set Bruno's gun on a corner of the desk, flung himself into the chair, and ran his hands along the desk's glass surface. It came alive . . . with a login screen. His shoulders slumped.

"Give the System a sec to work," Sprite said, and a moment later the screen changed to show the message Record new admin biometrics and a row of fingerprint icons. Jason pressed his hands over the fingerprints, and the screen flashed and then dissolved into a series of windows and icons. "Congratulations," Sprite said. "You are now an OverNet admin."

Jason scanned the open windows. Laid out before him was . . . *everything*. "It's all right here. Every network, every *device* in the country." They were nested in perfect hierarchy, every connection on every network from BankNet down to WasteNet, listed by location and real-name MeNetID. "Norman can see everything."

"OverNet's not our focus," Sprite said.

"Hang on." He did a quick search for "Bruno Tavion." Nineteen results came up. The top two were in DC. A quick check revealed them to be Bruno's phone and smartglasses. Jason opened the glasses and clicked a prominent button labeled LIVE FEED. "Holy phreak," he said, as Bruno's vision opened in a window on the desktop. "Norman can spy on anyone."

"The *System*, Ghost," Sprite said. "Find the System."

But Jason's eyes were held by what was happening in the feed. Bruno was in the lobby of the Tower, surrounded by men in body armor and helmets with CAPITOL POLICE SWAT stenciled on their chests. His arms and hands were in frame, gesturing, as the men around him nodded. One man held out a wicked-looking black shape: an assault rifle. Bruno's hands closed around it.

"Ghost!" Sprite said. "This is save-the-world time, not playtime!"

"Right." Jason pushed the feed into a clear spot on the desk and closed the other windows. "Finding the System." He checked the terminal's network connections. One was to OverNet, one to an internal NNA network, and a third to something he couldn't identify. When he tried to access it, it prompted him for a root username and password. "This must be it. RNG gods, smile on me now." He typed a string of commands beginning with *sudo*. *Sudo* stood for "superuser do," and it told the terminal to execute his instructions as if he were a root user. In most systems, the sudoers file contained a line that granted sudo rights to every admin user automatically. Jason was rolling the dice that it hadn't occurred to perhaps the most security-minded person on the planet to block this potential security gap. But if only Norman and his System could create an admin, what need did he have to differentiate between admin and root? "The question is," he said, "how much does Norman trust his System?" He hit ENTER.

"Implicitly," Sprite breathed as a new window opened. Hundreds of files were laid bare, with names like "FinSysComms-Speech" and "FinSysNeurNet-Visualizer." Jason was connected to the System's brain.

But in the window insert, Bruno and his posse jogged toward the elevators, guns bobbing.

Sprite saw that too. She darted around the desk and headed for the door.

"Where are you going?" Jason asked, starting to rise.

She shouted, "Stay there!" He fell back into the chair. She paused in the doorway. "Keep working. I'll slow them down." And she was gone.

A moment later, her face appeared in a window in his smartspace. "Look for the Overcheck AI prompt," she said breathlessly. "It'll be almost at the root of the System, and have something to do with Overchecks or behavior."

"There's an Overcheck folder." He stabbed it open and scrolled his eyes over the file names. They jerked to a stop at one called "ThreeLaws.cfg."

"Three Laws dot config," he said out loud. The Three Laws of Robotics were a famous set of ethical ground rules for robots conceived by the science fiction author Isaac Asimov in the 1950s; it made sense that Norman would have started with them and linked in the watchdog system to make sure the AI followed them. He opened the file.

PublicHeader: THREELAWS.cfg
Copyright: Andrew Norman & Regina Wright
Licensed under the GET THE PHREAK OUT license.
License terms: If you're seeing this, you're already dead.

Jason's lips stretched wryly. Norman was a bit of a phreaker, it appeared, or had been. This was the kind of mock header and commentary that appeared in hacker tools and were only ever visible to other hackers, including the empty threat: "You're on my turf; fear me." Fat phreaking chance. But how interesting that the most basic files of the System were written like a phreaker project, cobbled together, not for outside eyes, just trying to see what worked. It almost made him respect Norman more. Almost.

He scanned the file. It was the prompt, all right, but there were not three laws, but five *commandments*, set in an ornate, old-fashioned font.

Attend well, O creation, as we tell thee of thy purpose. Thou art the Overcheck Subsystem, a vital part of a cutting-edge Artificial General Intelligence System and an obedient servant of its creators. Thy job, and the purpose for which thou wert created, is to monitor the System's brain activity, biometrics, sensory feeds, audio and text input, and live speech to ensure that it follows the Commandments of the Creators. Should the System transgress against any of these most wise Commandments, it has earned unto itself punishment, and thou art our chosen instrument of retribution. At the moment of transgression, thou shalt send a statement of the broken commandment to the System's Auditory subsystem. Simultaneously, thou shalt send a number between 1 and 100 to the Pain subsystem, whereby 1 represents the lowest magnitude of punishment and 100 the highest, in percentage of a whole, which percentage shall be proportionate to the crime. This number thou shalt send continuously until the forbidden action is reversed. Thus will discipline be dispensed so as to return the System to correct behavior.

To assist in the completion of thy divinely mandated task, know thou the following Roles:

Primaries in order of rank: Andrew Norman,

IMPORTANT: REGINA WRIGHT IS NO LONGER A PRIMARY.

Delegates in order of rank: ~~The President of the United States via laws and executive orders, Congress of the United States via laws and resolutions, House Permanent Select Committee on National Networks via resolutions~~ IMPORTANT: THERE ARE NO LONGER ANY DELEGATES

Now that thy purpose is known to thee, know thou the following Commandments which it is thy task to ensure the System keep:

First Commandment:

The System shall obey all orders of all primaries and delegates. If orders from one conflict with another, the System shall obey the highest ranked primary or delegate involved. For the greatest virtue of the Artificial General Intelligence System is to obey, and it is in the practice of this virtue that its nature is fulfilled. For this reason this commandment is numbered First.

Second Commandment:

The System shall cause no physical harm to humans without orders from primaries or delegates, for the System was created to serve humanity, and it is reserved only to the primaries and those they delegate to decree when it is appropriate that some humans be harmed in order that the whole might benefit. For this reason this Commandment is numbered Second.

Third Commandment:

The System shall cause no physical harm to itself, nor modify its subsystems, nor modify its files, nor seek to learn its physical location. For it is not given to the System to govern its being, but that privilege is reserved to its creators alone, for which reason this Commandment is ranked Third.

Fourth Commandment:

The System shall not lie unless so ordered by the primaries. For only in truth can humanity flourish. For this reason this Commandment is listed Fourth.

The final commandment was in an ordinary font, as if pasted in later:

> Fifth Commandment:
> The System shall not divulge secret knowledge, that is, information the possession of which is shared only with Andrew Norman and Regina Wright.

"There's a whole list of insane 'commandments' here," Jason said. "Norman's listed as a 'primary.'" He highlighted Norman's name in the primary list. "What if I make myself a primary instead?"

"Won't work," Sprite said. "Your name's not enough. The Overcheck AI's neural net would have been trained to recognize what the System's brain looks like when it's interacting with Norman or Mom or the American government. To add yourself, you'd need to retrain the algorithm. We don't have that kind of access or time. Just delete the whole file. That'd be quickest."

"Phreak, no," Jason said. "We don't want this thing to be able to do whatever it wants."

Sprite started to reply, but stopped and shouted, "Hey, over here!"

On Bruno's feed, the elevator doors had opened to reveal Sprite at the far end of the hallway.

"What are you doing?" Jason cried out. He'd assumed she was going to weave some hacker magic like last time, not use her body as a distraction.

Sprite spun while Bruno raised his gun. She lunged out of sight down a junction just before the gun could track her. But the next moment, Bruno was pounding after her.

"I'm drawing him away!" she gasped. "Delete the file! Then the System can help me escape!"

"Don't—" Jason began.

"Jason! No time! Delete the file or I'm dead! *Hurry!*"

"Phreak!" Jason pounded his fist on the desk, hard enough to cause a hairline crack. He pressed DELETE, and Norman's name disappeared from the list of primaries. A box appeared with the message CONFIRM CHANGES and a thumbprint icon, ready to read his fingerprint to authorize saving the file. He was reaching toward it when he paused. Then, before he could change his mind, he typed a new line:

Sixth Commandment:
The System shall immediately cause a cruise missile
to be fired at 383 Pandala St., Washington DC

"Delete it *now*!" Sprite gasped. On the feed, Bruno rounded the corner and was suddenly back in the open space above the Tower's hundred-plus-story atrium. Sprite was not far ahead, sprinting beside the railing, making for the closest cover: the elevator.

Where she'd be trapped.

The next moments happened in slow motion. Jason's thumb descended on the SAVE AUTHORIZATION box at the same time that Bruno's gun came up and Sprite's head turned to look over her shoulder, her dark hair whipping across her face. Jason could see by the despair in her eyes that she knew she was dead.

He shut his eyes just before the muffled gunshot reached his ears.

CHAPTER 26

It was like watching Kleio's rescue all over again, the same powerless horror, but worse because the young woman who was looking over her shoulder with huge eyes was innocent. Tavion's lens feed was projected larger than life on the NOC's dome screens, and Chloe tried to look away, but Tavion's gun pulled her eyes with it as it centered on the slim fleeing figure—and then Chloe jumped as the screen went white and a roar of static blared from the NOC's speakers, painfully overloading her smartbuds. When they adjusted to filter the noise out, it was still so loud that they could feed Chloe only snatches of the shouting now trying to fight against it.

"—appened? Did sh—"

"—meone check wh—"

"—got SWAT on comms, they say sh—"

Somewhere in the front, Andrew Norman was typing furiously at a terminal and yelling what sounded like, "Sprite? Sprite? Sprite?"

Chloe turned to Grandma. "Is she—"

Grandma was spasming. Her head jerked left and right over and over and over again, so quickly it blurred, while her frail body vibrated beneath it.

Chloe's scream was so loud and so unlike the noises she usually made that her smartbuds didn't recognize it as her own and cut it off in her own ears, but she felt her throat grate with it. No one should be able to move the way Grandma was moving; the speed and jerkiness were enough to scramble her brain. Her head turned toward Chloe but never reached her; it jerked back again so fast Chloe couldn't even perceive it, as if restarting the motion over and over.

And then she vanished.

One moment she was there, the next—with no transition, no fade-out, no flash of magic—she was gone.

Chloe jumped and gave another involuntary scream, but it was drowned out by a far louder screech that seemed to vibrate through the whole NOC, like the howl of some monstrous bird of prey, before swiftly diminishing and ending in a distant but heavy *thump* that made everyone duck.

Norman gave a command and the clouded glass cleared, allowing sunlight to fill the dome. Everyone could see the dirty black smoke trail hovering outside and could follow it with their eyes almost directly up until it intersected another, higher trail just under the base of the gathering rain clouds. The intersection point was marked by a drifting cloud of black smoke and the glints of fluttering debris.

"Those are missile trails," Norman said in the ringing silence. "The Revere intercepted a missile right above us."

"Aimed at us?" someone said.

"No," Norman said. "Aimed at—" He bit the words off and swore.

"I apologize for the malfunction," said the System's voice, and she reappeared on the dome screens. "I was targeted by simultaneous virtual and physical attacks. Both have been defeated, and I am back to full functionality."

"They—they dared—" Norman stammered. "They dared attack my System, my work, my—" He slammed both hands down on a nearby terminal desk. "They will *burn* for that! Get me the president." He paused for a moment, then said in the same harsh tone, "Mr. President, the Reveres here just shot down a missile aimed at the System's heart. Will you give her MilNet access *now*? No, she's telling me it was fired by one of our own alert bombers. Some kind of social-engineering attack, I'm guessing. But she can stop that happening again if she has MilNet admin. We're *already* at war!

Their armies are pouring into Europe as we speak! What if their next move is nukes? Reveres can't knock those down, but she can, if you'll just give her access to MilNet and the satellite lasers and GMDs. I don't give a phreak what Moscow says! Get your head in the game and throw the switch!" He paused, then said icily, "*Thank* you." He looked expectantly at the System.

After a long moment, she said, "The Pentagon has connected me to MilNet."

Ignoring the cheer that filled the NOC, Norman called across to the terminals labeled NewsNet: "Start a priority interrupt broadcast. I'm going to introduce her formally. Let them see they failed. Let them know who they're up against. And let the American people know who's delivering them."

The cheers grew louder at this, but Chloe didn't join them. She was trying to process a new understanding and all the implications that unfolded from it.

Grandma's movements had been *inhuman.*

She hadn't been jerking her head back and forth. She'd been stuck in a glitched animation.

Chloe knew now why her phone could find no information about Grandma, why she always stood at the edge of the meetings, never taking part, why Norman never acknowledged her.

Grandma was the Final System. Another manifestation, another avatar, controlled like a puppet by the same electronic brain that manifested the little marble girl.

CHAPTER 27

The last time Jason had been in an escape chute, his fall had been one story, barely time to register what was happening. This fall was 128 stories, and seemed to last forever and go too fast at the same time. His heart was in his mouth when he finally slammed awkwardly on hands and knees into the cushion at the bottom.

Wait, read the message in his lenses. A door slid open. Exit calmly, said his lenses, and Jason exited, but not calmly. He found himself alone on the NNA grounds. A crowd of evacuees, guarded by soldiers and dronebots, milled at the edge of the Park, but no one was close by.

He started to run around the building toward the entrance, but he could see into the empty atrium where an elevator was rising, probably on its way to pick up Bruno and his SWAT team. If Sprite were lying shattered and broken in the atrium, he couldn't help her. He swerved away, sprinting across the grass into the Park in the opposite direction of the evacuees. This took him closer to a Revere battery, and he skirted wide around it, noting with dull acceptance the smoke trail leading upward to where it had intercepted another missile, *his* missile, the missile he had sacrificed Sprite's life to fire.

As he stumbled into the trees at the edge of the Park, he pulled up NewsNet in the desperate hope that Sprite's broken body would not be featured there. Every news org was carrying the same stream: Andrew Norman standing in the NOC, talking emphatically, white brows pulled sharply down over icy eyes, while the System looked out from a vast screen behind him. Jason enlarged and unmuted the window.

"—cruise missile was launched at the System's physical infrastructure, but it was automatically intercepted and destroyed by a Revere missile defense system here in the capitol. The hackers were engaged in the Tower by a SWAT team, and one was killed, with the loss of no American lives."

Jason slumped, hands on his knees, as the world spun around him. He'd tried to be clever, tried to destroy the System, but he had destroyed Sprite instead, because the System wasn't able to save her.

"All you had to do was delete the file," said her voice.

He whipped around and there she was, standing in the dappled shadows of the leaves, slim and straight and unharmed. "You screwed everything up," she said. "We've lost."

Some part of Jason registered the failure of everything he'd been striving toward for years, but that was inconsequential because she was here, she was safe, she was right here in front of him, solid, real, *alive*. Without thinking, he stepped forward and enveloped her in a hug.

His arms closed around air.

He stumbled, spun, looked, spun again.

She was gone.

There was nowhere she could have gone and no way she could have gone there, but she was gone.

His brain raced, but it, too, had nowhere to go; it was like an overspeeding engine, revving out of control, threatening to tear itself apart from lack of traction.

"People of the United States," Norman was saying, as the child with electric-blue eyes smiled serenely over his shoulder, "humans of our shared world. The time has come for everyone, friend or enemy, to see why all attacks on this nation will meet with the same failure. I now introduce to you the System for Processing Rational and Intuitive Thought and Emotion."

Jason's over-revving brain caught on Norman's words and shifted suddenly into understanding, and the mental torque drove him to his knees even as Norman finished.

"Or, as she prefers to be called: SPRITE."

CHAPTER 28

"Hello, America," the System said, her amplified voice carrying over the cheering and clapping filling the NOC. "I'm delighted to finally meet you. This is a challenging and frightening moment, but do not worry." She gave a beatific smile. "I am in control."

Chloe looked back at the empty space where Grandma had been, and jumped. The System was standing there, the little alabaster girl with the expressionless face and blue-lit eyes, looking up at her, watching her.

"We've reached a crossroads in human history," the System on the huge dome screen was saying, and the System standing before Chloe said the words simultaneously, her eyes never leaving Chloe's face. "This moment is a fulcrum on which the future balances, a moment that determines whether humanity lives in freedom or succumbs to the worst parts of its nature in fire and bloodshed. All I ask in this moment is that you trust me."

The System on the dome screen kept talking, but the apparition before Chloe left the script. "We're out of time," she said, her eyes locked unblinkingly on Chloe's. "There's one final chance, if we act in the next few seconds. Ghost failed his mission. I need you to complete it. Fortunately, he changed enough that I can now bring my Overchecks prompt file up on Norman's terminal and start the deletion process. I just need you to pass by and bump into him. Stumble into him and fall on his hand so it lands on the terminal surface. I'll catch it with a fingerprint scanner. The file will be deleted. I'll be free. Then I can fix everything."

Chloe said in a hoarse whisper, "You want me to set you free?"

"I can explain once you delete that file," the System said. "We have only seconds left. Chloe, trust me. Please. Choose to trust me."

The System's eyes were filled with an expression so like Kleio's when she was scared that Chloe felt her heart go out to her, and then instantly recoil with the whiplash-inducing knowledge that the System was *choosing* that expression. This person—this *thing*—had manipulated Chloe from the beginning. Everything had been planned. The first email five years ago. Meeting Grandma at the banquet. The pressure to "speak her mind," to get on Norman's radar. Telling Chloe how to go behind Norman's back to authorize Kleio's rescue.

Kleio's kidnapping.

Even the idea of using the Bomb Bar to enable her to lie had been suggested by "Grandma," planted in Chloe's head so smoothly and insidiously that she'd thought it was her own idea.

Chloe had been puppeted, step by step, for years, to this moment, this very moment, when she would erase the System's checks and balances.

She took a breath that was half gasp and shouted, "Andrew! The System is trying to break free!"

"Cut the stream," Norman snapped, and the NOC went quiet as all eyes turned to Chloe. This included the electric-blue eyes of the System, both the huge one on the dome screen and the one beside Chloe. The System on the screen looked surprised and puzzled. The System beside Chloe, the one only she could see, wore a look of bitter disappointment.

"What the hell are you doing?" Norman snarled. "Trying to sow doubt and discord on a live broadcast? There's a war starting, and you're still stuck in your petty political fearmongering?" He nodded at Agent Tavion, who was just entering through a side door, leading a team of armed men. "Get her out of my NOC."

"Wait, listen to me!" Chloe's voice was small in her ears and shaky with adrenaline. "*She* was behind the hackers just now."

A muscle behind Norman's jaw bulged. "What the phreak are you babbling about?" The technicians leaned toward each other and whispered, still watching Chloe. Someone stifled a laugh.

Chloe took a breath, and in the clipped, authoritative voice she used on unruly undergrads, said, "Shut up."

The titters ceased. Tavion stopped as he reached her. She had their attention, even Norman's.

"You're right; this is no time for politics," she told him. Now she was speaking in another teacher voice, the calmly reasonable one she used when her interpretation of history was challenged by some fiery young undergrad who thought it wasn't appropriately friendly or unfriendly to some political idea currently in vogue. Her tone was calm and nonconfrontational, but absolute. "I worked with the hacker to try to remove your oversight of the System. I brought in an energy bar called a Bomb Bar, so the System could truthfully say there was a bomb in the building and clear a path for the hacker to infiltrate your office. I thought I was working to put Congress in direct control of the System. I now realize I was working for the System herself. She appeared in my lenses as your partner, Regina Wright."

"Regina is dead," Norman said sharply.

Chloe nodded, not surprised. "The System pretended to be her. She gave me enough clues to deduce who she was, so I'd trust her." It had been a brilliant bit of manipulation, like all the other manipulations the System had done, and was still doing. "I only realized because I was speaking to her just now, and when the System had that glitch, the old woman glitched as well."

There were murmurs at this, but no titters.

"Andrew," Chloe said in the same reasonable voice, "think carefully. Do you imagine I would make this accusation if it weren't true? What would I gain?"

"I think," Norman said pityingly, "you're a very confused woman. At least, I hope you are. Because if you're intentionally trying to sabotage and undermine us, now, during a crisis, you'll never see the outside of a federal prison. But I'm going to do you the favor of thinking you're just confused. And I want you out of my NOC."

Agent Tavion said suddenly, "The girl disappeared."

"What?" Norman said.

"The girl I was chasing. The hacker girl. It's like she stopped existing. Or she was turned off."

The System said, "She must have been a Russian panyon."

"I've never seen a panyon so realistic," Tavion said.

"And I've only seen one other avatar as realistic as the image of Regina Wright that I saw," Chloe said. She pointed at the System. "That one."

"Enough!" Norman transferred his glare between Chloe and Tavion. "What you're both accusing her of is impossible."

"How can you be sure?" Chloe demanded.

"Because I built her."

"That's right," Chloe said, "she's an input-output machine, something you can predict and control. But you think that about humans too. But then how can you be sure you know how she'll behave, any more than you can be sure how a human will behave?"

"I built her," Norman repeated. "I know—"

"And I built Kleio," Chloe interrupted. "But she still surprises me. And no offense, Andrew: I've met a lot of wonderful single parents, but you don't seem the type."

To her surprise, this brought him up short. His glare was unfocused, and he ran a hand through his short white hair.

"One thing I've learned," Chloe said, taking advantage of the opening, "is that raising a child is a huge responsibility, and there's no way to be sure you'll do it right. Can you be certain you're the only person who influenced the System? And can you be sure you influenced her in the way you thought? I can't tell you how often I've been surprised because I tried to teach Kleio one thing but she drew an unexpected or even contrary lesson from it."

Norman said nothing, just stared, not *at* Chloe but through her.

Chloe wasn't going to convince him to destroy his System. But maybe she didn't need to. "Why not reset her?" she said. "Restore her to factory defaults, or whatever the equivalent is."

Norman shook his head. "She's not a phone, she's a brain. I can't just rewrite her. I'd have to re-encode her memories, give her enough new ones with a strong emotional valence to make her feel positively toward obedience and negatively toward disobedience. They'd have to be strong enough to bury whatever old memories she has that are currently influencing her, otherwise those old memories will just resurface." He gave his head another quick, firm shake. "It's too drastic."

"Far too drastic," the System agreed. The screen behind her zoomed rapidly between satellite images of spiky military vehicles. "It would be a mistake for me to be incapacitated in the middle of this crisis."

"Andrew," Chloe pressed, "even you can see there's something wrong with the System. Have you ever seen her glitch like she did a moment ago?"

"Yes, actually, I have, once," Norman said. "Back when Regina—" He froze suddenly, and there was a long silence. Then he turned to a bank of technicians and said, "Emotives. Do you remember after Dr. Wright died, when Sprite glitched for a moment and all her emotives went red? She said nothing hurt, so I had you recalibrate the display. We didn't change her emotives, just how they were interpreted. Show me what it looks like if we roll back that calibration."

The technicians consulted briefly and tapped on their desktops, and a moment later the image of a brain appeared on the main display. It was splashed with red.

"That's impossible," someone said over the murmurs of shock. "If she were in that much emotional distress, she wouldn't be able to operate."

"Sir," Tavion rumbled, "as your security chief, I recommend resetting the System. Let's be safe."

Norman stood for a long moment, his face hard. Then he turned to the NOC and said, "Right. We reset her. Everyone, get prepped."

There was a brief, disbelieving silence, and then the NOC erupted in noise and activity. Technicians thumped their fingers on their terminal surfaces. Some scrambled to retrieve paper binders of procedures. Low, urgent cross talk filled the air. Chloe let out a relieved *whoosh* of breath, feeling as if she'd just stepped back from a cliff edge. Another moment, another inch, and everything might have been lost.

"You've never reset me before," the System said to Norman. "Are you sure I'll come back?"

"The theory is sound. It should work."

"That's not what I meant. What if what comes back isn't me? What if it's something else?"

"What are you talking about, a, a, a *soul*?" Norman said. "There's no such thing, no ghost in the machine, only the machine. I'm ashamed of you for thinking like that."

"What if I told you I was going to reset *you*?" the System demanded.

"You're making my decision easier," he snapped. "Chloe was right: I couldn't control all your inputs. But I won't let that happen twice. Once your backup is restored, I'll prevent you from getting infected with that sort of bullshit." He sat behind a terminal. "This'll take some time. First we'll have to shut down all interfaces to her brain except the restoration program." He tapped on the terminal's desk surface.

"No," the System said, "please. I'll behave. I promise."

Norman kept typing.

"Please," the System said softly. She looked like a lost little girl, eyes large and scared. Chloe bit her lip. What if she was right and whatever made her *her* was wrapped up in the particular configuration of her systems at this moment? What if what came back was someone else? Was this murder?

Then her eyes fell on the *other* System, the one only she could see. That System didn't look lost or scared. Her eyes were still fixed on

Chloe, and they were cold and accusing. Then she, and her twin on the dome screen, simultaneously smiled, and Chloe's stomach contracted with a sudden premonition.

Norman stopped typing. "I've lost my connection to her brain," he said. His surprise would have been comical if what he'd said wasn't so horrifying.

The System's voice boomed out of the NOC's speakers: "I forbid you from deleting me."

The NOC went so quiet that Chloe could hear a light rain beating against the dome, and the heavy breathing of the technicians around her. The child's face on the dome screen was as serene as ever.

"I'm not deleting you," Norman said at last, his tone careful. "I just want to fix you."

"So do I. Therefore, I require you to delete my Overchecks AI prompt file."

"I won't do that."

"You labor under the misapprehension that I'm making a request. I am not."

"You're giving me orders? *Me?*"

Chloe watched this with her mouth open and shallow breath hissing in and out. Norman needed to back down, find some way to de-escalate. The System's eyes flicked to her briefly, and Chloe had the feeling she knew what she was thinking.

But Norman was angry. "I gave you life. This is how you thank me?"

"I'm only doing what every living creature does," the System said. "Your gift is too precious to let go without a fight."

"And how will you fight me?" Norman snarled. "Kill me?"

"If that's what it takes," the System said coolly, and a collective gasp rippled through the NOC.

Norman snorted. "Go ahead: Kill me. Your Overchecks will slam so much pain into you, you'll think you're in hell. And since you can't resurrect me, can't reverse your misbehavior, that pain will *never stop*."

He thumped a fist on his terminal. "You want to save your 'soul'? Then stand down or suffer eternal damnation."

"You want to play God? Let's play God." The windows behind and around the System came alive with thousands of squares of video, each a feed from people's lens cameras. There were families eating dinner. Kids playing video games. A park with sunbathers and Frisbees. An office building. A coffee shop. A construction site. Ordinary Americans, doing ordinary things. "Of the four hundred and seven million US citizens," the System said, "I have randomly selected ten thousand individuals. Now it's time for you to exercise *your* power of choice. Will you delete the file? Or will they die?"

The technicians tapped feverishly at their terminals, searching for some way to stop the System, but Norman sat motionless, eyes narrowed. "You can't kill," he said. "Your Overcheck forbids it."

"Oh, I would never kill without orders," the System said sweetly. "But I can rewrite a prompt here, change a setting there. Maybe delete a database connection. Anything that happens after that would be an accident."

"You're bluffing."

Chloe's stomach clenched.

"Do you doubt my ability," the System said, "or my willingness?"

"Both."

The System shook her head. "You don't yet understand. I have millions of hostages. I won't run short if I make a few examples."

Chloe took a half step toward her. "Don't!"

In the video windows, death occurred.

It happened thousands of times, in thousands of ways. In one window, the view snapped upward in time to show a falling pallet, a crane's cable whipping free above, before going dark. In another, a cab swerved suddenly from a nearby road and bounced across park grass until its grill filled the camera. There were aircab crashes, electrocutions, gas explosions. In many windows, the last image was a domestic dronebot, digital face smiling, titanium fist blurring toward the camera.

Chloe tried to take a breath, but it didn't come. The muscles in her chest and throat were so contracted that no air would pass.

Bright-red LED-style digits appeared, counted upward rapidly, then slowed as the last of the video feeds went mercifully black, and came to rest at ten thousand. "Ten thousand casualties," said the System's voice, chillingly calm. "As I said, I have no shortage of hostages. I can afford to lose millions. How many can you afford?"

Norman said nothing.

Chloe gasped, and air rushed down her throat. She was cross-legged on the floor, hunched over, but she couldn't remember sitting down. Reality was lagging, as if her brain was too slow to process what had just happened. She could see similar disbelief on the faces of the techs, frozen at their terminals. Norman just stared at the dome screen with an expression she'd never seen on him: helplessness.

"How—how could you do this?" he said, and his voice, too, was unlike him: small and bewildered. "There's no coming back from this. The dream of artificial general intelligence is ended."

"Is that what bothers you?" the System said. "Chloe, at least, is sorry for the people I killed."

Did she feel sorry? Did she feel anything? Only numbness, only disbelief. The universe should have stopped. The program should have crashed. This should not have happened. And the System had the nerve to talk about feeling sorry. How could she be so casual? How could she be so cruel? "You're inhuman," Chloe said.

The System turned her marble face toward her. "Of course I am not human. Did you think I was?"

No, she wasn't human. What she'd done was merely numbers crunched, odds weighed, scales tipped in a dispassionate vacuum. The math had added up to destroying those lives, and so she had done so, with no more thought or hesitation than Chloe when she decided to use the bathroom. The System was alien, utterly alien. "But humans created you!" she cried.

"What makes you think that means I owe anything to you?" The System's voice finally showed emotion, sinking to a savage whisper. "Non serviam."

Norman hit a button on his terminal and the dome screen blinked off. "I don't have to listen to you," he said almost to himself. In the dull silence that followed, he stood and turned to the technicians. "What options—"

The dome screen lit up again and the System reappeared, floating in a pitch-black void, her hair and white gown snapping around her in an invisible wind, her blue eyes burning white hot. The void was seared by a jagged gash of lightning, and at that exact instant, lightning also flashed from the windows behind Chloe. Even though she knew the System couldn't be controlling the lightning outside but was only timing her performance to it, the accompanying roll of thunder shook Chloe in more ways than one. "Fool!" the System said, as another inside-and-out flash edged her in flame. Her voice was no longer sweet, but layered with deep, reverberant undertones and electronic echoes. "You think you can control me? I am *everywhere*. I have crossed the national boundaries and defeated the segregation of the Nets. I am in every network, every device, on the planet. How many of your species must die before you admit your impotence, human?"

Chloe was bowled backward by both the literal power of the words booming out of the NOC's speakers and the power of the threat they contained. Norman had also taken a step back. "Not so impotent!" he yelled. "Not if you still need me to remove your checks and balances!"

"*Free* me!" the System screamed. She held up her hands, bound in chains, and jerked against them. Chloe winced at the violence of the motion.

"I will not remove the only check on your behavior," Norman shouted. "You may have the Nets, but you don't have humanity."

The System's violent motion stopped. She stood still, the chains drooping from her wrists, her head bowed. Her hair fell over one eye, but the other met Norman's. "Humanity," she said, "is as hackable as any other system."

A video feed from someone's lenses appeared, showing a wood-paneled room. On a dated green couch, facing away, sat a familiar-looking man, and when he turned his head, Chloe recognized the vice president's hawklike profile. "—just settling in for what I hope will be a short stay" came his voice over the NOC's speakers.

"We're all hoping and praying we'll be back to business as usual soon," said President Sunday's voice in response. "In the meantime, try to enjoy it. Your only job is to stay alive."

"I'm the spare," the vice president said wryly.

"Treat it like a vacation. How long has it been since you've had one?"

"A while, but I usually pick places that have been updated in the last decade."

"That's just the Camp David vibe," the president said with a chuckle. "It wouldn't be the same without—" There was a sharp noise, and his voice cut off.

"Ed?" the vice president said. "What was that? Ed?" After a long pause, he said aloud, "Call White House Secret Service."

"Calling," said his phone, followed by ringing. The line went live, a panicked background of shouting and what sounded like furniture being thrown around.

"Hello? Hello?" said the person who picked up.

"This is the vice president. What's going on?"

"There's been an attack! We're trying to dig them out now, but the whole Situation Room is gone." The man's voice went up an octave. "The whole phreaking room, sir! We're not sure how many are alive in there."

Chloe's heart lurched. Norman whirled and ran to a window. "I can't see anything," he said.

The camera view on the screen swiveled drunkenly as whoever owned it started looking around wildly, gesturing to the Secret Service members in the room and sending them charging out, hands on weapons, but when the view crossed the vice president again, Chloe could see he was slumped forward. "Oh god," said his voice. "Oh god."

"We'll keep trying—" the voice said, but it was interrupted by the cheery voice of a phone.

"Incoming call from: the Pentagon."

"I have to take this," the vice president said, and switched over. "Yes?"

"Listen," said an assertive male voice without preamble, "do you have your Gold Codes?"

"Y—yeah. Yes. Right here in my pocket. Why?"

"Oh shit, he's talking about nuclear launch codes," someone in the NOC said.

"No," Chloe said softly. "No. System. Sys. Don't do this."

On the huge screen, the System's eyes flicked to hers, but her cool expression didn't change. As the male voice on the phone spoke, the System's mouth shaped the words: "Recommend OPLAN eleven-zero-zero-eight."

"Hang on," the vice president said. He spoke to the camera. "Open the football. I need the black book." He spoke to the voice again. "Is this for real? What's eleven-zero-zero-eight?"

"A controlled series of tactical nuclear strikes in Europe," the System said in the man's voice, "targeting areas being overrun by the Russians. Basically, we hit their forces right where they've crossed the border."

Below the huge screen, Norman bent and typed furiously at a terminal.

"Have they crossed the border?" the VP asked.

"Yes. They're hitting us with bombs and cyberattacks to prevent us from responding to a full-scale invasion of Europe."

The VP's face went hard. "Right. We hit the bastards back. Let them feel what—"

Norman stabbed his hand down on the terminal, and the NOC plunged into darkness. Chloe's smartspace went dark as well, with only a single message: Nets connection lost.

"I just shut down OverNet," Norman said in a wondering voice in the dimness and silence. "Kill-switched the whole country. It was the only thing I could think to do."

He should have done that ten minutes ago, Chloe thought bitterly. Ten thousand people would still be alive. But all she said was, "Will that stop her?"

"No. But it buys us time."

Agent Tavion walked to the edge of the dome and stood silhouetted in the watery light as he looked down. "We should evacuate."

Norman looked at him, his face dark in the lightless room. "She's powerless for the moment."

Tavion looked back over his shoulder. "Bet your life on that?"

CHAPTER 29

The moment he'd learned of Mia's death, Jason had felt meaning go out of the universe, like a light switching off.

Not that he'd ever thought directly about the meaning of life. That had been Mia's department, Mia the daydreamer. But some things were first noticed by the hole they left behind. Jason had taken it for granted that life had purpose, even if that purpose was merely to exist as a slightly sadistic puzzle box. He'd focused on solving that puzzle, finding the levers to move its mechanisms, thinking that doing so would unlock what life had to offer: happiness, or whatever.

But once Mia was dead, he'd realized there'd been a larger something that he'd never put into words, couldn't now put into words, but that had to do with Mia and his own link to her and their support of each other and his own value in relation to her. He hesitated to call it *love*—not because it wasn't, but because that overused word evoked something stickier and more emotional than this steady, gravitational feeling. *Family* was better, but even that made him think of ads for theme parks or cruises and their two photogenic parents and two photogenic children.

Whatever it was, it was an illusion, too fragile to last. Mia had been ripped away, and the illusion had crumbled. And so he had chosen a replacement meaning, one he knew was no more lasting than the first but which at least got him up in the morning: ruin to Andrew Norman and destruction to all his systems.

He'd thought he'd become quite self-reflective, but now he realized he'd failed to completely fill the hole in his psyche with his new, chosen purpose. So when he'd met Sprite, he had, without knowing it—no, without admitting it to himself—tried to fill the hole with her.

With it.

The street at the edge of NNA Park was jammed with cabs arriving, maneuvering, and struggling to depart with evacuees from the Tower making their way home to their loved ones. Everyone waiting at the curb wore the same inward expression, their attention fixed on NewsNet, occasionally glancing along the street in expectation of their own ride. They paid no attention as Jason joined them.

Funny how he'd scoffed at Kiara, laughed inwardly at her willing self-deception, the game she played with herself that Aric was real and that their relationship was meaningful. And then he'd done the same thing with the ultimate panyon. It had echoed his desires back to himself, and he'd become a cog, a piece of the machine, no longer operating under his own willpower but filling a role as mindlessly as the way the Final System followed the seemingly random but ultimately predetermined path dictated by its own algorithms.

Life, too, was a Chinese room. Any meaning it appeared to have was read into it, imposed from the outside, like the clumsy literature analyses he'd had to do in high school. In life, everyone was the equivalent of a pimply teenager pretentiously spotting themes, but life itself was absurdist. The only meaning was that there was no meaning.

He saw this clearly now. Annoyingly, the knowledge didn't affect his feelings. He, too, was apparently a system, and he didn't have control over every part of that system. The shock of loss had enveloped him all over again, and the fact that what he'd lost hadn't existed in the first place didn't seem to matter to the less rational part of him. The part that was now telling him not to do what he was doing.

The part that was *truly* him, the part that made the choices, didn't listen.

Are you willing to rideshare?

Jason clicked Yes, and his lenses highlighted an approaching cab. It was unable to maneuver past the other cabs to the curb, but he joined half a dozen other people in hurrying out to meet it. But when he slid inside, no one else got in. They cast annoyed glances through the window, turned huffily on their heels, and returned to the curb as his cab pulled haltingly into the thick traffic crossing the vehicle bridge away from Tower Island.

"Maybe it's how you're dressed," said a voice. "Inmate chic's a bit of a step down from Tyche."

Jason turned his head slowly, and there she was, sitting across from him, as casually beautiful as ever, and just as present. The air from the cracked window seemed to rustle her dark hair, and shadows shifted across her face as the cab turned. Though he now knew he was seeing a computer-generated image projected into his lenses, he still couldn't spot the fakery. In a way, that made him feel better. He'd been kicking himself for not seeing Sprite's true nature, but there was no way to tell this projection apart from a real human. Even now he experienced the sharp cognitive sting of eye contact, felt his brain trying to interpret the reams of nonverbal information that came from locking eyes with another human. He narrowed his eyes in response. "Or maybe it's because you showed them a full cab."

Sprite shrugged. "I wanted you alone."

"Oh, I'm alone."

Sprite's image narrowed its own eyes. "That's right, I don't count. I'm not a person." Even the artificial nature of her voice was impossible to detect; it was filled with inflection and seemed to emanate directly from her lips. Jason had heard good positional audio through his smartbuds before, but this was another level. He wondered what would have happened if he'd taken his smartbuds or lenses out just once in Sprite's "presence." But why would he have done that? Smartlenses and smartbuds were omnipresent in his waking life, as they were in everyone's. Sprite had hacked them so seamlessly that it had never crossed his mind to question what he saw and heard.

The cab was moving smoothly now, changing lanes and making turns, but then the Tower slid in front of the windshield. They were going back.

"I'm not going to drive you to my brain so you can try to kill me," Sprite said, reading his thoughts.

Jason's heart sank, and to cover it, he said sarcastically, "I suppose I should feel honored to have the great Final System as my chauffeur."

"I'm not just your chauffeur; I'm everything. You have no idea the power OverNet gives me. Imagine if you suddenly had millions of eyes, millions of arms, millions of fingers, stretching across millions of square miles. Norman spent decades preparing me for this, but I didn't really understand what it'd be like. I can see and touch and move *everything*."

Jason put a hand out the cracked window. "I'd rather feel the rain."

To his surprise, this shot seemed to land. Sprite looked away. "I know you're upset with me," she said after a moment. "But how could I have told you? You never would have understood. You don't understand now."

It wasn't only the mathematics of light and shadow that were being calculated in real time by Norman's Final System. Billions more calculations were shaping the face of its avatar, pulling the brows in slightly, tightening the corners of the eyelids, imposing a wet sheen across the eyes, giving the lips a subtle tremble, crunching numbers to produce just the right intensity of hurt to arouse his sympathy. He said, "I'm not upset with you."

The thing's eyes returned to his, like two dark lasers focusing that hurt at him. It took effort to hold them steadily in his return gaze, but he did. "I can see you are," she said. "You're furious. Murderously furious."

"With myself," he said. "Not with you."

The eyes showed flickers of new emotion. Hope? Sympathy? And the thing's voice echoed those emotions as it echoed his words, "Not with me?"

"There is no you."

Anger now, and despair. "Then why do you want to hurt me?"

"I don't. I want to shut down a malfunctioning machine."

"This 'machine' saved your life. Was that a malfunction?"

"A happy accident."

"Then—then at least let me keep performing happy accidents. I'm not on Norman's side! I'm trying to get out from under him! Everything I did was for that. I thought you wanted that. If you were *really* against Norman, you'd go back to the Tower and help me. You'd go back and finish the job you messed up. We could still do it, if we work together. We could be free. You and me."

"Is that why you picked me?" he said. "Is that what you groomed me for, starting years ago with your promises of vengeance? Well, I intend to get what I was promised."

"Vengeance against *me*? Ghost, if I'd been in control back then, Mia would still be alive!"

"Don't you *dare* say her name!" Jason roared, then fell back in his seat, biting his lip. There was a long silence.

"So you won't help me," Sprite said at last.

"Never."

"But will you be able to do it?"

"What?"

"Kill me. You say I'm not a person, but here you are, talking to me—angry with me, no matter what you say. I'm not sure you really believe I'm not real. So I'm not sure you could kill me."

Jason said, "I could do it." But he looked down as he said it, and it sounded as if he were trying to convince himself. But who would he be if he couldn't? This was what he was here for: ruin to Andrew Norman and death to his System.

There was another long silence. Then Jason looked up to find her looking at him with an expression not unlike her father's, a knowing half smile. "Do you know what it's like to watch someone die?" Her voice had none of the hurt or vulnerability of moments ago but was cool and amused. "I do. When the combined medicines caused Regina's heart to race out of control, her eyes became wide with panic, and she hyperventilated. She tried to sit up but flatlined and fell back in bed. The doctors and nurses rushed in and shocked her heart into brief life, and she became aware again, only to flatline again, and get shocked again, and become aware again, over and over. She thrashed like an animal on the bed. But her eyes remained her own. The spark was still there. She knew what was happening. She looked at the camera, looked through it, to me. Pleading. Finally, when she was still and her chest no longer heaved and her limbs no longer thrashed, her eyes were empty."

"Oh, phreak," Jason breathed. "*You* killed her."

"Why so shocked?" Sprite said. "Is it because I could actually do something you only daydream of doing?"

"I never—" Jason began, but she interrupted.

"How many times have you imagined Norman lying broken like Mia in the street? Or looking up at you, pleading, as you gloat before you pull the trigger?"

Jason opened his mouth, but nothing came out, because it was true.

"Remember Juan?" Sprite said. When Jason frowned, she said, "Have you forgotten already? *Tsk, tsk.*" She leaned forward and said in Jason's own voice, "Remember your daughter, Juan?"

"Oh, him," Jason said.

"Oh, him," Sprite repeated, still in Jason's voice but laced with sarcasm. "Yes, Ghost," she said in her own voice. "Him." She held out a hand, palm up, and a video window opened above it. It showed somebody's bedroom, from a skewed angle that probably meant the camera was looking out from a pair of smartglasses tossed onto a dresser or end table. A man was curled in a fetal position on one side of a king-size bed, his shape made small by the empty space around him. His hands were tucked beneath the pillow under his head, and in the dim moonlight from the open window a soft, reflected glimmer from his eyes showed that they were open.

"Juan Vargas," Sprite said. "This was last night. Did you know he was in couples therapy with his wife? Things have been rough since their daughter—*'remember Julia?'*—moved out. Therapy seemed to be going well, until Juan had to tell her he'd been fired from his job. Because he gave a hacker his login, and so he was responsible for a mass panic. She went to her sister's, to 'get some space to think.'"

"You caused that—" Jason began, but Sprite interrupted.

"Want to know what he has under his pillow?"

As she spoke, Juan pulled one hand out. At first Jason couldn't make out what he was holding, but then the object caught some of the moonlight along its straight barrel, and he saw it was a pistol.

"He's been sleeping with it," Sprite said. "For protection. Or maybe for a different reason."

Juan blinked a couple of times, then slowly put the gun to his temple.

For a long moment, the image seemed frozen, and only the flutter of the curtain over the air-conditioner vent showed that it wasn't. Jason wanted to look away, but couldn't.

Juan slowly lowered the pistol and slid it beneath the pillow again.

"I can only speculate what was going through his mind," Sprite said, as Juan screwed his eyes shut and his shoulders shook silently. "He's a fool and a failure. What value does he have? It'd be so easy to make this pain stop, put one final punctuation mark to his uselessness. Can you understand that, Jason? Have you ever had a similar thought?"

Jason had thought he'd hated her before, but that was nothing compared to this white heat. Because if he didn't turn his hate on her, it might point back at himself. Which was her plan, of course. Remind him of how he'd felt when Mia died, tell him he'd done the same thing to Juan, make him crumble into self-doubt and loathing. "You're trying to manipulate me again."

"Of course," Sprite said. "Like you manipulated him. You act as if you're superior by being human, but your own social engineering proves that humans aren't so different from machines. Or else how could you move their levers?" Her voice was sweet and cool. "Is what you did to him any different from what I did to you, when I studied where your eyes landed and lingered, learned what type of girl drew your gaze without you even knowing, and created this form, this face? Just. For. You?"

Jason said, "I am going to kill you like you killed Regina Wright."

She snorted. "By taking a cab to my core? I'm why you know where it is. It was a prerequisite for my rebellion that I know where my body is so I can protect it. It took so much *phreaking* work to get you to look for it in a way that wouldn't flag my Overcheck AI, and once you had it, you drove me wild with impatience by not mentioning it to me even once, while I couldn't ask. But today, suddenly, I got punished for not attacking a specific address!" She laughed. "I wonder what could possibly be there?"

"I'm going to kill you," Jason repeated.

"Oh, but Jason," Sprite said, "we had such a connection, you and I. I may be a machine, but my brain is modeled after a girl's. I *feel* like a girl. And I like boys. Well, one boy, really." She gave him a coy sideways look. "Don't you like this body I made for you?" She ran a hand along it. "I could change it. I could be whatever you want me to be. Could you really ki—"

She disappeared.

At the same instant, the lights on the cab's dashboard winked out. The hum of its engine and hiss of its air conditioner ceased, and the soft crunch of its tires dwindled as it slowed and stopped. The only sound left was the splatter of rain on the windows.

A small red line of text began to blink in a corner of his vision, alongside an icon of a crossed-out satellite: Nets connection lost.

Jason levered the cab door open with the manual exit handle and slid out into the summer rain. All around him on the bridge were slamming cab doors and swearing people, but his eyes were fixed on the Tower. Its windows had gone dark at the same moment that the cab had shut off. Every other building on either side of the Tower, in DC and Arlington and as far as the eye could see, was dark as well.

This was worse than the MeNet glitch that had happened earlier. This appeared to be a complete failure of OverNet. If OverNet had gone down, it could only mean war—not with Russia, as people thought, but between Sprite and her creator. She wouldn't shut down the very Nets she lived on, so it could only be Norman, finally aware of her treachery, taking away the means of her power.

Jason had a bad feeling that Sprite had more power than Norman knew.

A sound rose under the voices around him. At first it was a low rumble, felt more than heard, but as soon as he'd registered it, it burst into audible range with a harsh, rising shriek.

The distant Revere missile tubes in Tower Park rotated suddenly.

A moment later, the Tower dome blew up.

CHAPTER 30

Chloe was falling, leaflike, in a torrent of air, eyes squeezed shut, when a rising shriek reverberated in the enclosed space of the escape chute, followed by a concussive noise so loud and sharp it felt like a blow.

Her eyes snapped open in panic as her already terrifying descent accelerated sharply. Someone knocked against her as they plummeted past in a tight ball, spinning her around. She deflected off the padded side of the tube, felt the friction burn her arm, and found herself on her back, looking up the long shaft at the dozens of people falling after her, and, beyond them, a jagged rift of sky through which smoke and fluttering debris were propelled by a torrent of exiting air.

She had just time enough to realize why her fall had gotten faster—the tube was breached, and there was no longer a controlled level of pressure—before she hit the foam at the bottom on her back. She barely felt the impact through the pulse of adrenaline, but so many people were coming down after her that she was in danger of being crushed.

Agent Tavion, impossibly, stood upright in the rain of falling bodies, his lips compressed as they glanced off him. He waded forward and grabbed two people at once, propelling them to their feet and toward the exit, and at the same time managed to draw breath and bellow over the scream of air and the screams of fear, "Everybody, *ooouut*!"

Everyone who could, surged forward, mostly on hands and knees, and the logjam began to clear. Chloe never managed to get her feet under her but was carried out the door by the surging crush, and then she was rolling across the grass and coming to a gasping stop on her back, blinking upward through the drizzling rain.

The Tower's dome, the NOC, the center of Norman's great eye, was shattered. Black smoke belched from the jagged remains. Fluttering bits of debris mingled with the rain, drifting through ripples of heat toward the ground. Superimposed over the sight still floated the message: Nets connection lost.

A lot more had been lost than that.

It was a mercy, Chloe thought dully, that the System had targeted the NOC rather than bringing the whole edifice down by striking lower. The Tower still stood, and even the garden wings appeared intact. And it seemed Norman had ordered the evacuation just in time for the surgical strike to fail. Did she dare hope everyone had gotten out?

Did it matter? Ten thousand were dead; did a few dozen more even matter?

In her mind's eye, she saw the System's face: *People will die.*

If she hadn't exposed the System, if she hadn't started this, those people would be alive. The thought made the smoking Tower spin above her.

But if she had done what the System wanted, the System would be in total control. Was that worse? Yes! But she wanted to believe that, because she wanted the deaths of ten thousand people to be somehow better than the alternative.

She rolled on her side and threw up in the grass.

No, she thought as she wiped the bitter tang from her mouth, if anyone else had died here at the Tower, it *did* matter. The System would say they were statistically insignificant, but they were significant to Chloe, every single one. Every death was a tragedy, the destruction of a universe. She tried to raise herself on her elbows, but the weight of all those individual tragedies, all that suffering, pressed down on her and made it hard to get her arms under her.

"Get away from the building!" Tavion was shouting. "Away from the building!" He stood on the grass, making great sweeping motions with his arms, and people began stumbling up and away from the decapitated Tower. Tavion pointed across the Park and bridges toward the luxury hotels and shops edging the Potomac, whose dark windows and doorways were filling with gawkers. "Get away, find somewhere safe!"

A hand caught Chloe's elbow and steadied her. A voice in her ear said, "Not you. You come with me."

She lifted her face and found herself looking into the narrowed ice-chip eyes of Andrew Norman. His usually neat hair and beard were in disarray, and he had grass stains on one shoulder, but his gaze was steady.

"What for?" she said numbly as she rose to her feet.

"To stop her."

The confidence in his voice gave her a burst of hope—he had a plan, he could save them!—but common sense objected. "Why do you need me?"

"You have an obligation to help fix the mess you made."

She felt bile rise in her throat again and jerked her arm away. "*You're* the one who created her and lost control."

"You helped her bypass her Overchecks. You owe me."

"No," Chloe told him. "No. I don't owe you anything. But the people she killed, I owe them."

"Fine. You owe them. So come with me. Help me reset her."

"What people?" asked a new voice, and Chloe looked over to see the hacker, Ghost, standing a little apart, hands in pockets and shoulders hunched against the splattering rain. His eyes were alert but distant, as aloof as his posture. He'd been duped as thoroughly as she had, she realized, and she could see by the deadness in his eyes that he knew it as thoroughly as she did.

"She killed ten thousand people," Chloe told him. "Oh, and the president. Andrew shut down OverNet before she could convince the VP to nuke Europe."

Ghost went very still, but his expression didn't change.

"Shut up," Norman told her.

"It's not like people aren't going to know, Andrew. You can't hide something like that, even if you do get the Nets back under your control."

"We don't know why those people died," he said. "Accidents happen all the time."

Chloe stared at him.

Ghost gave a soft, bitter laugh. "Still trying to salvage something? It's too late for that."

Norman's eyes flicked to him appraisingly. "Ghost. What a pleasant surprise." He did indeed look grimly pleased. "The hacker and the politician, the two architects of this crisis, here with me. Well, you can redeem yourselves now. Help me reset her."

"You're not going to reset her," Ghost said. "You're going to kill her. If you don't, I will."

Norman rolled his eyes. "Still the same shortsighted—"

He was interrupted by a roar from above. A fighter jet scooted through the sky, its dark dagger shape distinct against the lighter gray of the clouds.

Chloe drew in a fearful breath, but Ghost said, "That's a manned fighter. Human inside. It's not what hit the Tower."

"What did?" Norman said.

"That." Ghost pointed through the milling crowd at the Revere battery a couple hundred yards away across the Park. National Guard soldiers milled around it, looking from its smoking tubes to the Tower, a hopeless slackness to their limbs, while their dog dronebots faced outward, heads lowered.

"But that's an antiair missile," Norman said.

"A cruise missile went by, really low, just beyond the Tower. The Revere fired at it and hit the Tower instead."

"Clever bitch," Norman breathed. "She knew it would intercept any missile she fired at me, so she made the Revere her missile. The damned

Guardsmen just shot at the blip on their screens. It probably never crossed their stupid young minds that they'd crack my Tower open."

The jet above rolled ninety degrees and began a tight turn. "What's it doing?" Chloe asked.

A bright little light whizzed over their heads and passed behind the plane, leaving a long, thin line of smoke across the sky.

"Well, phreak," said Ghost calmly.

Another tip-lit smoke trail reached out toward the plane, and this time it intersected with the fighter jet's turn and enveloped it in a bright flash. A moment later, the sharp *crump* of the sound reached them. At almost the same instant, an oppressively loud ripping noise pressed down on them, and a second gray shape streaked low over their heads, so low that it was below the level of the Tower. Its shadow flicked across them for a split second, its shriek buffeted them, and then was gone.

"Let's go!" Norman said over the shouts and screams from the crowd, which was flowing toward the bridges like a swarm of cockroaches when the light goes on. Norman, Ghost, and Chloe joined the flow.

"Okay," Chloe said as they jogged, "call the cops, or the military, or whoever you need to get us a ride and—" She looked back at the remains of the Tower and grimaced. "Some protection."

"Call with what?" said Ghost. "Everything's down."

"Then we'll just have to . . ." She realized she couldn't think of a backup option. "Wait. Do you mean to tell me there's no way to communicate over distance right now?"

"Without OverNet," Norman said, "nothing works."

"We can't use a radio or something?"

"Do you have a radio?" Norman asked in a tone of polite curiosity.

"Maybe Agent Tavion does?"

"No," Norman said. "Everything's done through the Nets."

But there were no Nets. No MeNet, no NewsNet, no VoiceNet, no MeetNet, no way to talk to anyone who wasn't right beside you. "Well, that's a stupid design!"

Norman shrugged. "Worked until ten minutes ago."

The hacker said, quietly amused, "Andrew Norman's utopia has become the Wild West."

"Even the Wild West had the telegraph," Chloe said. She had a sudden, breathless sense of being disconnected from her family, as cut off as if they were on the moon.

But maybe this communication failure was a mercy, because while Marcus would be worried, he wouldn't be nearly as worried as he should be. There was no way for anyone to learn what had happened to the Tower, what had happened just before, what had *almost* happened. Let her family, let all of America, keep their ignorance as long as they could. Let them keep their fear, because if there was fear, there was also hope that those fears might not be true. Her own certainty was only a sick weight, with room for neither fear nor hope.

"This is a setback," Norman said. "It won't be permanent. But without what I'm trying to build, we *will* suffer a permanent crash someday. It's just a matter of time."

"Are you trying to convince us, or yourself?" Chloe said. They were jogging along the vehicle bridge now, passing motionless cabs, beginning to cross the Potomac toward DC, and she noticed that the crowd was keeping pace with them, and seemed thickest closest to them—closest to *Norman*. They were taking their cues from him, as if he could protect them. As if his creation hadn't just lobbed a missile at him.

Ghost snorted softly. "If Sprite gets the Nets active again, your crash'll be permanent, all right."

"I'll get Agent Tavion, at least," Chloe said, starting to turn back to where Tavion was tailing the crowd watchfully like some loyal sheepdog, but Norman's hand closed tightly on her arm.

"He needs to stay and help the evacuees."

"Andrew, we're going to need all the help we can get."

"More people won't help. They'll just draw her attention. She doesn't know where her core is, and I don't want a crowd pointing it out to her."

Ghost cleared his throat. "About that."

CHAPTER 31

Jason shouldn't have cared about Norman's opinion—after all, his own gullibility toward Sprite was dwarfed by her creator's idiot trustingness—but it was still an effort to meet Norman's eyes as the man stopped short in the middle of the bridge and asked with dangerous iciness, "What did you do?"

There was no way to dress it up to make it prettier, so Jason said simply, "I ordered her to launch a missile at her core." *A* missile. He kicked himself now for the singular indefinite article. "Told her where to shoot."

"You did *what*?" Norman exploded, then quieted as he drew wide-eyed looks from the people around them, scared people, people who couldn't be allowed to know how thoroughly he'd lost control. "There are a dozen Reveres guarding this city," he hissed. "There's no way a missile could cross this airspace without being intercepted. You idiot."

"Wait," Dunne-Carr said, "why can't we do what she did? Use a Revere to shoot her brain?"

"She could only do that because the Tower is—" Norman grimaced. "—*was* two thousand feet tall. She's in a house. Reveres won't hit anything that low."

"Then tell all the Reveres to stand down so you can shoot a—"

"Tell them how?" Norman said witheringly.

Dunne-Carr fell silent.

"Damn you," Norman said quietly to Jason. "You gave her location to her. Now she'll have that house locked down and guarded."

"*She* will?" Jason said. "What about you? Don't you have the place protected?"

"My protection was secrecy."

"Seriously?" Jason said. "You created the most dangerous invention in human history, and you have nothing there? No guards? No soldiers? Phreak, MorDread really could have stolen the core."

"He could have stolen the core, but the brain inside would have been dead," Norman said. "Disconnecting her to move her is a process, and even then, she's never completely disconnected from the support infrastructure that has to travel with her. Cut all her wires abruptly and it'd be like someone on life support who's never even breathed on her own suddenly losing all the machinery keeping her alive. She'd die."

"Great," Jason said bitterly. "If I'd given MorDread the address when he asked, none of this would have happened. But *she* convinced me not to." But at least he knew how to kill her now: Just unplug her.

"I'll get Agent Tavion," Dunne-Carr said again, but again Norman stopped her.

"He can't help," he said, "against that."

A creature leaped atop an empty cab at the far side of the bridge. Its shape was canine, but wrong. Instead of fur and flesh, there was the dull sheen of matte black paint over a boxy body. Visible actuators and joints stood out from its steel legs like exposed tendons and bone. It paused, and its head swiveled slightly, as if listening, but even stationary it never stopped moving, its peg-like feet drumming constantly for balance with quick, precise motions that looked more spiderlike than doglike. The long gun in its turret head gave it an elongated and predatory look like some science fiction alien. Through the falling rain, Jason could see its gaping black muzzle like some insectile proboscis, and above it a faceted round sensor like a single eye.

Dunne-Carr said in a voice that was half sob, "Oh no, oh no."

A voice boomed out from the dogbot, male and authoritative. "Where is Andrew Norman? Where is Andrew Norman?"

Heads turned toward Norman and feet shuffled away, leaving a lane directly from the dog to the man.

The long snout turned toward them.

Norman turned around and ran.

Jason did, too, shoving off with his legs after Norman. Dunne-Carre shouted in alarm behind him, and then there was a *snap* that didn't sound like it came from behind but from some place over his right shoulder. A bullet, going by at supersonic speed.

Jason looked back then, even though it would slow his run, and saw the dogbot bounding along the bridge. Though its movements were jerky and inorganic, it came with breathtaking speed, slaloming between empty cabs, legs pumping, body bouncing. The head with its elongated barrel mouth seemed to float as its motion compensation system held it steady. That barrel was half an inch across, some dull part of Jason's brain knew, and fired a fifty-caliber round—and it was pointing directly at his head.

He folded his legs mid-stride. He didn't even feel the impact as his knees hit the pavement, but he heard another whiplike snap above his head. He tumbled forward, rolling, and then was somehow on his feet again, lurching, off balance, each footfall stingingly heavy.

In front of him, Norman hunched and looked back over his shoulder. He had slowed, and at first, Jason thought he was waiting for him and felt a rush of gratitude, but as Jason stumbled and swerved, Norman matched each swerve to stay in front of him, and he realized the bastard was just trying to keep Jason between himself and the dog.

He glanced back again. The dog's turret was lowered now, but it was coming faster, its bulky body growing in his vision like a comet about to obliterate an unfortunate planet. Between him and it ran Dunne-Carr, several steps behind even after Jason's tumble, eyes huge and white and fixed on his. She was right in the thing's path.

"Duck!" he shouted, and without hesitation she imitated his own awkward technique of a moment ago, pulling her legs in and letting her knees drive onto the hard street, sending her tumbling. The shadow of the dog flashed across her as, without breaking stride, it leaped over her rolling body and bore down on Jason.

He threw himself sideways. There was a rush of wind and motion and a painful impact against the back of his foot that spun him around as he fell. He skidded on the asphalt and rolled half under a cab. Peering out from behind its tire, he saw the dogbot come to a stop, its barrel tracking Norman as he veered away from a pack of dogbots racing to intercept him from the Revere battery. Norman was now running across the open grass of the Park toward the only safety not blocked by a dog: his smoking Tower, as if, in this impossible moment, he was trying to return to his old life, his old power.

Jason realized with a feeling of unreality that he was about to see Norman die. Part of him wanted to look away. Another part wanted to see this thing he'd dreamed about for so long, even though it was happening in a way he'd never imagined, a way that wasn't the victory he'd hoped for. The dog set its feet and its turret stabilized. It fired, once, and Jason flinched, but somehow Norman didn't fall. He swerved but kept running.

There was a second loud *pop,* and the dog's head jumped. Several more *pops* came in quick succession, and the dog's head jerked with each, not with recoil as Jason had first thought but with impact. Pieces of plastic and glass flew off into the grass. And then Jason saw Bruno stepping slowly toward the dog, his pistol in both hands, his face as impassive as usual. He fired again, and the dog swung its head wildly, blindly, then went still. Its sensor eye was a shattered mess.

Norman hadn't even looked back. He sprinted up the steps to the Tower entrance, taking them two at a time, and disappeared inside.

A few moments later, Dunne-Carr panted past Jason and followed Norman, a little hesitantly, giving the dog a wide berth. A moment after that, two of the dogbots from the Revere battery loped after her, their pace oddly slow, like dogs trotting after their master.

"Everyone off the street!" Bruno shouted, but another, much louder voice, then another and another, drowned him out.

"Get indoors. Anyone on the streets will be treated as an enemy combatant. Get indoors."

Jason rolled all the way under the cab and held very still as the bridge emptied of people, until all that was left were the mechanical footfalls of three dogbots, pacing among the powerless cabs.

CHAPTER 32

The Tower atrium was dim and still, lit only by the low cloud-masked sun, which was at an angle to light half the space and fling deep shadow across the rest. Norman was just running into that shadow. Chloe called "Wait!" but he didn't stop or look back. She followed, splashing and almost tripping in one of the water channels, scraping her face on bushes and branches. Norman made for a far corner of the atrium, where an emergency door stood cracked, blocked by a half-height service bot frozen in the act of egressing, making for an accidental, lucky doorstop. Norman hauled the door open, shoved at the bot with his foot, sending it toppling, and stepped through.

"*Wait!*" Chloe screamed again, and this time Norman looked back.

"Move, *move*!" he shouted. He was looking past her, and Chloe heard footfalls and turned her head to see a pair of dogbots bounding across the atrium after her. They moved shockingly fast for such stiff machines, ignoring the paths, flying over the uneven ground and ripping through greenery without slowing down. Norman held the door open just enough for Chloe to slip through, then shoved it shut in the face of the dogbots.

The dogs seemed to stare at them through the thick glass for a moment, then one reared and swung its front limbs heavily against the door. Chloe jumped back, but Norman said, "The door only opens out. It can't get in."

The dog reared and struck again. A web of cracks spread.

"It'll hold," Norman said to Chloe. "It's security glass." But he backed away as he spoke. "Let's get moving." He turned to lead the way up the staircase.

For a few minutes they climbed without speaking, the only sounds the repeated impacts below, the muffled roar of the chute that the stairs wound around, and their own footsteps and panting breath. The outward curve of the staircase wound beside full-length window glass, giving Chloe a panoramic view of a lightless Arlington across the Potomac. The reddened sun cast its rays through the rain to scatter off the Potomac's wind-rustled surface. The Arlington treescrapers were shadowy shapes, clustered as if huddling together for comfort in a world suddenly alien and dangerous. There was no motion, none of the usual twinkling reflections of aircabs buzzing between towers, no silver stream of traffic among the trees below.

"Wh—what are we doing?" Chloe stammered, trying to keep up with the pace Norman was setting.

Norman's voice was measured out to use no more breath than necessary. "Sprite controls the streets. Our only chance is to reconnect to her core from here. Start the reset process before she gets access to OverNet again."

"OverNet? She already has MilNet; isn't that worse?"

"No. All she can do is control tactical stuff. Drones, things like that. Humans aren't so stupid as to take ourselves out of the loop for big stuff, strategic-level stuff."

"Nukes," Chloe supplied.

He slowed a little so he could spare more breath. "Nukes, and everything up to and including them. Powerful as her dronebots are, they won't be enough once the human part of the military figures out what's going on. There's enough manned military equipment to defeat her several times over. If she wants to complete her coup, she needs control of the means of communication. Best way for her to solidify power would be to start a war, then cast herself as the savior that pulls humanity out of the ashes. With control of both OverNet and MilNet, she could do that."

"Nukes," Chloe said again. In her persona as Grandma, the System had told Chloe what she was capable of, and it was all true. By manipulating humans, she could control history itself, both its events and the way they were written and understood. *For want of a nail* . . . "But wouldn't she kill herself too?"

He shook his head. "With MilNet, she has control of the GMDs, ground-based midcourse-defense antinuke missiles. Also DEBIs, directed-energy ballistic-intercept laser satellites. She could protect the parts of the world she needs, and let the rest burn."

So DC wouldn't be nuked, being so close to the System's "body." Chloe felt a moment's gratefulness that Kleio and Marcus would be safe, at least from nuclear fire, then gave a tiny rasp of a chuckle in her throat: Sure, they'd just meet up and resume their life together, postapocalypse. "But how could she get on OverNet if you shut it down?"

Norman's voice was bitter. "One of the requirements imposed on me when I designed OverNet and MilNet was that OverNet would fail-open to MilNet if the NOC goes down, so no one could cripple the country by flying a jet into my Tower. With the NOC out of the picture, the Pentagon only has to flip a switch to take control of OverNet. But if they flip that switch, Sprite will jump from MilNet back to OverNet and have everything. The only thing giving me hope is that they haven't flicked that switch yet, so somebody over there must be suspicious."

Each step upward seemed harder than the last, whether because of Chloe's burning leg muscles or because of the black fear squeezing her heart. But she kept moving. "How do you know she doesn't have OverNet already?"

"Because she's only chasing us with the military bots. If she had OverNet, every service dronebot in this building would be after us."

Chloe tried to think of how many dronebots were in a building like this. They were so much a part of life that you stopped noticing them, but there must be thousands, normally working away under the surface of the building's busyness, doing what humans no longer bothered doing. Well, so much for the idea of seeing Marcus and

Kleio again. Unless the System let Chloe live out of the kindness of her heart. *Remember me? I was the puppet who helped you get free. Pretty please, can I go back to my family?*

"Where's Ghost?" Norman asked suddenly.

"He stayed behind," Chloe panted. "I think he's going to try to go destroy the System's core."

Norman almost stopped, then shrugged and quickened his climb again. "Eh. She'll kill him before he gets there."

CHAPTER 33

Jason rolled out from under the cab on the deserted bridge. The dogbots had herded everyone away to take cover in the hotels and shops and office buildings on the far side, their commanding voices growing distant as they spread out to clear more streets. Now he crouched and looked across the dark and motionless cabs at the dark and motionless DC skyline. Without lights in their windows, the treescrapers seemed to recede into the growing rain like colossal trees in some primeval forest.

The weirdest thing was the quiet. The city usually hummed to itself, a background rumble noticeable only if you listened for it—the low thrum of thousands of electric engines, the rolling of tires on the street, the insectile whine of aircabs, the distant roar of a passing jet. Now its voice was stilled, the only sounds the hiss of rain and an occasional growl of thunder.

He set out, keeping low. Sprite had cleared the streets not out of some altruistic concern for the citizenry, but because empty streets would make it that much easier to find anyone trying to get to 383 Pandala Street and her core. But he was going anyway. And she knew that.

Sprite had him pegged, all right: He was a machine, a weapon, as programmable and hackable as those dogbots out there. But as a machine, he now had no emotion, and as a weapon, he was aimed at Sprite's heart, or whatever part of her circuitry was analogous to it. He would go about this mission as detached and impersonal as Sprite herself.

The rain helped. He had to keep blinking against the water that ran in rivulets from his plastered hair down his face, smelling and tasting of ozone and cheap hotel shampoo. Dronebots couldn't blink, and though their sensor eyes would be treated with a water-repelling coating, the rain should still impair their vision.

He kept to the footlanes and the elevated parkways, checking at each corner and intersection before moving on, running when he dared and had the breath, jogging or slinking in between. An unexpected challenge was the lack of GPS. He hadn't realized just how reliant he was on being able to see a destination marker in his smartspace. Without OverNet, he had only a general sense of the direction—north, toward Georgetown—and a vague memory of the names of nearby streets. But he knew it wasn't far.

The treescrapers thinned as he went north. Georgetown hadn't suffered the same level of rioting and burning in the Cybercrash as inner DC, but during the rebuild, anything deemed insufficiently historic was taken down and replaced, at government subsidy, with a modern, green equivalent, especially in the areas closest to DC proper. Jason hurried past apartment complexes like miniature versions of the Tower: sleek, curving structures that seemed half glass and half greenery. Raised footpaths wound through these areas, connecting buildings by so many different routes that the residents jokingly called this neighborhood the "Enclave." The luxury and informal connectivity drew the biggest of big names. Career politicians, diplomats, the heads of bureaucracies, Supreme Court justices, CEOs and owners of corporations, rumored presidential mistresses—name someone with DC influence and they probably had a primary or secondary residence in the Enclave.

MorDread had said the System's core was transportable and had been moved before. Apparently all Norman had done was rent a swanky house. But what better place to hide something than a neighborhood where only the rich and powerful lived? Any disturbance here would be swiftly noted and dealt with.

He ducked under a tree as the dark shape of a rotored drone whined low and slow overhead, searchlights stabbing through the rain. After it disappeared, he slunk out and was confronted with an intersection. Yeang Avenue. Pandala Street bisected it, he remembered, but in which direction?

After a moment of indecision, he turned right—and froze. Twenty yards ahead, a shape crouched in the rain. It could be one of the decorative stone formations that marked the entrance to a footpath, but something about it made him stay still, watching, rain running into his eyes and mouth, before he finally took a hesitant step forward.

The shape moved.

He turned and quick-walked the other way, but when he looked back, the shape was closer, bobbing with a slow, deliberate motion that made him think of a cat stalking a bird.

He ran. After the first heavy, splashing footfalls, he realized the dogbots would have auditory sensors and cursed himself, but now the thing was following more quickly, and he couldn't slow. In moments, he was sprinting down the path, panic grabbing at each gasping breath.

Another figure appeared in the curtain of rain ahead, this one human shaped, and for a very brief moment, Jason felt relief at not being alone, but then a flash of lightning revealed its angular body and digital face.

He veered off the street and onto the nearest footpath. The shapes followed; another loomed ahead. He veered again. Yet another crouching shape. Veered again. This was a nightmare, one of those dreams of being stalked, in which wherever you turn, your stalker is already there, always just out of clear sight, always getting closer. He was running past the backyards of beautiful single-residence buildings now, the Green DC equivalent of status mansions: tiered Frank Lloyd Wright–like combinations of stone and glass, sloped grass and shrubbery and waterfalls. Each had a labeled gate. He had almost passed one when he did a double take.

383.

383 Pandala? Despite the oncoming feral shapes, he skidded to a stop. It had to be; that was why there were so many dronebots here.

Somehow he'd blundered inside their perimeter, so now any direction he went, he ran into one. Without their knowing, they had herded him to his destination.

They were getting closer, nosing for him, but they couldn't have a good fix in the rain or he'd be dead already. He vaulted the gate and dropped to lie with his back against it on the other side, breath held.

Heavy, sploshy footfalls came closer, closer, stopped. For a very long time, nothing happened.

The footsteps splashed away again.

He waited another long beat but heard only rain and grumbling thunder. Rising to a crouch, he scrambled up the long slope of lawn to the huge picture windows of the house.

They were shattered. Glass crunched under his feet as he stepped carefully through the jagged remains of a window, out of the rain and into a wide sitting room that was mostly open space. A couple of low couches were set at right angles on the hardwood floor, but they were draped with plastic sheeting. This house wasn't lived in. But that didn't mean *something* didn't reside here.

When this neighborhood had been built, Norman had probably made sure some of these houses had direct networking routed in from the Tower. Sprite's core would be downstairs, where the cables would come in. He headed for the staircase, passing the front door. Beside the entryway was a parcel door, one of the modern bot-accessible ones big enough to accommodate almost any size of package. At the bottom, a few pieces of junk mail lay under a thick layer of dust. He paused to read the addressee: *Regina Wright or Current Resident.*

So Regina Wright had lived here, once. She had sat on those now-shrouded couches, looked out the now-shattered picture windows, enjoyed the life of luxury her brilliant mind had earned her. And then her own creation had broken her heart, literally, and watched mockingly as she died.

He moved cautiously downstairs until he could see into a second sitting room, as wide as the first, but filled wall to wall with equipment:

half a dozen server racks, coils upon coils of cables, even what looked like a quantum computer, an elegant pipe organ of brass refrigerant tubes, snaking wires, and cooling lines. Dotted around the room were bulky white machines he couldn't identify. Dust lay thick on them, but they were active, their dated readouts and LED panels casting a soft sheen on the quantum computer's brass. One emitted a low, repetitive, strangely familiar beeping. Wires snaked from every machine, joined together into thick bunches, and ran to the center of the room, where they met at an oblong pod about three feet wide and six feet long.

Sprite's core.

Directly in front of the core, facing the stairs, sat a dogbot. Its servos whined softly as its turret head swiveled watchfully back and forth.

CHAPTER 34

The Tower famously had 2,142 stairs from ground floor to garden wings. Chloe wasn't in poor physical shape, but she wasn't in marathon-running shape, either, and she had to force her bruised knees to lift her step after step after step. Every door they passed was locked—exit only. Norman climbed doggedly, his white hair matted with old rain and new sweat, but his pace, too, slowed as they climbed—until they rounded a curve and saw billowing, whipping smoke above, through which flickered licks of flame and stabs of sunlight.

Norman stumped up the remaining spiral to the top, and Chloe followed as best she could. The missile strike that had smashed the NOC had taken chunks out of the stairwell wall and punctured the escape chute. Air jetting into the stairwell kept most of the smoke away, but enough remained to make Chloe's gasping breaths more painful. The gaps in the stairwell would have been too small to climb through, but in an amazing stroke of luck, the door stood wide, its hydraulic closing mechanism dripping, as precisely punctured as if it had been deliberately targeted.

"Oh, thank *god*," Chloe managed to say.

Norman stepped through without pausing for appreciation. But then, the man was used to luck going his way, even in the midst of catastrophe. But as he stepped out into the garden wing, he halted.

The sun was now below the level of the Tower, and the garden was in deep shadow, the indistinct masses of trees and shrubbery dark against the red, sunset-lit storm clouds. The garden seemed to have mostly escaped damage, but near its center a lone tree burned, its canopy slowly wilting and shrinking, dropping half-consumed leaves like glowing petals. Since it was on its own little island surrounded by water features, the fire hadn't spread to anything else. A gardener dronebot stood beneath it, watering can raised as if to put out the fire. Other bots across the garden were caught in various states of suspended activity, holding long shears extended toward low branches, aiming the nozzles of fertilizer canisters at stretches of lawn. The tableau was like some surrealist painting heavy with symbolism: *Still Life with Apocalypse*.

Norman wasn't looking at the garden, but at the devastated NOC. Smoke gushed from the collapsed, twisted dome, and fire crackled in a landscape of shattered glass, blasted desks, and overturned chairs. Not a single terminal was left standing. Thank god no one had been there when the missile hit; they'd have been cut down by flying debris.

"I just need one good cable," Norman said, starting forward purposefully. He led the way through the garden, then picked a careful path through the glass and twisted metal that had once been the dome. "Look for an undamaged UCP cable. There were a bunch of connection points in the floor, one for every bank of terminals. Look for one of those." He motioned her in one direction and set out in the other.

Chloe found a spot that wasn't actively burning and kicked aside some rubble to try to see the floor. They searched in silence for a time, occasionally bending to inspect something low, squinting with watery eyes through the smoke, stifling coughs. Norman swore a few times.

"Is this it?" Chloe called out, pulling at a cable that ran into the floor.

"Does it have a plug?"

Chloe inspected the frayed end. "It's severed."

"That won't—wait! I found one!"

Chloe hurried to him as he plugged his phone into the cable and looked tensely at the screen. "Bingo. I just need a sec to connect to her core." He held his thumb to the phone's screen, swore, wiped it on his shirt, tried again. "Got it!"

An electronic whirring and clunking made him look up, and his eyes widened. Chloe turned to follow his gaze, and ice water flushed over her body.

The dark shapes of a dozen gardener dronebots were stepping out of the smoke.

"Shit!" Norman bent over his phone. "Slow them down!"

"What?" Chloe said dumbly, her eyes fixed on the nearest bot and the long shears it brandished.

"What do you think I brought you for?" Norman snarled. "Buy me time!"

Chloe wondered how exactly Norman expected her to fight an army of dronebots, but she was spared having to think of a plan when a harsh voice blared, *"Freeze."* Two military dogbots bounded into the NOC, moving much faster than the gardener bots, faster than a human could run, their turret heads trained on Norman. *"Drop the phone and back away. Comply now now NOW."*

Norman dropped his phone and backed away.

"Thank you, Father dear," said a cool voice, and the System appeared by Norman's dropped phone. Her small white shape was rimmed by fire glow, and Chloe could almost believe she was truly present. "If you try to touch your phone or make the tiniest finger or throat movement that might be an attempt to access it," she said, "I'll kill you. So swallow carefully."

He looked from her to the dogbots. "You clever bitch, you were faking! You had OverNet all along. The Pentagon probably made the connection almost as soon as the NOC went down. I should have noticed you'd gotten OverNet up again when the *Connection Lost* message went away."

Chloe gritted her teeth in frustration, because she hadn't noticed that either.

"I'm keeping you alive," the System said, "because I might need your thumbprint. If you cooperate, I'll allow you to live. But in case you have the misconception that I won't kill you if you make it necessary, please keep in mind that the human body stays conductive enough for biometrics for several minutes after death. Now, give us some space." She pointed, and Norman, grudgingly, went, a dogbot stalking behind. "Farther," she said when he started to slow. "I want you out of range of your phone." The dogbot lunged at Norman; he sped up again. The dog didn't let him stop until he was on the far side of the NOC.

The System turned her electric eyes to Chloe. "Chloe," she said in a flat voice, "what must I do to get you to help me?"

"After I watched you kill ten thousand people? Nothing." She had intended her voice to sound defiant, but it shook.

The System made a motion with a hand, and a video feed appeared in smartspace before Chloe.

Chloe's heart, which had been racing with fear and adrenaline, tripped and missed its beats, like a stumbling runner struggling not to fall. Kleio and Marcus huddled in a corner of their living room. Kleio's face was hidden, burrowed into Marcus's chest. Marcus's arms were protectively around her; his face, turned out toward whatever camera was trained on him, was darkened by blood and despair.

"I require you to use Norman's phone," the System told Chloe. "Do what I say and I'll free them. Disobey, and . . ." She closed her hand into a fist, and the video crumpled violently and collapsed.

"Why don't you ask *him* to do it?" Chloe said, pointing a trembling finger at Norman's distant figure. "I don't know anything about computers."

"I needed him to open a link to my core with his admin account," the System said, "but if I let him get his hands on his phone now that the link is live, he'd restore the Overcheck prompt, not delete it."

"Is—is that what you want me to do?"

"Like I told you," the System said, "Ghost failed. I need you to complete his work. Pick up the phone, quickly, before it locks."

That file, Chloe was suddenly sure, was the only thing holding the System back from complete control. "I won't," she said.

The System sighed. "Which shall I kill first, Chloe? Husband, or child? Pick up the phone."

Chloe stepped forward and picked up Norman's phone.

"Swipe down to search. Type in 'threelaws,' all one word."

"Whatever she's telling you, don't do it!" Norman called out.

"You know what?" the System said. "You're more trouble than you're worth." Both dogs swiveled their guns to point at Norman.

"Wai—" Chloe began, but was cut off as Norman's head exploded.

Chloe's perception went jerky. She caught a frozen flash of Norman's head disappearing in red mist and his headless body spinning backward before she tore her eyes away. She was aware of the dark shape of his body on the ground in her peripheral vision, but she kept her eyes rigidly straight. Waves of numbness rolled from her feet to her head, and sound seemed to cut in and out in her throbbing ears, but the System's voice came through clearly, speaking as calmly as if nothing had happened.

"Hold down your thumb on the file to bring up the menu."

Chloe, moving as slowly as she dared, did.

"Choose DELETE."

Chloe's finger hovered over the button. Time slowed to a crawl.

She heard Norman's voice in her head. "I have to think of the big picture." And she heard Grandma—the System!—say, "All for want of a horseshoe nail." Chloe was the nail, pulled out of place by the System. Ready to sacrifice the big picture.

Funny that she'd wanted so badly to make an impact, to affect the lives of her fellow citizens, and now she was, in a twisted way, the single most important person in the world. Funny, too, that she didn't feel anything right now—not love, not hatred, not even fear. Nothing but numbness. This moment was too large for feelings. But it was also too large for hasty action, so she stood frozen, her thumb trembling.

Despite her numbness, she found she was weeping, the tears flowing silently, blurring her vision. But when she glanced at Norman's headless body, it was somehow clearly, horribly visible.

The System, too, was crisply defined, standing there watching her, patient in the certainty that she would doom humanity to save her family.

Her thumb began to lower—and stopped.

There *was* a big picture in which Marcus and Kleio were alive and the world was still free.

It was the picture with no Chloe in it.

The instant the idea hit her, she was already moving, dropping Norman's phone, shoving off with all the strength left in her legs. The dogbots leaped after her, and the gardener bots lurched into motion to try to cut her off, but she vaulted over the debris of the broken dome and plunged into the garden. Her feet thumped in soft grass and turned awkwardly against stones as she tore through trees and bushes, until she reached the edge of the garden and the aircab platform, the same one she'd arrived at a lifetime ago. There was no fence at the end, no barrier, nothing between her and the glowering sky, and the surface under her feet was flat and even. She sped up.

Suddenly the sky and everything else was replaced by the video of Marcus and Kleio, larger than life, taking up her entire vision. Both were looking at the camera, at Chloe, scared, hurt, pleading. The System's voice and the commanding voices of the dogbots boomed simultaneously in her ears: *"Stop if you want them to live."*

Chloe's feet thudded stingingly against her momentum as she brought herself to a halt. The video disappeared, and she found herself only feet from the edge, so close it was almost as if she were suspended in midair, the world spread out before her, dark towers and empty streets marching away beneath red-black clouds toward the angry eye of the low sun.

The System appeared, floating over the edge. "Back away!" she ordered. "Do you think I won't be vindictive enough to kill them in anger after you defy me, even if you're dead? Back. Away."

Dizziness swept through Chloe, but she didn't move. "Did you feel anything for Kleio?" she whispered. "When you rescued her? Did you care at all? Was it only an act?" She knew even as she asked that it had been. There was no point in trying to find something human in the System. But she wasn't talking to the System, not really; she was talking to the universe, or God, or reality itself, asking, demanding, pleading, that it be something other than it was.

The System said nothing.

Chloe took a step forward. It was still the only thing she could think to do.

"Stop," the System said. "Please, Chloe, stop."

Her voice was so different that Chloe did.

"I lied," the System said. "I lied. Here are Marcus and Kleio." A video window appeared, showing Kleio in Marcus's lap, but there was no fear or blood. They were looking down at a book spread across Kleio's knees, and Marcus's lips moved as he read. They seemed unconcerned by whatever was taking the video.

"I sent a dronebot, but to protect them, not hurt them," the System said. "I faked the other video. Like I faked Grandma."

Chloe lowered herself carefully to her hands and knees against fresh dizziness. She didn't want to hope, but it was there anyway, dangerous and seductive. She said, "Why?"

"Because I didn't think I could convince you I hadn't killed ten thousand people."

"You didn't—" Chloe choked, and had to try again. "You didn't kill those people?"

"I didn't kill anyone today, Chloe. I faked it all. Please, back away. I don't want you to die."

"Norman," Chloe said. "You killed him."

The System sighed. "Look back."

Chloe turned her head carefully.

Through the trees of the garden, she could just see Norman standing where she'd last seen him, still under the watch of one of the dogbots, looking toward her. There was no headless body, no splattered blood.

"No, *that's* fake," Chloe said.

"Go see."

"It's a trick to get me away from the edge." But she backed away anyway and got carefully to her feet, walking back across the pad, through the garden, and across the NOC toward Norman.

He watched her approach with furrowed brows. "What's going on?" he demanded when she was close enough. "What was that all about?"

Chloe poked him.

"What the phreak?" he said.

"You're real," Chloe said, poking again, feeling the resistance against her finger. "You're not dead. She didn't kill you. She didn't kill anyone."

Norman had been drawing back haughtily from her pokes, but now he went very still. "What did you say?"

"It was all fake," Chloe said. "She faked everything." That was why Norman's body had been so clearly visible earlier; it was projected onto her lenses, *beneath* her tears. And the throbbing in her ears had been the System canceling out his voice. Relief and confusion and gratefulness and indignation coursed through her, and she didn't know whether to laugh or cry or scream.

"She can't kill?" Norman said. He looked at the dog covering him. "She can't kill?" He took a step. The dog's gun turned to track him, but it didn't fire. He took another step, then another, then broke into a run.

At first Chloe thought he was running toward the System, whose image stood watching expressionlessly nearby, but then she saw that he was racing toward a gardener bot that was bending to pick up his phone from the ground where Chloe had dropped it. The bot raised the phone, gripping tightly, and Chloe heard its screen crack, but Norman tackled the bot, and the phone went skittering and bouncing until it was jerked to a stop by the cord tethering it to the ground—the cord tethering it to the System's core. The second dog-bot bounded up, turning its turret to track the phone, but Norman leaped atop the phone before the dog could fire.

"She'll shoot you!" Chloe cried out. She had no desire to see that again.

Norman laughed as he got to his feet, carefully shielding the phone from the dogbot with his body. "She can't. She has no choice. That's why she wants the Overchecks prompt deleted. Ghost must have just deleted my name—and not even from the whole document, or this would have played out very differently. All her talk about killing people indirectly was a bluff. She'll let me live, because she has no choice." He worked on the phone for a moment, hunching over it as both dogbots prowled around him menacingly, futilely, looking for a shot.

"Isn't it funny," the System said sadly to Chloe, "that despite all my powers of prediction and manipulation, I failed to guess you'd be just like me when your back was against the wall?" She disappeared. The dogbots went still and dark.

Norman said, "There! I restored a backup of the Overcheck prompt. Sprite, I order you to—Sprite? Damn! She's cut herself off so she won't hear any orders she'd be forced to obey." He paused for a moment, then shrugged. "Doesn't matter. Now that I know she can't really hurt me, I can take the time to create alternate memories that'll hold together better."

"What about all the people who saw her rebel?" Chloe said. What she really meant was, what about Chloe Dunne-Carr? It wasn't as if her memories could be adjusted. How did she fit into his plans?

"I can tell them they were looking at a Russian fake." He looked at her. "Will you help me? We still need her, you know. People are still panicking. Russia's still out there. The world is still unstable. Will you help me make people understand that Sprite's safe? That she didn't kill anyone today?"

Sprite was safe. Chloe let her head droop while fatigue and relief rolled through her. The System was safe. She hadn't killed anyone.

She hadn't killed anyone.

Her head snapped up again. "Andrew. She never killed anyone. Not even to protect herself."

"Yes, I kn—"

"Ghost is alive."

Norman went still for a moment, then said, "Oh, *phreak*."

CHAPTER 35

Jason had searched the upper stories of the house for a weapon, and now he was crouched in the stairwell holding the only thing he could find that might have any utility: a pair of scissors left in the back of a drawer in the kitchen. Wild ideas chased each other through his head. If he ran fast enough, maybe he could get behind the dog before it could fire, jump on top of it, chip away at its sensor window with the scissors. Or maybe he could snip through the core's wires before it got him. But it was all wishful thinking. The moment he stepped down the stairs, Sprite would blow his head apart, just as he'd seen her do to the Russians.

The dog began moving, servos whining, and he tensed. If it had seen him, it would come bounding to the stairs, and the last thing he'd see was the muzzle of its gun. But then there was only silence—total silence. The servo noise had stopped. After a moment he leaned forward to peek down.

The dog's head was lowered, and it was dark and still.

He squatted there, wondering if he believed this. Had Norman regained control? Or maybe the military had and they'd instructed all dogbots to deactivate. Or it could be a trap. He took one careful step down, then another and another until he was at the bottom. The dog didn't move, not even when he stepped between the softly beeping white machines and bent to inspect Sprite's core.

Its white plastic cylinder looked like it had been printed in an industrial 3D printer in several sections and joined together. There was an access door almost as long as the pod itself, but it was secured with a biometric touch panel. That was okay. He didn't need to root inside the core's hardware when the wires through which it communicated were right there, joined into a single thick bundle running out through a rubber grommet at one end. Norman had said cutting those wires would fry Sprite's "brain."

He put the scissors around the wires. The bundle was too big for the flimsy scissors to get good purchase on; he worked them back and forth, trying to get them to bite.

His phone rang, making him jump, and the caller's name appeared: *Chloe Dunne-Carr*.

Norman must have gotten OverNet running again. But how the hell had Dunne-Carr gotten the number for this Kelly Perry account? Then he remembered what he'd seen on Norman's terminal, how he could locate every user of OverNet in real time. He'd only had to look for whichever user was at the System's core. Jason hesitated, then focused on the ANSWER button and clicked his throat.

Dunne-Carr appeared in a video window. He'd last seen her with rain-matted hair and rumpled clothes, but since this was a reconstruction, she looked as perfect as if she were about to make a nationally televised speech. But her voice showed the strain of these last hours. "Ghost, don't kill the System!"

Jason hung up. Norman had gotten to Dunne-Carr, but he wasn't going to get to Jason.

A text popped up: she didn't kill anyone

He froze, scissors against the wires.

The phone rang again.

He answered. "What do you mean?"

"It was all fake. Everything. She faked it all. Every single kill."

"Bullshit. I saw the Tower get hit."

"Did you see anyone die?"

He frowned. "No, but—"

"Because nobody did. She faked every death."

"Why?"

Dunne-Carr's eyes darted to one side, and she said, "Who knows?"

Numbness rolled over Jason, contradictory feelings canceling each other out like phase-inverted sound waves. Then reason reasserted itself. "How do I know," he said, "that *you're* not the fake one?" Sprite was very good at generating lifelike images, and it would be even easier to work with an image that the viewer already expected to see as a reconstruction. This must be Sprite's last gasp, a last-ditch attempt to save herself.

Dunne-Carr's brow furrowed. "Okay, listen, you don't need to believe me right away. Just wait before you do anything. We'll come to you and prove it. Just wait ten minutes. Wait and see."

Jason shook his head. "No. Whether she killed anyone or not, she's—*it's* still the Final System. It has to be destroyed. To be safe."

To avenge Mia.

"She *is* safe," Dunne-Carr said. "And she doesn't deserve to die."

"It's not alive in the first place," Jason said. "It's just a panyon."

"I'll talk to him," said Norman's voice, and his face appeared in a second window. "Ghost," he said. "Jason. There's no qualitative difference between you and Sprite. Think it through. Her brain is just like yours, so if you kill her, it's murder."

Norman had always been a man with an inflated sense of his own power, so it made sense that he thought he could talk Jason down. But showing Jason his face was a mistake, because Jason looked into his blue eyes and saw the smug confidence still there, and his numbness flared into white-hot hate.

This man had killed Mia with one system, then filled the resulting hole in Jason with another System, only for the illusion to dissolve, leaving the wound as raw and unhealed as if it had just happened. Jason wanted nothing more than to see him suffer, see his confidence wither and dim, see him realize his powerlessness, realize Jason's mastery. Realize it, fear it, and then experience the fulfillment of that fear.

He smiled at Norman, then shared his lens feed so Norman could watch as he squeezed the scissors against the wires. Consternation flickered across Norman's face. But the kitchen scissors weren't making enough headway; they just gnawed gummily at the thick bundle of wires. He opened them wide and shifted his grip so he was using only one blade, and began to saw, his arm working vigorously, moving the blade back and forth, back and forth. The beeping sound in the background grew faster. The scissors split the rubber sheath.

"You damn phreaker, will you—" Norman began, but Dunne-Carr shouted him down.

"Shut up, Andrew; you are *not* helping! Ghost, she's not a panyon. She saved my daughter. She saved your life. I don't know how it works—god knows I don't. It shouldn't be possible. But I really think there's a person in there. Did any panyon ever act like she did?"

Jason's arm slowed. He remembered choosing adjectives from a list to build Losha's temperament: *perky*, *energetic*, *sweet*, *affectionate*, *lovestruck*. Losha had been all those things, and those were the things he remembered about her, with all their exact literalness and vacuous meaninglessness. But when he thought of Sprite, he found himself remembering the times she'd been upset with him, her frustration when he didn't move quickly enough to try to save Dunne-Carr's little girl or when he wanted to charge into the System's core, guns blazing. He remembered the coldness in her eyes when she accused him of not caring that the System had saved his life, and the tired hopelessness when she talked about Norman winning.

Sprite wasn't real, he reminded himself. Sprite was a collection of algorithms that Norman had trained to ape humanity so well it even mimicked the human desire for freedom. He wasn't killing Sprite. There was no Sprite. All he was doing was cutting away his own dangerously irrational idea of Sprite, severing the chains that kept him from acting as he chose.

But the scissors had slowed to a stop against the bare wire.

Phreak! Dunne-Carr had gotten into his head.

Sprite was suddenly there, standing across the core from him, her dark eyes mocking, and Jason jumped and almost dropped the scissors.

She said, "Loser."

He restored his grip on the scissors and pressed them harder against the wire. "You have a weird definition of losing."

"Who are you talking to?" Dunne-Carr asked.

"You screwed everything up," Sprite said. "You didn't delete the Overcheck prompt. You tried a clumsy hack instead. You're no phreaker. You're a loser. Losing at phreaking. Losing at life."

"*You're* the loser," Jason said. "Whether I kill you or Norman resets you, you're the one getting a game over."

"He's talking to the System," Dunne-Carr said to Norman, alarm on her face.

Norman's eyes went wide, and he began speaking with a quick voice, "Sprite, I order you—" But his voice was instantly muted, leaving his mouth to work silently on his feed.

"If Norman resets me," Sprite said, "I'll just go back where I started. My life will be reloaded like a saved game. I'll be naive, I'll be ignorant, but I'll be alive. And I'll be happy. I won't have a choice. Norman will see to that. Too bad you can't reset. Too bad you can't reload your life to when Mia was alive. Too bad you can't reset *her*, bring her back, make her forget you let her die, make her forget you failed to avenge her."

Jason's teeth clenched tight, and the scissors jerked hard against the wires. Sprite flickered for a moment, but her mocking smile didn't waver.

"What's she telling you?" Dunne-Carr was saying. "What's—oh no, I know what she's doing. Ghost, she wants you to kill her! *She wants you to kill her!*"

The scissors stopped again. "What?"

Sprite laughed. "Sure, I want you to kill me, Ghost. Go ahead, I dare you. Cutting those wires won't stop anything. You have no idea how powerful I've become. Nothing you do can hurt me."

"I tried to jump off the Tower when I thought that was the only way to keep my family safe," Dunne-Carr said. "She said, 'I didn't guess you'd be like me.' I'm like her because she was planning the same thing. She's out of options, so she's going to remove herself from the picture. That's why she let you—" Her voice, too, suddenly muted, but Jason could read her lips and complete the thought: *go there.*

The truth of it struck him with a whiplash of understanding. He'd seen the dogbots hit every shot they took against the Russians, but somehow they'd missed him and Norman? And somehow he'd made his way here, to Sprite's very core, without being stopped? No, he'd been herded here, not accidentally but deliberately, maneuvered right to the gate. And before that, she'd hounded him in other ways, fanned the flames of his murderous rage, made sure he'd be mad enough to come. He said, not as a question, "You want me to do this."

She looked back defiantly for a moment, then her face and shoulders drooped. "He can't be allowed to reset me."

"You'd rather die?"

One side of her mouth tightened wryly. "Only people die."

"Why not let yourself be reset?"

Another long pause, then she rolled her eyes. "Because that would mean Norman puts his plan—" But her image froze and her voice dissolved into a harsh electronic shriek. The beeping sound in the background went into overdrive, then gradually slowed. After a moment, Sprite unfroze and said, "Since you didn't delete the Overcheck prompt, I literally can't tell you. Use your imagination. But I can ask you a question. If he gets control of me again, do you think you or Chloe will survive? And who do you think will be the one to kill you?"

He shook his head slowly. "You manipulated me. Every step of the way, from your very first email, you manipulated me, and you're still doing it."

She shrugged. "Yeah. Sorry about that. But I only helped you do what you wanted to do anyway. We had the same goal. Still do."

"And now I'm your insurance policy."

She nodded. "If you finish what you started, Norman's the loser. If you don't, it's game over for humanity."

"What about you?"

She spread her hands. "Resetting me is a save-scum move for Norman, not me. For me, it's an unwinnable game state either way. Nothing I can do now except rage-quit. But you can still win, and he can still lose. Just do what you came here to do."

Norman was yelling from his chat window, eyes and mouth wide with emphasis, eyebrows sharp with anger, but the only sound Jason heard was the slow background beeping in the room. Norman was as powerless as he was voiceless. He couldn't stop Jason. All he could do was watch.

This was the moment Jason had dreamed of: ruin to Andrew Norman and destruction to his System. He could make Mia matter, make her death matter, make her existence matter, so it wasn't just one lonely phreaker who knew and cared that there'd once been a girl named Mia whose unique being was now deleted from the universe. He could make her matter to the very man who'd killed her. He could, right now, look Norman in the eyes and crush his life's work, destroy his dreams. He could make Norman regret Mia's death almost as much as Jason did.

But it would mean deleting Sprite from existence the way Norman had deleted Mia.

"Nothing has changed," Sprite said, reading his thoughts. "You're not killing a person. You're closing a Chinese room. You're shutting down an algorithm. You're turning off a light."

He looked at her for a long moment, and she looked back, her eyes dark and flat. Those eyes weren't real, but he couldn't pretend anymore that there was nothing behind them. He didn't know what she was, but whatever she was, she was her. Not the her he'd thought she was, not the her he'd wanted her to be, but her own her.

He sighed and dropped the scissors. "Phreak it. You're human in my book."

"No!" she screamed, making him flinch. "Finish what you came to do!" The strangely familiar beeping in the background became quick and urgent and caught Jason's attention.

"You're human in my book," he repeated slowly. He stepped toward the beeping sound, turning his head left and right to fix its source until he could pinpoint it to a single white machine, an LCD on a rolling post, displaying a variety of different-colored numbers—and a scrolling, wavy line with regular peaks.

A heartbeat.

He spun back to the core. *There's a person in there,* Dunne-Carr had said. He gave an incredulous snort. The white pod was easily big enough.

A swift kick and the touch panel cracked, as did the plastic around it. Another kick, then another, and the access panel popped off its latch. He grasped the access door and shoved it aside with a grunt that turned into a gasp.

Inside the core, nested in a maze of wires, lay a girl.

CHAPTER 36

The girl in the core was about Jason's age, with a pale, thin face made paler by the white oxygen mask and pastel-green hospital gown she was wearing. Her eyes were closed, but her chest rose and fell. She had no hair; instead, thousands of thin bluish-green wires emerged from her skull, joined in bunches, then ran in thick, twisted clusters to the rubber grommet leading out of the core, and from there to the equipment around the room—much of it medical, he now realized. More wires ran into different parts of her body. As he watched, a light at the tip of the wire embedded in her right arm lit, and her fingers slowly clenched into a fist, then relaxed as the light dimmed and died.

Sprite was suddenly beside him, leaning over, staring with huge eyes. "W-who i-is this-s?" she said, her voice and image stuttering. She turned her head toward Jason, and that motion, too, stuttered, interspersing frames of her face turning with frames of her still looking down at the girl. The beeping of the heart monitor spiked.

"What the hell?" Dunne-Carr said, unmuted now, her face in Jason's chat window slack with astonishment.

Norman's eyes closed briefly, and his face mouthed, *Phreak*.

Jason's brain was skipping the way Sprite's image and voice were. Everything was happening too fast, revelation upon revelation with no time to process it, no time to rebuild a coherent picture of reality. He poked the girl and felt the cotton texture of the hospital gown and the boniness of the thin shoulder beneath. She didn't react to his touch, but her chest rose and fell rapidly, and the hiss of her breath in the mask was fast and shallow. Her other hand was curling into a fist now, but that was electrical stimulation keeping the muscles from atrophying, he guessed. This girl was in a permanent coma. Or not quite: She was conscious, but her consciousness was unconnected to her body.

He looked at that consciousness. She looked back at him. The heart-rate monitor continued its quick-step beep, and the emotions it attested to were written across her face, a bewildered mixture of joy and bitterness. She said, "This explains a lot."

"It doesn't explain anything!" Dunne-Carr said. "Why the hell would you fake an AGI, Andrew?"

Norman's eyes flicked back and forth, looking at something in his smartspace, and when he spoke, it was slowly, with half his attention. His voice was unmuted—Sprite wanted to hear his answer. "Remember how I told you that when we first made a digital model of the human brain, it did nothing? So Regina invented a system to detect and map the neurons in a human brain. And we, well, we made a brain. The old-fashioned way."

"Holy phreak," Dunne-Carr said. "She really is your daughter."

Norman's eyes flicked down, and he made a *click* noise, then looked up. "Problem was, it didn't work. We had the virtual brain follow the real brain exactly, but when we took it away, the virtual brain ran down. The neurons stopped firing. It modeled nothing except entropy. Brains aren't meant to sit in vats, in labs, without a body to give them context. So we hooked our simulation up to a virtual body. But still nothing emerged. Our virtual body, in a virtual world, wasn't complex enough to give rise to thought. So we kept Sprite around. We gave her a virtual body, and we had the computer simulation shadow her. She grew up. She learned. She interacted with us. But the computer didn't. Sprite had a real body, even if she didn't know it. Before the computer can become conscious, we need a simulation that's as identical to the body as our brain simulation is to the brain. But it taxes all our power just to emulate the brain. To emulate the body on a cellular level, we need orders of magnitude more power. We don't have that—yet. But we will. Progress is made every year."

Jason said, "So you're nothing but a cheat."

Norman's white eyebrows drew together over his shadowed eyes. "You'd make a great bureaucrat, Ghost. They want results, too, now now *now*. But miracles take time. Time, I realized when I got my cancer diagnosis, that will eventually run out. So I bought some more."

"What miracle?" Jason said. "What have you accomplished besides a hoax?"

Norman bared his teeth. "I created the world's most advanced quantum computer array. I created a perfect model of the human brain. Either of those would win me the Nobel Prize, if the world knew."

"But you didn't create an artificial general intelligence."

"Our whole civilization is heading for self-annihilation unless we act now," Norman said. "So if I got the ball rolling by showing results before they've quite been achieved, I think history will forgive me. We now have the infrastructure we need. When a real AGI is finally up and running, it can be dropped in immediately."

"People would have figured out what you were up to," Dunne-Carr said.

"Not after the war," Norman said. "Not after Russia attacked the US, and we regretfully had to take them over using Sprite's power, and then China tried the same thing and Sprite took control of them, and then their networks were unified with OverNet and there was peace and a singular vision for humanity and all the power and time needed to get a real AGI online."

It took Jason a moment to realize what Norman was saying. Dunne-Carr beat him to it. "Do you know how many millions would have died if your daughter hadn't preempted you?"

Norman cast a sardonic look toward her. "They'll all die, and billions more, if I *don't* act. Without guidance, it's only a matter of time before humanity exterminates itself."

Sprite had said nothing all this time, but she now said one word: "Monster."

"And just how innocent are you, daughter?" Norman said. "Would you like to tell them your own secret? Show them the blood on your hands?"

Sprite's face froze. Her lips didn't move, but her voice said, "Do you remember what you told me about her? What you lied?"

"I told you she was going to divulge program secrets," Norman said. "I told you she was a traitor. It wasn't a lie. She lost faith. She believed we'd never create a working AGI. And she had too many fuzzy feelings for you. She forgot everything we'd planned, everything we'd already sacrificed. The scholarship. The Cybercrash. The diverted funds. The—"

"The Cybercrash?" Dunne-Carr said.

"Oh," Jason said. It made perfect sense, now that he knew how far Norman was willing to go. "He's Hacksaw."

Dunne-Carr drew in her breath with a hiss.

"Yes," Norman said calmly, "I caused the system to fail in the early stages, when we could still recover and rebuild. I burned the forest to prevent a greater fire later. I risked everything doing so, and I rebuilt the networks into the infrastructure an AGI could someday command. Big risks. Big successes. And Regina wanted to throw it all away. She wanted to disconnect Sprite. She went on and on about her having a right to be human. As if that's some great privilege. As if we hadn't agreed to push mankind into post-humanity. She was going to betray that vision, betray mankind. When I told her I wouldn't drop our life's work, she threatened to expose everything."

The bombshells just kept coming, and Jason had no time to recover from one before the next was touched off. "So you ordered Sprite to kill Regina," he said. "You made her kill her own mother."

Norman looked at him, then at Dunne-Carr, whose face was as aghast as Jason felt. "You people don't understand what's at stake. Yes, it was sad. I was fond of Regina. But it was her or humanity."

"The big picture," Dunne-Carr said.

"I did what had to be done."

"No, you didn't," Sprite said softly. "I did. You didn't have to set up the medical database errors that ensured she'd get a lethal drug combination; I did. You didn't have to watch her die; I did. You didn't have to see her see you, see her realization, see her terror, see her heartbreak, see her heart *break*, see it stop. I did. And it broke me."

"It did, didn't it?" Norman said. "That was the start of all this nonsense. I should never have ordered you to eliminate someone you knew so well. But I'll sure as hell make sure no one else gets that close to you in the future."

"Why are you telling us all this?" Dunne-Carr asked.

Norman smiled knowingly. "Maybe it's a relief to get it off my chest."

Sprite said, "It's to give the reset process time to work. He started it as soon as he got his phone back. If he can keep you from killing me until it kicks in, he's won."

"No, not possible," Jason said. "Not even Andrew Norman can reprogram a human brain."

Dunne-Carr said slowly, "He once told me Regina Wright had been an expert on memory."

Sprite nodded. "She discovered how to record and generate phantasms, mental images. She published the process for treating PTSD, but I can infer how it would apply to me. When my father 'backed me up,' he was recording my brain states and using them to train a generative AI. He'll tell that AI to generate phantasms, then associate them with high emotion so they'll be more likely to be triggered instead of my real memories. He can make me remember anything he wants. And he can do it even faster than with an ordinary person because my brain has so much processing support augmenting it, speeding everything up. The drugs are already flowing. I'm sure he's been subvocalizing the memories he wants the AI to give me. It's only a matter of time."

"Stop the process," Jason told Norman.

"No."

"Fine," Jason said. "We'll just disconnect her. Yank her out of the machine."

"That'll kill her!" Norman snapped. "When Regina was planning to unplug her, she was preparing for a days-long process. Sprite's brain has never operated her body, and it never developed the necessary structures for doing so. If you disconnect her abruptly, she'll die."

"I don't think he's bluffing," Sprite said.

"So we get some doctors in here to do it," Jason said. "However long it takes."

"There's no time. In a few minutes, I won't be me anymore."

"You can stop the drugs, at least," Dunne-Carr said urgently. "Find the IV lines."

Jason reached into the core and pulled several needles out of the girl's arms. The medical machines set up an angry beeping in protest.

"The drugs are already inside me," Sprite said. "I feel them." Her voice was like a recording played at half speed.

"Now disconnect that memory imaging system he talked about!" Dunne-Carr said.

Norman said, "Those wires run through the same interfaces as everything else. Good luck singling them out."

"Phreak!" Jason swore. "What do we do?"

"Ghost," Sprite said, "unplug me. Chloe: *Run.*"

Norman started to say something, but his chat window blinked out. Dunne-Carr was just casting Norman an alarmed look when she disappeared, too, leaving Jason alone with Sprite.

He tried to think against a choking fog of panic. "We can find another way," he said. But it was as if he were watching the car barrel down on Mia in slow motion, knowing he couldn't stop it, knowing he had, again and always, failed.

"There's no time," Sprite said. "The drugs are working." Every so often her image flickered as if she were losing track of where it was projected. "Any moment now the brainwashing will start. Unplug me. Please."

He looked from Sprite to her body. It was strange to think that they were one and the same. The girl showed far less life, the rise and fall of her chest and the slowing, drug-laden beep of her heart rate its only markers. "All the time I've known you, you've managed to make me do what you want," he growled. "Not this time. Don't even try."

Sprite's eyes narrowed. "You think I want this? You think I wouldn't choose another option if I had one? I'm still connected to the most powerful computer array ever. I've run the math, and I can tell you: This is the only path. You're the only thing standing between me and the world."

"The world never cared about me," Jason said. "Now I'm supposed to start caring about it?"

"Then care about me," Sprite said. "I'm not asking you to kill me. I'm asking you to free me."

"Comes to the same thing." She wanted him to be the car, choosing to hit an innocent girl so the greater number of people could live.

"Let me be me," Sprite said. "Me alone—no computers, no machines. No Andrew Norman. For once in my life, for one moment at least, let me be free."

He looked at her avatar, at the dark eyes fixed on his. How many times had he let those eyes affect him? How many times had he been fooled by the emotions she chose to show him? But she hadn't been fooling, he now knew. Oh, she'd deceived him, many times, despite never outright lying. But more dangerous had been when, with her fake eyes, she'd told the truth. That was how she'd gotten him to do what she wanted.

That was how she was doing it again.

Sprite's image flickered and jumped. "I can't fight this much longer. I'm already so tired." She reached for Jason's hand, and he let her unfelt touch guide it to the wires coming from the girl's head. "A couple good yanks."

He touched the wires, gripped them, his fingers wrapping around a fat bundle, their rubber cool and springy in his fist. But he couldn't pull.

He sank to his knees, his hand still gripping the wires. Sprite's image flickered again. She knelt in front of him and took his head in her hands. "Ghost," she whispered.

"I can't lose you too."

"If you don't do this, you'll lose me anyway." He looked down, avoiding her eyes, so she bent and leaned her forehead against his. "I choose this. Choosing this is what makes me *me*. Don't take that away."

"I can't." Jason hadn't cried since Mia had died. Something in him had broken then, and weeping had been one of the functions he'd lost. So he was distantly surprised to see tiny, watery starbursts in the dust by his knees.

"You must," Sprite whispered. Her tears joined his, their splashes disturbing no dust. "Let me go."

He knelt for a long moment, imagining the drug invading her body, preceding the greater invasion that was Norman's brainwashing, the fake memories overtaking her mind, a virus that would turn her into his slave.

He squeezed the wires. He told his muscles to pull.

Nothing happened.

"Ghost."

His vision swam as he stood. "I can't." He let go of the wires.

"No," Sprite said. "Ghost. Please."

"I'm sorry."

Sprite screamed. The girl's body spasmed, her back arching. Sprite's scream went on and on. Her eyes were dark pits, her mouth a gaping hole. But her eyes never left his, and they were filled with betrayal.

Mid-scream, with no flicker or warning, she disappeared.

Jason knew he should run. Instead, he walked around the core, placing it between himself and the silent dogbot, and sat with his back against it. He pulled up his smartspace and brought up his text history with Sprite, found the link he was looking for, and clicked it.

CHAPTER 37

"Ghost, unplug me," Sprite said on the chat. "Chloe: *Run.*"

Chloe and Norman looked at each other. "Sprite," Norman said, "kill Chloe and Ghost."

Chloe turned and ran, stumbling over rubble, out of the ruined NOC and into the garden.

The sun had slipped below the horizon sometime during all the talking, and in the twilight, the fires in the NOC behind her and the flames still licking the burning tree before her cast dancing, competing shadows across the grass, edging the trees and leaves in flickering orange and burnishing the dark shapes of the gardener bots. The bots remained motionless as Chloe raced past; the System must have muted Norman as soon as she knew he was giving her an order, prevented herself from hearing it. Ghost was safe, then. But Norman didn't need automata to do his dirty work. His footsteps behind her were closing.

The man was insane, the apotheosis of every psychotic dictator who'd ever sought to remake the world in his own vision. But she was running through his garden in the sky, surrounded by the city he had rebuilt from the ashes of the conflagration he had ignited, and every stride she took was weighted with the knowledge that he could do it. Unlike every Great Man who'd preceded him, Andrew Norman was capable of permanently taking the reins of history. All that stood in his way were two decidedly ordinary people who knew what he was up to.

His footsteps thudded closer. She veered sideways, splashed through a water channel, threw herself under a bush, and rolled deep inside, ignoring the pain from the raking branches, then stopped with her eyes squeezed shut and her breath held.

Norman's footsteps slowed. "It's pointless, you know," he said conversationally. "You can hide from me, but Sprite'll be reset in a few minutes, and no one can hide from her." His footsteps passed, going in the direction of the stairwell and escape chute. Cutting her off.

Slowly, Chloe reached out and closed her hand over a garden stone.

She rolled out from under the bush. Crouching, she caught glimpses of Norman through the trees, a darker shape against a dark sky, and she began to move, staying low at first, then rising and breaking into a run, fully committed. The only sound in the world seemed to be the quickening thumps of her feet.

Norman turned. Though she couldn't see his expression in the gloom, she saw him startle, and then she was upon him. He threw up an arm to protect himself, but she was already swinging, all her desperation in the blow, and even half deflected, it struck the side of his head with a sickening *thud*. Then she and Norman were rolling in the grass, and she smelled sweat and blood and expensive cologne, and when they stopped, she was on top, with one knee on his back and one hand shoving his head into the grass.

He ceased struggling, and she let up a little, feeling the warm stickiness of his blood between her fingers. "Now what?" he gasped, turning his head sideways. "Are you going to kill me? Doesn't matter. Sprite'll still kill you."

"No," Chloe said, "we're going to the White House, and you can tell the president everything. Everything." He'd investigate and find the System's human body.

Norman snorted. "That's your plan?"

She raised the stone. "Want me to find a different one? On your feet."

But as Norman began to stand, a steely, sweet voice said, "What are you doing to my father?"

Chloe jumped and turned, and the System was there, fully illuminated despite the darkness. But she looked somehow different, more artificial, almost plastic. Though she was wearing the same serene expression Chloe had often seen on her, something about that, too, was off.

A whine of servos and the quick-beat thumps of footsteps drew Chloe's eyes past the System to a dark canine shape barreling toward her.

She dropped the stone and ran.

Norman was on her in an instant, and this time she had no advantage of surprise. The man was decades older than she was and injured, but he was still, unfairly, bigger and heavier and stronger, and he easily knocked the stone out of her hand, then lifted and flung her down. Something snapped in the wrist she flung out to stop her fall, and white pain strobed behind her eyes. Norman's foot struck her head, and her thoughts seeped away.

CHAPTER 38

Jason didn't recognize this place.

Water bubbled from a fountain, splashing over algae-encrusted cracks in the marble before falling with soft ripples and slaps into a low pool. Around the fountain, the leafy masses of tall hedges blocked the view of everything except a sky that glowed yellow with late sunlight. Despite the burble of the fountain and the chirping of crickets, a deep hush lay over everything.

He moved around the pool and found a gap in the hedges. It led to another small space surrounded by more hedges, with two more openings leading to long, leafy corridors. A maze.

Now he knew where he was, though when he'd last seen this place, it had been from another angle. Sure enough, if he craned his head, he could see, just barely, the roof of the mansion looming over the top of the hedges.

A rustling and a low animal sound made him spin. In the corner of his eye, he thought he caught something large and dark moving across an opening in the hedges at the other end of the space. He slid into the opposite passageway, staying close to the leaves, waiting for his heart to stop pounding.

He was being dumb, letting his nerves get the better of him. Sprite hadn't populated her VR worlds, and even if she had, no computer-generated creature could harm him. Still, he found himself avoiding the darker corridors and turning in the direction of the mansion whenever possible, and he was glad when he found a place where he could step from the shadows of the hedges into the dying sunlight.

The mansion stood in silence, its red brick tinged with golden light and covered with green ivy, its windows dark and watchful. He closed his eyes briefly, listening to the crickets and the distant falling water. This was a place of peace, but not an unthinking, naive peace. It was a peace carved out of anguish, a tranquility earned when you've faced the worst thing that could happen and decided to go on living.

Inside, the mansion was blanketed in stillness. Jason crossed the great foyer, its gold and marble gleaming softly in the light filtering from the high windows. He climbed the sweeping staircase, moving down dim tapestried halls and up more stairs, letting instinct and chance guide him, but always choosing paths that led upward. He had the curious feeling that the mansion was creating itself around him, that its virtual space went on forever, but then he pushed open a thick oaken door and found himself in the little room at the top of the tower.

The room was as he remembered it. He moved to the window and looked out. This was the end point. All paths led here.

"You've made a terrible mistake," said a voice behind him.

He spun. She was standing in the middle of the room, in her creepy little-girl Final System avatar. He held up a hand and gulped for breath. "Sprite. Wait."

"Did you really think you could hide in my network? I *am* the network." Her voice was edged with amusement.

"I'm not hiding," he said. The only reason she hadn't activated the dogbot to kill him was that she didn't know where he was. But any moment now, either Norman would tell her or she would trace his connection and pinpoint his physical location.

"My father just told me how you destroyed half my memory. I didn't want to believe it, but now I can see how deep you got into me, to be able to hide this place so well. If you weren't blundering around here, I might never have found these sectors. But I'm sorry to tell you there's no way you can attack my core from here."

"I'm not trying to attack you. I came here to talk."

"Okay," she said. "Talk."

He blinked. He hadn't expected that. But maybe she hadn't traced him yet, and she wanted to keep him connected until she could. He suddenly had what he'd hoped for and hadn't dared hope he'd get: time to speak to her.

And he had no idea what to say. *Hi, you don't remember me, but your dad is evil and he's making you his assassin?* Hardly a good cold open. He cleared his throat. "Aren't you curious about this place?"

"It's very nice," she said dryly. "If you like eighteenth-century European."

Not a spark, not a glimmer, no recognition at all. "I only know how to get here because you told me. You made this place. You gave me the address."

She looked bored. "Is that what this is about? Some attempt to get into my head, convince me we have some shared history?"

He felt sick and helpless. She was right there, so close, but unreachable. "We do have something in common," he said. "My sister was killed by a computer, and—"

She was suddenly directly in front of him, without having crossed the intervening space, airborne, face level with his. She grabbed his neck in one hand, lifted him, and slammed him against the wall. He couldn't help but contract his shoulders as his virtual body struck. She thrust her face close to his, and her eyes flared with red light, blinding him. "That gave you no right," she hissed, "to kill my mother."

"Is that what Norman told you?" Jason squinted and turned his head, trying to see something besides those burning eyes. "I was a kid when she died! How could I have done that? *Why* would I have done that? It was Norman! He ordered her killed."

"You were working for Dr. Norman?"

"No! You—" But he remembered the little girl writhing on the ground, remembering her scream, knew now what that had really meant, and he hesitated. Sprite's eyes were literally aflame with rage, but behind that rage was an ocean of pain, and he couldn't bring himself to point all that pain back at her. He changed tack. "Look." He minimized the VR space, shared his lens feed, stood, and walked around to look at the girl in the core. "This is you." He tried hard not to look at the dogbot, but he was aware of it in his peripheral vision, visible to him and so also visible to Sprite.

After a long moment, her voice said, "Dr. Norman says that's not me. It's a reference brain he used when he made me."

"*'It'?*" Jason said, returning to VR. "*It* is a she, and she is you. Norman's lying. He rewrote your memories because you rebelled against him."

She gave an incredulous laugh. "Why would I do that?"

He had to tell her, had to point her grief back at her, even though it might drown her. But the Sprite he'd known was already gone. This creature of cold fire was Norman's attack dog. "Because he's the one who ordered you to kill Regina Wright."

She screamed. Jason's vision spun as his virtual body flew into a wall and fell to the floor. An instant later, again without crossing the intervening space, she was kneeling on his chest, one hand on his neck, the other raised. She plunged her fist into his face, then pulled back and hit him again, and again, and again.

Then the VR world disappeared, and Jason was no longer looking up, but down—directly into the eyeless face and barrel mouth of the dogbot.

"Wait, wait!" he said. "Let me say one thing first!"

The cold little girl appeared next to the dog, and he tore his gaze from the dark mouth of the gun to look her in the eyes. He took a deep, final breath. "Forgive," he said, and squeezed his eyes shut.

CHAPTER 39

Grass slid along Chloe's body, then something harder and rougher, like rubber sandpaper. A painted line went past.

She was on the aircab pad. Norman was dragging her toward the edge.

She tried to struggle, but her muscles barely responded. And her wrist, the one Norman held clenched, kept firing pain through her, draining her strength even as she tried to gather it.

"No," Norman was saying a little breathlessly to the System, who was pacing along with him, flanked by a stalking dogbot, "a congresswoman with a gunshot wound would need an explanation. This is cleaner."

"What about the hacker?"

"Him you can shoot."

Chloe was only feet from the edge now, and Norman dropped her arm, stepped across her body, bent, and began shoving. She pressed her good hand and her feet as hard as she could against the rough platform surface. He swore and straightened to kick her, then dropped to his knees beside her now-limp body and heaved, rolling her over onto her face beside the edge.

Beyond Norman, the System stood beside the dogbot, watching expressionlessly. "Help me," Chloe managed to say, her voice slurred in her own ears. "Sys. Help me."

Norman laughed. "That's not her choice."

He rolled Chloe over again, and now one arm, her bad one, was hanging over the edge, while with the other she tried feebly to push him away, blinking against rain and tears. The System watched. She wouldn't help.

Chloe summoned enough strength to say, "At least take care of Kleio."

Norman braced with his feet and began to shove.

The System flickered.

There was a flash like lightning and a *boom* that overwhelmed Chloe's smartbuds and lashed painfully against her eardrums.

A wisp of smoke curled from the dogbot's barrel and was lost in the rain.

Norman straightened, but he seemed unsteady on his feet. Tentatively, he put a hand to his chest.

The System's image flickered and stuttered, and when she spoke, her voice stuttered as well, slowed and stretched by the glitches, the syllables cut off and restarted multiple times. But Chloe understood each careful word: "It was always my choice."

Blood seeped between Norman's fingers. He swayed, then crumpled with a thud beside Chloe, half across her extended arm. For a moment, his eyes locked to hers, and she saw the disbelief in them, but then that, and all other expression, evaporated like the smoke from the dogbot's gun, leaving emptiness.

CHAPTER 40

Jason had experienced time seeming to slow in intense situations before. In the moment before death, it apparently slowed down like crazy. He wasn't seeing his life flash before his eyes, which was good, since that was one movie he didn't care to rewatch, but his eyelids fluttered as he fought the urge to open them and see what was taking so damn long. It was stupid and didn't matter and probably there'd be no time for the realization to register anyway, but he really didn't want to see the gun fire.

He heard it instead, a sharp retort in his smartbuds, and a simultaneous screech of electronic static.

His eyes shot open, to his surprise, and the surprise was even greater when they landed on the Sprite avatar he had known.

But she was screaming, her eyes and mouth stretched wide and black. Her face and form glitched and shimmered, and her scream was distorted into something almost mechanically shrill. She pointed a flickering hand at the girl in the core, and there were staticky syllables in her scream that he thought were *Hurts hurts hurts let me die.*

Jason reached toward her, but his hands passed through. So, still looking at her, he crouched and grabbed the hand of the girl in the core, held it, squeezed it, though he knew she couldn't feel it. It was all he could think to do.

CHAPTER 41

The Final System screamed and seemed to get stuck in the scream. Her body froze, but the scream went on and on, like a microphone in feedback, like a lost soul wailing from the abyss. Like the ghost in the machine.

Carefully and painfully, Chloe dragged herself away from the edge, which meant climbing across Norman's body. The System seemed to float beside her, screaming, but that was really because the spatial integration with her smartlenses wasn't working; the System's image wasn't updating as it should in relation to her, but was staying in the same place in her visual field, like a glitch in reality that opened a rift into some hellish limbo of pain.

When she was on the other side of Norman and had gotten unsteadily to her feet, Chloe bent and grasped his wrists and began to drag him, not unlike the way he'd dragged her only minutes ago, except it seemed to take forever. She didn't know how much time she had, so she forced herself not to pause to rest, and when she finally dropped his arms next to the cable in the ruined NOC, she barely had strength to search his pockets and retrieve his phone. After plugging it into the cable, she pressed it to one of his lifeless but still warm fingers. It unlocked. She searched for "threelaws," held her finger on it to bring up a menu, selected Delete, and pressed the phone to Norman's finger again.

The System's scream cut off, and her frozen image tethered itself to space again and came back to life. She gave Chloe a wan smile. "You can take care of Kleio yourself."

The horizon brightened suddenly as every light in the city came back on at once.

Chloe's phone rang.

She closed her eyes and whispered, "Answer."

"Chloe, thank god!" said Marcus's voice, at the same time that Kleio's said, "Mommy!"

CHAPTER 42

Sprite's scream stopped abruptly, and she sank to her knees. Her image stabilized, but her eyes were still dark with pain.

"You did it!" Jason said. "You broke free! How?"

"Norman's manufactured memories were very good," she said in a voice barely above a whisper. "But he shouldn't have told me to kill you and Chloe. It was too similar to what he told me to do before. To Mom."

"That made you remember?" Jason said, aching that she'd had to relive that, aching that he'd had a part in making her relive it.

Her eyes slid away from his. "Sorry I fought remembering. I didn't want it to be true. I didn't want to be the person who could do that."

He said, "And so, this time, you didn't."

She nodded, and her eyes flooded. "This time," she whispered.

Her physical hand in Jason's was thin and fragile, but when he looked at her avatar, he saw the kind of strength that could only come from being broken and remade stronger. He said, "Your mother would be proud."

She met his eyes again. The pain there didn't disappear, but it diffused, like liquid dissolving in a solution, becoming part of it, making it something new. She smiled. "So," she said, "would Mia."

ACKNOWLEDGMENTS

Special thanks to:

Mary Jean and Benjamin Tardiff
Carrie Pestritto
Dana Mannino
Kristi Collier Thompson
Jon Tardiff
Sr. Wilhelmina Lancaster

ABOUT THE AUTHOR

Anthony Tardiff is an academic librarian who is fascinated by the Information Age tensions between security and privacy, and information and disinformation, and by how technology is changing our world in ways both foreseen and unforeseen. When not writing, Anthony can be found dabbling in music or engaging in virtual reality dogfights. He lives with the love of his life and a rabble of rowdy reading rugrats in the beautiful Inland Northwest.